EROSABEL

Nicole Plumridge

THE WOODLOCK CURSE

THIS BOOK IS part of what will be a collection of novels within the Woodlock Curse Series. While each book is a self-contained story, the novels interweave and link together through characters, times and settings.

Each individual novel can be read separately, in sequential order or scattered and at random. Whatever approach you decide to take, all stories will converge and connect, creating a tapestry of tales for you to delve into and explore.

Also by Nicole

Erosabel

Healing House

Table of Contents

PART IV: MADNESS

PART I

THE CURSE

East London, 1823

EVEN AS A child, I knew a curse hovered over the slums of East London where I spent a forgotten, empty childhood. It lurked patiently in the shadows, rising with the sun at dawn and settling like dust when darkness cast its liquid shadows across the godforsaken place I called home. The curse was a perpetual chill in my bones, an ever-present shadow by my side. No matter how hard I tried to dislodge it from the corners of my mind and dispel it into the realm where fantasies and dreams lay scattered and broken, I felt its caress, its icy breath on the back of my neck. I knew, one of these days, someday soon, it was coming for me.

Chapter 1

CHILDHOOD FELT LIKE a dream, or should I say nightmare, away. A distant memory swirling in a mirky pool I dared not peer into. It felt like millennia had passed since I was that frail, feeble child whose mother used to knock about. I was rarely comfortable discussing my past, but it felt different with Willowen, a cup of broth clasped in my hands, its warmth embracing me.

I had travelled a great deal to reach this gypsy campsite, both in terms of physical distance and psychic. I had journeyed to the edge of my own sanity, looking into an abyss that was threatening to consume me whole. At the very last moment, I had been pulled back, saved by the steady hands of Willowen.

Willowen was head of the camp. He had taken me in, a lonely, stray orphan with nowhere to go. When I had first arrived, brittle and broken, he had asked no questions, only focused on my health and healing. Now, however, he wanted to know. He wanted to know about my past, who I was, where I came from. Dread tied itself in knots in the pit of my stomach.

As if in deliberate contrast to my inner world, the caravan in which I had been convalescing had a sleepy, calm aroma to it. A stillness hung in the air. Willowen was perched on a three-legged stool opposite me in the bed, wrapped in thick fur blankets.

"You don't have to tell me your story tonight," he said kindly, noting my pregnant pause after he had asked where I was from. "You must still be exhausted."

Mother's face floated into my mind from the ether. I had tried to bury the image; pretend she had only been a figment of my macabre imagination. Suddenly, I felt words, rising like bile, creep up my throat. I needed to talk. I had to tell someone my story. I desperately wanted someone to understand. Someone to tell me that I wasn't going crazy. Someone to forgive the evil I had done. The smudged windows and thin walls of the caravan melted away, replaced by the dank, rotting walls of Mother's flat in East London. With the familiar taste of fear metallic in my mouth, I began to tell my story.

The slap stung the side of my face. A blood-red tear trickled from the gash, burning my cheekbone. I tried to stifle the sobs heaving through my chest.

"You ungrateful little beast!" Mother shrieked, brandishing her broken, dagger-like nails, threatening to strike again.

I recoiled into a corner like a wounded animal, trembling in fear. My eyes were glued shut as I waited for the final blow, waited for her to cut through my skin and pierce my very heart with her claws. It was only when I heard the sound of muted crying that I squinted through one eye. In that instant I wished Mother would continue beating me until she cracked my bones and scratched me to shreds. It would have been infinitely better than what I saw.

Mother was curled up in a ball, rocking backwards and forwards, mumbling through her streaming tears, "I'm sorry, Erosabel. I'm sorry. It's the Devil, you know. The Devil whispers in my ear. You know how I suffer. I'm sorry." Mother repeated this over and over again, her eyes unseeing and glassy.

Barely able to stand on my shaking, scrawny legs, I stumbled over to the rocking lump that was my mother. I sat down cautiously next to her, never sure of what to expect. Slowly, I put my arm around her shoulders. Her once luscious fiery red locks hung in limp strands around her waxy, pale face. A shiny film of perspiration coated her skin, giving her the appearance of a distraught wax doll.

"It's ok, Mother," I said, my voice high-pitched and trembling with uncertainty.

"No, Erosabel, you deserve better than this," Mother said, her eyes puffy and swollen with tears. "I can't protect you. The demons will have their way."

Her eyes had a faraway gleam in them, as if she were half in this world and half in another, a world invisible to me. Although I couldn't peer into that strange world of hers, I knew it to be one haunted by dark corners, winding mazes that led nowhere, shadows and eerie echoing voices. I was terrified when Mother was drawn into that world.

"What did she mean when she said the Devil talks to her? Could your mother actually hear voices?" Willowen asked, his brow furrowed.

I am no gypsy, but I have heard they can be superstitious about these sorts of things. I wanted to put his mind at ease but didn't know how. I decided to go with the honest truth.

"I believe she thought she heard the Devil talk to her. She was tormented by it and then she transferred that torment onto me," I said as plainly as I could.

Willowen nodded thoughtfully. I took his silence as a sign to press on.

It wasn't the first time Mother had spoken to me like this. The previous week I had come home after delivering linens and fabrics to a nearby shop. I had hesitated before entering the room as I thought someone was there with her. She had been shouting at someone or something to leave her alone. My first thought was that the rent collector had been pestering her again.

I pushed open the splintered wooden door to find Mother standing by the fire. At the sound of the creaking, Mother spun around wild-eyed. A blank film coated her eyes and there was no hint of recognition when she saw me. She was alone.

"Who were you talking to?" I asked timidly, my voice barely above a whisper.

Mother stared at me before tipping what would have been our dinner, a broth she was heating in a pot, into the flames. It hissed like angry snakes just as my stomach growled in hunger.

"That's what you get for not holding your tongue. Only troublesome devils ask questions!" Mother spat at me.

I nodded, wishing I had never said anything, wishing the broth would wind its way back into the pot and from there into my hollow, aching stomach.

"The devils will get you too, you know," she said, pushing past me into the only other room in the hovel we called home.

We lived in a tiny flat above what used to be Mother's apothecary. My grandparents had run the shop, selling herbal medicines and ointments for refined ladies with white, delicate hands ensconced in fine silk gloves. When they had died Mother took to running the shop. From the few stories Uncle Benjamin told me about Mother, she had been a different person back then.

"Where's your Uncle Benjamin now? Are you still in touch?" Willowen cut in.

I shook my head slowly, a hint of bitterness in my voice as I continued.

Uncle Ben had made promises to us, promises he swore he would keep. He had escaped the squalor of London and sailed off to the new lands and with them, a new life, in America. I remember him letting me sit on his knee with a sad, wistful expression clouding his eyes the day he was set to travel.

Uncle Benjamin said, as if to himself, "I wish you knew your mother before. Before... things changed. The strength of her spirit could rival the sea itself. I always thought she would marry well and get out of this dump. She didn't lack suitors, that's for sure."

"I thought she married Daddy," I said, wide-eyed, staring up at Uncle Ben.

Uncle Ben looked down startled, as if surprised by my presence. "Of course. I meant after your father died. I thought she would marry again," he said, clearing his throat and shifting me off his knee. "You take care of your mother now. She's not well, so you have to do everything you can to help her get better," he added, his eyes misting over with tears.

I didn't understand what he meant. Usually when people weren't well they were in bed, coughing and sneezing. Mother wasn't like that. She never got sick. I simply nodded as Uncle Ben patted me on the head.

"You be a good girl. I'll send you treats, lace and dolls every month. It's a new world out there, a better one. And who knows, maybe once I'm settled you and your mother can join me!"

He planted a long kiss on my forehead before leaving the room to find Mother and say his farewells. I heard a pot smashing and peeped around the door to see what had happened. Mother was standing in the middle of the bare room as Uncle Ben hurried out. I remember his shoulders were hunched over, as if he were carrying the weight of a thousand worlds on his back. A delicate painted clay pot lay shattered on the floor.

"Good riddance. We don't need your charity anyway, you good-for-nothing layabout," Mother shrieked after him.

As she slammed the door behind Uncle Ben, I felt my small world close in on me. Curtains of darkness descended, and I knew then in that bleak winter of 1818 that my childhood had ended.

Willowen and I slipped into silence. I could feel his brain working, whirring away, processing all I had told him. Usually I would feel panicked; wonder what he was thinking about me, but today I was feeling too mentally exhausted for that. I was being honest, perhaps, for the first time in my life. I was stripping layer after layer of my soul, leaving it bare. Somehow, it felt good, a welcome reprieve.

"Where was your father during your childhood?" Willowen asked, softly peeling back the fabric of silence that enveloped us.

"Father?" The word was unfamiliar in my mouth. All I knew was Mother. The word had encapsulated hope and wonder in my childhood, only to turn to bitterness, disappointment and then apathy as I grew older.

The story was my father had died before I was born. I wasn't sure if I believed the story as it frequently changed, depending on Mother's mercurial moods. She sometimes told me he had been trampled by a horse and carriage one day on his way to work at the factory. Other times, he had drowned in the murky waters of the River Thames as he was scouring the banks for valuable fragments. When Mother was in a good mood, he had heroically died from smoke inhalation after rescuing a family trapped in a burning building. Occasionally, she would curse him, brandishing her fists in the air, muttering furious words as if he were still alive. When I confronted Mother about these discrepancies, she would slap me so hard I felt my teeth rattle.

"You hold your tongue, girl, before I cut it out of your mouth," she would hiss.

I learnt never to question her. She would glower at me, saying that I was the ruin of her life. If it hadn't been for me she would have escaped the doom of the slum we lived in. Sometimes I would catch her staring at me, a look of disgust contorting her once fine and beautiful features.

"You have his dark looks," she would say, shaking her head. "Anyone would mistake you for a heathen."

It was true. I had dark skin and hair blacker than the night itself. Before, when we used to leave the flat, people would stare at us. Mother, a tall, willowy, red-haired beauty, with skin so pale it was almost translucent alongside this small, scrawny, tanned urchin. The only reason Mother wasn't called a baby-snatcher was our eyes: they were unmistakeably the same, passed down the generations like precious sapphires. Our eyes were a deep swirling ocean blue with large inky black pupils dotted in the centre. A peddler of feathers and trinkets had once grabbed me by the arm and stared at me, frowning. "You have the eyes of a witch," he spat. "Cursed." He then flung me with all his force away from his wares, sending me flying into a puddle of muck and filth.

I remember avoiding my reflection for years growing up. When I looked into Mother's eyes, I saw nothing except a hallow emptiness, as if her soul had already transcended to the world beyond. I was scared that if I saw my own reflection, I would see the same lifeless gaze staring back, like the glass eyes of an empty china doll.

Mother's rage, and later what I understood to be madness, ruled our lives whilst we lived in the two dingy rooms above the shop which had fallen into disrepair. All I remember feeling was an incessant guilt, gnawing at my soul. Because of me, her life was in tatters. Because of me, we lived in a ramshackle hovel. Because of me, she lost her mind.

"You can't blame yourself for your mother's unravelling," Willowen said gently. "You never did anything wrong. Whatever was troubling her had nothing to do with you."

I was about to agree when I felt a lump in my throat. To my surprise, tears had gathered in my eyes and were threatening to spill over. Although I had rationally told myself that I was not responsible for her downfall, I couldn't help but feel the weight of ephemeral guilt press down on me. Somewhere, deep down within me, I blamed myself for everything that had gone wrong in our lives. To hear a perfect stranger say otherwise and have it ring true made every fibre in my being quiver with this new realisation.

Willowen handed me a plain white shred of cloth. I hadn't realised I was crying. The gentle tears turned into heaving sobs, and before I knew it, I had lost control and my entire body was shaking. But it wasn't with sadness. Willowen put his arms around me and drew me close. He didn't say anything, just let me cry it out. As the tears were tumbling down, I searched within myself to understand what emotion was bubbling to the surface. It wasn't sadness or fear. Nor was it worry or heartache. I then realised what it was: relief. It was washing over me and within me, cleansing me from the inside out. I was relieved to know that it was not my fault. Someone outside of myself had validated me for the first time. As the tears ebbed, I felt more alive than I had ever felt in my entire life. Just as this new vitality surged through me, a heavy physical exhaustion settled within my limbs, making it difficult for me to move.

As if reading my mind through my movements, Willowen said, "I think we ought to call it a night. You must be tired."

I nodded. The very act of speaking felt like too much of an effort.

"Goodnight, Erosabel. Rest well," Willowen said, as he opened the door of the caravan. "You'll be all right?"

"Yes," I managed to say. "Thank you for listening to all that."

11

"Of course. I can't believe everything you've been through. But don't worry. I'm glad you found us. It's all about to get a whole lot easier," he said with a warm smile.

I managed a weak smile in return as I waved him goodnight. I hadn't realised how much I needed that release, how much I needed to tell my story aloud. But I wasn't done. Now I had a taste for it, I needed to continue. I needed to tell my story and for it to be heard.

* * * * *

The next morning, I woke up feeling refreshed, lighter than I had ever felt in my life. I wanted to find Willowen. Just then Betty stepped into the caravan. She had been taking care of me, fixing my broth and medicine since I arrived.

"Oh my, you are looking so much better," she said. "You're practically glowing."

"I feel much better. Thank you for taking care of me. You've been so kind."

"Of course, it's nothing. You poor mite, you were all sallow and bruised up when you got here. But look at you this morning. It really is a miracle!"

I smiled. "Is Willowen around?"

"No, dearie. He left at daybreak to meet up with Jackson, the head of another camp to see which direction they are heading in. He'll be back by evening," she added, seeing my disappointment. "It must be difficult not knowing anyone around here. But don't worry, everyone is friendly round here."

"Of course, I can feel that already," I replied. I would just have to wait until evening before I could continue my offloading.

"Do let me know if you need anything. Perhaps a walk in the fresh air would do you some good? I can introduce you to a few people if you like?"

"I think I'll go for a walk on my own just to gather myself together. Then I'd love to meet some of the others!"

"Of course, you just take your time," she replied. "Eat up that broth now. Clearly it's doing you wonders."

As she bustled off, I gulped down the broth and quickly fixed my hair and clothes. Slipping into the past always gave me goosebumps. The memories I thought I had banished from my mind swept through with such accurate detail I felt as if I was reliving every moment.

By the time evening rolled around, I felt desperate. I was itching to tell my story to someone who wanted to listen. I hadn't left the caravan. I was scared to interact with anyone who wasn't Willowen. When I heard a knock at the caravan door, I nearly jumped out of my skin.

"Come in," I said, rather too quickly.

Relief flooded through my veins when I saw it was Willowen. He was back and I was ready to talk.

"How're you?" he asked.

A heavy weariness hung over him. An inkling of guilt tugged inside me as I had no intention of asking him how he was. I just wanted to talk.

"I'm doing ok," I replied. Due to social niceties, I continued, "And you?"

13

"A little tired. But it's fine. Have you been in here all day?"

"No," I lied. "I went out for a walk. But I haven't really been up to meeting anyone yet. My brain still feels fogged up most of the time."

"Of course," he said, warmly. "No need to rush."

I smiled wanly, hoping he would urge me to continue. When he sat there in silence, I blurted out, "Do you think I'm crazy?"

Willowen stared at me, perplexed. "Where did that come from? Of course I don't."

I allowed myself a small sigh of relief. People used to say that all the time about Mother. I didn't quite understand what that meant. After a while, I wondered if I was the same as her. If I was also crazy.

"Why would you ask such a thing?" Willowen repeated, slicing into my thoughts.

"No reason. I think I'm still not feeling too well," I replied hastily.

"Of course, you've been through a lot. Would you prefer for me to leave and let you rest?"

That was the last thing that I wanted; to be alone with my thoughts. "No, no. Please stay. I've been alone all day. I'd be happy to have the company."

"All right. I must say I am curious about where we left off. Please don't be afraid to tell me if I'm overstepping the mark. I know it must be difficult recounting all those memories."

At last, the hook I had been waiting for.

"No, it's fine. I actually find it strangely relieving telling you about my life up until now."

"Then please, continue..." he said.

The first time I heard someone say Mother was mad I couldn't understand what they meant. Since Mother was unable to keep a job for more than a month, I was sent all around East London doing odd jobs and errands at all hours of the day. I was ten years old at the time and had stitched five dolls and a blanket for the seamstress's daughter down the road.

I entered the seamstress's shop cautiously, aware of my grubby appearance and ragged clothes, and found myself surrounded by beautiful flowing silks, embroidered gowns and tangles of brightly coloured ribbons. I wondered what it must feel like to be able to hold one of those smooth pieces of ribbon and wind it delicately in one's hair. Uncle Ben's packages had stopped coming shortly after his arrival to the promised lands and he had never sent the lace and dolls he had promised all those years ago. Mesmerised by the vibrancy and beauty of the wonderland of cloths, I didn't notice the seamstress, Mrs Perkins, materialise from behind a heavy, velvet curtain.

"Erosabel," she said kindly. "Would you like a biscuit?"

I nodded enthusiastically. The last thing I had eaten was a plate of thin watery porridge the morning before.

"Thank you. I made the dolls and blanket for your daughter's baby," I said, pleased with myself as I handed over the basket.

"Oh, how lovely," Mrs Perkins replied, taking the basket and placing it behind the counter. "And how are you, dear? How's your mother?"

"Fine, thank you," I said, a few biscuit crumbs spraying from my mouth.

She nodded, a fixed smile plastered on her face.

"Thank you very much, but I must be off," I said, hopping to my feet after finishing the biscuit. *"Mother doesn't like me staying out too late."* The last part was a pure fabrication. The majority of the time Mother didn't know where I was, nor did she care. She had once told me to come home with coins or not come home at all. By that time, I was in the habit of lying, especially when people asked about Mother.

"Well, here you go, dear, for the dolls," Mrs Perkins said, slipping a few coins into a velvet purse which she pressed into my hand. *"Make sure to buy some food with that."*

I nodded and thanked her again. I slipped out of the shop into the dark gloom of the streets. I then decided to go back inside and ask if her daughter might like an initialled handkerchief or little shoes for the baby.

I entered the shop and heard Mrs Perkins talking to her assistant behind the heavy velvet curtain.

"Poor mite, she looked worse than ever today. So thin and fragile. I mean, I could have sewn these dolls much better myself, just look at that frayed edge."

I heard a muttering of agreement and tutting from the assistant.

"But you know, I just feel awful for her situation with her useless vagabond of a father and a mother who ought to be locked away in an asylum. The girl is little more than an orphan. And I knew her grandparents so well, such kind, gentle people, God bless them. What a

tragedy that railway accident was. They would have cared for the girl so much better than their insane daughter."

More mutterings of assent rustled through the thick fabric of the curtain, but I couldn't listen any more. I suddenly felt winded, as if I had been punched in the stomach. I had heard of asylums just as I had heard of workhouses. Both had the same effect of sending cold shivers down my spine.

I quickly left the shop and tumbled back into the street. A biting autumn wind blew dead leaves in eddies at my feet. I watched them swirling for what felt like an eternity, mesmerised by their sprightly dance. Finally I tore my gaze away and looked around the streets where I grew up, bathed in the shadows of the setting sun. Crowds of people bustled down the street, hawking and selling their wares. A stream of sewage constantly flowed through the thick, sludgy ground. Shoeless street urchins, like me, hovered in the shadows, eyes peeled for the possibility of earning a coin. My eyes drifted upwards as I glanced at the street name which was meant to read Hopefield End. The last five letters of the first word, however, were blackened with smog and dirt so thick that it read "Hope End." In that moment, I had never felt more abandoned and hopeless in my life. With the velvet purse stashed safely in my undergarments, I dragged my feet through the narrow, dark cobweb of alleyways, and made my way home.

Willowen's mystical eyes were transfixed on me. The horrors of my childhood melted away in those eyes. When those eyes were on me, I felt like the most important person in the world.

"I'm sorry to hear that about your grandparents. Those railways are dangerous. They should never have built them. Utter monstrosities," Willowen exclaimed with passion.

I mumbled assent, not caring either way about the railways. I had never met my grandparents; therefore, could never miss them.

I cleared my throat before continuing. I wasn't done for the evening. I still had more I needed to say. Willowen seemed to notice my cue and settled back into listening posture. His chin rested gently on his hand whilst his head was tilted to the side. I continued...

That next morning, Mother had been so pleased with my earnings that she gave me a couple of pennies to get myself a little treat. I was surprised at the gesture but then again, Mother always surprised me. Sometimes she was as light and happy as a fluffy white cloud in the sky and at other times she was as dark and brooding as an impending storm creeping along the seas shore. I never knew which Mother I was getting in the mornings. The worst was when neither appeared. Several times I had gone into the room where she slept only to find her sitting bolt upright on the bed, staring at the grubby, peeling wall with patches of mould festering in the corners. I remember waving my hand in front of her face so closely I felt her clammy breath. Her eyes, however, maintained their glassy unseeing stare. Occasionally she muttered under her breath incoherent words jumbled together.

I would usually leave her, too scared to do anything else. Once, her strange trancelike state lasted for two full days. She had neither eaten nor drunk anything in that time. I was too scared to tell anyone for fear they may accuse her of harbouring the devils she so often spoke about in her mind and soul. My mother was strange, mysterious and terrifying to me, but she was still Mother and I didn't want her carted away from me to some asylum filled with unknown horrors.

That morning, I left Mother brewing some strange-smelling concoction in the dark flat as I went out into the world with several pennies stashed in the inner lining of my threadbare dress. I looked about for where to spend those jangling coins. It was still early in the day and the cold sunshine drenched the mud-soaked roads. I dodged the stinking puddles and piles of dung that oozed along the road, as I made my way to the market.

I passed hunched women balancing platters of pickled salmon, others hawking at passers-by to try their "cherry, ripe, ripe, ripe". The aroma of sweet pastries mingled with the stench of sweat and manure in the air. The scent of food was intoxicating and made my stomach rumble loudly. I wound my way through the maze of alleys and side streets that wove the tapestry of East London together.

Swaying gently in the breeze was the sign I had been looking for. It was a picture of a curled-up badger with a fierce expression, baring its sharp pointed teeth. Naturally, I couldn't read but had been told that the large, bold writing underneath the vicious-looking creature said Badgers Den. It was a crowded, rowdy public house. I slipped inside, hoping to see my friend. Despite the hour, several men were already slurring their words, drunkenly swaying in their seats. It was the drinking hour of the poverty-stricken and unemployed. Desperate men with empty pockets and ragged clothing congregated here. Hopelessness and resignation hung damp and heavy in the air, almost visibly weighing down the mumbling drinkers. In one of the side rooms I heard a familiar voice.

Lucifer the storyteller. Lucifer the thief. Lucifer the criminal. Lucifer the light bringer. Lucifer the Devil. Lucifer my friend. I never found out if his real name was Lucifer or if the stories they told about him were true.

He was an enigmatic man with skin paler than pearls and a mop of black hair, darker than a raven's coat. He had large, clear grey eyes, orbs of wisdom that looked as if they had witnessed the sufferings of several thousand years. I never asked how old he was or where he had come from. He had an ageless face that reminded me of a vampire. All I knew was one day he didn't exist and the next, as if he had tumbled out of the sky, he was on the streets of London with his haunting puppets and their tales of turmoil and apocalyptic disaster.

"He sounds like quite a character," Willowen cut in.

My mind was so full of Lucifer's stories and intense imagination that I had all but forgotten I was recounting this to Willowen.

"He was... is quite a character," I said, a sad wistful note tinging my words.

"You miss him?" he continued.

"Of course. Him and Tommy. Even Mother sometimes," I said slowly. A curtain of memories divided me and Willowen. I knew no matter how much I told him, how much I spilled my heart out, he would never truly understand.

Willowen nodded. "Hopefully you'll see them again. Just because you left does not mean it's goodbye forever. It's the way we live over here after all. Sometimes we don't see family and friends in other camps for years. But we always meet again."

I tried to feel uplifted by his words. I so desperately wanted to grasp that thread of hope he dangled so temptingly before me. But I knew it was only a fool's hope. In the depths of my dark heart, I knew I would never see them again.

Swallowing the lump that had begun to form in my throat, I continued...

I met Lucifer during one of his shows. It was a creepy drama brimming with supernatural powers, of fallen angels and cunning devils. So full of horrors was his show that the other children ran away in tears, terrified of going to bed that evening. I, however, was entranced. His words wove a story unlike any I had heard before, a story which spoke to my soul. Each word was stitched together so beautifully, I knew it was more than just a puppet show he was creating. It was a work of the most exquisite art, a true masterpiece.

"You do not scare easily, child," he had said in his deep voice, a voice which had initially startled me as I hadn't expected such a voice from a man with his slender build.

"No, keep going with the story! What happens to the Fates?" I asked, mesmerised.

"Ah, my storytelling powers have been bled dry for the day. I suggest you go home," he said, indicating the darkening sky.

"Ok, will you be here tomorrow? What is your name?"

"Curious child. You may call me Lucifer, bringer of light to the shadowy underworld in which we live," he said with a wink before packing up his limp, lifeless puppets.

I made sure to see as many of his shows as possible after our first encounter.

I strolled into the room where Lucifer was sitting in the Badgers Den, expecting to see someone with him as I had heard multiple voices. To my surprise, he was the only one in the room.

"Erosabel," he said, his unblinking eyes landing on me.

"I was wondering if you were doing any shows today," I said, smiling. "I heard you talking to someone."

"Ah no, my puppets were the ones talking to me," Lucifer replied. He was what they called a ventriloquist, a complicated word I was proud to know.

"What lives and worlds are you creating today?" I asked excitedly. Lucifer never told the same story twice. There were always bizarre twists and turns to his tales that left the audience on tenterhooks. The audience that was brave enough to stay, that is.

"Oh, you shall find out this afternoon, when the show starts," Lucifer said with a wink, taking a sip from his glass.

I slumped in a chair, pouting, wanting to know the essence of the story before everyone else got the chance to hear it. Knowing the story ahead of time made me feel like I was part of a magical secret. It made me feel special.

"Ok, I shall throw you a titbit of the story before the others crowd me in and prevent the creative juices from flowing," Lucifer said, seeing my desolate expression. He suddenly sprang into action as if a magic switch had been flicked. His fluid motions and eloquent speech immediately had me captivated.

"The Gods in their ever-enduring wrath and jealousy cast from the heavens an illegitimate babe with a dark prophecy hovering over its head, hoping for its quick death. Unfortunately for them, the babe was cast outside a hovel where the witches dwelt. After hearing the raucous noises of a screaming babe crashing through the trees, the witch..." he paused, *grabbing one of his pale puppets with cunning eyes and dark threads of matted hair, before continuing, "cast a spell so that the little infant landed softly on the earth, like a petal fluttering to the soft, dewy grass below.*

"Immediately it stopped wailing. The witches sensed the prophecy the babe had brought with it. Although they had immense powers, they couldn't read the prophecy the Gods had so desperately tried to destroy. The witches decided to raise the babe in comfort and joy and hope one day they would understand why it was sent their way from the ether."

Lucifer's witch puppet was now cradling a lumpy blanket that was supposedly the fallen baby.

"The babe grew tall, strong and handsome. His fine features glowed as if chiselled from the purest marble. But his heart was a dark, foreboding place. The witches kept no secret from him and told him of how he came into their path. They stirred their cauldron, brewing within it trouble and mayhem. The babe, no longer a babe, let's call him," Lucifer paused, making his puppet adopt a thinking pose, "Samael. He was a brute of a man with the face of an angel, with nothing but vengeance pulsating through his veins. Every day for twenty years of his life, he would gaze to the heavens and curse the Gods who had rejected and cast him down so cruelly. He grew blind to earthly pleasures and was only able to see the devious plots forming within his mind's eye.

"He began to erect a tower, a tower so tall it reached the heavens. With the witches by his side, they unleashed all kinds of horrors and evil. Samael tore the heavens apart with his bare hands. All the Gods were destroyed and the world fell into an endless night, filled with demons and devilish critters unlike any you have conjured in your worst nightmares. And that is how the world remains for as long as the vengeful Samael clutches the

reins of power within his mighty fists. Whilst the Gods in their vain glory thought they were destroying the prophecy all they did was ensure it came to pass. It is not the immediate but the unintended consequences that forge our life's stories and reveal our destinies."

I listened wide-eyed at the detail of ever-increasing despair. "Will the world ever get rid of the everlasting night?" I asked.

"Only a force of genuine truth, beauty and light can ever attempt to shine a beacon of hope onto the desolate land of Samael's. Only a person of true nobility and strength can banish the witches and provide an antidote to their poisonous creations. The power to restore the world to rights lies within this unknown, noble person who must convince Samael of his wrongdoings and show him the way of light."

I sat open-mouthed, in awe of this deliciously terrifying tale. "But will this noble person kill Samael or lock him up forever in an unbreakable tower for all the evil that he did? Or will Samael get away with it?" I asked, anxious to know the ending.

Lucifer paused, tapping his chin thoughtfully. "What do you think would be a fair punishment?"

"Well, he did destroy the Gods and throw the world into darkness," I mused, taking the question very seriously. "But if they hadn't been cruel and banished him in the first place, he wouldn't have done so." I sat back on the hard bench feeling thoroughly perplexed by this seemingly unsolvable riddle.

"Indeed. Are we what we make ourselves or do we enter this world already made? Do we have volition or are we under the control of invisible masters, much like my puppets on strings?" Lucifer asked.

"*Maybe a bit of both?*" *I suggested, hoping this was the right answer.*

Lucifer smiled, baring his sharp, pointed teeth. He had a strange smile that never seemed to reach the swirling grey pools of his eyes. His long slender fingers ruffled my hair.

"*You're a sharp one,*" *he said.*

I smiled inwardly, feeling the warmth of the compliment glow within.

He sipped the remainder of his drink and surveyed me. "*Now, to more important matters. Have you had breakfast?*" *he asked in a mock serious tone. I shook my head just as my stomach concurred by rumbling loudly.* "*Neither have I,*" *Lucifer whispered conspiratorially.* "*Let's fix that, shall we?*"

Lucifer went up to the barmaid and whispered something in her ear that made her giggle. A few minutes later, we were served a platter of delicious, hot, steaming food. There was an assortment of hot and cold bread buns, boiled eggs, hot cakes, juicy glistening sausages, fried potatoes and two beers, one large and one small.

I immediately devoured the food, shovelling the hot, sticky cakes into my mouth, licking my fingers as I snatched the oozing sausages and gulped down my small beer. Lucifer watched me with a quizzical expression playing on his fine features. Whilst I gorged myself on the feast, he merely picked at the food and nibbled it slowly.

"*Better?*" *he asked once the plates had been licked clean and I reclined back on the uncomfortable wooden bench.*

"*Yes, thank you,*" *I replied quickly, hoping Lucifer wouldn't mistake my gluttony for ingratitude.*

"You looked as if you hadn't eaten in weeks," he replied, fixing me with his perturbing unblinking stare. "How are things at home, Erosabel? How's your mother?"

The question floated from his lips, a featherweight, only to land on my shoulders, heavy as lead. This insurmountable despondency spread through my veins. The ever-perceptive Lucifer sensed the subtle shift in my mood and put his spindly arm around me.

"We all have a cross to bear in this life," Lucifer began, looking directly into my eyes, giving me the uncanny sensation that he was peering deep into my soul. "That cross can make itself apparent early on or later in life, but it will always be there, waiting for you. It is our trial, our ultimate test. Yours has become apparent during the beginnings of your life. This will help you build strength and resilience for the years to come. You will be able to bear the might of it as you progress through life whilst others, others whose crosses come to them later, would not have the tools to forge onward as you have. They become crushed by the weight of their burden. As long as you cultivate the strength in your body, mind and soul, you will be able to battle whatever comes your way. One day, this inner strength will set you free."

Willowen melted into the background of my mind. I was transported back to London, 1823, where my story really begins. I was no longer in the gypsy camp but sitting with Lucifer in the grubby public house. I was back home.

I cannot lie. I was mystified by what he had said. I could barely comprehend anything past the first line of his speech. It did, however, leave me with an unsettled feeling, a feeling akin to nervous butterflies in the stomach. It felt like a prophecy. I felt as if one day, I would be faced with a fork in the road and my fate would be entirely based upon that one, defining decision and the unintended consequences that unwound like a loose thread afterwards. The strength of my mind, body and soul would be tested in that one truth-telling moment. Was it at this moment, over empty plates in the Badgers Den, when the shadowy curse that would haunt me for my entire life settled so gently within me that I barely felt its arrival, like a butterfly landing on the soft petals of a flower? His ominous words sent shivers down my spine, culminating in a pool of dread in the pit of my stomach.

"Anyway, enough darkness for one day," he said, baring his fangs again in that perturbing smile. "You, child, should go out into the light of day and enjoy yourself. Where's that friend of yours, Tommy?" he asked.

Tommy was a good friend, about two years older than I was at eleven years old. He came from a big family with six brothers and sisters. He was lost somewhere in the middle of the tangle of siblings and was often forgotten about by his mother who was sick and his father who was out all hours collecting coal. His mother had been sick for a while. I wasn't sure what was wrong with her but Tommy had told me that when she coughed, her handkerchiefs and bed sheets were soaked with deep, dark red stains. He had told me in a matter-of-fact manner but I had known Tommy a long time and could read the fear that lurked behind his eyes.

I had an idea where he would be on a cold sunny morning such as this one. "I think I know where to find him," I told Lucifer.

"All right then, until next time," he said, lifting a pale, long-fingered hand in farewell.

I waved goodbye and scurried off, leaving the heavy atmosphere of bleak hopelessness behind me. I felt all those men in Badgers Den were bearing crosses heavier than mine and I could see their souls were being slowly crushed to death by them.

I headed to the river. Like me, Tommy always did odd jobs here and there to earn a few coins. Today I had the feeling he would be mudlarking in the Docklands. In between jobs he often waded into the river's stinking, muddy depths in search of anything of value. Occasionally he found a coin or expensive handkerchief gliding on the river's surface but more often than not he was confronted with nothing more than slimy pebbles, rotten fragments of timber and floating rubbish.

I dodged past the stalls, beggars, shoe polishers, sandwich board men and weaved between the horses and carriages. It was quite a long distance, but I was fast. There was a biting chill in the air which made me move even quicker to keep warm. I darted through a dark alley, the natural light blocked by so many washing lines draped with tattered rags undulating slowly in the breeze, resembling defeated flags from a sunken pirate ship.

I heard glass smashing from right behind me. I ducked into a shadowy corner, my senses on high alert. A woman with hair wildly loose, clutching what looked like dirty bed linen around her naked body, was rushing out of a dilapidated house. The smashing glass had come from a man who had thrown a bottle at the woman but had missed, hitting the lamppost instead of his moving target.

"Filthy hedge whore!" he slurred, his face a blotchy red. "I'll kill you next time I see you!" he yelled, fists raised drunkenly in the air. He spat on the ground and mumbled something under his breath before stumbling back into the house. He slammed the door so violently, the windowpane shuddered and looked as if it was about to shatter. The woman's footsteps echoed off into the distance as the white billowy figure turned a corner and disappeared, a ghost disappearing into the maze of tattered clothes and shadows.

As my heart began to slow, I regained my composure and slid out of the shadows. I could smell alcohol wafting in the stagnant air of the narrow, claustrophobic alleyway. I continued on my journey. This was by no means an unusual occurrence. I had seen much worse fights and outbreaks of violence on the streets. Poverty plagued every corner of these wretched slums. It infected the city and spread like ink bleeding through paper. No one could escape it. I saw how people tried to break free from their collective dreary realities as they stumbled into dingy public houses, overcrowded music halls, watched backstreet penny gaffs and drank copious amounts of gin and other spirits. And yet, when they awoke the next day with heads pounding and pockets even lighter than the day before, their realities merely tumbled back into focus. It was a miserable cycle no one seemed to be able to break free from.

Lucifer's words crept back into my mind. "One day, you will be free," I heard his voice echo, reverberating through my mind.

As I slunk through the shadows of the alley, to find my good friend Tommy, I made a pact with myself. I would get out of this slum if it killed me.

Chapter 2

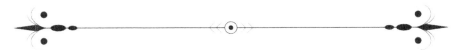

I FOUND TOMMY, as I suspected, by the docks. Instead of mudlarking, he was carrying heavy crates filled with timber and other weighty materials from one ship to another.

Although an icy wind blew off the misty surface of the water, Tommy was dripping with sweat from the exertion. He managed a smile as he saw me approaching. With a heavy sigh he carefully placed the crate on the ground.

"What are you doing here?" he said breathlessly, bending over with his hands on his scrawny knees. As he lifted his hands to stand up straight, I could see the skin had peeled off and was torn and bloody. Following my gaze, he said quickly, "Don't worry about these," as he waved his hands in the air nonchalantly. "I'll be earning a couple of shillings today for all this work," he added, managing a feeble, tired smile.

"That's good," I said, trying to hide my concern for his bleeding hands and scraped arms. "Now I'm here, I can help you!" I took his calloused, rough hands in mine and dabbed away the blood with the corner of my tatty dress. "I'll bandage these up properly when we're done," I tried to say in a carefree manner whilst staring at the deep gashes.

"All right," Tommy said, wincing in pain as I pressed his skin. "Where have you been this morning?"

"I was with Lucifer," I said excitedly. "He was telling me another one of his stories. It's a really good one. I think he'll be performing later. You should watch it!"

Tommy smiled. "You and your stories. I don't get why you like them so much. Lucifer and his puppets give me the creeps," he said, shuddering. "Mother doesn't want me watching them either." A sudden sadness seemed to wash over Tommy at the mention of his mother. His eyes were downcast and his strong, sinewy shoulders slumped.

"How is she?" I asked softly.

"Worse," he replied. "She was coughing so much last night she could barely breathe. I overheard a neighbour telling Father that she wasn't long for this world."

I put my arm around Tommy. I couldn't think of anything comforting to say to such devastating news. Death stalked everyone around here, snatching babies from their cradles, children from their mothers and grandparents from their loved ones. Nevertheless, it didn't attenuate the pain when it affected someone you knew, someone you loved.

We worked together in silence for the rest of the afternoon. Once the sun started to set, leaving a fiery trail on the water's surface, Tommy collected his wages for the day and together we headed home.

"Here you go, take half," Tommy said, trying to slip a few coins into my hand.

"No, I only helped you. You keep it, you did more of the heavy lifting," I said, digging my hands into my pockets, poking my fingers through the multitude of holes.

"That wouldn't be fair," Tommy said, his brow creased.

"Really, you keep it. I've been making money selling dolls and sewing blankets lately. So we've been doing fine. Besides it's only me and Mother at home. You have all your brothers and sisters to think about."

Tommy nodded, conceding to the logic of my argument. There were a lot of hungry mouths to feed in his household and his three younger siblings were not old enough to work yet.

"But how about we get something small to eat? I'm hungry and you must be starving!" I said, knowing he had probably not eaten anything all day.

"All right," he said, his tired face breaking into a smile.

We left the grimy docklands behind as we headed to the dark, overcrowded streets of the city. It was not safe to be wandering the streets at night, but two tired, scrawny, tatty children with dirt under their nails and holes in their shoes slipped easily into the gloomy patchwork of the city after dark and we were hardly noticed at all.

A trio of prostitutes shoved past us, nearly knocking me off my feet. One of them laughed loudly. I observed them as they sashayed down the street. Their dresses looked as if they had once been luxurious and beautiful. Now, however, I could see the ragged hems and the different shades in the skirts from where holes had been patched up and mended.

The women themselves were not young and were plastered in heavy make-up. On a youthful face, the look could pass for daring or striking. On them, however, it simply looked garish. They were all wearing bright red blush and rouge on their lips. One of them even had on what looked like sooty eyeliner, which was crumbling down her face, leaving streaks of black tears.

I stared at them, wondering if that would ever be my fate. So many poverty-stricken women and orphaned young girls turned to the madams and their brothels for shelter and money. A girl I knew and used to play with, Lizzie, at twelve years old had been snaffled off to work for a madam in a particularly grotty brothel. She had been orphaned when her parents had died within days of each other after a drawn-out stretch of illness. Her brothers had been taken off to the workhouse right after the funeral. Lizzie had been sitting in a nook of a tree, crying when it happened so they hadn't seen her. I didn't know which fate was worse, that of her brothers in a godforsaken workhouse or that of Lizzie at the mercy of the madam and the whims of the men who visited. It was heartbreaking. But these streets were overflowing with similar stories of tears, tragedy and trauma. It was a way of life. And all I wanted was to escape it.

"You ok?" Tommy asked, concerned.

I realised I had been staring blankly at the backs of the prostitutes, a world away. "Yes, I'm fine. What do you say to hot potatoes?" I said, pointing at a stall nearby selling fluffy hot potatoes in newspaper cups.

"Yes, sounds good," Tommy replied.

The warm, comforting smell made our mouths water. We ordered a cup to share. We continued to walk and eat in companionable silence, savouring every bite. When we had finished we licked the newspaper to ensure we had eaten every last morsel.

"That was good," Tommy said, stopping by a ramshackle house.

Shouts and screams were coming from an upstairs window. A group of ragged men were sitting on steps nearby, muttering and taking long swigs from a bottle they were passing around. I took several careful steps away from them.

"Well, I'll see you tomorrow, Rozzy," Tommy said.

"Sure. Hope your mother's feeling better," I replied.

"Thanks," he said, and we hugged goodbye.

I lived on the street parallel to him. As quietly and inconspicuously as I could, I crept through the alleyways making my way home. As I was walking, I passed a toothless old woman with a hunched back, swaying slightly where she sat. In a quick fluid motion, she grabbed my foot with surprising strength with one hand and with the other she gestured for food. I recoiled from her touch and tugged free from her clutches. In my haste to get away, I tripped and stumbled on a man lying on an old, filthy sack. He was either drunk or dead for he didn't stir despite me landing heavily on his leg. I dodged a bucket of rancid-smelling water that was being chucked out a window and sprinted the rest of the way home. By the time I reached the creaking wooden door my heart was hammering, ready to burst through my chest.

I slipped through the door and tiptoed through the shadows of the apothecary with its dust-lined shelves and old phials with sludgy discoloured liquids festering inside. Thick blobs of goo were suspended within several of the slimy jars. Sometimes the goo would drift slowly up or down, making it look as if it were alive.

The floorboards of the stairs creaked underfoot. I skipped the step of the rotten, splintered floorboard and reached the top. To my surprise, I heard soft voices whispering from inside the room. I strained to hear what was being said but could only capture bits and pieces of the conversation. I then heard a gentle, faint sob.

I knocked carefully on the door before pushing it open. Mother was sitting cross-legged on the floor, gently rocking a sobbing woman. The room had a strangely sweet aroma and the fire was blazing. There seemed to be an aura of calm around Mother and the woman despite her tears. It was as if they were wrapped in a halo of light, protecting them from the darkness of reality. The woman stopped sobbing as she heard me come in.

"Don't worry, that's just my daughter, Erosabel," Mother said. "Come here," she said, gesturing to me.

I went closer and kneeled by her side. It was warm on the threadbare carpet by the fire. I could see where the sweet smell was emanating from. Mother had crushed flower petals and placed them in a bowl by the fire. Mother placed a thin, wiry arm around me and hugged me close to her. I could smell lavender from her recently washed hair which hung in damp strands around her face. Mother then started to sing a low, wistful tune in a language I did not recognise. It was a song that came from another world. Mother's clear voice melted into the atmosphere so that the reverberations of the song not only echoed in my ears but also in my soul.

When I look back on my life, this was probably one of my happiest memories. As I sat there, with Mother holding me and this unknown woman together, I knew this was a special moment, one that would end too soon but would be treasured for eternity. This was one of the few moments in my life where I felt warmth seep through my very bones and into my soul, where I felt comfort, peace and safety.

Soon, Mother stopped singing. She unwrapped the strange woman from her embrace and spoke to her softly. I looked at the woman who had visited Mother at this odd hour of night. She had dark clear skin, a warm coffee colour. Her hair was in a thick braid and had a fluffy, pillowy texture. I wanted to reach out and touch it but restrained myself. She had soft eyes and full lips. Her cheeks were stained from crying but it gave her a frail, mellow sort of beauty.

"Remember," Mother was saying, "it's thirteen white stones you need. And only perform the spell on the first Friday of the full moon. You remember how?"

"Yes," the woman replied timidly. "Lay the stones in a heart and place my heart over them whilst thinking of Albert and do the same whilst thinking of myself. Then wrap the stones in a white cloth and carry this with me until the next full moon."

"Correct, but don't forget, after thinking of Albert, arrange the stones to make out his initials, AF. And when you are thinking about him, remember not to force your love on him. Just think about why you love him, his qualities, his livelihood, his features, his characteristics and such," Mother said softly.

The woman looked close to tears again. "Thank you, thank you so much. I just hope he falls in love with me before..." Her voice trailed off as her hand rested on her small, flat stomach.

"Have faith. By the next full moon, he should be drawn back to you and you must work your charms from there. And here, take this as well," Mother said, handing over a fistful of herbs. "Sprinkle this in his food and wine. Also add it to your bathwater and take a long bath allowing your skin to soak it in."

"Thank you, Esther. You are so kind," she said, taking the herbs and placing them carefully in her pocket. "I must leave now."

"Good luck," Mother said in hushed tones.

The woman gave her a watery smile and got up to leave.

I sat, watching this strange scene unfold. I felt disconnected from reality, as if I had stepped across a threshold and entered into a waking dream. Once the woman had left, Mother turned around and let her gaze land on me sitting in the centre of the threadbare carpet. She sat down next to me.

"I'm sure you have questions and I will answer them but you must promise me one thing. You will never tell a soul what you saw tonight or what you may see in the future." Mother's tone was gentle but her eyes were penetrating, searching mine to ensure I understood the gravity of the promise.

"Yes, I promise, Mother," I replied.

She let out a sigh. "Well then. Ask anything you want, my darling," she said, suddenly weary.

At first I was too shocked to say anything. For years Mother had berated me for asking questions and not holding my tongue. And now, Mother was allowing me to ask her anything. I knew this was not an opportunity I would get again anytime soon, if ever. I thought carefully before asking my first question.

"What did that woman want from you? And why was she so sad? And what was that stuff about stones that you were talking about?" I asked, the questions tumbling out, one after the other.

Mother gave a small smile. She laid my head gently in her lap and started stroking my thick, dark waves of hair. "She is with child. The father is the master of the house where she works. She's in a bind as she doesn't want to get rid of it but doesn't believe Albert will do right by her. Knowing men, I'm sure he won't," she said bitterly. She looked down at my confused face and continued more softly, "I'm just giving her a little hope that her love for him may one day be returned."

"Is that what the spell was for? To make him love her?" I asked.

"Well, you can't make anyone fall in love, and I told her as much. It may help him notice her, cherish warm feelings towards her. There's no knowing really what course fate will take," Mother replied wistfully. "But we can try to nudge it along the right path as much as is within our powers."

"Do you have powers?" I continued with my interrogation.

"We all do, sweetheart," Mother replied. "You do, I do, that woman does. We just need to learn how to cultivate them, nurture them and let them grow within us. The more we pour our time and energies into one thing the stronger it becomes, whether that be in love, work, friendships or vices, gambling, stealing and the like."

I nodded silently. Mother's thin hands were interlacing themselves between thick strands of my hair. It was an alien sensation to me. The sweet smell and warmth of the fireplace made me feel light-headed and sleepy but I had to continue asking questions. I had to stretch out this moment for as long as I could, extending it through time and space.

"Why must I promise not to tell anyone? If you are doing good deeds, shouldn't other people know?" I asked.

"Not everyone sees it that way. Some small-minded people see it as an evil. They believe free thinkers, open-minded people, wanderers, travellers, unorthodox healers, gypsies all need to be caged and forced to walk one path and one path only. They want to quash our freedoms, our minds and our souls. They believe the road to heaven is a dark, gloomy journey devoid of all life's pleasures, a colourless existence. They are the real devils, not us." Mother's gaze was lost in the dying flames. The deep blue of her eyes reflected the fire and I could see the turbulent, unsettled mind that was eating away within.

"Did Father teach you these things?" I asked, my voice barely above a whisper.

Mother tore her gaze away from the dying embers to look down at me, an unfathomable expression playing across her delicate features. "You're a smart one, Erosabel. You will go far. Get out of this place. Don't leave it too long and become like me."

I felt a wave of sadness wash over me. Mother's disappointments and regrets seemed to pour out of her and, like a sponge, I absorbed them. I felt her anger, her sadness, her losses.

"What about the voices? Does this have anything to do with them?" I said before I could stop myself.

Mother's fingers instantly froze, intertwined in a lock of my hair. I felt her thin, frail body become tense and rigid. "I think that's enough for one day. You look exhausted. It's time for bed," she said softly but sternly.

I could see the shutters close on the golden window of opportunity I had been granted. I wondered when, if ever, they would open again and shine light into the deep gulf that separated mother and daughter. I nodded, taking my cue to leave. Regretfully, I heaved myself up and looked into her face before going to bed.

"Good night, Erosabel. I hope you know that you are precious to me. You cannot fathom the evils I battle with every day, the wars waged within. If I were religious, I would pray to God that you are never able to understand the turmoil that exists within me. It is a curse best left to be born with my life and carried away with my death," she said, turning her face back to the fire.

I stared at Mother, questions and confusion swarming within my brain. Partly, I felt elated. It was the closest Mother had ever come to saying she loved me. And yet, part of me felt broken by her sadness. I wanted to fix her and thus heal myself. The helplessness, knowing there was nothing I could do to make things right, weighed heavily on my conscience.

Tears, like a film, clouded over my eyes. Before Mother could notice, I quickly kissed her on the cheek and scuttled to the other room where my thin, dilapidated mattress lay on the floor. It was a dark room with no windows or light. I shivered as I snuggled under my thin blanket. That night, I had a deep, dreamless sleep. I slept like the dead, barely moving a muscle. When I awoke the next day, I felt I had aged a hundred years.

Chapter 3

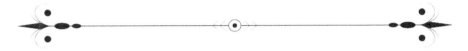

THE COLD, EMPTY winter melted into a dreary, uneventful spring. At last, a weak summer sun infiltrated the heavy, swollen clouds and hazy smog that blanketed the city. I had a regular job as a washer in one of the many brothels that dotted London. I had finished my last load of soiled bed linen. My hands and arms were stinging as the soap seeped into the cracks in my peeling skin. I threw out the soapy water and hurried off to find the madam to collect my day's wages.

I found her in the reception room where guests were invited to sit as she offered them wine or spirits of their choice. She was rearranging the topless figurines that lined the mantelpiece. I let out a meek cough, announcing my presence. She turned around slowly. Her grey-streaked hair was piled high on her head. She always wore elaborate gowns in deep, dark shades of scarlet and purple. Her dark, angular eyebrows gave her a permanently cross expression. Aside from a dab of powder, the only other make-up she wore was a statement rouge on her lips. I had never seen her without her blood-red lips painted on.

She surveyed me and said slowly, "I suppose you want your earnings for the day?"

I nodded in response.

As if moving in slow motion, she reached for a pouch inside one of the many folds of her dress. She pulled out what looked like a black velvet drawstring purse and let two shillings jangle out. Without saying a word, she dropped them onto the oak table between us.

"Thank you," I said, averting my gaze as I pocketed the coins. "Thank you. I'll be back first thing tomorrow."

She did not speak but continued to burn a hole through the crown of my head with her penetrating stare. Feeling perturbed, I scrambled to get away as fast as I could. I didn't like the way she eyed me. I couldn't help but feel as if she was making plans for me, calculating my worth or potential in her establishment. Fortunately I was small for my age. At eleven I could still easily pass for a seven-year-old with no hint of a swell in my chest or curve of the hip. I was all bony appendages and coarse dark skin. With another mumbled "thank you" I scurried out of the house, leaving the heavy silence behind.

I set off to find Tommy. I found him by the river, knee-deep in muck.

"Tommy," I called out from the banks, waving. Normally I would go in with him, wading through the filth that constituted the river. The thought of doing any more washing, however, made me shudder. My hands were still burning from the last load I had done.

Tommy glanced up, smiling. I noticed a small, soggy bundle in his hands as he trudged through the mud towards me.

"What did you find?" I asked excitedly.

"Nothing much," he said, displaying his wares to me in his mud-streaked palms. His dingy collection consisted of a broken fragment of crockery, a frayed bit of knotted rope and a sodden scrap of material which could have been torn from a dress or handkerchief, there was no knowing.

I nodded encouragingly. "Not bad for one day."

Tommy shrugged, looking unconvinced. "How was your day?" he asked.

"Good," I replied, showing him the coins I had earned. "I've been working from morning to night most days and I've actually managed to save up a few!"

"What are you saving them for?" Tommy asked as he rubbed the dirt off the trinkets he had pulled out from the sludgy river.

I thought about Tommy's question. What was I saving them up for? The thought of buying a warm pie or pretty trinket was tempting. Yet something made me hold back. I clutched on to the belief that there was more to life than this. That Mother and I could escape, and these coins could be the key. I answered Tommy's question with a casual shrug of the shoulders.

"Should we see if Lucifer has any shows today?" I asked excitedly.

Tommy's face broke into a grin. "Sure, let's go!" He wrung out his trousers as best he could and placed his findings into a tatty pocket. Together we made our way back to the streets in search of Lucifer and his penny gaffs.

Lucifer stood out amongst the crowd, his dark hair and spindly frame towering a head above the majority of the people. He was preparing his puppet set for a show.

"My two favourite audience members," he said, smiling. "You're just in time."

"You're starting a show?" I asked. "Can we help set anything up?"

"Just rally up a few children and collect some coins for me," Lucifer said, tossing a cloth hat in my direction.

Immediately I set off to work, searching out children who may have a penny to spend, or a tired-looking parent looking for a moment's entertainment for her little one at any cost. Within a quarter of an hour, I had rallied up a decent crowd and the hat already had a few coins jangling in it. I placed the hat by the puppet stage, allowing for people who enjoyed the show to toss in a bit extra before leaving.

"Ladies and gentlemen. Boys and girls," Lucifer said in his deep rumbling voice, his arms flung open wide in a dramatic gesture. "This is not your ordinary backstreet puppet show. This is not going to be your ordinary tale. This is a tale about a sorceress, a dark prophecy and a girl who turns into dust. It is a fairy tale to listen to and take heed. We will begin as all good fairy tales begin, with Once Upon a Time..."

Lucifer had his audience captured, staring up at him, drawn towards his natural magnetism. The story he told that day stayed with me for many years to come. I couldn't help but feel that it was this story that set the course of my destiny.

The story was as follows:

45

Once upon a time, there was a middle-aged couple who lived in a cottage tucked away deep in the woodlands. Rarely did they leave their humble abode as they had everything they needed. It was a beautiful corner of the world where flowers blossomed and the lands produced the freshest, most sumptuous fruits. In the summers the sun dappled through the trees, scattering shards of crystal light on the river's surface. The ripples scintillated like dancing diamonds as the soft breeze gently caressed it.

During autumn, the land turned into ribbons of scarlet and gold until the quiet hush of winter descended on the earth. The couple would watch from their window as fresh snowflakes sprinkled down from the sky like pale confetti. Their life was nearly perfect, except for one thing. They were childless. All either of them had ever wanted was a child to love, teach, nurture and watch grow. Every year they wished, hoped and prayed that their luck would change. Yet with every passing year their disappointment became ever more bitter to swallow until one day, they decided to take fate into their own hands.

It was spring, the season of birth and renewal. Lambs stood on uncertain spindly legs in the fields, bunnies tripped and hopped after their mothers whilst fluffy ducklings wiggled their tufts of feathers as they paddled along the river. The couple had not openly discussed what they were planning to do, yet there was no need as they had been together for so many years, indeed they had even lost count. It was as if their minds were connected and thoughts traversed openly between them without the need for spoken words. In that way, they came to realise what they had to do.

A sorceress lived near the banks of the river. She lived in a mud and straw hut under the bent arms of a weeping willow tree. One fine morning, the couple journeyed their way to her. It took the better part of the whole morning for them to find their way. Although they had seen and passed by the hut many times it was as if its location was constantly shifting. It was nothing dramatic, sometimes it was a barely noticeable shift such as a change in angle. Other times, the hut was like undulating sand dunes in a desert, there one minute and swept away the next.

When they finally stumbled upon her abode, they knocked on the earth door. Although from the outside the appearance of the hut was crumbling and dilapidated, the couple drew breath as they stared at the sumptuous decorations inside. It was equivalent to a palace with marbled floors and ribbons of silver and gold lining the walls and furniture. So busy were the couple admiring the furnishings, they did not notice an old, stooped woman emerge from the shadows.

"Welcome, welcome, dear travellers and friends. What can I do for you this fine spring day?" she said in an old, creaking voice. Despite her fragile exterior, her eyes were sharp as pins and surveyed the couple without blinking once.

"Pray, help us, sorceress. We have prayed to our Gods but they are merciless and cruel. All we want is a child to love and raise. Can you help us in this request?"

"But of course I can, if that is what you wish," replied with sorceress, an enigmatic smile playing on her lips. "I am here to help where your Gods refuse. But you must understand what you wish for as well as the consequences that will ensue."

"Yes, yes, it is our deepest desire, our most heartfelt wish!" the couple replied in unison.

"Ah, let's not be hasty. I have not detailed to you how it will work as of yet. You must listen, and listen well," the sorceress said, raising a crooked finger.

The couple, only hearing what they wished to hear, half listened to the cautionary tale of the sorceress.

"I can bless you with a babe, and it will be yours to raise. I can create a fair beauty with a spirit from the purest air, a body from the lush bounty of the earth, wisdom from the great depths of the sea and a heart borne from the passionate flames of the sun. All these elements will converge together, creating this miraculous life. But be warned, the elements creating your most darling daughter will only be able to bind themselves together for sixteen years before splitting apart and disintegrating back into the air, earth, sea and fire. At this point, your beloved daughter will have a choice: to allow nature to take its course and to let the elements constituting her return to nature. Or to visit me where I can cast a spell to bind the elements together forever. But this will be forever. She will be cursed with everlasting life. She will be cursed to watch all her loved ones pass on and die. She will be cursed to walk these godforsaken lands for all eternity. She will be cursed to be immortal." The sorceress finished her tale with her head bowed awaiting the couple's answer.

Without hesitation, they replied, "Sorceress, we have heard your talk. Now bless us with a daughter."

"Very well. Although I fear this will only multiply the heartache that already exists in the world, I shall do as you wish." She closed her eyes and began to recite:

"Breath of the breeze, drift my way, sail through the skies,

Bounty of the earth, raise thy ground, within you miracles lie,

Dark depths of the ocean, float to the surface, let wisdom ripple through,

Combine with fire, flames of passion, behold this babe I bring to you."

Within moments of the sorceress's chant, a crying babe appeared. The couple snatched it from the old woman's gnarled arms and rocked it gently to sleep.

"She's perfect. We'll call her Theodora, our divine gift," the woman said to her husband. Without a word of thanks to the sorceress, they left with their bundle and returned to their cottage.

Sixteen happy years passed as they watched their little girl bloom into a beautiful, elegant young woman. The couple had forgotten all about the prophecy until the sorceress paid them a visit a week before the girl's sixteenth birthday.

Hunched and aged, she knocked on the cottage door of the happy family. The woman answered. Instantly recognising the old sorceress, she slammed the door in her face.

"Go away! We want nothing from you! Leave us be!" she yelled through the oak door.

"I wish it were so. And yet it is not within my powers to halt the prophecy. Once the die is cast, there is nothing we can do except watch the game unfurl."

"This is no game! This is my daughter, my life!" yelled the woman, near hysterics.

"In one week the girl will have a choice to make, a choice of the utmost importance. Either she chooses to follow nature and return to the air, earth, sea and fire, or she should choose to lead an unhappy, immortal life. You should have no sway in her decision. I beseech you, let her make it of her own free will."

"Leave us in peace!" yelled the woman once more.

With that, the sorceress vanished.

On the day of Theodora's sixteenth birthday, she received a message. A raven sent from the sorceress found its way into her room whilst she slept. Attached to his leg was a scroll of parchment.

"Now what have you there, little birdie?" Theodora muttered, tossing a thick lock of golden hair aside. She untied the scroll and spread out the parchment. She read the words over and over whilst tears flowed from her eyes. In spidery writing, the sorceress had detailed the entire prophecy.

Upon hearing Theodora's sobs, her parents swiftly entered the room. They took one look at their weeping daughter and told her they knew what to do. They would find the sorceress.

"But does that not mean I will be immortal? I would be cursed to watch you and all that I love die?" Theodora said through sobs.

"But child, you will see us die anyway. That is the natural order of things," her mother said, in comforting tones.

"But I would see the world age and wither and all I love turn to ash," she continued.

"But darling, you do not know that for sure. Surely, the sorceress will have another spell by then to put you into a sweet everlasting sleep," her father soothed.

"But would it not be better to have enjoyed this life as I have and put all to rest rather than meddle in the natural way of things?" Theodora beseeched.

"But love, there is so much you have not yet experienced. It would be unjust to cut a rose when it has only just bloomed," the couple said in unison.

With their voices resounding in her head, Theodora sought out the sorceress. She found her hut by the river and told her she had made a decision: she wanted the spell for everlasting life.

"Child, is this your desire or that of those who raised you?" the sorceress asked, her sharp eyes fixed on Theodora.

"I am convinced. It is my choice," Theodora said as bravely as she could manage.

"Then may your will be done," replied the sorceress quietly.

"Child so bright, so young, so beautiful,

May you age not a year more,

May your body, spirit and soul,

Continue to walk this earth forevermore."

Thus the spell was done, the die cast.

Theodora thanked the sorceress with tears in her eyes, kissing her hands and feet. "My parents will be so happy. Thank you, thank you," Theodora gushed.

"Please do not thank me, child. Never thank me for this," the sorceress said, her eyes also brimming with tears.

The couple welcomed their daughter with open arms when they saw her return, overflowing with light, youth and beauty. As the years crumbled and aged, Theodora remained the same. The couple grew old and tired and died a happy death in the comfort of their home. With a heavy heart, Theodora buried them in the woods. Theodora married and fell in love. She bore children. But it was her curse to outlive them all. As years turned to decades, decades turned to centuries and centuries to millennia, Theodora roamed the earth, weary and broken. When earth burst into stardust, Theodora remained, drifting through galaxies and far beyond. She had experienced everything possible as well as impossible. She had lived a thousand lives and more. She wept into eternity, lamenting the decision she had made in youthful ignorance.

One day, as she was drifting from one ethereal planet to another, she came across a crater, within which sat an ancient woman. Theodora called to her as she hadn't seen another member of the human species in millennia.

"Hello, down there," Theodora called, her voice unfamiliar to her as she hadn't used it in so long.

"It is you, child. I've been waiting for you," the old woman called back, her voice barely above a hoarse whisper.

"Do I know you, kind woman?" asked Theodora.

"Yes, you know me and you have every right to curse me into oblivion. I am the sorceress who gave you everlasting life," the sorceress stated plainly.

"But it was not your fault, it was mine. It was my wrongful decision," Theodora wept, clasping the old woman's wrinkled, papery hands. "I should have gone as nature intended. This existence is a worse evil than any death you could endure me to suffer."

"Child, your heart is good. After all these years, I still see the fire in your heart, the light in your spirit, and the wisdom in your eyes. I have been working all this time to break the spell. To put an end to the prophecy, to end the evil that man and woman subjugated you to."

"And have you found it, dear sorceress?" Theodora asked.

"Prophecies and spells are impossible to reverse. But I believe I have found a way to end your misery. I can rip you to pieces, split your very atoms, tear the water, air, fire and earth from your body. With all the spell's energy entering your body, you will combust and explode into stardust. You will continue to exist as specks of shimmering light, but you will be non-sentient, non-seeing, non-feeling. You will know not of your own existence. Your molecules will glitter in space for all eternity but you will have no knowledge of it."

"Yes, please, sorceress. I beg of you, cast your spell!" Theodora replied.

"Very well, child," the sorceress said.
"Heart of fire, passion be ceased,
No longer give this maiden breath,
The time has come to rest in peace,
I bestow upon your body, the likeness of death."

With those words, the air, water, earth and fire that had created Theodora came apart in a flood of energy. Heat, light and stardust radiated out of her skin. Within seconds, her earthly body exploded, scattering orbs of light into galaxies near and far beyond.

The tired sorceress smiled and exhaled her last breath. All these years, she had been fighting death with spells of her own until she could figure out how to lift the curse the couple had bestowed upon the girl, for her love for the girl was pure and unselfish. Once she had worked it out, she closed her eyes and let nature take its course. Her last sensation was that of the warmth of a thousand pinpricks of light caressing her face as her inner light slowly flickered, faded and died.

The End

As Lucifer finished the tale, he drew the curtains of his stage of wonders and gave a low bow to his audience. It took several long moments of silence before the audience realised the story was over. Once reality seeped back in, there was a loud round of applause. More people had gathered during the storytelling and shiny coins flew in shimmering arcs into Lucifer's cloth cap.

Lucifer bowed several more times. "Thank you, thank you, good people of London."

Slowly, the crowd dispersed as the magic of the story settled like fairy dust on the dirt roads.

"What did you think of that one?" Lucifer asked us.

"It was a real good one," Tommy said. "I wish I could live forever with everything I could ever want!" he said, with a wistful gleam in his eye.

Lucifer gave a slow nod and then turned his gaze to me. "And you, what did you think?"

At first I was lost for words. I couldn't quite formulate a sentence that did my feelings justice or expressed the powerful impact the story had had on me.

"It's a beautiful fairy tale about true love, I think. The parents did not genuinely love their daughter otherwise they wouldn't have made her choose everlasting life. It was the sorceress who loved her and worked all those centuries to put things to right. She healed her with her spell and her love."

The corners of Lucifer's mouth twitched. "I'm glad you liked it."

"I feel sorry for the sorceress," I continued.

"Why the sorceress?" asked Lucifer.

"Because she was only trying to do good and help people. But the old couple took advantage of that. They made her do something bad even though she didn't want to. How do you know when you've gone too far, even if you're trying to do good?"

"That's a good question. As long as you are guided by your moral compass and do what you believe is right, you will be fine. You have a strong moral compass, Erosabel. Most people are guided by fears, doubts, jealousy, the whims of others, greed, but as long as you stay true to yourself and keep those vices at bay, you have nothing to fear."

I nodded, trying to take it all in. Lucifer's words of wisdom always made my head spin. "I want to help people," I said without thinking, "like the sorceress!" Or like Mother, I thought silently to myself, remembering the crying woman sitting on the carpet. Had Mother helped her? I hadn't thought of that night in a long time but the memory came rushing back to me now.

"I'm sure one day you will. You have a great power within you, Erosabel," Lucifer said with a smile as he ruffled my hair.

"I have a question, Lucifer," I continued.

"Ask away," he replied.

"You said she exploded into molecules. What is that?"

"Ah, you picked up on that. I guess I shouldn't be surprised. You notice almost everything."

I smiled, enjoying the warm sensation the compliment gave me.

"Well, there's new science out there. It's truly a fascinating thing. If you think my stories are interesting, you will be blown away by the things science can teach you. There's something called matter and we're all made of it. Everything you see and touch is matter. And that matter is made up of tiny particles called atoms and molecules. These are not visible to the human eye. So when she exploded into molecules, she exploded into tiny, nearly invisible fragments of herself."

I nodded, trying to keep up with him, as usual. It was not an easy task. "So, we're all just little molecules and atoms sewn up together?"

"Pretty much," replied Lucifer.

"How do these atoms stay glued together?"

"Well, they don't always stay glued together, as you say. If a certain amount of energy is applied, the matter can change. Take water, for example. At a certain temperature water is water. When energy, in the form of heat, is added to it, the particles become unfastened and it turns into steam. We're all made of matter and energy."

"And the stardust? When she turned into stardust, does that mean they are just matter and energy as well?"

"Yes, they are." Lucifer smiled mysteriously. "We are all ultimately stardust."

I nodded, liking that analogy. "How beautiful," I reflected.

"It truly is a beautiful world out there, if only everyone was able to see it."

Tommy, who had been chatting to another boy, turned and said, "Hey, what are you two talking about?"

I loved Tommy but I somehow felt this discussion was over his head.

It was late afternoon when Tommy went back home and I made my way to the apartment above the disused apothecary. My mind was swirling with Lucifer's stories, morals, rights and wrongs. I felt like it was all part of some strange universal puzzle where I had been given the pieces but could not quite arrange them in the correct places.

I opened the creaking wooden door to the apothecary. Usually I would dart upstairs, skipping the rotten step since I did not like being alone in the apothecary for long. It always filled me with a deep sense of melancholy to see thick carpets of dust layering the shelves, cracked vials which someone had once spent so much time preparing, as well as the nasty little spiders and insects that filled the corners and scuttled between the cracks of the floorboards.

Today, however, felt different. I let the door close gently behind me as I stood in the middle of the abandoned shop. Shafts of ethereal light blanketed the floorboards in a golden honey hue. I watched, mesmerised, as tiny dust particles like flecks of diamonds floated and scintillated in the air. I took my time, slowly walking around the shop, as if discovering it for the first time.

I let my hand rest on one of the shelves, exciting a plume of dust. As I traced the outline of a cracked bottle, the peeling label crumbled under my touch. I examined the bottles closely, all of different shapes and sizes, as though they were priceless jewels. With the utmost care, I picked up some of the less fragile-looking ones. Several gave off foul pungent aromas when the stopper was uncorked.

I then turned my attention to the drawer of a thick, sturdy desk with chipped wood and dark stains on its counter. Immediately I recoiled as a spider the size of my hand sprung out the drawer, scuttled down the table leg and through a gaping hole in the floorboards. Waiting for my beating heart to return to its normal pace, I remained rooted in place, terrified to look at what else lay in the dark corners of the drawers.

As a cautionary gesture, I gave the table a gentle kick and then rapped on the counter firmly, hoping to expel any other nasty surprises that may be lurking within. When nothing happened, I opened the drawer wider and peered inside. There were two books, one on top of each other. Carefully, I lifted up the first one. As gently as I could, I placed it on the counter of the desk and wiped off the dust with my bare hand.

I flipped through the thin, fragile pages, noticing lots of numbers and notes scrawled in the margins. I had no idea how to read and therefore no idea what any of it meant. I continued to flip the pages in the hope of finding some pictures or illustrations to help me decipher what the book was about, but there were none.

I was then struck with an idea. I could take it to Lucifer. He was one of the only people I knew who could read. Perhaps he could tell me what the book meant.

The second book was heavier than the first. Dark mouldy stains spread like a disease on several of the pages. This book contained some numbers but mainly writing and, to my satisfaction, pictures. The pictures were hand-drawn in a careful, delicate way, surely by a feminine hand. There were various pictures of herbs, flowers, bottles and equipment. It didn't take long to figure out that the pictures were describing how to make certain remedies and medicines. There were drawings of various ailments next to each remedy. One drawing revealed a man with an extensive rash all over his body which he was scratching furiously. Another showed a picture of a fainting woman with her head held in her hands. The next showed a child coughing into a handkerchief.

There were words next to the pictures, which I decided I would ask Lucifer to read to me later. However, it was easy enough to figure out a lot of what was being portrayed by following the steps in the pictures and checking the corresponding ailment portrayed in the drawings.

I was fascinated by it all. As carefully as I could, I peeled the damp pages apart and pored over each page. I was so engrossed in the book that I was not aware of the sun setting and darkness pooling into the room. I knew Mother would never let me light a candle for such frivolous activities. Regretfully, I closed the book and placed it back in the drawer. I would return to it the moment I finished washing the following day. I could not help but feel the warm glow of a secret kindle deep within me. I would become the sorceress from Lucifer's story. I would help and heal people through remedies found in the tome of treasures I had just discovered. With Mother's help, we would restore the apothecary to its previous splendour, and by doing so I would no longer be the burdensome curse Mother believed me to be.

Chapter 4

"YOU WANT TO what?" Mother asked, glaring down at me.

It was the next morning, before I was to head out to the brothel to work on the endless stream of washing.

"I thought we could re-open the apothecary. You have your healing spells and we could make herbal remedies and elixirs for people who don't believe in spells but want to feel better and get well," I said timidly, my voice drifting into a whisper under Mother's harsh stare.

"And where would we get the money to buy all the ingredients for that? My spells can do more than any ridiculous herbal potion," Mother said drily.

"I've got some money from the washing work I've been doing. I can start buying the flowers and herbs that we need. I can also get the material we need to make the equipment to crush and mix them."

To my shock, my last statement was met with a sharp slap across the face.

"You've been hoarding money from me, you sneaky little rat," Mother spat in a dangerous whisper.

My lip was swelling and I could taste blood pooling in my mouth. I simply shook my head, trying to hold back tears. Mother was still a moment. Suddenly she knelt down next to me. With the corner of her dress, she dabbed at my cut, bruised lip.

"I don't know where you've been getting these far-fetched ideas. Perhaps Lucifer has been filling your head with his ridiculous stories," Mother said. "We don't need the apothecary. We are doing just fine as we are."

I nodded silently. I was already planning ways in which I could get things started by myself. I knew it was a good plan, and I would see it through with or without Mother's help.

"Perhaps you need more honest work to keep your mind busy. Isn't it time you were off to Madam Stark's brothel?"

Again I nodded silently and made my way downstairs. Seeing the dilapidated apothecary created a steely determination within. I would see my plan through. I would work longer shifts at the brothel, not only doing the washing but also scrubbing the floors, dusting the surfaces, running errands for anyone in need, mending the sheets and any other job they could think to give me so I could earn a few extra coins to re-do our apothecary.

I could even picture the name, Rose's Remedies. Erosabel was too long and too strange a name. It wouldn't work as the name of the apothecary. But Rose, that was an elegant, simple name and an easy one to remember. I had always wished Mother had called me Rose, not

Erosabel. The sign would have a painting of a blooming rose within a glittering vial. Once it was up and running, Mother would have to see what a success it could be and how it could be the key to lifting us out of this ever hungry, ever lurking, ever cruel spiral of poverty we were in.

I went to work that day with a newfound vigour and intensity. I scrubbed sheets until my hands were raw. I picked up extra loads of washing and once I'd finished with that, I scrubbed floors until my back ached. Madam Stark watched me with sharp curiosity.

The sun began its nightly descent into the underworld whilst I was huddled in a cramped corner, mending a tattered piece of bed linen. Suddenly a dark shadow stretched itself over my work, making it impossible for me to see where the needle had to go.

"You are still here?" Madam Stark's cold, hard voice penetrated the gloom.

"Yes, Madam. And if you don't mind, I would like to keep working until I finish this. I know I'm just a washer, but if there are any other tasks, any at all, I can do them!" I said as enthusiastically as my weary countenance would allow.

Madam Stark raised her thin angular eyebrow. "Go home, Erosabel. Now. I don't want your tired eyes miscalculating a stitch and ruining my linen."

I looked down to hide the tears welling up in my bloodshot eyes. Madam Stark then threw down several coins. It was nearly double the amount I usually got for just washing the linen. I looked up dumbfounded.

"I recognise hard work when I see it. But it's no good being a hard worker if your work is rubbish. Go home, Erosabel, but come back tomorrow bright and early. I have plenty more for you to do."

When I finally found my voice, Madam Stark had already turned away. "Thank you, thank you so much!" I gushed.

She stopped in the doorway but didn't turn around. I could barely hear her whispered reply: "I do not want your thanks, just your work. This is a transaction, Erosabel. One day, you will curse me for it." Without further explanation, she swept up the creaking stairs.

Too tired to try to understand the meaning hidden within her enigmatic words, I got up on shaky legs, pocketed the extra coins and made my way home.

The next day, I arrived at the brothel bright and early as promised. Madam Stark had a long list of chores and errands that I was to complete. I was to do my regular washing, continue mending torn sheets, scrub all floors and surfaces, pick up packages and deliver several messages to all sorts of men, women, stragglers, urchins, shopkeepers and prostitutes all over London.

From then on, my days started as soon as the sun rose and ended long after it had set. I was exhausted but kept going. The burning desire within fuelled me when I went without food for days at a time. My dream breathed air into my lungs when they were searing from running from one end of London to the other carrying all sorts of boxes and parcels on my narrow shoulders. My hope for the future was my beacon of light when I felt I was being consumed by darkness.

I had been suffering through these gruelling days for several weeks before Tommy and Lucifer commented on my absence from their lives. Lucifer was performing at his usual spot near Badgers Den. I had managed to attend one of his shows as it was next to one of the shops where I was picking up a delivery. Usually I was his most rapt and avid listener; however, today, perched on the delivery box, my eyelids started to droop. Several times I was about to slip off the box before I was startled awake. Tommy squeezed himself next to me on my perch.

"Roz, you ok?" he said, looking at my tired face in concern.

"I'm all right, Tom," I replied. "I've just got a lot I need to do."

"What's going on? You've been so busy lately."

"Yes, I was meaning to ask you that myself," Lucifer chipped in.

I hadn't realised his show had ended and the crowd had dispersed. The same concern I saw in Tommy's face was reflected in Lucifer's eyes.

"I've been picking up more work and more chores for extra coins," I said simply.

"What for?" Lucifer asked. "You look exhausted."

I hadn't told anyone else of my plan to refurbish the apothecary. After Mother's response, I was scared to tell anyone for fear they would also mock my decision. I could take it from Mother as I was used to her bizarre reactions, but I wouldn't be able to continue with the plan if Tommy and Lucifer felt the same way. Their opinions mattered.

"Well, it's all part of a bigger plan," I ventured slowly.

Both Lucifer and Tommy looked at me expectantly. I heaved a sigh before continuing. I told them all about the dusty old book I had found in the apothecary, about my plans of fixing it up, about how I was trying to earn more so that I could buy the necessary materials and ingredients to get started. In an attempt to convince myself as much as them, I told them how it wouldn't be so difficult as things were already set up. It just needed dusting down, freshly stocked shelves and a new name. I was staring at the palms of my grubby hands as I finished, not daring to look up into their expressions of derision and ridicule.

"Wow," Tommy finally said.

I peeked up at him. There was no mockery in his tone. He seemed genuinely astonished at my plan.

"Erosabel, that's amazing," Lucifer said. "You are an ingenious girl. Any help you need, I'm here for you. I can take a look at that book and see what the notes are. I could even teach you to read some letters and words if you like!"

Tears of joy sprung in my eyes as relief washed over me, mingled with utter exhaustion. Someone believed in me. And not just one person, but two. Two of the most important people in my life believed in my plan.

"I'll help too wherever I can," Tommy added enthusiastically. "This is going to be great! We'll get it up and running in no time!"

I nodded and smiled. "I will see if I can get off a bit early today and show you both the apothecary and what I've got planned. Maybe you could help me out with the books, Lucifer," I said, hopeful.

"Yes, yes! Let's see the place," Tommy said, springing up from the box. His enthusiasm seemed to outdo my own. I laughed at his overjoyed reaction.

"I have several more shows to do this afternoon. Let's say just before sunset we meet at the apothecary?" Lucifer said.

"Perfect!" I replied. I then realised I had been sitting for a good half an hour and still not only had the package to deliver but a list of errands as long as my arm to complete. I sprang into action, startling Tommy.

"Sorry, I just realised I have to run, but I'll see you later," I said, lifting up the box with one hand and waving with the other as I began to wind my way through the crowd.

Several hours later, at the agreed time, we all met in the apothecary. I felt a slight wave of embarrassment as I looked at the place through their eyes; a complete wreck as opposed to my sparkling dream.

"Obviously it needs loads of work and I'm going to fix it up. I mean..." I started babbling.

Lucifer simply raised his long-fingered, slender white hand in the air to quiet me. "This is going to be perfect," he said solemnly. "Now, show me that book."

I took the two books from the drawer and gave them to him. "This one is how to make the remedies. I can understand most of it with the pictures," I explained.

Tommy looked curiously over my shoulder at all the ailments. "Ugh, that's disgusting," he said, pointing to a picture of a man popping what looked like a pus-filled blister on his foot.

"And this one," I continued, giving Tommy the book so he could gawk at the hideous array of diseases portrayed. "Looks like it has numbers and writing but I can't make head or tail of it."

"Ah," Lucifer said, nodding. "It's a ledger. This is vital," he explained, looking at me. "This is a record of all the expenditures you will have to make, how much each remedy will cost you to make, how much you will sell them for, your profits and such."

I swallowed. I had no idea how to compute numbers. All of a sudden the project seemed much more daunting than I had expected. I thought I would simply save enough money, buy some of the basic ingredients, make several remedies and sell them. All this number crunching and profits had not even occurred to me. I felt overwhelmed at the prospect of having to be responsible for all this.

"Don't worry," Lucifer said calmly, sensing my increasing desperation. "I can teach you the basics and take care of the numbers myself."

"Really?" I asked.

"Absolutely," he replied.

"So when can we start fixing the place up?" Tommy piped up. "I've been helping mend old pieces of furniture and have learnt a few tricks. I can fix up that desk, that old chair and maybe even the shelves if I can sneak out the toolkit from the shop I've been working at."

"Let's start tomorrow!" I said, hardly believing that we were actually going to get the place restored and turn my dream into a reality.

* * * * *

We set a regular time and as often as possible met to work on rebuilding the place. During these sessions, Lucifer also taught me to read numbers, letters and basic words. Tommy tore out the original shelves with Lucifer's help as they were all rotten. He then put up new ones with timber he had "found" (I believed this meant stole) from the docks.

Mother continued to ignore the project happening under her very roof. I never spoke about it with her and she never asked what Lucifer, Tommy or I were doing or the raucous noise we were creating. She strode right past us when she saw us scrubbing the walls and floors and throwing out the rotten wood. She turned away as we dusted everything down and removed the broken vials from the shelves, to which some of them were nearly glued. She breezed up the stairs as Lucifer showed me the books and how to read them. She belligerently refused to believe in my dream or that I could make something of the disused place.

Mother continued to conduct her strange spells and practices upstairs as I fixed the downstairs room. Over the years I had noticed a change in her spells as well as the people who visited her. No longer were there weeping, fragile-looking women. The spells seemed stranger and darker and the people who sought them reflected that change.

One evening, I heard eerie chanting. It wasn't musical, like the time I heard Mother singing. It sounded deep and ominous. I then heard flapping and the soft coo of what sounded like a dove. As quietly as I could, I pushed the door open a fraction so I could see what was going on. Mother was dressed head to toe in black, as was the woman sitting opposite her. I heard the wild flapping of a dove's wings again and then saw the glint of a sharp needle. Mother handed the needle to the woman and whispered something to her. In a flash, the woman grabbed the needle and pierced the dove whilst uttering what sounded like a name three times.

I looked away in horror as blood spurted from the poor creature's limp body. Mother wrapped the corpse in a handkerchief, handed it to the woman and whispered a final instruction. I quickly left my hiding spot and went downstairs as quietly as possible, trying to avoid the creaks in the floorboard. Just as I reached the bottom I began to fiddle with the desk and drawers as I heard the other woman hurrying down the stairs with the bloody bundle in her hand. Black lace covered her face so I couldn't define her features. She was very tall and walked so elegantly she looked like a black ghost gliding by.

Mother was standing at the top of the stairs. The way she stared down at me I was sure she knew. She knew what I had just seen. She knew I had been hiding behind the door, horrified by what I was witnessing. She turned and closed the door behind her.

Chapter 5

I CONTINUED TO work long hours, keeping Madam Stark's brothel spick and span as well as completing the endless list of errands she prepared for me. This had been my routine for the better part of a year and a half, and I was used to the gruelling work.

This morning was a morning like any other. The weak summer sun was making a shaky appearance, darting in and out of the clouds above. I had just started my load of washing when Bessie, another washer girl, came up to me.

"The Stark lady is looking for you," she said, her brow furrowed in concern. "She said she wants to see you immediately."

I swallowed hard, trying to think of some errand I had forgotten or linen I had left unwashed. Madam Stark was a woman of few words. If she was unhappy with something, with lips tightly pursed she would snatch the cane by the fireplace and lash us several times. Fortunately, the majority of my work was up to her standards and in the two years I had worked for her, I had only been caned once.

I entered the stuffy reception room. The topless figurines on the mantelpiece had multiplied over the past couple of years. Madam Stark had her back to me when I entered the room. The hair piled up high on top of her head was slashed with multiple streaks of grey, and she was wearing a faded purple gown. She turned slowly to face me.

"You wanted to see me, Madam?" I asked, speaking to the ground.

Madam Stark did not respond. She appraised me as you would appraise a slab of meat at the market. She walked slowly towards me and then, like a vulture, circled around me, her prey.

"Tell me, how old are you, child?" she said brusquely.

"Soon I will be thirteen," I answered.

"And how would you feel about doubling what you earn now?" she said, raising a quizzical eyebrow.

My first feeling was elation at how much quicker I would be able to buy the things I needed for the apothecary. It was almost ready to go. Lucifer, Tommy and I had fixed it up to the point where it was unrecognisable. I had started buying ingredients and making simple herbal remedies which I had bottled, ready to line the shelves. Lucifer had even spoken to a friend who was painting the sign for us as well as making some of the labels for the bottles. It had taken the better part of a year to get this far but it was finally all coming together.

My elation quickly deflated, however, when I realised this was Madam Stark I was talking to. She would not do a favour for nothing. There was a catch of course, which became apparent with Madam Stark's next words.

"You're not pretty. But you are growing into your body, willowy, like your mother. Luckily you have her eyes; there's magic in them. That feature alone will make you popular with many men I know."

I stared in horror at her proposition. I was to become her latest whore.

"I know what you're thinking, Erosabel," Madam Stark said. "And it's not as bad as you think. You've seen the girls here and how well they are taken care of. How they are never hungry, never want for a warm bed, and never have a sickness left untreated. There are not many people in this city that can boast about the same care. You are lucky to be offered this opportunity. The extra money, I'm sure, will not only benefit you, but also that witch of a mother of yours."

I was startled by her last comment. I stared up at her in disbelief. I had never breathed a word of Mother's incantations and spells. In my naivety I had not realised that what Mother did was common knowledge in these parts.

"I'll give you some time to think upon my offer. Have an answer by tomorrow. You may leave your duties for the rest of the day," she said in a dismissive tone.

Shock coursed through my veins. I turned and left Madam Stark's brothel. It felt strange being out in the sunlight at mid-morning with no chores and no errands to frantically run. I wondered if I should find Tommy or Lucifer but then decided against it. This was a decision I needed to make on my own. Madam Stark was right. The girls who lived and worked there did have comfortable lives. Madam Stark was a better madam than most as she would screen the gentlemen who came through her brothel, expelling the overly drunk, boisterous, violent ones into the street. She was protective of her girls to a certain degree and did ensure they were relatively well taken care of. And the wages. The wages would be better than anything I could ever earn doing the work I was currently doing. The hours would be nowhere near as long. Many of the prostitutes I knew would lounge around until mid-afternoon, eating biscuits, smoking, gossiping and laughing.

Besides, what were my alternatives? I could continue to earn a pittance being a washer. I could join the mudlarks and search in the filth of the river for scraps. Or I could act on my dream. Although it would be earlier than I had imagined, I could see what would happen if I fully applied myself to the apothecary. I had a decent bundle saved up. Lucifer had done all the necessary calculations and was monitoring expenditure costs. The apothecary itself had been cleaned and refurbished. It was rather plain-looking but the wooden shelves sparkled, the desk had several ornaments placed upon it and we had bought a thin pale pink carpet which was laid out in the centre of the shop. All I had to do was put some of the tonics and remedies on display, see if the sign was ready and start advertising our new business. Advertising would be easy as I knew half the population of London with all the errands Madam Stark had sent me on. Word of mouth would spread quickly. Perhaps Mother's infamous reputation may also help rather than hinder the news that the apothecary was again open for business.

Before the day was over my mind was made up. I did not wait until the next day to give Madam Stark my answer. With my heart in my mouth I went back to the brothel and told her what I had decided. I waited for her response. She stood completely still, staring at me, an unfathomable expression in her eyes. The silence continued, growing heavier with each passing second. I had never said no or refused to do anything Madam Stark had asked me. The weight of the silence between us was slowly crushing me. I felt a trickle of sweat drip down my back. The stuffy air suddenly felt suffocating.

"The offer stands until the end of the month after which, if you still turn down my offer, you are never to come crawling back to this establishment under any circumstances," Madam Stark finally stated. Without giving me the chance to respond, she whipped around and disappeared up the stairs.

My stomach was tied up in knots. A part of me wanted to call after her, tell her that I would accept her offer as well as the stability that went with it. However, another part of me, the stronger part, had already decided what to do. I would find Lucifer and Tommy and tell them the news. It was time to open up shop.

* * * * *

We opened the apothecary on my thirteenth birthday. Lucifer and Tommy arrived early in the morning, and even Mother came down from her lair upstairs to see what was going on.

"Well, this is a special day," Lucifer said as he entered the shop, his arms outspread wide in a grand gesture. In one hand he carried a single lush red rose and in the other a wrapped rectangular parcel. Tommy followed, carrying a box of cakes. At fourteen years old, I couldn't help but notice Tommy had grown tall and strong. He was nearly as tall as Lucifer but twice as broad in the shoulders. After years of lifting heavy boxes and doing manual work, his arms were muscular and his hands calloused and rough.

I smiled widely as I saw them enter. I was pleased with my decision to wear my best dress for the occasion. It was a thin, gauzy, pale-yellow dress which I believed offset my coffee-coloured skin quite favourably. It was my favourite summer dress, the colour of liquid sunshine with a high waist. It covered my shoulders but left the rest of my arms bare. It was loose-fitting, only just hinting at my budding figure beneath. My thick dark hair, on the other hand, was another story. It had always been difficult to tame. It rolled down my back in heavy waves. I had added an oil to it which I had sneaked out from one of my remedies to smooth it down and add shine. I had even attempted to run a comb through it the night before but soon gave up when several of the teeth snapped due to the thick tangle that was my hair.

There was an embarrassing moment when Tommy caught sight of me. He stared, his mouth slightly open. We usually saw each other in the street, our clothes faded and torn, grime under our nails with smears of dirt on our arms and legs. This was the first time in a long time where I had taken care of my appearance, used the basin not only to splash water on my face and hands but also to scrub the backs of my ears, under my nails, even between my toes. I had used the grime-smudged window to gauge my appearance and was surprisingly satisfied. My skin radiated a healthy glow and my eyes shone brighter than usual. No longer would I be running around the smog-filled streets of London, its grime leaving a sticky film on me like a second skin. I would be ensconced in my shop, selling oils and ointments to fair ladies. Things would be different from now on. Things would be better.

Lucifer saved the day as ever, noticing Tommy's sudden trance. "So gifts first?" he said loudly, breaking the spell.

I saw my mother smirk as she surveyed the scene from a shadowy corner.

"Yes, gifts first!" I said enthusiastically.

"For you, my lady," Lucifer said, presenting me first with the rose and then the parcel wrapped in a purple swirling cloth.

"Thank you, Lucifer!" I said, overjoyed. I caressed the softness of the rose petals which were a deep crimson. I set it down gently on the desk and turned my attention to the parcel. "It's wrapped so beautifully and the cloth is so smooth! I almost don't want to open it. Could it be a book?" I asked, as I felt the hard edges and corners.

"Open it and see," Lucifer replied.

I carefully unfolded the cloth and let the book slide out. It was heavy and had elaborate gold lettering on the cover. Slowly and carefully, as Lucifer had taught me, I made out the words. "Lucifer's Tales from the Beyond", I read aloud. It took a moment for the meaning to sink in. "Lucifer," I said slowly. "Are these all your stories? The ones from your puppet shows?"

"Every single one is in there. I had my friend who created the shop sign illustrate the pages of this book."

I turned the pages in disbelief. I had never seen anything so beautiful. On each page, in the most elegant calligraphy, the stories Lucifer told were printed for posterity. On the opposite pages were illustrations of fair maidens with flowing, golden locks, dark, foreboding forests amidst a swell of hills and fields as well as furious Gods striking humanity in their endless wrath. Lucifer had created another world which I could delve into whenever I wanted to. I stared in awe at the gold- and scarlet-rimmed pages, unable to put it down.

"So, do you like it?" Lucifer asked.

"It's the most beautiful thing I've ever seen," I replied in hushed tones. It literally took my breath away. "Here's the one about the girl who turned to dust," I said, pointing enthusiastically at the illustration of an ancient, wrinkled sorceress casting a spell on a maiden who was disintegrating into the stars around her. "And there's Samael," I said, as I turned a few more pages and found a picture of a muscular man tearing open the night sky, revealing the terrified Gods hiding behind tufts of wispy cloud.

Lucifer nodded, clearly pleased with my reaction. "I'm so glad you like it."

"Must have cost a pretty penny," Mother jibed from the shadows.

I could feel her bristling. There was an electric current of energy radiating malevolently from her corner. She continued to mutter under her breath to herself. I thanked and hugged Lucifer again, ignoring her comments.

"Tommy here helped me remember some of your favourite stories," Lucifer said, patting Tommy on the back, who suddenly looked shy, shuffling his foot on the earthen floor.

"Just wanted it to be perfect," he said, shrugging his shoulders. "My turn now for your gift!"

I looked at his hands. He had set down the cakes and wasn't holding anything. "Where is it?" I couldn't help but ask.

Lucifer and Tommy laughed at my impatience.

"It's outside," Tommy said, opening the front door for me.

Looking around, I saw something covered in a large, rough piece of brown cloth. It was almost my height and was slightly wider than me if I had my arms outstretched to the full.

"Is it under here?" I asked, curious as to what this bulky present could be.

"Yup," Tommy replied from behind me.

I hauled off the heavy covering and for the second time that day had the breath taken right out of my lungs.

"Tommy..." I began, unable to finish my sentence.

It was a dark cherry wood cabinet with large panels of smooth, shiny glass. Below the glass section were several wooden shelves. There were two heavy locks, one for the glass section as well as one for the shelves.

"I thought if you have any more precious or expensive remedies, you could put them in here and keep them extra safe. It might also encourage people to buy them if they think they're more exclusive and special that they need to be kept in a locked cabinet," Tommy said quickly, filling my stunned silence with explanations.

"Tommy," I said again. "You made this?"

"Yup," he replied. "For you, for the shop. You deserve the best."

I spun around and hugged him tightly, tears welling up in my eyes. I had never felt so fortunate in my life.

"Thank you, Tommy! It's perfect!" I said into his shoulder.

"You're welcome, Roz," he said, squeezing me in his strong bear hug.

Lucifer and Tommy then hauled the cabinet into the apothecary and set it down towards the back.

"I can't wait to line up some bottles on it. It's going to look so good!" I gushed.

"Don't think Mother forgot your birthday," Mother suddenly barked from the gloom.

She hadn't moved from her corner whilst all of us had gone outside, admiring the cabinet. She had remained where she was, stock-still, like a spider waiting in the centre of its lair. It was only then that I noticed a very small, lumpy bundle in her arms.

"Oh," I said, not knowing what to say. I had not expected a present. Mother had never given me a present on my birthday.

"You seem surprised. It's a special day. Not only is it your birthday but look at all you've created," she said, gesturing to the apothecary.

I nodded and forced a smile, noting the heavy hint of sarcasm in her voice. She was dressed in her usual rags. Her red hair fell beyond her waist in a knot of tangles. Her gait was strange as she approached from her shadowy corner.

"Here you go, daughter," she said, thrusting a scratchy grey drawstring bag into my hands.

I opened the bag carefully, half expecting spiders and insects to come crawling out. I emptied the contents of the bag to find three gruesome-looking dolls, each about half the size of my hand. They were made of rough, splintered wood, and their arms and legs stuck out at odd, twisted angles. They had black twine for hair and black, white and grey woollen string for clothes. What disturbed me most about the dolls was the bizarre expression painted on each of their flat wooden faces.

The first doll appeared to be in the utmost agony, with what looked like blood-red tears trickling down its face. The wood was cracked through one of its eyes, giving it a semi-blind look. The second doll to tumble out of the bag wore an expression of fury. Mother had gone to the trouble of scratching what looked like popping veins into the doll's face and neck. And the last wore a desolate expression of heartbreaking sadness. Its thin line of a mouth had small vertical lines painted over the top, giving it the impression it was stitched up.

I did not know how to react to this hideous sight. "Thank you, Mother," I finally said quietly.

Both Lucifer and Tommy were staring at the dolls in disgust.

"Three worry dolls," Mother said. "You tell one of them your worries and then tuck it under your mattress at night. You need to think, dwell and dream about your worries and troubles throughout the entire night so the doll can properly absorb it. And by morning, like magic, your worry will have disappeared."

I stared at her in disbelief and nodded slowly. I would never tuck one of these monstrosities under my bed. I wondered to myself at the irony of the situation. Did she really not realise that one of my biggest worries, since as long as I could remember, was her? Did she want me to wish her away with one of these nasty little dolls of her own creation?

"There's three of them," she said, picking them up and flipping them backwards and forwards in the palm of my hand.

I could smell her stale breath and sour skin. I could feel that volatile energy that pulsated around her and scared me. I felt suffocated by her proximity. All I wanted to do was run.

"Three," she repeated. "Three. Yes, three," she muttered. "Three is the number of the universe. Three signifies birth, life and death. Three is the number of existences on this hideous earth." She started mumbling to herself, "Three is half of the Devil's number. By cutting the Devil in half, you stand a chance of killing him. But adding another three will only bring him back." Suddenly she grabbed me by the wrist and hissed in a flurry of madness, "Never add three to this collection. You will only be welcoming the Devil himself into our house and you will kill us all! He will breathe his putrid breath into the dolls, and they will come to life and slay us as we sleep!" I tried to shake off her tight grip, but she only drew me closer. "Swear you will stay away from the Devil's number!" she growled, not breaking her stare.

"I promise, I promise," I said.

At that moment, Lucifer gently prised my wrist out of Mother's vicious grip. "Wonderful dolls, absolutely lovely," he said, as he led me to where the cakes were. "I think it's time we all had some cake."

Mother glared at him, her blue eyes frozen over in hate and fury. "None for me," she whispered in a low, threatening tone. With that, she went back upstairs, continuing to mumble and mutter to herself as she went.

Everyone was silent for a moment, waiting for Mother's heavy presence to clear.

"She's getting worse, isn't she?" Tommy said quietly.

I sighed and nodded. She had been steadily getting worse over the years. She was almost constantly talking to herself now, unless she had one of her strange visitors. Devils constantly seemed to plague her mind. She had even started swatting mid-air, although there was nothing there, claiming that there were so many bats flapping about in the house.

"Today is your day, Erosabel. It's about you," Lucifer said gently, handing me a cupcake. "We're going to eat, celebrate and then open up shop. I've told some of my friends to pass by around mid-morning and to tell people they know, so I'm expecting quite a crowd," Lucifer said.

I devoured my cupcake quickly, licking the icing off my fingers. "I need to finish setting up!" I exclaimed. "I have to fill that beautiful cabinet with some of my finest-looking bottles!"

Once we'd finished eating, we set about arranging the bottles so that they looked aesthetically pleasing. I organised the bottles on the shelves based on ailments. There was a section for stomach aches and cramps where I placed my *Genuine Ginger Cure* which consisted of ginger syrup I had derived from boiling ginger root and adding a dollop of honey. I also laid out my *Peppermint Panacea* which was simply bottles of peppermint oil. For coughs and sore throats, I arranged jars of honey and horseradish syrup, labelled *Soothing Syrups*. For skin-related concerns such as rashes and cuts, I had several containers of black oak bark and an oatmeal paste I made through mixing together honey, lard, oatmeal and eggs, called *The Cure-All Cream*. To make skin smooth and supple, I had large bottles of *Bathing Oats* which consisted of ground-up rolled oats which were to be applied to a warm bath. For stings I had mixed clay and warm water, calling it *Rose's Sting Relief*, and for muscle sprains, I had mixed cold water, clay and vinegar, calling it *Sprain Away*. I had several vials of lavender oil for sleeping concerns, labelled *Rose's Essence of Lavender*. I also had some bars of *Rose Soap* and hair powder called *Rose's Pure Hair Powder*. Finally I had sewn together cloths of varying sizes with which to wrap injuries. They were folded neatly and placed at the end of the shelves, labelled *Rose's Clean Comfort Wraps*.

I had chosen easy remedies to make, whereby obtaining the necessary materials had not proven too difficult. Tommy's nineteen-year-old sister-in-law, Anna, was also going to be helping out in the shop and had promised to come later that day.

Just as we were making some final arrangements, the bell Lucifer had hooked next to the door gave a light tinkle. We all looked at each other for a moment and then towards the first-ever potential customer at Rose's Remedies.

I recognised the two women who entered. They were two of the more popular prostitutes at Madam Stark's brothel. The sweeter one, who was short with generous curves was Lydia. She had a plump face with angelic features. Her eyes were large and doe-like, whilst her skin was fair with flush cheeks and a wide smile. She had full lips which she occasionally rouged. Her face was framed with gentle blonde curls which she took fastidious care of, always brushing her hair with a soft brush fifty times before she went to sleep. She would also wrap damp rags in it overnight to keep the curls full and bouncy. Throughout the afternoons, before it was time for customers, she would twiddle and curl her hair around her fingers absent-mindedly.

Clara was taller and slimmer than Lydia and much less pleasant. There was no denying she was stunningly beautiful with her large, almond-shaped green eyes and heavy eyelids, giving her a permanently sleepy or bored expression. She had delicate thin arching brows, small bow-like lips and an upturned pointy nose. She was wearing an olive-green dress, which made her emerald eyes sparkle all the more. Lydia wore a fluffy pink dress with unnecessary bows and ruffles around the hem and collar giving her the appearance of a cupcake with too much icing.

"So this is it?" Clara said in a loud whisper to Lydia.

Lydia ignored her and said in her loud, cheerful voice, "Rozzy, look at you! This place looks great! A little birdie told us what you were up to!"

I smiled. Lydia had always been kind to me, slipping me little treats here and there. The majority of the other girls simply dumped piles of washing on my head without so much as a word of acknowledgement of my existence under those heavy, stinking piles.

"Thank you, Lydia," I replied. "Are you looking for anything in particular that I could help with?" I asked excitedly.

"Oh, look how professionally the little washer speaks," Clara sneered.

Lydia elbowed her sharply in the ribs, to which Clara rolled her eyes and sulked by the front door.

"I'm just having a browse," Lydia said, eyeing the vials and cordials, letting her fingers brush over the slick and shiny shelves. She paused at the hair powder, unconsciously twiddling a lock of her own fine hair around her finger, allowing the curls to spring to life. "I think this may come in handy," she said. "I try not to wash my hair often but the other powder I use seems to leave a sticky residue in my hair."

"No sticky residue with this at all," I said quickly. "This just absorbs some of the extra oils to give it a clean appearance and leaves your hair sleek and shiny!" It felt strange advertising my products. I noted the hint of desperation in my voice, pleading to be believed.

Lydia nodded. "All right, this one it is!" she exclaimed.

Clara gave an exaggerated eye roll from her corner. Lydia slipped a couple of coins in my hand. She had given me double the cost of the powder.

"Just wait one second, I'll get you some change," I said, feeling the weight of the coins in my hand.

"No need, just add it to my credit. I'll be back here again, with more of the girls," Lydia said, winking.

I couldn't help but beam. I had a regular customer already. "Thank you so much, Lydia!" I said.

"I'll never be stepping foot in here again. I wouldn't trust anything that grubby little street urchin makes," Clara said in a loud whisper as they left the shop.

Ignoring Clara's comment, I squealed in delight, jumping up and down. Tommy was grinning from ear to ear. He grabbed me and wrapped me in a big hug. I squeezed him tightly. He broke out of the embrace looking slightly flushed.

"Well done, Roz," Lucifer said from behind the desk. He was making notes in his accounts book. "Our first successful sale!"

Just then another woman entered the shop. It was Tommy's sister-in-law, Anna. I didn't know her well but I had seen her around, always doing chores and working odd jobs to help support the family. There was nothing particularly special about her features. She had mousy brown hair, clear brown eyes and a thin line for a mouth. I almost felt as if the more I stared at her, the blurrier her features would become, like she was blending into the background. She had the type of face that you could forget immediately even if you had looked right at her a second ago. She would make a good criminal, I found myself thinking. She would be undetectable, becoming a part of the furniture of the scene around her.

Tommy told me she was clever and had managed accounts before. She had also worked in a cousin's bookshop before getting married and could help with the business side of things.

"Hello there," she said in a warm friendly tone. "Tommy told me what you've been up to. This place looks amazing."

"Thank you," I said, a small glow of pride kindling deep within.

"Well, whatever you need, I'm here to help," she said enthusiastically.

"Thank you so much, Anna," Tommy replied. "Once we start making some profits, we'll be sure to split everything evenly!"

Anna shrugged good-naturedly as she looked over Lucifer's shoulder at the accounts.

"Lucifer," Lucifer said, introducing himself. "These are the accounts, the cost of raw ingredients, the cost of making the products, how much we plan on selling them for and such."

Anna nodded. "Mind if I take a look?"

"Be my guest," Lucifer replied, sliding the book over to her.

"Anna's amazing with numbers," Tommy piped up. "I think she dreams and thinks in numbers!"

Anna rolled her eyes playfully. "No need to exaggerate, Tom!"

Several more customers drifted in that day. They seemed more curious than interested in purchasing anything. I noticed how their eyes would occasionally flit to the stairs leading to where Mother was. It was as if they could feel the dense energy that surrounded her, oozing through the cracks in the floorboards, slithering down the stairs. She was both absent and omnipresent at all times. Little did I know back then that the shadow she cast would darken my existence my entire life.

It was getting late and I was exhausted. The adrenaline that had been coursing through my body for the majority of the day had seeped out, leaving me more tired than ever.

"Let's call it a night," Lucifer said, eyeing me as we talked. "I would say that was a success. We had plenty of customers and made four sales. Once word spreads that our cures and panaceas are the best East London has to offer, they'll be flocking to us!"

I smiled weakly, the energy drained from my body. "It was a good day," I said.

"You get some sleep now, Roz," Tommy said. "You've done so much today. Rest up so we can be ready bright and early tomorrow."

"Thank you so much," I said, surprised that my throat felt constricted. Unbidden tears welled up in my exhausted eyes. I tried to brush them away discreetly.

"Good night, Roz. And happy birthday," Lucifer said, kissing the crown of my head.

"See you tomorrow," Tommy said, half hugging, half patting me on the back.

Anna gave a small wave and a smile as she and Tommy left together. Lucifer tipped his black hat to me as the bell tinkled, leaving me alone in the dark.

Mother had been quiet today, too quiet. Rarely would a day go by without some outburst from Mother. I had been panicked that she would storm down the stairs like a ball of fire, scorching the potential customers, burning them to dust with a mere glare.

I tiptoed upstairs as quietly as I could. I pushed the door open slowly when I reached the top. It breathed out an agonisingly loud creak. Mother was sitting bolt upright, facing the small, smudged window. Her back was ramrod straight and her hair hung like rags, creating a dying pool of flames around her.

"So how did it go, my pretty petal?" she said in an eerie, harsh voice that sent goosebumps up my arms. The voice that spoke sounded deeper than her actual voice.

"It was fine, Mother. It went rather well," I replied nervously, never knowing if I was giving her the right or wrong answer.

"It was fine, Mother," Mother echoed, in a high-pitched lilting voice that sounded nothing like my own. A heavy silence descended between us. "Come sit here, with Mother," she finally said, in a poisonously soft voice.

With legs like lead, I walked over to where she was and sat down beside her on the bed. She smelt stale. When she opened her mouth, she exhaled a cloud of gin. I turned to look at her, surprised. Mother had problems, but she had never been a drinker. Could things be getting even worse?

"Tell me, what do you see out there?" Mother said, pointing at the grimy window.

I stared. It was nearly impossible to see anything other than the shadowy reflection of her impassive face alongside my fear-filled one. I shrugged. "Not much."

Mother ignored me and continued in the harsh voice she had used earlier. "I see the withered hands of a curse, clutching around your dark, heathen neck. The curse has blossomed and bloomed inside me, and it needs to spread. It needs space to grow. I see the curse, as we speak, sliding its way out of me, tearing through every inch of my skin." She paused, tracing an invisible path in the air with her index finger.

"The curse needs something to latch on to, to feast on." She grabbed my hand tightly, making me jump. "Like a parasite it will suck all your thoughts out of you. Everything you once believed in and held true will be a lie. It will slowly eat away at your skull and burrow through your brain." She prodded my head hard with her finger.

"Once it has found your brain, it will nestle there and populate. Goblins will dance around in the prison of your mind and drive you mad. They will laugh and taunt you. There will be thousands of them all crammed up in your little head making it impossible to think straight or own a single original thought. They will shift and morph, forever out of your grasp. They will turn into thick, oozing, shapeless demons with ruby red eyes and fangs dripping blood.

"Their poison will trickle through your brain, to your fingertips. Everything you touch will be smeared with its toxicity. Everyone you know will be tainted and cursed. You should never have children, Erosabel," Mother said, turning my face to look directly into hers. Her piercing blue eyes melded into mine, fusing our souls together.

"Never. The demons in your head will convince you that they are real and the world outside is a mere figment of your imagination. The more children you have, the stronger the curse will become. It will become an avalanche of black mud, a tidal wave of filth that will be out of your control. Never have children, Erosabel. Never. The demons destroy everything in their path. They carry torches in the dark and set fire to everything in their wake. A mass of impenetrable smoke and swirling chaos is all you will see. That's their way of blinding you to reality. They stuff your ears with decaying filth so you can no longer hear reason. They cut out your tongue so you can't cry for help. Those demons are coming for you. And they will kill your children, gobbling them up with their knife-like teeth. They will kill them, just as my demons will kill you one day."

I didn't realise that tears were streaming down my face as Mother told her grotesque story. My face was clutched in her pincer-like grip. I yanked her hands away from me, leaving claw-like nail marks on my skin.

"I hate you," I whispered. The words felt like dry ash in my mouth. I spat them out, wishing they could solidify into acid, knives, fire, anything that could silence her forever.

Mother stared at me blankly. She turned back to the smeared window, as if I no longer existed. I got up from where I was sitting and grabbed a blanket. Although it was cold and draughty downstairs, I preferred it to the thought of sleeping next to her. This way, I would be able to hear her creaking footsteps down the stairs if she decided to visit me in my sleep. I would be ready.

Chapter 6

TO MY SURPRISE, Mother did not interfere with the running of the apothecary. It ran smoothly and business started to pick up. Tommy and Anna were relatively permanent fixtures, along with me. Lucifer came to help in between his shows.

Occasionally, strange customers would enter. They walked differently from the usual customers. They would glide along the floor, their eyes darting about shiftily in their sockets. They spoke in a different manner, using hushed tones as if fearful of being overheard by invisible ghosts drifting through the shop. They had no interest in the products I was selling but would specifically ask for Mother. As they went up the stairs, I could feel their presence linger. I tried to ignore the muffled voices trailing through the cracks upstairs. I was reminded of the slaughtering of the bird I had seen. It sent chills down my spine whenever one of them came to the shop. They exuded an ominous miasma which remained, like a foul aftertaste, even once they left.

Tommy was stacking the shelves with some new concoctions I had whipped together. I was thoroughly enjoying the creative side of my new work. I loved reading my grandparents' remedy book. Repeating the names of the ingredients felt like I had diamonds and rubies spilling out of my mouth. I could feel the texture of the names, I could smell the fragrance emanating from the mixtures and see the subtle changes in colour they made when combined in the palette of my mind. The new concoction was supposed to reduce inflammation and redness in the skin. It was called *Rose's Redness Eradicator* and contained soothing oils and softening creams.

"So what are you going to do when you get rich?" Tommy asked, flashing a grin at me as he stacked the shelves.

"Hmm," I replied, thinking about it. "I'm not sure. I'd like to expand the shop and make more healing remedies. Maybe I would buy more tools and equipment to make more advanced things. What about you?"

"I'd like to build a boat and go exploring for at least a year, or even forever!" Tommy said immediately. "I'd like to go treasure hunting and travel to far-off islands full of barbarous savages and battle with pirates along the way. I want to go on long sea journeys where there is nothing but an endless ocean in view. Wherever I go, I want to get as far away from here as possible," he finished, resignedly.

My heart felt sober and heavy. I knew he had a lot to manage, with his ill mother and trying to take care of the family.

"How is your mother?" I asked. She had been hanging on by a thread for months.

"She can barely talk for coughing," he said sadly. "She's pretty much turned into a skeleton and can't keep anything down any more."

I sighed, nodding. I couldn't think of anything comforting to say. It was clear she was going to die soon and there was nothing anyone could do about it. At that moment I wished I could turn to religion, but Mother had never instilled a sense of believing in anything and I didn't know how I could believe in an almighty, all-powerful God when I had seen the destitution, disease and poverty that suffocated the slum I lived in. I felt we lived in the belly of a monster which was slowly ingesting and eroding us until there was nothing left.

I put my hand on Tommy's shoulder. "Do you want to go home and spend some extra time with her?" I asked gently.

Tommy shook his head. "No, I'd rather be here with you. I feel bad saying it, but I actually can't stand being at home."

As I did not know what to say or do, I wrapped my arms around him and hugged him close to me. His big arms locked around me in a tight embrace. He then lifted my chin to face him. I felt a strange, unfamiliar current of energy pass between us, like an electric charge zapping back and forth. He leant down and clumsily kissed my lips. My thoughts scattered in a million different directions, and I couldn't think what to do next. I kissed him back lightly, like a fallen feather caressing the earth. I withdrew and stared up at him wordlessly, feeling adrenaline flow through my veins. I had never been kissed before and didn't know how to do it. His hands were planted on my slim waist. He cleared his throat and ruffled his hair.

"Sorry, Roz. I... Umm, it's just you're so sweet and pretty... I just, I don't know, I just felt like I wanted to kiss you," he stammered, his gaze flitting between the floorboards and my face.

I smiled, feeling a jolt in the dynamics of our relationship. The tectonic plates which had been solid and steadfast were splitting apart, slipping under my feet and I didn't know how to keep my balance.

"Are you ok? Is everything ok?" Tommy asked, concerned.

"Of course I'm ok," I replied, squeezing the palm of his hand in what I hoped was a reassuring manner. "Should we close up?" I asked, injecting a forced light-heartedness into my tone.

It was starting to get late, and I wanted an excuse to be alone and try to gather my thoughts. I had just been kissed by my best friend. Did this mean things would change forever? Or would everything settle back to how it always was by tomorrow? Was it because he was sad that he kissed me? Or did he really think I was sweet and pretty and he wanted more from our friendship? I felt dazed and confused.

"Sure, let's close up," Tommy replied.

Quietly we went through the motions of sweeping the floor, putting away anything valuable in the locked cabinet and straightening up the items on the shelves.

"Well, I guess I'll see you tomorrow," Tommy said, concern lingering in his eyes.

"Yes, see you tomorrow," I replied. I didn't know if I should hug or kiss him goodbye. I settled with a small, awkward wave, which Tommy mirrored as he left the shop.

I let out a long sigh, then locked up and went upstairs. I contemplated what had happened. I really liked Tommy, but I had never thought of him as more than my best friend. An additional layer of complexity had suddenly spread across my life. I decided I would act normal tomorrow and take my cues from him. That would be the easiest thing to do.

Mother was sleeping, curled up in a ball on the mattress. I slipped inside the room and fished out Lucifer's book of fairy tales from under my blankets. I crept back downstairs and decided to light a candle and read a story before bed. When life got too complicated, I could unlock the gateway to another world by delving into Lucifer's stories. I could escape from my world and free-fall into another.

I lit my stumpy candle which already had thick teardrops of wax frozen down its length. I sat on the hard wooden chair, let Lucifer's book fall open and decided to read whatever story I found there.

"Adeline's Imaginings"

Once upon a time there was an ordinary girl, Adeline. Everything about her was ordinary. She wore ordinary clothes, had ordinary straight hair and lived in an ordinary house with ordinary parents. She attended an ordinary school, had ordinary friends and ate ordinary food. Her features were ordinary. Her toys were ordinary. Everything about her was ordinary, except her mind. For within the labyrinth of thoughts and passageways that created her mind nestled an extraordinary imagination.

Ever since she was able to talk, she told tales of faraway lands, castles in the sky and princesses flying on the backs of butterflies the size of dragons. Her stories were so vivid that anyone who heard them could swear they came to life before their very eyes. They felt as if they were watching the moving pictures inside the little girl's mind. Adeline's imagination was impossible to quiet

or subdue. Even as she slept, she would mumble the stories under her breath.

Her parents, who were unimaginative and coarse by nature, were fearful of her storytelling. They prayed she would grow out of it. Their fear infected their relationship with their only daughter. They grew austere and cold towards her, rejecting what they did not understand. They thought her mad or possessed by demons. As her stories grew in intensity, unfurling into the most colourful and vibrant of tales, their anxiety grew in equal proportions. They started beating her and threatening her. They lashed her back for every new story told. They taped her mouth shut when she slept to force her to swallow her words. Yet no matter what they did, the stories poured out of her, like sunlight caressing a field of flowers. It was an unstoppable stream, a waterfall of words woven together in the most intricate, dazzling patterns.

On her sixteenth birthday, her mother died. Her father told Adeline that her mother had died from a broken heart. She was so distraught at her daughter's madness that her heart stopped dead, frozen over in grief. Adeline wept for her poor mother, broken by the news. Immediately, her father re-married a cruel woman, Hagar. Hagar took one look at the willowy beautiful Adeline with the doleful eyes that misted over, creating a veil between the world in her mind and the real one. The hatred Hagar felt was instant. It gripped her heart with a vice-like clutch making it difficult for her to breathe. If she were to live, Adeline had to die.

One evening, after the girl returned from the countryside, Hagar slipped a venomous poison into Adeline's tea. She set it by her bedside and crept like a shadow out of her room. Adeline, weary from her wanderings, took the dainty teacup in her hand. As she settled into her bed, teacup raised, her imagination took flight. She opened her eyes blearily and saw a figment had sprung to life. A small butterfly she had been daydreaming of fluttered next to her nose. It was electric blue with a web of black lace adorning its wings. It fluttered to her ears and whispered what her stepmother had slipped into her tea. Adeline immediately dropped the cup, letting it splinter into a thousand pieces on the floor.

Hagar heard the crash with glee, assuming Adeline had drunk from the tea and was now lying dead in her bed. She skipped up the stairs, humming a jolly melody to herself. As she opened the door, a white fury blinded her. Her last vision was that of Adeline dusting the gleaming shards of the teacup into a cloth.

With her lost sight, her hatred for the girl only grew. She hired the best hit man in town to finish the girl off using any method at his disposal. She paid him a thousand gold coins to kill her. As Adeline was strolling through the forest she heard a whistling sound speed past her right ear. She turned in shock to find a man as tall as a tree bearing down on her, bow and arrow in hand. The sharp end of the arrow glittered malevolently in the setting sun. Just as she had been sauntering along, she had been imagining a wolf strolling by her side, protecting her from harm's way. Just as the burly man was about to release the instrument of doom, a huge white and grey wolf leapt in front of Adeline. It snarled so viciously and glared so violently at the man that he whimpered, stumbled and fell to the ground. He snapped the arrow in two and pleaded for mercy. The wolf growled at him to leave and never return. In a flash, the lumbering man vanished forever.

When Hagar sensed Adeline returning from the woods, she screamed such an ear-splitting screech that her voice was lost forever. With no sight or voice, her resentment towards the girl festered like a disease in Hagar's mind. She realised the only solution was for her to kill the girl with her own bare hands. She fashioned a dagger out of the strongest steel and cut the blade sharper than a diamond. One swipe would be enough to slice the girl in two. Since she could not see, she would have to strike the girl at the easiest possible moment, when she was asleep. Adeline slept so heavily and dreamt so deeply, Hagar knew she would not be disturbed from her slumber.

One calm night, Hagar stole up the stairs as quietly as a whisper. She drew the dagger upon the sleeping maiden, poised to plunge it into her breast. Just then, the girl had been dreaming of a tremendous dragon breathing out a cloud of flame. From the depths of her mind, sprang the dragon. Hagar, sensing something was wrong, faltered in her quest. In an instant, the dragon obliterated Hagar with a gust of fire. When Adeline woke up, she cried at the sight of a pile of ash by her bed. Her imagination told her that the feathery ash was her stepmother. She knew she would have to leave before anyone else got hurt.

Adeline packed a small bag with basic provisions and left the town she had called home for her life thus far. She travelled night and day. She travelled for so long her shoes disintegrated and her feet bled. After she had eaten all the food, the only nourishment she had was the breath of the wind. Time collapsed around her. She no longer noticed if the moon hung in the sky surrounded by a carpet of stars or if it was the sun cushioned by her feathery clouds. She starved her body and her mind, hoping to quiet her imagination. Months bled into years and still Adeline journeyed on, alone in her heart and mind.

One day she stumbled upon a quiet town perched on the edge of the earth, its inhabitants living in a desolate area which even the sun couldn't reach. It was perpetually dark and there was neither arable land nor fresh drinking water anywhere nearby. The residents were slowly withering away and dying, like silent crumpled leaves dropping from the trees. Despite this hardship, the townspeople had only warmth and generosity in their hearts. Although they had no food, they offered her the scraps they had when they saw she was starved. Although they had no water, they filled a goblet up to the top from their reserve. Although they had no clothes, they fashioned shoes for her out of the earth and leaves.

Adeline cried at such generosity which she had not known in years. As her body was nourished and soul replenished, thoughts, dreams and stories began to bubble within the cauldron of her mind. As she cried at the kindness of the townspeople, her tears started pooling together. They continued to collect even after she stopped crying. They travelled deeper into the ground until they had formed a well of fresh water for all the townspeople to drink. When the townspeople cheered for what Adeline had done for them, she let out a great sigh of relief. Her breath travelled on the wind, all the way to the once barren fields. As it caressed the surface of the earth, it grew warm and fertile. Within days, crops were blooming from its depths.

When there was food and water for the townspeople, Adeline's heart felt so light she started singing songs of pure joy. The vitality in her songs created a lush oasis of blossoming flowers, sturdy trees and twittering birds. The townspeople cried with joy as their town became richer and more glorious than ever before.

Adeline started telling her stories again to the little girls and boys of the town. They were immediately enraptured by their truth and beauty. Her creations mirrored her pure thoughts and soul. She told stories until her heart was content. She continued telling stories until, at the ripe age of one hundred, she lay on her deathbed. She let out her final breath, a gentle kiss sealing her love for the town and its people.

Her story became embedded in the myth and lore of the town. She was forever remembered for all her good deeds and rich stories for generations to come. Her soul, along with her stories, was woven into the fabric of the town perched at the edge of the earth.

The End

I closed the book, feeling my eyelids droop. I imagined what it must be like to have such a vivid imagination that whatever you thought of could potentially spring to life. I let the book close with a heavy thump and blew out the candle. Cloaked in darkness, I made my way upstairs to bed. Mother was still exactly where I had left her. I snuggled up in my own small mattress and drifted off to the land of dreams.

The next day, Tommy's mother was found dead. She had passed away at some point during the night. Tommy told me he had brought her breakfast only to find her slumped over and stiff as a wax statue. Her eyes were closed, and a dribble of blood leaked from her parted lips.

Chapter 7

AUTUMN WAS ROLLING around again, bringing with it harsh winds and crisp leaves. We were all working hard, and the business was doing well. I was creating more lotions and potions and getting ever more creative with my remedies. It came naturally to me, deftly mixing herbs and pastes, concocting soothing and healing elixirs.

When Tommy's mother passed away several months ago, he seemed to have aged a decade. At fifteen years old, a heaviness descended upon him, which try as I might, I couldn't lift. I could tell he was stretching himself thin with the shop and other odd jobs to help keep the family afloat and prevent anyone being snaffled off to the workhouse.

I noticed more of what I called "Mother's Minions" entering the shop. They were getting creepier and creepier with each passing day, draped in black shawls and lace. Sometimes they carried large, bulky parcels under their arms. Once I was watching a tall, thin woman as she entered the shop with a large package under her arm. I jumped and nearly tripped backwards when the parcel started twitching uncontrollably. The gaunt woman flashed me a look of anger as if I had something to do with her moving parcel. I didn't know what Mother was doing up there, but it disturbed me. More worryingly, it disturbed several of my customers. I could sense a dusting of unease settle on anyone in the shop when one of Mother's Minions entered.

"Who do you think they are?" I whispered to Lucifer as a tall, strong man dressed head to toe in black strode past me and up the stairs. He had thick dark hair and a rough, tangled beard. There was so much hair obscuring his face, I could hardly make out the small beady eyes embedded deep within.

"I'm not sure, Roz," Lucifer replied, his gaze trailing after the huge man. "Better you stay away from them."

"I am, but it looks like our customers are as well," I said, nodding in the direction of two older ladies who had been browsing the shelves. They were whispering amongst themselves, sending furtive glances upstairs. They then bustled to the door, scurrying away from the menacing aura that trailed after the man.

"She's going to give this place a bad name," I continued.

"Well, it's not necessarily such a bad thing to be infamous," Lucifer replied thoughtfully. "It'll certainly get your name on everyone's lips and people will be bound to come out of mere curiosity. When they see what you're selling, they'll probably also remember an ailing friend or relative and end up buying one of your remedies. But I agree, it doesn't sit well with me what is going on up there. I don't know what kind of black magic or voodoo she's got going on, but I sense it will get us all in trouble one of these days."

I swallowed hard. It was a premonition. Something bad would happen. It was just a matter of when.

"Where's Tommy today?" I asked, trying to change the subject. He had told me he was coming in late that day, but he still hadn't turned up.

"I'm not sure," Lucifer replied. "He told me Anna's baby, Alfred, wasn't well yesterday. Perhaps he's with her helping out."

"Do you mind if I quickly run to his and check?" I asked. "I've been worried about him lately and he's just down the road."

"Of course, Roz. I can hold the fort here. It's not a particularly busy day," Lucifer replied.

I smiled, grabbed a few of my towels and a soothing oil for babies, and dashed out. Tommy was not one to confide in others when he needed help. Annoyingly he would clam up and act like big, tough man. It drove me crazy when he did this. I just wanted to know how to help, and his cross demeanour and folded arms were not forthcoming.

I skipped over the muddy piles and horse dung as I weaved amongst the peddlers and sandwich board men. It only took me a few minutes to reach Tommy's place. I came to a small cul-de-sac and immediately heard the wailing coming from an upstairs window.

I knocked on the door before letting myself in. It was crammed and chaotic inside. A little girl of about six had her hands plunged in a bucket of soapy water and was scrubbing at dirty rags. The sight of her tugged at my heartstrings as I realised that was what I was like at her age. My hands and arms had been covered in blisters and sores from the constant washing. An even smaller boy was crawling on the floor, pushing a rough wooden car along the floor and slamming into surfaces. I recognised

Emily, Tommy's sister, who was a couple of years younger than me. She was stirring a pot over the fireplace. Sweat shone on her brow which she dabbed at frequently. I walked over to her.

"Emily, how are you?" I asked.

"Hi there, Roz! I'm sorry, I didn't hear you come in," she said, as the racket around her seemed to increase a notch.

"That's ok. Where's Tommy?"

"He's upstairs," Emily said, gesturing to where the wailing sound was emanating. "Freddy's not doing well." Tears shone in her eyes.

"I'll go check on them," I said, giving her arm a squeeze.

Several of the planks in the stairs were broken, their edges jagged. The bannister was also hanging off the wall at a precarious angle. I made my way up the rickety set of stairs and called out for Tommy.

"In here," Tommy yelled back.

I entered a room which had a shabby curtain in place of where a door should be. Anna was sitting on a thin mattress on the floor with her screaming son in her arms. Tears streaked down her face as she tried to rock the baby to sleep. Freddy was just under one year old. Tommy was sitting next to her, anxiety lining his face.

"He hasn't stopped crying all night and he's burning up," Tommy said in a flat voice.

I looked around the room. Apart from the mattress on the floor, there was a desk with a broken leg and a wooden chair in the corner.

"Is there a bucket or something I can use to fill water in?" I asked.

Tommy heaved himself up. "Yes, over here." He lifted the flap of the curtain and grabbed a tin pail that was in the corridor.

"Let's fill this with cold water and try to get Freddy's temperature down."

"Are you sure that'll help?" Tommy asked.

"Well, it's worth a try," I said.

Tommy went to fill the pail and headed back to where Anna was desperately rocking Freddy. Whenever I saw Anna she was always so calm and composed. Seeing her in this distraught state made me feel numb inside, like the equilibrium of the world was off kilter.

"Anna, let me take Freddy. We're going to give him a sponge bath to try to cool him down," I said.

Anna nodded, shakily handing over the bundle of screeching baby. I carefully unwrapped the thin blanket covering him. His small face was scrunched up and red. His hands were balled into tiny fists as he wailed. I took out one of my cloths and dipped it in the water and started dabbing him. The wail was a constant ringing in my ears. A stretched out, elongated, tortured note. I continued sponging the baby until he gave a slight shiver.

"Let's dry little Freddy now," I said, softly drying him with a clean towel. I wrapped the light blanket around him loosely and gave him back to Anna who started rocking him and singing lullabies to try to get him to sleep. The high-pitched wail seemed to have reduced in intensity.

"He must be tiring himself out, poor thing," I said to Tommy, who looked like he hadn't slept in days.

"Well, he seems a little better," Tommy said, allowing a hint of hope to nudge its way into his voice.

"I think he just needs to sleep and hopefully when he wakes up he'll feel better," I said. "You also look like you need some sleep."

Tommy smiled at me weakly. "I am pretty tired."

"Hey, listen to that," I said, finger at my mouth, gesturing to be quiet. Freddy was still sniffling but the wail had subdued. "I think he's falling asleep," I whispered.

Anna continued singing in hushed, gentle tones, lulling Freddy off into a dream world.

"Here, lie down," I said, directing Tommy onto the narrow mattress. Anna shifted over slightly, making room for him.

Tommy stretched out and closed his eyes. "I'll just lie down for a minute. Then I'll come help out at the shop, Roz, I promise."

"Right," I replied. I found myself stroking his thick, sandy hair as he lay. The worry lines melted from between his brows. Anna watched me curiously as I continued to brush away the anxiety from his face. I ran my fingers through his hair and applied gentle pressure along his temples. Within seconds he was breathing deeply, fast asleep. I continued to watch him as he lay. Without the stress and anxiety, he looked like the fresh young boy he had always been to me.

"He's lucky to have such a good friend like you, Roz," Anna whispered to me.

I smiled, not wanting to speak, not wanting to disturb the peaceful aura that enveloped the room. I was the lucky one. I didn't know where

109

I would be without my good friend Tommy by my side. We had never mentioned the kiss we had shared that night several months ago. Perhaps if his mother hadn't died the next day, something might have happened. But with that tragedy, everything else was overshadowed and unimportant. I felt the pull of that strange undercurrent of energy that I felt that day he kissed me. It drew me to him like a magnet. It kept me stroking his hair and face. I observed the micro expressions that flitted across his faced as he dreamed. I touched the rough smattering of stubble that appeared like a shadow across his face. I blushed as I noticed that Anna was still staring at me. I quickly withdrew my hand.

"I better head off. It's getting late and I asked Lucifer to manage the shop without me," I said, without meeting Anna's eye.

"Thank you so much for your help today," Anna said, gratitude hanging on her every word.

"Of course," I replied, as I slowly got up and crept out.

It was cold and dark out on the streets. I felt a pang of guilt for having left Lucifer for so long. I mingled with the shadows and slunk through the pools of darkness as I made my way home. Prostitutes lined the walls, forming a picket fence of gaudy colours. Leering men shoved past me as they made their way either to the prostitutes or the public house.

Before I opened the shop door I felt an ethereal pull, as if I were a puppet on invisible strings and a master puppeteer was manipulating me at that moment. I turned and looked up. The moon was gazing down at me with a feverish glow. It was a full moon, a perfect circle hanging in the sky. It was shining so brightly, I couldn't make out any star companions near it. In fact, I had never seen the moon so luminescent before. It sent a chill down my spine. I didn't like it when things were out of the ordinary. There was something extraordinary about that moon. That was not a normal moon in the sky. With my head still cranked towards the moon, I entered the shop.

"Sorry I took so long, Lucifer. I think Freddy will be fine..." My voice trailed off as the scene unfolded before me.

I felt as if I had entered a nightmare. The moonlight streamed in from behind me, lighting up the spectral scene in an icy blue glow. The centre of the room had been cleared and twelve shadowy figures sat in a circle, cross-legged. Thin, lace veils shielded their faces which were directed towards me. Eleven faceless statues. Mother was at the head of the circle, propped on a floppy cushion with the stuffing leaking out. She was not wearing a veil. When I saw her face, I wished there was something separating her penetrating stare from me. Her skin was shiny and taut, pulled over her skeletal frame. Bones jutted out at odd angles. Her eyes were manic and wide, sinking into their shadowy sockets. Her lip curled when she saw me.

"I told Lucifer to go home. He wanted to wait for you, naturally, but I insisted. Come, Erosabel, sit with us," she said in her dangerously soft voice, a voice that signalled trouble. "Sit with me," she said, patting the space next to her.

I moved slowly, eyeing the faceless crowd around me. I felt as if I was walking under water, at the bottom of a dark, black ocean. There was an unearthly silence hanging like a dead man in the room. Once solid objects seemed to take on a blurred quality in the dim hazy candlelight. I finally made my way to where Mother was sitting and ever so slowly folded my legs and sat next to her. I was hardly able to breathe.

"Relax, Erosabel," Mother said. "What we are doing here is healing. You see, all these people here have lost someone of importance to them. We're going to see if we can bring their spirit back from the underworld." She flashed a toothy smile. I noticed how her canine teeth gleamed bone white in the dark, reminding me of a bloodthirsty vampire.

"Everyone join hands. Let us sing together," Mother ordered the faceless group.

There was a light rustling as motion rippled through the circle. Everyone joined hands. As if by an invisible cue from a conductor, they all started humming. I was holding Mother's clammy hand on one side and a strange woman's soft wrinkled hand on the other. I started to sweat as the incantation increased in volume. They started chanting in unison, with one voice. It wasn't in English and I couldn't understand what was being said. I felt a line of sweat form down my back, one drop tracing after another.

I looked around. I couldn't tell if the faceless people had their eyes open or closed. They were all gently swaying from side to side, like tendrils of seaweed underwater. Mother's eyes were closed, her brows slightly furrowed. The flames from the candles started flickering manically. I couldn't tell if it was my imagination or fear, but each flame seemed to glow brighter and jump higher as the chant continued. Long ghostly shadows danced across the floor. My eyes darted from one patch of darkness to the next, fear creating monsters hunched in the shadows, their hungry eyes glued on me.

Suddenly it stopped. The chant was cut short by sharp invisible shears. Mother started shaking. Then I heard heavy thumping noises, as if we had awakened a giant from its slumber with the chant. The sound was coming from everywhere and nowhere. The faceless bodies turned their heads left and right, trying to source the location of the sound. Muffled gasps whispered through the circle.

A total and complete silence swept through the room when Mother opened her mouth. I could not ever remember hearing such a silence. It was tangible. It was so dense I could feel it and taste it in my mouth. It tasted metallic and heavy, like a solid lump weighing on my tongue. I strained my ears but not even the burning candles sizzled. We were at the bottom of an inky black ocean where I couldn't hear anyone and no one could hear me scream.

At first Mother didn't say anything. Her mouth simply hung open, abnormally wide, like a gaping fish. She then croaked in a broken, cracked voice, "I'm here, Mother. It's your son, Jacob."

One of the faceless women let out a small shriek, nearly breaking the circle. The other faceless sentries on either side of her clutched her hands tightly in their grasp.

"What happened? What happened to you, my son?" the woman cried, leaning closer towards Mother.

"I never meant for it to go that far, Mother. I got into debts and gambling. I drank and frittered away our savings." Here, Mother paused for breath as if uttering each word was agonising. "Yes, I sinned and gambled but I also won. I was doing it to save our family from wreck and ruin and I won a lot during one of our gambles. When I left the gambling den with my winnings I was set upon by two big, burly men." Mother gasped again, sucking air into her lungs as if she was on the brink of drowning.

"They strangled me and took the money." Mother clutched at her throat with a trembling hand. "But when my spirit floated out of my earthly body, I saw who they were working for and who they gave the bag of coins to. The thief who still lives, breathes and walks free whilst I rot in my grave is Robert Simmons. He lives in a comfortable part of London near Dove Cross Lane."

Mother's breath became shallow and her head started rolling in circles. It looked as if it might snap right off her thin, spindly neck. Her eyes flashed open. They were bloodshot, the red veins cracked and bulging. Several gasps of shock rippled through the circle. Mother's voice changed. It became lower, deeper and harsher. Each word dripped with malevolence.

"Seek revenge upon my soul. Unleash the Devil's work upon his godforsaken soul. He sinned and the Devil must collect his dues. Take back what rightfully belongs to our family."

Froth was bubbling around Mother's lips and trickled down her chin. I was staring transfixed at her terrifying countenance. She started rocking violently, her body shaking, the entire circle was trapped in the vortex of movement. I could no longer see her eyes. They had rolled back in her head, revealing only the whites of her eyes. Several sickening cracking noises split through the room. The candles, which had been dimming and becoming fainter, suddenly flared up again, thrusting their orange spikes in the air. Several of the women jumped back, fracturing the circle. Mother stopped rocking, her head hanging limply in front of her. A curtain of matted flame red hair was draped across her face.

The faceless people all appeared to be staring at Mother. Fear rocketed through my body. My dress was drenched with sweat as if I had run a hundred miles in the desert. My hair clung to my shining forehead. I slowly freed my sweaty palm from Mother's weakened grasp, and with a trembling hand I parted the curtain of hair blocking her face. I could see she was breathing evenly. Her eyes were closed and her white lips slightly parted. The foam that had bubbled from them was dripping off her chin.

"Mother," I said, in a weak voice unrecognisable to me.

Her eyes snapped open. She lifted her head slowly. "I felt someone's spirit enter my body. It worked, didn't it?" Mother said in yet another voice. This one sounded light and feeble, almost childlike.

The mother of the dead Jacob was sobbing quietly. "Jacob told me what I need to do. Esther, you must help me carry out his dying wish."

Mother nodded. "Of course, anything. You must tell me what Jacob told you. Naturally I have no recollection of what was said or what I did. Perhaps come back tomorrow. My spirit is drained for today." She hung her head again, limp and lifeless.

"Of course, I completely understand. I will be back tomorrow," the mother said in hushed tones.

The shadowy faceless crowd rustled and like a liquid bruise evaporated from the shop. I was left alone with Mother. Her head immediately snapped up, a smile pulling at the corners of her lips.

"Well, that worked like a charm," she said wickedly.

"What do you mean?" I asked, a fog of confusion engulfing my mind.

"I mean that worked well. We, me and you, will be doing more of those," she said. "Next time, I'll increase the fee."

"They paid you to do that?" I asked, trying to wrap my head around what was going on.

"Of course, I don't do seances for free. It's hard work talking to the dead, Erosabel," Mother replied.

"But it was real, wasn't it?" I asked, thinking of the noises, Mother's eyes rolling back and the froth dripping down her face.

"It's real if you believe it is," Mother whispered. "Now I must prepare for tomorrow. We'll be having a returning customer and she won't be after your little lavender scents or skin buffers. She will want something which only I can give her. She will want a curse," Mother said, her eyes shining like the abnormally bright moon in the sky.

Mother creaked up the stairs, muttering to herself under her breath. A chill shimmied its way down my spine. A new chapter of life was revealing itself to me and I didn't like what I saw. A cursed hand was extending out through a dark abyss. It had long blackened fingers with singed, grimy nails. It was grasping wildly at anything within its reach. No matter how much I tried to push back, I could feel a force drawing me closer to the hand. Sooner or later, it would have me in its talons and I would be stuck, a pierced voodoo doll. When that happened, my life would no longer be my own. I knew I had to leave. If I stayed here, in my home, in the slums of East London with Mother, the hand would reach me and I would die.

Chapter 8

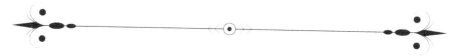

THERE WERE MORE seances. After the first one, more of these deathly faceless spectres swept in and out of the shop, leaving their gloomy shadows lingering behind them. Mother's fits became more violent and shocking. She carried knives in the many folds of her pockets and would slit her hands, arms or any other appendage within reach for dramatic effect, making it appear as if the wounds stemmed from supernatural entities at work. She also used me. I was responsible for hiding away upstairs and creating unearthly, spooky sounds with handmade instruments and pots and pans. I wanted to refuse, to stop playing trickster. But I couldn't refuse Mother. Money was also flowing in like never before. I was able to buy more equipment and make more remedies. Despite the improvements in my cures, I felt a black stain spreading like an inkblot on parchment through my apothecary. The reputation of Rose's Remedies was being tarnished, dragged through a haunting underworld, generating fear and whispered gossip.

It all came hurtling to the brink of collapse one night when Mother was conducting a seance for a group of people who were from out of town. Since they weren't local, Mother had another use for me. Instead of being tucked away in the safety of the upstairs room, she was going to use me as part of the seance. Mother always acquired the list of names before the seance and would do a background check on the participants. She had connections with the dregs, criminals and crooks of society. She would have them run around and find out information on her newcomers. Through their field research, she would discover which of the group had the most tragic, heart-shattering story, and that person would be her target for the seance.

For this seance, Mrs Mary Carlisle would be joining the sinister carnival of exploitation and madness. Mother quickly learned that her only daughter had been murdered and buried by her father. In a fit of manic rage, he had sliced the girl's head open with an axe. He then hung himself from the tree in their garden. Mrs Carlisle was well-to-do and was not facing poverty or destitution, but no amount of money could mend her broken heart or bring her daughter back. Except, that was exactly what Mother planned to do that night, to resurrect the daughter, Annabelle, from the grave. Annabelle was eight years old when she was murdered.

"You're still quite scrawny. All we need to do is bandage your chest tightly and you can pass for an eight-year-old," Mother said, eying me with undisguised disdain.

At fourteen years old, my chest had finally crept forward and started to swell, revealing two shy bumps under my thin clothing. I was also getting taller, my legs elongating and my hips starting to jut out.

"But I'm sure I look nothing like her, Mother," I said.

"That doesn't matter, Erosabel. Have you learned nothing from me?" she spat. "It's going to be dark and shadowy. People see what they want to see. We will douse you in powder from head to toe, so no one can see your coarse brown skin or dark hair. You will look ghostly white and ethereal. You will probably look the prettiest you have ever looked in your life. You will wear a long white dress with flowing ruffles and a train, and your hands will be covered in white gloves. You will be entirely unrecognisable. These newcomers will have no idea who you are, or the little business you've got going on here."

I nodded, seeing a thousand ways in which this could go wrong. "Why don't you just do your usual thing? Pretend to talk to her and pretend as if she is talking through you?" I asked.

"These people are paying real money and they will get a real show," Mother said stonily. "They will talk about it and spread the word. People will hear about my seances not only in London but all over England."

"Do I need to speak?" I asked.

"No, perhaps just mouth the word 'mama' or something," Mother said, waving her hand, swatting away my unimportant question. "They'll be coming soon so go out and buy the powders, gloves and necessary materials."

"Yes, Mother," I replied. As I made my way downstairs I heard Mother talking in the background.

"It must be done. The Devil's work will spread across the world, bathing it in death and ruin."

119

A morbid laugh resounded through the walls and into the very heart of our dingy dwelling. It rattled my insides as I quickly grabbed my money pouch and headed out to buy the necessary paraphernalia for the charade.

I went to a second-hand fabric shop to buy the material to stitch together an angelic lace gown fashioned out of deceit and treachery. I entered the shop and greeted the assistant, scrutinising the rolls of fabric flowing from the walls, tables and chairs.

"Can I help you with anything?" the assistant said, a forced smile plastered on her lips.

"No, I know what I'm looking for." I stroked several white silk sheets and ran my hands over lacy, beaded material. The assistant's eyes were glued to me. I decided to combine the lacy beads and the soft, white silk for my dress.

I let my hands glide over the water-smooth fabric, imagining who had used or worn this before me. This shop took the gowns of ladies and either sold them as they were or unpicked them, returning them to their original fluid state. My mind drifted to expansive mansions with huge dance halls, the servants tucked away in the corners. A lady with a mysterious smile and silky golden-brown hair floated into the ballroom. She had an energy about her that drew in the stares of men and women alike. The silky dress she wore skimmed the floor with all the gentleness of a mother caressing her infant.

I then saw the delicate fabric in my coarse, cracked hands and remembered my deceitful mission. The honour and nobility the material contained from its previous life drained out of it. I could feel its lifeless energy as it hung limp in my clutches.

I snaffled up the material, paid the assistant and left the shop with my bundle. I traipsed around other second-hand stores and bought a pair of elegant, porcelain-coloured gloves and a jar of white powder as well as silky white slippers in which to hide my growing feet. I sneaked in a hot potato which I wolfed down out of a newspaper, and took my purchases home.

Tommy and Anna had opened up the shop and were busily going through the accounts and chatting.

"There you are, Roz," Tommy exclaimed. "I was wondering where you'd got to. You must have been out pretty early to have missed us coming in."

"Yes, I was out early," I confirmed. "Listen, I'm just going to be upstairs working on something so I won't be able to help out much today. Feel free to close early if you like."

"You're working on a new best-selling remedy?" Anna asked light-heartedly.

"Yea, something like that," I replied. I bounded upstairs with my packages, feeling Tommy's scrutinising stare on the back of my neck. I had never been able to lie to him and I was sure he could sense something was amiss.

I didn't have time to contemplate what Tommy was thinking and immediately set to work making a dress fit for an angel. I made rough measurements of myself and began cutting up the fabric. It was so soft I felt like I was cutting through butter. I then carefully started stitching bits and pieces together, altering the positions of the beads and faux pearl teardrops that littered the fabric. I didn't realise time collapse around

121

me. The sun unleashed a blood-red stain through my window as it folded itself away. The dress was nearly finished. I quickly slid out of my old, tatty clothes and slipped into the dress to see what final alterations I needed to make.

Immediately I was transformed, I was a different person. The silk cocooning my skin was so soft I felt I was being embraced by feathered angel wings. It cascaded to my feet, pooling in crumpled, pearlescent ripples. My toes only just peeped out from underneath the waterfall of silk. The lace section clung to my bodice, revealing a figure I did not know I had. My waist was small and tucked in whilst my chest appeared full, pushed up by the tight folds of material. I would definitely have to bandage my chest well if Mother and I were to pull off this stunt.

Suddenly I felt eyes on me. I spun around. I had been so engrossed in examining each fold and stitch in the dress that I had not heard Tommy come in. He was staring, speechless at me.

He cleared his throat, which seemed to be dry and scratchy as sandpaper. "So this is what you were working on?" he managed.

"Yes, it's something I have to do for me and Mother," I replied, watching as his gaze trailed the length of my body, pausing at my newly discovered chest and hips. I felt an intense heat land wherever his gaze fell. That undercurrent of energy was back, pulsating through my body. I couldn't tell if I felt uncomfortable or if I enjoyed the sensation.

We remained quiet a few moments longer.

"You're so beautiful, Erosabel," Tommy said in a surprisingly calm, almost sad way.

"Thanks," I said, shrugging, feeling the weight of the beads on my arms and shoulders.

"You won't stay here long, will you?" he said, tears wavering in his eyes.

I was taken aback by this comment. I had no plans to leave. I was not a willing party in Mother's seances but I didn't have anywhere else to go as of yet.

"Of course I'm staying. I don't have anywhere else to go."

Tommy nodded, unconvinced. He reached into his pocket. "Here, I made you this a while ago. I couldn't think of the right time to give it to you but I want you to have it," he said, taking several steps towards me. He took my small hand in his large, rough one. Tommy was sixteen now. He had grown up and I hadn't realised. Tommy was no longer my best-kid-friend who I used to play with in the mud and roll around the city with in tattered clothes and shoes riddled with holes. He was a man now.

Gently, he pressed a necklace into the palm of my hand. I drew the pendant closer to my face. Tiny crushed flower petals were preserved in a small circular orb, dangling from a silver chain. Where the chain connected, I saw "T & E" engraved in beautiful swirling calligraphy.

"Wherever you go in the world, Roz, don't forget me," Tommy said with a melancholy that punctured my lungs and withered my heart.

A lump rose in my throat, making it impossible for me to refute him, to tell him that I would go wherever he went. I stared hard at him, trying to let him know that we would never part. He had been my life thus far and without him, I would lose a significant part of me. It was like being separated from my shadow or staring into a mirror with no reflection to greet me. I knew from this moment on, I would always be half a person, never whole.

"Good luck with whatever you're planning on doing tonight," he said, giving my dress and body a final once-over as if trying to burn the image in his memory forever. "I'll always remember you like this, a fallen angel."

"So catch me," I stammered, managing to swallow the lump in my throat. I collapsed into his warm, strong arms and cried silently. I wasn't sure what I was crying for. Perhaps for lost time or the innocence of childhood which had been snatched away from both of us all too soon. I cried for a future I knew we would never have, a life which would never be. I cried for the shattered dreams and hopes that had been stolen from us and for the way this city, this life, seemed to swallow anything pure and good, regurgitating a putrid mass of decay in return.

We remained locked in an embrace where time seemed to weep around us, seconds, minutes, hours splashing around our feet on the floor. Finally, Tommy pulled away. He gently kissed my forehead and without another word turned and left. I don't know how he knew, if the world had given him a secret message, but that was the last time I ever saw my best friend. His slumped shoulders as he ducked under the crumbling wooden beams of the doorway to my room was the last image imprinted of him in my mind. In that moment I felt part of my soul being ripped out from inside me. The gaping hole of loneliness that had started as a pinprick when Uncle Ben left was growing, stretching its long dagger-like arms, piercing anything in its path.

Mother arrived shortly after. I did not know where she had been all day, nor did I ask. She took one look at my dress.

"That'll do quite nicely," she said, her lips carving into a bleak smile.

I had bandaged my chest, put slippers and gloves on and was powdering my hair and body, turning into a spectre of myself. I felt with each shake of the powder jar, I was slowly disappearing, erasing the Erosabel the world had known thus far. Soon I would cease to exist at all.

The sound of horse hoofs and a carriage being dragged through the muck outside rang through the night.

"They're coming. You will hide behind a screen downstairs. On my cue, you drift out," Mother said.

"What's the cue?"

"I'll say, 'Annabelle, we beseech you, come to your grieving mother and give her some peace at last'," Mother said, in a deep, dramatic voice. Without warning, Mother clutched her head with her hands and slammed it into the wall. I jumped back, startled. Mother smiled as a serpent of blood trickled from her forehead and into her tangled nest of hair. "Just trying to get some peace and quiet so I can focus tonight. No need to be frightened," she said in a sugar-sweet voice.

I swallowed hard. I was frightened. Trepidation and dread settled like weights in my bones. This was not right. This was not going to go well.

Mother traced the blood with her finger and then put her finger in her mouth. She sucked hard on it, licking every drop of blood as if it were the fountain of youth. "Showtime, my petal," she whispered.

This group of newcomers were not faceless. I watched as they trickled in. They wore dark clothes but their eyes darted around, fully visible, observing their surroundings. I hid behind a black curtain Mother had hung up in the apothecary. There were just as many men as there were women, which was unusual. The groups Mother entertained were usually all women. The men had thick beards and tall, black hats. There were ten people in total. Once they had all settled in a circle, the show began.

"Let's begin by holding hands and sharing our collective energies, spirits and memories," she said sombrely. I noticed she was twitching strangely. This wasn't part of her usual act.

What sounded like a sceptical mumble rumbled throughout the circle. Nonetheless, everyone held hands and waited. Mother started her usual chanting and humming, interrupted by the odd whisper or comment. My nerves were frazzled, balancing on a razor edge. Usually there was either deathly silence or obedient chanting. Typically there was a reverential respect for the dead soul Mother was calling forth and for her power as a medium between the world of the living and that of the dead. This group seemed different. My heart was thumping in my mouth as I continued to watch the murky scene unfold.

As if on cue, Mother started shaking and trembling violently. Several gasps of concern bubbled to the surface from the pool of sceptics. Mother's eyes rolled back as froth trickled from her mouth.

"She's here," Mother stammered in a quivering voice brimming with emotion. "What is your name, child?" Mother paused for a strangled breath and became limp, like a rag doll. "Annabelle," she whispered, letting the name float through the circle like a dark cloud, landing deftly on its target.

Mrs Carlisle's head snapped up. She was a slim woman with pinched features from what I could see from behind my shadowy veil. She was eying Mother closely.

"My Annabelle?" she said in a voice that I thought was much too sharp and brittle to be heartbroken.

"Annabelle," Mother continued. "Poor child, whose life ended before it had begun. Annabelle, we beseech you, come to your grieving mother and give her some peace at last."

That was my cue. My legs shook as if I was walking on toothpicks. I slowly crept forward. The tight bodice and bandages were gathering sweat. I couldn't look at the crowd at first, planting my eyes to the floor. When they caught sight of me, there were several gasps and hands clapping over mouths in fear. My eyes flitted up to Mrs Carlisle's and I did as Mother had instructed, mouthing the hallow word "Mama", looking as intently as I dared into her small, pinched eyes. Those were not the eyes of a grieving mother. Whilst the rest of the crowd seemed to tremble in fear and awe, this woman merely stared. What looked like anger seemed to bubble underneath her calm exterior.

"Annabelle, you suffered a brutal death by your father's hand. He murdered you cruelly and is paying for his sins in the bowels of hell. We know your story now, and your soul may rest in peace," Mother was saying, as she rocked from side to side.

I stood still, within arm's reach of Mrs Carlisle. Her eyes were hard like stones. She then snorted in mirth. Fear froze my veins. This had never happened before.

"He didn't kill you," she said in a voice that could cut steel. "This is a sham. I killed you because you ruined my life," Mary Carlisle said, her voice rising to a shriek. "I found that axe lying around and there you were, screaming your head off about some nonsense about how you'd tell Father that I'd beat you the other day. You and your endless lies! You needed to be silenced once and for all," she spat. The deranged Mrs Carlisle then lunged at me, planting her claws around my neck. "You demon from hell, you're the one that should be punished!"

Her grip tightened around my throat. I felt every last drop of air being squeezed out from me. I caught a glimpse of Mother staring dumbfounded at the attack. I tried to call out for help but could only whimper. I felt my arms and legs flailing uselessly by my sides as my vision dimmed, like a tunnel leading me to the end of the world. Suddenly the iron grip was released from my neck. I choked in lungfuls of air as I struggled to sit up.

"That's not your dead daughter. It's just some girl," a man was yelling, holding a writhing Mrs Carlisle by the waist, having pulled her off me.

They had all discovered I was a live, flesh-and-blood girl, not a haunting spectral eight-year-old who had journeyed from the other side. I managed to get to my feet. The world was spinning around me with dizzying speed.

"This is all a sham. She's no ghost, and she's no medium," the man continued to yell.

I wished he would shut up. He was still gripping a thrashing Mrs Carlisle firmly, saying something about calling the police. I felt the world crumbling around me in great chunks.

Mother now began to yell, adding her shriek to the confused fray. "Get out, get out this instant!" She grabbed several of the vials lining the walls and starting to hurl them at the group. Explosions of shattering glass sent the group tumbling towards the door. Mother wasn't done with the vials. She grabbed heavier jars of bathing oats and salts and flung them across the room, their contents spraying everywhere. I watched, unable to speak or move, as Mother continued in her blind destruction of the apothecary even after the group had left.

"This is all your fault," Mother hissed as she turned on me.

I shook my head, still unable to speak. My tongue felt like a heavy, immobile worm dead in my mouth. I could feel a ring of bruises throbbing around my neck. My dress was torn in several places, the rough stitching splitting open.

"It's all her fault," Mother repeated, her voice increasing in pitch. Her eyes took on a manic gleam. "We told you this would happen! But did you listen to us? We told you to kill the little beast whilst she was still in her cradle and now look! Look at what she's done!" Mother was staring blankly at me, as if she could no longer see me. She could only see the demons tormenting her mind, speaking to her with their forked tongues. She slowly picked up another heavy jar, weighing it in her hands. Quicker than lightning she hurled it at me, aiming at my head. I dodged it but felt shards of glass shower my back.

"Oh, she's a cunning one, she is," Mother was saying in yet another unrecognisable voice. "Hangs on to life as if there's something worth living for. Well, I've got a secret for you. There is nothing worth living for. Hell is empty and the devils are here, some wise man once said. Death is a mercy. A mercy which I shall bestow upon you sooner rather than later."

Another jar whizzed past my ear, adding to the necropolis of splintered vials, spilt tonics and smeared pastes. The floor was a sheet of sparkling glass. Mother then grabbed the sharp scissors I had used to trim my dress.

"It's time we kill her, wouldn't you say?" she said quietly, approaching me with the scissors held up high above her head.

"Mother," I managed to stammer. I fell to the floor, paralysed. I couldn't run. I couldn't move. There was nowhere to hide. Horror rippled through me in waves as I stared at my own mother with a demonic glint in her eyes. Was this how it would end, me stabbed to death amongst the wreck and ruin of my shattered apothecary?

Mother's hand was shaking as she loomed over me, a shadow of death. I closed my eyes and turned my face, waiting for the final blow, the excruciating pain. I then heard the quick slicing sound of a dagger cutting through air. Instead of feeling the sharp blades I heard a sickening sound of skin being punctured. I opened my eyes.

Mother was kneeling next to me, the scissors plunged deep in her stomach. Thick red blood oozed from the wound.

"Leave now, Erosabel. Get out," she whispered in her own voice.

I shook my head. Tears were flowing down my face, mingling with Mother's blood. "I can't leave you like this. You need a doctor," I stammered between sobs.

"The medical world abandoned me long ago, just as you must do now. It is too dangerous for you to stay here. You know what will happen if you do," Mother whispered. Her voice was ebbing, like a dying tide. Her face shone marble white in the glimmer of moonlight.

I continued to shake my head, refusing to believe this was how it was to end between me and Mother.

"Go now. You have no place, no home here any more. The only thing for you here is death..." Mother's voice trailed off as she collapsed in the pool of blood.

I can't remember how or when I was able to stand up. I do not remember grabbing my cloth bag from the shelf. I have no memory of packing it with essentials, spare clothes and the few surviving remedies. I have no recollection of saying goodbye to Mother, planting a kiss on her cold cheek. I do not remember leaving my home, shattered in glass, oozing with potions, lotions and blood.

It was the darkest night of my life. Usually sound emanated from the public houses, street urchins, prostitutes and other night walkers. On this night, it was as silent as an abandoned tomb. The streets were still. Not a single leaf stirred. It was amidst this deathly silence that I heard it for the first time. A fear I had never known before froze me to the very depths of my soul. I felt I was suspended at the bottom of a glassy lake and I could see the layer of ice freezing over its smooth surface. I was trapped and would never see the light of day again.

It was the first time the whisper of madness crept inside my head. A voice that was not my own lodged itself firmly within my mind, growing roots, wrapping its tentacles around my brain. I felt an intense pressure squeeze my head, strangling and warping my thoughts.

"You left her to die. You're a monster. But you're not alone. We're with you now," the poison whispered in my mind.

The curse was breathing. It was inside me and it was alive.

PART II

REFUGE

The Open Road, 1828

Chapter 9

I HAD BEEN traipsing on the open road for nearly a month, with nowhere to go. I was lucky that spring had come early this year, melting away the icy breath of winter. If I had left my home earlier I would surely have frozen to death on the cold, unforgiving roads. There was still a marked chill in the air but when midday arrived, my numb toes and fingers defrosted, getting some relief. Nothing except my tears and memories kept me company. The pernicious voice which had infiltrated my mind on the night I left had withdrawn, but I could feel its thick presence lingering in the folds of my mind, biding its time, waiting to strike. I would shake my head occasionally, trying to expel its fuzzy presence. When I caught myself doing this, I reminded myself of Mother and her bizarre twitches and spasms. Fresh tidal waves of fear and regret would smother me until I felt there was not enough air in the world for my lungs to inhale. During moments like that, I would have to kneel down, rest my pack on the earth and just focus on breathing. I would be dripping in cold sweat. My palms shook violently and I felt my heart might burst from its cavity. Pinpricks of light blinded me and I couldn't see my own hands resting on the damp earth beneath me. All I could do was breathe and wait for it to pass. Everything passes in the end. Everything.

I had been creating more potions and cordials on my journey. As I left the cramped, fetid streets of London, I found myself in more open, country roads. I picked wild flowers, crushing and mixing them with herbs and berries I found along the way. My pack was weighed down with all the new concoctions I had made. Occasionally I was able to sell my wares to passers-by. I had taken all the money Mother had made from the seances as well as everything I had saved up on that last fateful night. For the most part, I slept rough, on hard benches or hidden amongst the barbs of bushes. Occasionally when I needed to bathe or have a hot meal, I would pay for accommodation in one of the nameless towns I drifted through.

My heart was empty and the black hole inside me was so large and all-consuming I couldn't tell where it ended and where I began. I felt I had left my soul behind in the slums of East London by Mother's dying body. As the white powder had been sprinkled all over my body, I had indeed erased myself. I was a blank canvas, a ghost with hallow eyes and no soul. I noticed wherever I went, whoever I talked to, everyone avoided my eyes. It was as if they were scared if they looked too deep they would catch the emptiness that lurked within me, as if it were a contagious disease leaking out of my eyeballs and snaking its way into theirs. I didn't attract trouble. I wasn't harassed by anyone. Beggars, thieves, madmen all avoided me as I wafted through the world. It was the loneliest existence imaginable.

The only refuge I had was in my memories. They embraced me at night and kept me warm. They were proof that I was real or, at least, that at some point in my life, I had been real. Tommy's smiling face would surface amidst the swirling whirlpool of the past. I wore his necklace around my neck and held it tight as I slept. My thumb stroked the T & E so often my skin started peeling. It was for him and Lucifer that I knew I had to leave. This curse, this cross I had to bear, was mine and mine alone. I couldn't let it harm anyone else. I was already weighed down with guilt over Mother's death. I couldn't add anyone else to that list.

Another relic I had saved as I stole away on that fateful night was Lucifer's book of tales. I didn't get the chance to say goodbye to him. The thought of him looking for me, trying to find out if I was ok, broke a heart which I thought could break no more. Whenever I could, I would open his book and slide into another world, another life where stories had happy endings, and misery and gloom were not always inevitable. I felt close to Lucifer as I read his book. His voice echoed in my head and his puppets danced in front of my eyes. Sometimes I would talk to him and Tommy in my mind. It was only when I was walking past fellow travellers who gave me peculiar stares that I realised the conversations I thought I was having in my mind were in fact slipping past the barriers of my lips. Mortified, at first, I clamped my mouth shut as the travellers continued with their journey. Without warning or reason, a bubbling laughter erupted at the back of my throat. I tried to swallow it, choke it down but it continued, like gooey lava, up to the surface. A sinister laughter, unfamiliar to me, met my ears. I tried to quiet it but the more I tried, the more delirious it became.

* * * * *

I was fast asleep under a tree when I felt a sharp prod on my arm. I jumped up as if a thousand bolts of electricity had been zapped through me. I looked around me. A dark silhouette of a giant loomed over me. I brought my hand to my eyes to shade them from the blinding sun that lurked behind this giant.

"Excuse me, Miss. I didn't mean to startle you, but your bag is open," the dark shadow said.

I blinked, letting my eyes and mind adjust to this unfamiliar presence. I stood up, getting a good look at him. He wasn't so much a giant as reasonably tall and broad-shouldered. He had a barrel chest and thick brown hair peppered with silver. Our eyes locked. He neither batted an eyelash nor blinked away as most people did. His warm brown eyes emanated kindness. I felt my muscles relax a notch.

"Your bag," he repeated, pointing to the scattered contents underneath the tree.

I realised then that I had been squeezing my bag so tightly in my sleep that half of my remedies had spilled out, along with several gold coins which glinted in the light. I looked at him, surprised. Any straggler or passer-by would surely have snaffled up the coins and probably slit my throat to see if there were any more in the bag I held so dearly.

As if reading my thoughts, the man said, "I have no interest in dishonest money. I'm walking to a village that's about a two-week journey from here. I've heard they're building a church and need some masons to lay the foundation. As luck would have it, that's what I do." The large man shrugged his shoulders, watching me.

I bent down quickly and scrambled all the fallen bits into my pack. I slung it over my shoulder and met his steady gaze.

"What about you? You're out here on your own? Where is it you're heading?" he asked.

Unsure of how to answer or engage in reciprocal conversation with a fellow human being, I merely met his questions with a steely stare.

"Not so talkative, huh," the man replied. "Well, I take it you're journeying along this way," he said, gesturing to the road which I had indeed decided by complete chance to take. "Let's walk together, look out for each other," he continued. "My name's John. It's been a while since I've had work. My mother, father and sister are all relying on this opportunity to work out. Pray to the Lord that it does."

I looked up at him. Did he really think there was a Lord listening to him and his worries? How could he think an all-benevolent Lord cared an iota about his troubles? Anger simmered deep within. I could taste its bitterness on my tongue like drops of cyanide.

"So, can I at least know your name?" he asked in his mild, open manner.

The wave of anger receded. I opened my mouth to answer but found my mind had gone blank. Did I still have a name? I remembered the E on the necklace Tommy had given me. I felt I was drudging up a hidden memory from the depths of a scum-filled pond as I answered.

"Erosabel."

John turned to me and looked surprised. Perhaps he genuinely thought I was dumb and mute. Perhaps he figured my tongue had been torn out by some tragic accident or my ears thumped so hard I had gone deaf.

"That's an interesting name. I've never heard it before."

"Mother was an interesting person," I replied flatly, my gaze fixed directly on the path ahead of us.

"Was?" he said, his voice tinged with melancholy. "I'm sorry to hear that. Are you travelling to extended relatives or family?"

"No."

"So where are you going?" he asked.

I shrugged my shoulders. "Wherever."

"Are you always so monosyllabic?" he asked, a small smile tugging the corners of his mouth.

"No."

He nodded, staring at the same patch of path just ahead of us as if it held all of the answers to life's unanswered questions. We journeyed on in silence. I sighed heavily. This was the first person throwing me some crumbs of kindness. Perhaps it wouldn't be so wrong to make some sort of conversation.

"I'm an orphan. I have no family. I'm completely alone in the world. I make healing remedies. You say there's a town two weeks' travel away. I'll probably stay there for a few days, earn some coins selling tonics and cures before wandering on."

I wanted to continue but restrained myself from adding that all I had ever loved in this world was lost to me. The very air I breathe is cursed. I'm barely fifteen and I feel I've lived a thousand years. My heart, if I still have one, is as ancient as the earth we walk upon and as empty as a desert wasteland. I decided he didn't need to know the particulars of my innermost thoughts. I finished my melodramatic speech in my mind with my gaze still fixated in front of me, although I could no longer see the pathway. All I could see was darkness, the black hands of doom reaching out towards me, pulling me to the abyss. My resistance to those hands, to that force, was whittling away. If I didn't confide in someone, if someone didn't help pull me from the edge soon, I knew I would fall into that gaping hole of nothingness, becoming nothing in the process. When that happened, I feared something, the shadow of a nightmare, would creep inside me to fill the void. The shadow would fill every corner of my being like a thick sludge and I would no longer be Erosabel.

I could feel John staring at me intently. He put his giant paw on my shoulder so lightly it could have been a feather.

"I don't know what you've gone through but clearly you have suffered. I'm sorry for that. Have faith in the Lord. Have faith in this life that things will get better," he said gently.

I felt my eyes welling up with tears. "Hope is a curse."

"Whether it is a curse or not we need it, like plants need sunlight, like fish need water. We need hope for our survival. I can tell you are a strong girl and you can survive almost anything. Don't let go of hope. If you let go of hope, you let go of your soul."

I watched as heavy tears splashed down on the pathway, leaving their tiny signatures on the worn earth. John kept his gentle paw on my shoulder. His touch gave me warmth and comfort. It made me cry all the more since he didn't realise that my soul was already gone. It had withered away like the dying embers of a flame into the slick sea of blood and glass coating the apothecary floor. There it would congeal, sealing itself within those four cursed walls, embedded within its eternal tomb.

We walked on, speaking little. It was a comfortable silence that settled between us, the kind that settles between old friends. John had a knack for catching food. He could catch fish with his bare hands if we passed a stream. He was also adept at catching rabbits, skinning them and cooking the meat. He built fires to keep us warm on chilly nights.

One night we were sitting by a smouldering fire, just off the pathway. We had just eaten dinner and I was feeling warm and content. The more time I spent with John, the more human I felt.

"Do you have a family?" I asked him. The weather was soft and warm, shielding us in a cocoon.

John smiled sadly. "I have my mother, father and sister. I also had a wife, Charlotte. She died in childbirth. My son died with her. He would have been seven years old if he had lived." He clasped his big bear-like hands together as if in prayer, sighing deeply.

"I'm sorry," I said. I reached out and touched his thick, muscular arm. His sorrow was tangible. I could feel it coursing through his veins, just like mine. "I'm really very sorry."

"The Lord giveth and the Lord taketh away," he replied in resignation.

"You really believe that, don't you?" I said, trying to hide my perplexity. "It must be nice to find comfort in religion, to believe that you will see them again in heaven."

John raised his head from his palms. "Religion is the only thing that makes sense in this world of madness. It is the only sturdy thing that I can rely on. Life takes everything and everybody you care about. Cruel things happen for no apparent reason. But with faith in the Lord there is a reason. Through following the Lord's words, practising kindness and gratitude, small miracles can happen if you know how to look for them."

I smiled and nodded, admiring his fervent belief in what he said. I wished I could believe in something other than the black hands of doom.

"Anyway, it's time we got some sleep so we can set off early tomorrow. I think the town is only two days away now. Nearly there!"

We settled next to the burnt embers and drifted off to sleep. John snored deeply, a relaxing rhythmic tone which lulled me into a deep slumber.

* * * * *

I was awoken by a cold blade pressing hard against my neck.

"Wakey-wakey, sweetheart," a harsh voice whispered in my ear.

I let out an involuntary gasp of shock. A man gripped my arm with an iron fist whilst his other hand held a knife to my throat.

John stirred and woke. "What is it, Erosabel?" He rolled over sleepily to face me. His eyes snapped open and he jumped to his feet when he saw the man behind me.

"Stand up, sunshine," the man said to me in his rusty low voice. "Now, you, big guy, just stay where you are and no one needs to get hurt."

"Let her go," John said, his voice quavering in anger. His fists were clenched and his eyes darted around him, searching for a potential weapon to use.

The man followed his gaze. "Now, don't do anything silly, son. Like I said, no one will get hurt. Just give me whatever money or valuables you have and I'll be on my merry way."

"We don't have any," I managed in a semi-strangled voice.

"I hope you're not lying to me, sunshine," the man retorted. I could feel his hot breath on the nape of my neck. "Big guy, tip that bag upside down." He gestured to my pack which contained my remedies, book and stash of money. Panic was surging through my body. The money pouch was perched on top of the bag. In that pouch was my entire savings and livelihood. Without that the man might as well slit my throat. I had been struggling day to day as it was. Without a regular customer base, selling remedies didn't make enough to scrape by. My survival depended on that money pouch.

Searching wildly for a distraction, I noticed the smell of rotting flesh. The arm which had been holding me in a vice-like grip had a huge gash which had turned the man's entire forearm a bruised purplish green colour. Pus oozed from the wound and smelt foul.

"I can help you," I claimed, trying to quell the desperation in my voice.

John frowned at me whilst the man barked a harsh laugh. "You can help me? Do you not realise the position you are in, sweetheart? I don't need your help, just whatever's in there."

"But your arm," I pressed. "It's dangerously infected. As you'll see, all I have in the bag are my remedies. I'm a healer." I widened my eyes at John as I said this. He seemed to notice my cue and shifted the bag ever so slightly in his hands. I continued on, feeling I had the man's attention.

143

"If you leave your arm in that state, it will have to be amputated. I don't think you'll get far robbing people with only one arm," I blabbered. I noticed John subtly shift the bag and slip the pouch up his sleeve. The knots in my stomach loosened ever so slightly, although I still had a knife pressed against my neck.

"I can cure your wound and then you can leave us be," I heard myself saying. In fact, I had never healed such a dire wound but I would have said anything at that point.

"Very well, cure me. But tip that bag over now or I'll give you a wound you won't be able to mend," he said.

John tipped out the contents of the bag. The remedies tumbled out, along with the hefty book.

Suddenly a fog settled over my mind like the morning mist over a deserted lake. With it a sense of calm descended over me. The fear that had pulsated through my very bones had been swept away like dead autumn leaves. Instead a bizarre neurotic laughter tickled the back of my throat. I couldn't explain or understand it. Although there was nothing funny about the situation I was currently in, the insane laughter rose from the toxic cauldron within me, sparks crashing against the barrier of my pursed lips. I let out a choked gurgle, a noise somewhere between a hiccup and indigestion.

"You're hurting her!" John exclaimed.

"Don't you worry about her," the man said. "What are all those bottles?" he said, gesturing to the bag's contents at John's feet.

"I told you I'm a healer. Those are my remedies and I can help you if you would just let me go. What is more valuable than your health after all?" I spat in a much harsher tone than I intended. What was more valuable than health? Although physically I was well, I knew something inside of me was off kilter. Something was wrong and was getting worse. Maybe this stranger should cut me down where I stood and I'd be done with this life and its maladies.

All of a sudden, the man released his grip on me. I stumbled and fell to the ground. John ran to my aid and helped me stand up, glaring at the man.

"Well, you are an interesting duo, if ever I saw one," the man said, his sharp eyes flitting between us.

He was very tall, taller than John and had icy blue, deep-set eyes that were razor sharp. He had high cheekbones and thin lips which curled on one side, into a half-smile. A sheet of blonde hair that was so light it looked grey flopped just below his ears. His clothes had a shabby elegance about them and hung off his thin frame. They were probably stolen from some rich man travelling down these parts in a fine, horse-drawn carriage. His rough tanned skin revealed that he spent most of time on the road. He was a highwayman, no doubt.

He met my intense gaze with amusement. "You have the eyes of a sorceress, sunshine."

"So I've been told," I replied, thinking back to that peddler in the sewers of London who had called me a witch before tossing me into a puddle of filth.

"I'll take some of that," the man said, gesturing to the remains of our meal from the night before.

John tossed him the extra rabbit meat we had been planning to have for breakfast. I could feel the anger radiating off him.

"Thank you kindly," the man said, stripping the meat off the bone with particularly sharp, pointed teeth. "Listen," he said between mouthfuls. "I have a proposition for you two. These are some dangerous parts you're walking through right now, riddled with violent highwaymen much worse than myself after dark. How about we journey on together and I can protect you from the vilest of the vile. And you, sunshine, will heal my wounded arm. And if you don't, well, we're back to the beginning then, aren't we," he said, twiddling the knife between his long fingers so that it glinted malevolently in the growing daylight.

"Fine," I said, my mind flitting through potential cures for the dreadful infection the man had acquired.

I looked at John and shrugged my shoulders, hoping he would be able to rein in his anger. I didn't feel particularly bothered if we strung this spider along with us until we reached the town. As long as the highwayman didn't find my secret stash of money, I didn't care what he did.

"We're going to have to light a fire so I can make sure my tools are clean. And I will need to gather some herbs for the soothing ointment after," I said, straightening up, formulating a cure in my mind.

"Well, lucky for you, I've got all the time in the world," the man said, kicking out his legs in front of him as he sat on a log. His eyes followed us as if we were the most entertaining thing he had seen in a long time.

I rummaged through my memory on how to make the soothing paste. "I'll need to see if I can find the ingredients for the remedy around here."

"We'll come with you, keep you company. Can't have you running off now, can we?" the man said, standing up on his long, spidery legs.

It was a wooded area and I was sure I'd find what I needed.

"So how did the pair of you come to be travelling together? A child witch and her... bodyguard?" the man said, raising an eyebrow.

"I'm not a child," I said, feeling the anger bubble to the surface. I had been through too much to be condescended to by this stranger.

"What's your story? Do you enjoy threatening girls with knives and not doing an honest day's work in your life?" John retorted.

"Not particularly," the man said, in a faux thoughtful manner. "But you got to do what you got to do to survive."

"Survive in this life but what about the afterlife? What about your soul?" John said.

"Ah, we have a believer, a man of religion and purity in our midst. I now see your halo, like a cloud of heaven rising above your head," the man said, pretending to bow down to John. "I admire your ardent faith, son. I wish I could have but a drop of it and perhaps change my ways for good. Alas, I was born empty and soulless and have but my wits to guide me in this life, the only life I am aware of."

"Do you always give such flowery speeches? Perhaps you missed your calling as a poet," I said flatly, feeling the strange calm descend upon me again.

"You think a highwayman cannot also be a poet?" he said, smiling at my sarcasm. "The two are not mutually exclusive. Those who live on the edge have more right to poetry than those lazy louts who pontificate in their armchairs smoking their cigars, occasionally gazing out their window to gather inspiration for an insipid, uninteresting verse. But they will be acclaimed and admired with their connections and riches, and the likes of me will be the forgotten dust that they sweep from the floor." He looked at my expression and winked. "Tell me, what is your name, sorceress? You have an intensity that piques my interest." John cast him a furious look.

"Calm down, cupid. It is only my interest that is piqued, nothing else. I do not have a penchant for mere children, witches or otherwise," the man said, smiling his half-smile.

"Erosabel," I said, as I gathered some flowers and a rock that looked like it would be good to crush them.

"The belle of the ball," he said. "My name is Alexander. You may call me Alexander the Great if it pleases you. And what is your angelic bodyguard's name then since we are all getting so pleasantly acquainted?"

"I wouldn't say this has been pleasant, but my name's John," John replied gruffly.

We stopped in a small clearing, and I started crushing together some herbs and oils from my pack with the flowers I had just picked, creating a thin, liquidy paste. John bent down and started the fire. I didn't know what it was about the highwayman but something about him reminded me of my lost friend Lucifer. As I thought about Lucifer, the hostility drained from me, like water pouring through the holes of a sieve.

"Here, this should give you some relief after I work on your arm. I can make a better paste when I get more materials from the town," I said.

"Right, so what is it you're going to do with my arm then?" he asked.

I took out a needle and thread. "Sew it back together."

"How do I know you're not just going to kill me and leave me for dead in this little forest?"

"Kill you with this?" I asked, gesturing at the minute point of the needle. "You're the one with the knife."

"Hmm," Alex said, looking at the needle sceptically.

I heated it over the fire and threaded it. "This will hurt a little."

"I am a soldier of the earth, in a constant state of war with everything that comes in my path. I have faced worse foes, deeper wounds and nearly died more times than I can count. No need to worry about me," he stated stoically.

Despite his effusive speech, I felt his muscles tense up and heard his teeth grind as he clenched them hard. I cleaned the area of pus and poured some alcohol that I had stashed in a flask over the wound. I then drove the needle into his skin and sewed up the gash.

"How did you get this anyway? Someone use your knife against you?" I asked.

"As if," he grunted, breathing heavily. "I was bitten by a wolf."

"There are no wolves around here," John said.

"A bear then." Alexander groaned.

"Almost done," I said, rather enjoying plunging the needle in with all the gentleness of a butcher. I cleaned up the wound and plucked a large, waxy leaf from a nearby tree. I used that to smooth the healing liquid onto Alexander's rough, scarred skin.

Alexander closed his eyes for a moment and let out a deep sigh. "Well, if that is not the very balm of Gilead," he said. "You have some talents, little Belle."

I scraped the leftover paste into a small empty jar and put it in my pack. Quite some time had passed and we needed to get moving.

"Well, let us journey on to better days ahead with a newfound health and vitality in our steps," Alexander said, reading my mind.

"Do you want to rest? We can get a head start and you can catch up with us when you're ready?" John said.

"No, no, you can't get rid of me that easily, son. I'm right as rain. Besides, little Belle here needs to monitor this stitching to make sure it doesn't get infected," he added, letting out a stifled groan as he got up. "Let us be on our way. Wouldn't you say fate has a cynical sense of humour? Here we are, a priest, a witch and a battered criminal forming the most comical trio I ever did see."

"We are not a trio. Once we get to the town I will be reporting you to the town sheriff the second I get my chance," John huffed.

"I'm sure you will, my priest, cook and friend. But, unfortunately, I will be long gone by then."

"Going to leech off the skills of some other poor traveller?" John retorted.

"Precisely," Alexander replied with a wolfish grin.

* * * * *

We were a strange group. Hostility bristled off John whilst Alexander remained calm and composed, occasionally spouting off his bizarre monologues which was completely uncharacteristic of what I imagined highwaymen to be like. For my part, I surprised myself by enjoying the added company. It was infinitely better than wandering aimlessly by myself, with nothing except my dark, dangerous thoughts for company. Perhaps it was because he reminded me of Lucifer that I didn't want Alexander to leave. I knew I was clinging on to a mere shadow of my lost friend, but to me it was better than nothing.

It was late afternoon and the sun was at its peak, a fiery orb strung up in the sky beating down on us with a relentless intensity. Sweat was dripping down my body, making my dress cling to every inch of my sticky skin. I noticed John swiping his brow, banishing the sweat only for it to return moments later. The only one who seemed blissfully unaffected was Alexander.

"How about we stop and rest for a couple of minutes?" I suggested, fearing John might have a heart attack and collapse if we continued walking in the blistering heat.

"Of course, if you need a break, we can certainly rest under that tree over there," John panted, squinting at the shimmering tree not too far away.

"As you wish," Alexander said in his gravelly voice.

John and I melted against the tree trunk, relishing the cool shade. Alexander remained standing, surveying the scene with the sharp look of an eagle searching for its prey.

"So John, how about you put your hunting skills to good use? I'm famished," Alexander stated.

John was still catching his breath and looked about as ready to hunt as a corpse was to do backflips in a travelling circus.

"I'll go," I suggested. "I may not be able to bring us back a rabbit, but I can certainly forage for some berries and other fruits around here. I know the poisonous ones from the safe ones. It won't take me long. I also heard a stream running nearby. I'll get us all some water." I gathered the goatskin flasks we were carrying and a cloth in which I would collect whatever edible substances I came across.

"A jack of all trades. Very well, Miss Belle. I'll guard the bodyguard over here," Alexander said, leaning his sinewy frame against the tree. He casually took out the knife and started spinning it around his abnormally long fingers.

I headed towards a clearing which dipped into a wooded area. The sounds of the gurgling stream reminded me of just how thirsty I was. My throat was burning and my mouth felt as dry as parchment. I would fill up our flasks first, I thought to myself, before going off in search for food.

I reached the cool, murmuring stream. Immediately I fell to my knees and took several long gulps of the delicious water, shimmering like crystals under the dappled gaze of the sun. I dipped my hands and face into its waters. When this wasn't enough, I kicked off my tattered, heat-filled shoes and plunged my feet beneath the surface. Before I knew it I had peeled off my sticky clothes and jumped into the refreshing pool. It was just deep enough to cover my body, up to my neck. I allowed the cool tingling sensation to spread until I felt numb all over. After the sweltering heat of the day I felt I was in paradise.

A rustling sound in the bushes stirred my attention. I looked around me. All I could see was the rushing of the river and my clothes tossed in a pile along the muddy edge. Suddenly I felt apprehensive, as if I wasn't alone. I swivelled around, feeling the heat of someone's gaze land upon me. Three figures lurched out from amidst the trees. My body froze in terror. I was naked and alone in the middle of the brook. These men smelt of desperation and had emptiness and other men's blood cradled in their souls. They leered at me.

"Come out, come out, we won't hurt you," the ringleader said in a flat voice, devoid of emotion.

"You are a pretty thing," said a shorter man, who walked with a slight limp.

"We'll enjoy her," the last one added. He had a malicious grin plastered across his face and was holding a large, heavy stick above his head. "Come out before we make you."

My body started to tremble. I couldn't talk my way out of this one. I was stuck and they were coming closer. I pressed myself against the opposite end of the brook breathing heavily, my mind drawing a complete blank. I had lost my voice, lost the ability to scream. All I could do was stare at my fate which lay in the hands of three brutal men.

They laughed, sensing my fear.

"We're not going to hurt you. Who knows, you might even enjoy it," the one with the malicious grin said.

They cackled like a pack of hyenas, loud and menacing. Their hooting laughter froze the blood within my veins. I tried to swallow, tried to fight back the tears gathering in my eyes. Whatever happened I did not want to show them that I was afraid. I took in a deep breath and felt along the side of the bank, trying to find a sharp, hard stone embedded within the soft mud. My hand found nothing but reeds and mushy earth.

Just as the ringleader dipped his toe in the cool waters I heard another rustling in the bushes. The men were all fixated on me and didn't see the shadow of Alexander appear from behind. With all the deftness and subtlety of a magician flicking cards, he quietly crept behind one of the men, gently slitting his throat with his knife. Blood spurted like a fountain as he choked and fell to the floor. The other two men, a few seconds too late, turned to see what had happened. Before the short one with a limp had time to realise someone was behind him, Alexander's blade had already pierced his stomach and he was dead. The last man, the one with the malicious grin, turned and sprinted from the scene dripping with death. His footsteps crashed through the undergrowth in their desperation to get as far away from his fallen comrades as possible.

"You were taking your time, Belle. I was hungry and starting to get a tad worried," Alexander said, as calmly as if he was commenting on the weather.

I tried to stammer a reply but found my throat was constricted, thick with emotion.

"Come on, out you get," he said, a note of kindness injected into his usual ironic, sarcastic tone. He took off his shirt and laid it by the side of the brook. "Dry off using that," he said. He turned his back to me to give me some privacy.

With shaking arms, I barely had the strength to heave myself out of the brook. I wrapped my naked body in his shirt.

"Dry up and get changed, Belle," he said gently. "We can go berry hunting together."

Again, I tried to reply but found myself still unable to speak.

The numbing shock was wearing off and I found it nearly impossible to dress with my shaking hands. Tears unwittingly started cascading from my eyes. I had managed to get my dress over my head and was struggling to pierce the sleeve with my arms when my body started convulsing in sobs. Alexander turned around. He took one wordless look at me and held my shaking arm. He helped place it in the sleeve and straightened the dress out over my shivering body. He then helped me sit on the ground, put my shoes on and tied my wet tangled mess of hair back with a ribbon. He did all this with the gentleness of a mother caring for her helpless infant, not a rough, heartless thief.

I couldn't say why I was crying. I didn't know. I wasn't sure if I was crying from fear of those three stooges or if it was for the train wreck that was my life. I thought I had numbed my heart to the past. I thought I had managed to tuck Mother away in the folds of my memory, where Lucifer and Tommy lay, waiting to be resurrected in dreams.

All I knew was that I couldn't stop sobbing. Alexander held me quietly in his wiry, strong arms as I shook with grief. I clutched his shoulders, pouring what was left of my heart and soul onto his bare skin. He held me close and rocked me gently. He didn't say anything. I couldn't say how long we remained in that strange embrace. Life was spinning out of control. I no longer felt I had any grip on reality. And what was reality? A day ago the very man I was finding comfort and solace in was the man who held a blade to my throat and would have cut me if I hadn't promised to cure his wounded arm. I felt reality was continuing to shift around me. Just when I felt I had things under control, my world was turned upside down once again, leaving me stumbling in the dark.

Finally, exhaustion released me from the cruel grip of reality. I lay on the warm, moist earth and surrendered to a tiredness only the dead could empathise with. I felt drained, a corpse wishing to sink into the bowels of the earth, forgotten forever. I felt Alexander cradle my head and place me in a more comfortable position. Voices floated overhead. John's disembodied exclamations of worry and concern burst through the ether of silence. I heard a muffled conversation between him and Alexander before I completely lost consciousness and drifted into limbo, suspended in a land between the living and dead.

* * * * *

It was dark when I awoke. I was no longer by the brook. I sat up, leaning on my elbow. Both Alexander and John were sleeping by the smouldering embers of a fire. I saw some meat had been left aside, presumably for me. My stomach rumbled loudly and I felt starved. As quietly as I could I crawled towards the meat and tore it from the bone. My body felt heavy, as if I had been through a bloody battle. With each mouthful I felt strength being restored to my frail, brittle self.

The moonlight shimmied its way through the trees, lighting up the clearing in an ethereal glow. I turned my face towards the crescent moon. I wondered how many people before me had sought some sort of refuge or answers in the silvery orb suspended in the velvet sky. I stared hard at it, willing it to send me a sign or guidance. Amidst the heavy silence only midnight has the strength to carry, I heard it. The voice had returned. A disembodied, unwelcome croak within my own head. I shook my head violently, tempted to smash it against a tree to rid myself of the voice.

It sneered, *"You can't trust anyone. Not anyone. Especially not those you travel with. You were born to be alone. To die alone. They will turn on you. They are not your friends."*

I was shaking my head, hitting it with the palm of my grimy, mud-stained hand as I willed the voice to stop. It continued to float, unattainable, unresponsive to my attempts to dispel it.

Alexander had saved me. He had helped me. He could have left me to be raped and slaughtered by those men. Better yet, he could have joined in. But he didn't. He saved me. I thought this over and over in my mind, replaying the thought like a broken record. I was not going to allow space for the other, unwanted thoughts to flourish and grow like weeds strangling a flower. As long as I kept thinking, I could squash the paranoid, delusional nuisances that were trying to infect my mind. I would not give in to them as Mother had. I would not.

Chapter 10

WE JOURNEYED ON. I didn't mention what had happened by the brook and neither did Alexander. It was a pact of mutual silence. The two dead bodies remained, unburied, left to the elements of nature and wild animals to pick apart.

We reached the town three days later. Once we reached the bridge connecting us to the entrance of the town, we paused, staring at one another. Despite our tremendous differences, a peculiar fondness had grown between us. We had come to appreciate each other's silence. With the exception of Alexander, we were not a particularly talkative group but we understood each other on a level beyond words.

"Well, here we are," Alexander said.

"Here we are, indeed," John echoed.

"So what's everyone's plan?" I asked.

"Well, you know mine. I'm going to see if they need a mason to help build their church," John said.

"I'm going to check out their public houses here before I make myself scarce." Alexander winked. "I must thank you for the hospitality and food you have shared with me along the way."

"It wasn't exactly optional," grumbled John.

Despite his initial dislike for Alexander, I felt him warm to the cavalier highwayman more after the night he saved me.

"What about you, dear Belle of the ball?" Alexander asked.

"I'll see if I can peddle my wares, I guess," I replied.

Alexander looked at me intently. "You are more than a mere peddler, Belle. One day you and the world will see that."

I nodded, looking down. I had already cried all over this man. I was not about to let myself lose control again.

"It's true, Erosabel. You have a talent not many people have," John said, resting his familiar paw on my shoulder. "I'll be lodging at the local inn around here. If you need me, you will know where to find me."

I nodded, smiling at them. Their kindness tore through my heart like a dagger, shredding it to ribbons. I was not used to such gentle words from anyone except Tommy and Lucifer after Mother's reign of absolute madness and terror.

We entered the town together before going our separate ways. John went in search of the building site for the church whilst Alexander's eyes darted around for the local public house. I decided I would find the local inn and have a long, luxurious sleep before freshening up and going about selling my tonics and remedies to the good people of this supposedly affluent town.

159

After Mother's death and leaving Tommy and Lucifer without so much as a goodbye, I felt my soul had hardened into a thick impenetrable hide that nothing could penetrate. However, as John and Alexander drifted to their separate destinations, I felt a tug at old wounds. A part of my granite soul crumbled, allowing a speck of light to shine through. I hoped I would continue to see them around town and that they wouldn't stray far. I hoped I could keep the voices at bay. I desperately wanted to welcome their friendship without the constant undercurrent of fear that one day I might do something to make them regret ever having laid eyes on me.

* * * * *

I had been staying at the Queen's Inn for just over a week. Each day I had been telling myself that it was time to move on, that staying here was too expensive for my meagre budget. Despite this, I couldn't find it in myself to go back to journeying alone as a lost soul, dithering on the brink of existence. I couldn't go back to being a mere reflection of a person, crossing the earth aimlessly with an empty heart and even emptier soul. Here I felt grounded. I knew people. John had been taken on as a full-time labourer for the church construction. Alexander flitted in and out of the town, usually under cover of night, flashing me a wink as the breaking dawn swept him away.

I had set up a small stand with the familiar name, *Rose's Remedies*. It had been doing rather well and I had sold a number of potions to several of the respectable ladies of the town. They had been open and welcoming when they saw me. The suspicion characteristic of most Londoners was absent in these sweet country folk. For the first time in a long time I felt like I belonged somewhere. No matter how small and insignificant the role I played in this part of town, it was still there. I felt like I was Adeline from Lucifer's tale, "Adeline's Imaginings". If I could only imagine myself living here, becoming an integral part of the patchwork quilt that constitutes this patch of the globe, then it would become real. All I had ever wanted, to be accepted and to belong, could be mine if I only had the power to believe in it.

I was selling a small bottle of lavender water to an old lady when I noticed a young woman by my stall for the second time. She had come by yesterday and bought a skin powder. Today she was fiddling with the oatmeal paste for sensitive skin.

"Hi, would you like to test it on your skin?" I asked.

"No, that's all right. I'm just looking." She smiled. She had soft green eyes, the colour of fresh grass after a summer storm. Small freckles were scattered across her nose and cheeks. Her glossy auburn hair was swirled in a bun.

"You look like you have great skin," I noted, looking at her healthy flushed cheeks and radiant glow. That certainly wasn't London skin. Even rich ladies and gentlemen in London had sallow, coarse skin that was clogged and couldn't breathe. The fumes and smog that billowed throughout the city suffocated the body as well as the soul.

"Thank you," she said shyly.

Suddenly a heavyset, sturdy woman planted herself next to the blushing beauty. "So, did you find out anything?" she whispered in a loud voice.

"Mother," the girl said, widening her eyes in horror.

"Oh, you are useless. Pretty but useless. If you want anything done, you have to do it yourself," the woman muttered. "Where are you from, girl?" she barked at me.

Slightly taken aback, I stumbled over my words. "Uh, um, I'm from—"

"Come now, we can't have any uhs or ums. Speak properly, girl," she interrupted.

"London. I'm from London," I replied.

"God help you. London, foul place to live," she said, scrunching up her nose as if an unpleasant odour had been sprayed in her face.

"Quite."

"I had a brother who went to London years ago. He died a month after arriving there. The core of that city is rotten through. As black as the Devil's heart!"

I stared at her, stunned speechless.

"Well, enough gawping like a glassy-eyed fish. What's your name?" she continued, hammering down questions with the force of a sledgehammer.

"Erosabel. But I go by Roz. Or Belle. Whatever you like."

"Three names! Who has three names! Here on your sign it says Rose. Well, Rose, my husband is a dreadful snorer. He's been snoring for years, and for years I've been getting by on no sleep at all. Do you have a remedy for that?"

I rummaged through several concoctions and lifted out a small vial. "This helps open the passageways. It's supposed to ease breathing when congested with the cold or flu but I'm sure it will work for snoring as well," I said. "Just put a few drops of it in his evening tea and perhaps dab a little under his nose at night and it should do the trick."

"You mean to say that little thing could potentially cure a lifetime's worth of suffering on my part?" she said, suspicious as she eyed the small bottle in my hand.

"Uh, potentially," I replied, with a slight shrug. I knew I wasn't selling myself well, but I felt I had been hit on the head with a ton of bricks. This woman was like a colossal tidal wave, drowning everything in her path.

"Right, I'll take it," she stated.

As they were walking away, the daughter mouthed, "Sorry."

I couldn't help but smile as I lifted my hand and waved at her. I could hear the mother's voice trailing after her as they walked away, as loud as a foghorn. I prayed the vial would work. That was certainly not a woman I would like to have as an angry, displeased customer. Not only would all the inhabitants of this town hear of her dissatisfaction, but it was highly likely all the neighbouring towns and villages would too.

I had a light supper at the Queen's Inn. I kept to myself and focused on my food. I liked it when John was there. I could relax and slip into easy conversation with him. Today he was nowhere to be seen and I felt unprotected. Two men were at the bar. One was swilling his drink and taking long sips from it. The other kept darting furtive glances my way. He was tall and big. He didn't seem particularly muscular, just big-boned and chubby. He had dark black hair and dark eyes that seemed fixated on me. I was on tenterhooks throughout my meal, hoping he would not approach me.

I soaked up the last bit of soup with a crust of bread before darting upstairs. When I was behind my closed, locked door I breathed a sigh of relief. It was strange. I had felt safe amongst the dirt-filled, thief-ridden, stagnant streets of London. I knew my place in the innards of that labyrinth. I could read the signals and understand the people who lived there. I knew what they wanted and how they intended to get it. I could see when a thief was going to slip his hands into a lady's petticoat and rob her of her purse before he knew he was going to do it. It was like a puzzle I had all figured out. These streets and these people were different though. They wore masks, concealing their true identities and desires. I felt like I was learning a whole new language.

I settled onto the hard mattress and did what I did every night. I slipped out Lucifer's book of tales and let the book fall open to a random page. It was my favourite pastime, my favourite form of escapism. I felt close to my lost friend Lucifer as I read the stories he had transcribed for me. Although both Tommy and Lucifer were a dream and lifetime away, the magic of the stories pulled me closer to them. I could hear Lucifer's deep voice resonating through my ears, his dancing puppets acting out the stories. I could hear Tommy's comments and gasps of surprise. He would sometimes put a protective arm around me during a particularly harrowing part of the show. I always sensed it was he who was scared and needed the comfort, but I never said anything.

A small, sad smile played on my lips as the book landed on a page with a picture of a man made from grainy, rough-looking sand. The expression on his face was of heart-breaking desolation. He was alone amongst an eternity of bleak rolling sand dunes. I hadn't read this story before. I adjusted myself, trying to get as comfortable as possible on the slate mattress and began to read.

"The Sandman"

Once upon a time the Gods looked upon an expanse of desert wasteland. The empty sand dunes undulated as far as the eye could see. Ripple upon ripple of unused grains of sand unfurled like an ocean. The Gods decided they ought to make use of this land and create something out of the fallow nothingness that it was. At first the Gods were in agreement and formed the first-ever sandman. They carefully picked out each granule of sand, creating eyes, a nose and a mouth. They furnished his head with ears on the sides and sand hair on top. They gave him arms and legs and a strong body. When the final speck of sand was placed on his body, the Gods fell into a ferocious feud, arguing over what other forms of life should be added to the deathly desert landscape. Should they build more sand people or a city? Should flowing rivers ripple through the dunes or a thick forest? Should animals be set to graze on sand granules or lush verdant fields? The sandman looked up and saw the heavens clashing. Thick angry clouds gathered and collided with lightning. It was a battle that knew no end.

The sandman got used to his new body. He roamed the abandoned desert in the hope of finding someone or something to share his life with. When nothing came, he decided he would create an oasis out of sand. If the wind whispered loud enough, perhaps someone might hear of the paradise he had created and be tempted to pay it a visit. Over the years, he built castles out of sand. He tirelessly worked to mould trees, vast lakes and exotic blooming flowers out of a fine mist of sand. Houses sprung up as well as libraries, schools and parks spreading over the rolling dunes. The sandman created an entire city without a single other inhabitant in it. He would spend hours, days and years wandering through the forlorn alleyways and streets. Time lost all meaning, floating around him in a haze of dust. He had no past or future, merely an everlasting torturous present. All hope of finding company faded and withered like a sun that was about to set forever, her rays of light kissing the earth for the last time.

The sandman collapsed in his castle and cried sand tears. Just when the last drop of sunlight was about to be consumed by an eternal darkness, the sandman heard a knock on the door of his grand sandcastle. At first he thought the wind was testing him, playing games with his sadness. Nonetheless, he rose from his puddle of sorrow and dragged his sand feet to the door.

As he opened it, his jaw dropped in disbelief. It was no joke of the trickster wind but an actual, sentient being. It was a monstrous scorpion, about twice as big as the sandman, its pointed lethal sting twinkling in the air.

"Can I help you?" the sandman asked, unsure of whether the thing he was seeing was a mirage.

"I need a place to stay for the night," the scorpion said in a sharp, rasping voice. "May I rest here?"

"But of course, come in, come in, kind sir," the sandman effused, pure joy radiating from his sand body.

"I have travelled far and wide. No one typically grants a home or resting place to a scorpion. You are most generous," the scorpion replied in his strangely strangled voice.

"I am over the proverbial moon that you chose to rest here. I have not had company since the day of creation. I have not spoken a single word to another being until this great, memorable day," the sandman said.

The scorpion nodded. "If it is agreeable to you, I would like to go to my quarters and rest. It has been a long, long day."

"As you wish," the sandman replied and quickly escorted the scorpion to his quarters. He gave him all he could need, fashioned out of the finest, purest sand. "Goodnight, dear scorpion," the sandman said as he left his guest to rest.

The next day, the sandman rushed upstairs to greet his guest with breakfast in bed. He knocked enthusiastically on the door. When there was no reply, he pushed the door open. The bed was neatly made and there was no scorpion. The sandman fell to his knees, crushed by despair. His one and only guest, his only companion had already disappeared into the veil of nothingness that engulfed the sandman's lonely heart.

Between sobs, he heard a soft fluttering sound from behind him. He turned and had to squint. The being in front of him was so bright with golden light streaming from its every particle.

"Hello?" the sandman said, directing his speech to the curious phenomenon floating in front of him.

In a voice of purest light, it replied, "Hello, kind sandman. You gave me a place to stay for the night. I was cursed to be a scorpion by the wicked Gods. The only thing that could break the curse was another's act of kindness. Since no one is kind to scorpions, the Gods thought I would remain a curse for all eternity. But you have shown me the light. I am now your angel. And as your angel, I can grant you one wish as a form of repayment for the kindness shown to me and for breaking the evil spell."

With a tremble in his voice, the sandman replied instantly, "I would like a family. I would like a sandwoman and sand babies. I would like sand friends to live nearby within this empty, heartless community I have created."

"Then that is what you shall have," the angel of light replied.

With a loud cracking sound that nearly split the sand town apart, the angel disappeared. In its place was a sandwoman and sand babies. Down the corridor, the sandman could hear a group of sand friends chatting and laughing. It was music to his sand ears. He ran up and embraced his sandwoman and their two sand babies. He tossed the babies in the air and caught them. The sound of their bubbling laugher melted away the fallow sadness in his heart.

For many years, light and laughter filled every corner of the sandcastle and the community beyond. No more were the streets deserted. No more was the mocking wind the only thing the sandman could hear. There was life and vitality within the town and the sand people were the friendliest people ever created.

One evening, the sandman was saying goodnight to his youngest sand child when he heard a knock on the door. He opened it and was shocked to see the angel of light hovering over his doorstep.

"It's you!" the sandman said. Joy filled his heart and tears peppered his sand skin. "I never had the chance to thank you properly, kind angel of light. How can I ever repay you? I merely gave you lodging for a night and you have granted me an eternity of happiness. There must be something more I can do."

"Dear sandman, you have shown kindness. That is all anyone can ever ask for. If I want anything from you, it is for you to continue showing kindness in your heart and in your deeds for as long as life is granted to you."

The sandman nodded. And for the rest of his life he practised kindness. The sand people were known as the kindest people to grace the earth. Their light and joy spread like the sun across the globe to every shadowy corner of the world. It became well known that as long as there was just a single sand person, there was hope for all. For the kindness held within one granule of sand was enough to change the world.

As I reached the end of the story, I felt my eyelids grow heavy. The book slipped out of my grasp as I slumped over in bed. Within a few moments, I was in a deep slumber, my dreams swirling pictures of people made from sand and monstrous scorpions roaming the earth. A bewitching angel of light appeared in my dream but I was afraid of her. For when she opened her eyes, they were the cold blue eyes of Mother.

Chapter 11

T HE NEXT DAY, the auburn-haired girl was back for a third time at my stand.

"Did the potion do the trick? Was your mother able to get a good night's sleep?" I asked, smiling.

She blushed a delicate pink. "I'm so sorry about yesterday. Mother can be very loud and forceful. But yes, I think it worked wonders. Mother woke up today saying she felt like a new woman. Be careful or you're going to have her as a returning customer." She giggled.

"Glad to hear it! Could always do with more customers, no matter how loud or forceful," I replied. "What's your name, by the way?"

"Emma," the girl said, holding out her dainty hand to shake mine.

I felt embarrassed taking her hand. Hers was as soft as the velvet petals of a rose whereas I had the rough, coarse hands of a bricklayer. She didn't seem to notice. She smiled and shook it.

"It's nice to meet you," she said.

The Sandman story suddenly crept into my mind from the other night. I felt purity and light radiate from her, just like the angel in the story. Unlike most people, I felt she was not wearing a mask. Her feelings were genuine, and a certain honesty was reflected in her expressions. I felt the usual tension I had whilst keeping my guard up relax and dissolve in her bright presence.

"Nice to meet you too," I replied.

"How did you come to be here, in this small town in the middle of nowhere?" she asked, curiosity shining in her meadow-like eyes.

"That's a very long story."

"I have time." She shrugged.

I eyed her, contemplating how much I could trust her. I knew the answer immediately. "You know what, let me close up shop for the day," I said decisively, folding up my sign and packing my ointments and jars into a cracked wheelbarrow John had given me to help me cart things around.

"Let me help," she said immediately.

Together we dismantled the stall and tucked it away in the wheelbarrow. We walked the short distance to the Inn where I stashed it behind the bar.

"How about we take a walk by the stream?" I asked, hoping for a bit of seclusion if I were to tell Emma the tale of my life.

"Ok, that sounds good," she replied, taking my arm. "I live just down that road," she said, gesturing to a row of houses neatly tucked away. "I live there with my mother, father and older brother. You must join us for tea today if you can!" she said enthusiastically.

"Are you sure that would be ok with your parents?" I asked, not wanting to intrude on the bossy woman's household without her written and signed permission first.

"Don't be afraid of my mother." Emma giggled. "She seems like she's made of iron but deep down she's as soft as can be."

"Well, if that's the case, I'd love to join you for tea," I said, smiling.

The girl's delicate arm was threaded in mine. I felt an unfamiliar wave of tenderness cascade over me. I was used to male friendship with its hard edges and rough mannerisms. Throughout my entire childhood Tommy had been my best friend, ruffling my hair and catching me in headlocks. Then there was Lucifer, certainly less rough but not soft and sweet like Emma. I felt a subtle dynamic shift within me as we walked towards the stream.

"I'm an orphan," I started, looking up to see her eyes melt in sadness. "It's ok," I said quickly. "My father died before I was born, and Mother…" A lump unexpectedly wedged itself in my throat, stubbornly refusing to move. Again I was surprised at the strength of the emotions I thought I was able to suppress.

Emma squeezed my arm reassuringly. "Sorry to hear that. That can't be easy, growing up in London alone," she said softly.

"I wasn't alone," I said, giving her a watery smile. "I had Tommy and Lucifer." I told her about how my best friend and Lucifer had helped me set up shop and how well it had done. I told her about my grandparents' book of remedies and how Lucifer had taught me to read it. I told her how I felt like I had found my calling in the world at last. I then felt my tongue twist and the words turn to ash as I found myself lying about Mother's death and the reason I had to leave. I pretended we had been burgled and Mother had been stabbed during the robbery. I said it with so much conviction I nearly believed it myself. I could almost see the masked face of an anonymous burglar thrust the knife into Mother's stomach whilst she faded away in my arms. I told her how they threatened to put me into the workhouse after that and how I knew the only way for me to live was to escape the turmoil of the city. I told her about how I met John and Alexander on the way and how we had helped each other on our journey to the town.

"And here I am," I said finally.

There were tears swimming in Emma's eyes. "You truly are the bravest person I know."

I looked down and shuffled my feet, kicking some stones into the river.

"Really, I can't even imagine going through half of what you've been through, and you're so young. You're incredible. I'm seventeen and I've just lived a dull, humdrum life here with my parents and brother, doing chores, learning my lessons and taking walks."

"That sounds like perfection to me, not in the slightest bit dull," I replied. "If I could live my life over as anything I liked, I would choose yours."

We continued to walk, a comfortable silence breathing around us. Birds twittered overhead, flitting from one branch to another. I looked up at the clear blue sky. The soft sun caressed my face, bathing it in its warm, golden glow. I felt a small burden lift from my shoulders after divulging parts of my life to Emma.

"Should we head to mine for tea?" Emma said, her soft voice cutting the silence as a knife cuts butter.

"Let's go."

On first seeing me, Emma's mother raged at not being told ahead of time. She scolded Emma for her negligence and then bellowed at me for not making her aware of my intentions of attending their family dinner.

Emma's father, an older man with a kind face, gave me a subtle wink. "Take no notice of her, she's actually delighted that you're here. She lives for entertaining guests!"

I stifled a giggle as Emma's mother scanned the room with a predatory gaze.

"I will tell Margaret to set an extra place at the table. I just hope there's enough food to go round and we aren't pecking each other's eyes out by the end of the night!" she exclaimed, flailing her hands in the air in a display of utter despair.

Once the food was ready and the commotion had subsided, everyone was in their place at the dinner table, eating the monumental-sized portions the maid Margaret had laid out.

"So Rose, what brings you here to this town?" The question shot out of Emma's mother like an arrow. I couldn't help but feel like I was target practice.

I told the brief version of the story I had told Emma earlier that day. I was shocked to see Emma's mother close to tears by the end of it. She picked up a large handkerchief and like a foghorn blew her nose for all her neighbours and beyond to hear.

"That is just tragic. You poor dear, Rose," she said, dabbing her eyes with a pillowcase-sized handkerchief. "And there I was thinking you were some wandering prostitute or something."

"Now, Ada," Emma's father cut in.

"It's true," she exclaimed. "I mean look at those eyes. Those are not normal eyes, my dear," she said, directing the latter part of her statement to me.

"So I've been told. They're my mother's. I've got the same colour eyes as her. I didn't inherit anything else from her, just her eyes. Everything else is my father." Or at least I should imagine it is, I thought to myself, having never met the illusive shadow figure that was my father. Strange to think I was wearing the man's features and yet he knew nothing of my existence. I felt like I was tipping into the surreal, as if I was being erased away, turned into a living, breathing ghost. An ephemeral sense of detachment descended upon me. The only thing that had any weight in my body and soul were the stony blue eyes of Mother. Everything else may simply cease to exist one day, my features melting off my face and evaporating into the black hole of oblivion. All that would remain of me would be a pair of floating sapphire blue eyes amidst a dark whirlpool of a starless space.

Emma's voice infiltrated my thoughts, grounding me back in reality. "I think Rose is the most extraordinary person I've ever met. Wouldn't you agree, Richard?" she said, enlisting her brother's support for her claim.

Richard was older than Emma by a year. He had the same soft looks and calm demeanour. Like Emma he was also quite shy and seemed slightly flustered that his opinion was being called to the table.

"Yes, of course," he replied quickly. "You've been through a lot," he said, flashing a modest glance and half-smile my way.

I smiled politely, hoping to steer the conversation away from me. "I heard there's a church being built around here. I know one of the masons working on the project," I said, switching the railroad tracks of the conversation in a not particularly subtle manner. I had apparently hit one of Ada's many, loud nerves.

"Can you believe it?" she blasted. "Another church! There's one not a stone's throw away from here. Why they need to spend years creating all that havoc and commotion for another one is beyond me! I have sensitive ears and can pick up noises from a mile away! Can you imagine what that building racket is doing to my nerves!"

Everyone at the table had to duck behind napkins or hide behind their glass to mask their smiles and giggles. Ada didn't seem to notice the collective struggle and continued. We passed the rest of dinner talking about events happening in the town or local gossip about the neighbours. By the end of the meal, I couldn't help but feel like I had found a little nook within the town to call my own. I felt warmth, ensconced within Emma's family, like a cat purring in its owner's lap.

"Where are you staying then, dear?" Ada asked in her most mild manner yet, clearly somewhat sedated by the good food and locally produced beer.

"At the Queen's Inn."

"You're staying there alone?" she asked, her voice rising a notch. "Now we can't have that. It's not right for a young girl, even if you're a penniless orphan. My Christian charity simply won't allow such a thing. We have a spare bed here for guests and visitors. You are more than welcome to stay in it as long as you keep making those tonics to stave off the wicked snoring of my husband. The one I bought earlier is a miracle worker."

"That's very kind of you, but I couldn't possibly intrude on your hospitality any further," I said, taken aback by her generous offer.

"Of course you must! I won't allow you to go back to that dreadful inn. No, no, Margaret will fix up the spare room."

At this point she bellowed for the timid-looking Margaret to make an appearance. When she popped her head nervously around the door, Ada was in full bossy flow.

"Margaret, change the sheets in the spare bedroom. Make sure it is dusted and clean. Ensure all the necessary toiletries are there. Rose here will be staying the night and who knows how many more with us."

Margaret nodded emphatically at each instruction, concentrating hard to commit each and every one to memory.

"Well, what are you standing around for, gawping like a lost fish! Off with you," Ada barked at Margaret.

Margaret jumped as if she had been electrocuted and immediately ran off.

"A bit slow on the uptake but she's a good girl," Ada said in a loud whisper to whoever was listening.

And that's how it happened. In a flurry of action and chaos, I had found myself transplanted from the Queen's Inn and plopped into the warm heart of Emma's family home.

Chapter 12

"*T*HEY WILL KILL *you... She's standing over you with a knife in her hand right now. It's dripping with your blood. Drip, drip, drip.*"

I woke up, bathed in cold sweat. The voices were whispering, echoing faintly in the background.

"We warned you. You know what they're planning. They will wring your neck and gauge your eyes out."

I writhed in bed, shaking my head violently. I slapped the palm of my hand against my forehead until I felt my hand sting. I rolled out of bed and splashed water on my face from the shallow basin propped up next to a mirror. I glanced up at my reflection. I squinted, trying to recognise the face staring back at me. My skin was sickly pale and my eyes wild. My hair was matted and tousled on top of my head. Its knots and tangles, like twisted bent fingers, reminded me of Mother. I breathed deeply and began to fix my appearance so as not to scare the members of the good Thompson family who had welcomed me into their humble abode several weeks ago.

I ran a comb through the bird's nest that was my hair. I could hear toothcombs cracking and flying off as I yanked as hard as I could. I scrubbed my face with the small bar of soap and sprayed some of the leftover water over my sweat-embalmed body. I dried myself with a towel and got dressed.

The weather was rapidly cooling down, preparing for the crisp downpour of autumn leaves. The trees were peppered with rich scarlets, flecks of amber and tawny brown colours. My eyes drank in the sight from the little window I stared out of. I could just imagine a giant painter's paintbrush dotting the finishing touches of those leaves. They were so still and perfect, it looked like a fresh canvas with the paint still wet to the touch. I reached out and touched the glass of the windowpane, watching my breath create a fog in front of me, my fingers smudging the glass. I felt trapped. I was floating outside myself, watching others relish in the joys of nature around me but I was not allowed to partake in that scene. I was meant for dark corners and shadows. The angel of light would never deign to visit me. I was trapped in my mind, shackled to my destiny. My heart was as black as the Devil's and my mind bent, twisted and broken. When I looked at my misty reflection in the windowpane, I gasped. It wasn't my coffee-coloured skin that I saw but Mother's pale, delicate skin and piercing blue eyes that gazed back at me, cutting daggers into my soul.

A knock on the door jolted me back to reality, or what I thought was reality. The line between my imagination and what was actually happening in the real world was becoming blurrier by the day. The knock on the door returned. It was an impatient knock, demanding immediate attention.

"Coming," I said as I twisted the doorknob.

"Sleepy head!" Emma accused playfully. "It's mid-afternoon, Rose! Don't you remember, the travelling circus is coming to the village green today for their last performance of the season! My brother and his friend are already there. Mother and Father will probably be coming along as well."

"Of course," I replied. It had slipped my mind entirely. The entire village had been talking of little else for the past month. Everyone was excited to see what tricks the travelling circus would bring with them today.

Emma grabbed me by the hand and dragged me downstairs. We had a quick bite to eat before flying out of the house. Her excitement was contagious and before I knew it, I felt my worries detaching from me, like a tree shaking off a flurry of autumn leaves. I felt light and new. Her excitement bubbled up within me and I found myself laughing as we made our way to the village green.

A crowd was growing in the spacious field. It was no longer the lush emerald green of the summer but a rust-tinged, dusty green. Young children yelped in delight at the fantastical sight. There was a large banner with spikey writing on it, "The Romany's Travelling Circus." I felt like I had left reality back at Emma's place and stepped into a dream world. A man balancing precariously on sticks tottered past me and Emma whilst another riding a unicycle juggled four oranges without faltering once.

I had entered a cave of wonders. Beside me, Emma was speechless. It was probably the most exciting event she had attended in months, if not years. Everywhere I looked flashes of bright colours and strange painted faces drew me in. Several canvas tents with splashes of colour were pitched up and dotted around the field. Someone stepped out of the tent closest to me, which exhaled a string of loud, cheerful musical notes. Emma and I walked farther along, drinking it all in. A group of children sat in a circle enraptured by a puppet show. I did a double take when I saw the small stage but quickly realised it wasn't my friend Lucifer pulling the strings. That life was gone. It was hard to believe it was ever mine. I couldn't help but feel I had toppled into an alternate reality where my real self was still in East London with Tommy, Lucifer and Mother. Only the shadow of myself existed here, in the small town with Emma and her family.

"You like puppets?" Emma's voice echoed somewhere nearby, jarring my thoughts.

"I used to, as a child," I said, tearing my eyes away from the show.

"Look over there," Emma said, eyes as wide as saucers. "What are those? Monkeys?"

An old man with a bent back was walking across the green with at least four monkeys draped over his arms, neck and head, all chattering loudly amongst themselves. The expressionless man seemed oblivious to their conversation as he trudged along, his eyes fixated on the few inches of earth in front of him.

"Looks like it! Wow, this really is spectacular!"

"I know! The travelling circus has come here before. I think the last time was a couple of years ago, but it's never been on this kind of scale before," Emma said.

We passed the musical tent and slipped into the one next to it. Music was also playing in here and there were several dancers wearing layered, ruffled dresses and long, colourful sashes that contrasted with their dark hair. Enigmatic smiles danced on their lips as they twirled in time with the music. They had dark, coffee-coloured skin like mine. Emma and I were mesmerised by their fluid movements and tireless energy. When their performance ended they bowed and curtsied, making way for the next act.

Three men wearing tight, brightly coloured suits did dramatic backflips into the centre of the tent where the dancers had been. One was standing in the centre whilst the second somersaulted, landing on the palms of the first. He stood tall and outstretched his arms, waiting for the third to catapult himself on top to make a very tall human tower. When the third was at the top, he whipped three balls out of what seemed to be thin air and began juggling. When he was finished he let the balls bounce to the ground where young children scurried to catch them. The man at the top then bent over and placed his palms on the second man's hands and stretched his legs above him, doing the splits. The crowd in the tent erupted in claps and cheers. The man flipped over and landed on the floor with a solid thud. The second man did a similar trick but instead of doing the splits he balanced on top of the first man with only one palm, the other hand outstretched, waving at the crowd. A second eruption of shock and excitement rippled through the crowd. Once he had landed, the third man did a small run-up and did two backflips over the heads of his fellow performers.

Whilst the crowd was cheering, Emma tugged at my shoulder. "Let's explore what else there is around here. That was amazing, don't you think?"

"Yea, they make it look so easy," I agreed. "They really are great!"

We tumbled out of the packed tent and into the fresh air outside. Warm smells of food wafted past us, making our mouths water. Food and drink stalls were dotted all around the village green. I was about to suggest we try one of them when Emma exclaimed enthusiastically, "Let's see what's in that tent!"

She was pointing at the farthest tent, perched like an afterthought at the corner of the field. I hesitated. It was a good distance from any of the other tents and was the only tent which did not have a large crowd spilling in and out of the entrance. It had an air of loneliness about it. But it wasn't just loneliness. It was foreboding. Although I was looking at it from a distance, I felt the air around it was thick and congealed, as if it were emanating a glutinous, tangible warning.

"How about this one here?" I suggested, pointing to the tent opposite the one we had just come out of. A sudden roar of cheers exploded within. I could hear the loud chattering of the monkeys and assumed there was some sort of animal performance going on inside.

"No, that one looks more interesting! Let's go," Emma said, her eyes misted over in a hypnotic trance. She tugged my hand like an impatient child, dragging me to the edges of the green.

As I stared hard at the tent, I felt reality wash away around me. I blinked several times. The image I saw was becoming ever more distorted. Everything around the green field melted away. All that was left was the island that we were on. Even the other tents became fainter and fainter, turning into empty, white ghostlike shells. Sound became muffled until all of a sudden, I felt I had entered a silent vacuum. Silence throbbed in my ears, the weight of it crushing my eardrums. All I could see was the grimy, brown tent perched at the end of the earth. It was balancing precariously, as if on a precipice. The flap to the entrance was rippling wildly in a non-existent breeze. Something was going to come out of that tent. Something I didn't want to see. I tried to turn away or close my eyes but I was paralysed, my eyes glued to the soundlessly moving flap. Red bloodied fingers grasped the edge of the tent. Fear pulsated through my body. A trickle of sweat was winding its way down my back. My nerves were on fire. All I wanted was to turn and sprint away from this waking nightmare. But I had no other choice than to stare at the gruesome apparition that was unfolding. A second hand reached out, grasping for something. It was as if the tent was giving birth to this red, bloody monster. Then her head appeared, a tangle of hair and clotted blood. I knew who it was immediately. Recognition slammed into me with the force of a ton of bricks, leaving me winded. She had been haunting me, stalking me from the moment I had left East London. Mother was dripping in thick, sludgy blood. She was dressed in tattered rags, and the sharp scissors were still plunged deep in her stomach. A leering smile spread across her face as her yellowing eyes with their cold stones dropped in the centre made contact with mine. The force of her presence knocked me backwards and I fell.

I blinked several times. A rush of sound swept over me, and I felt Emma's warm, soft hands pull me to my feet.

"Rose!" she was calling loudly. "Can you hear me? Are you ok?"

I looked up at her, dazed. "Yea, I'm fine. I just lost my balance," I said, looking around me. Everything was as it should be. The other bright tents, the loud crowds, the heavy scent of food hanging in the air. I looked into Emma's face and saw concern etched in her eyes.

"You went completely still. It was as if you couldn't see or hear anything. I even put my hand in front of your face but you didn't so much as blink. Where'd you go?" she asked.

"I don't know. I think I was just a little overwhelmed, is all," I replied, not knowing the answer to her question. Where did I go?

"We don't have to go to that tent if you don't want," Emma said, shrugging. "We could go home if you don't feel well."

I shook my head. Destiny was calling me there. I found my legs moving mechanically in time with Emma's as we headed to the tent. I had no choice. Perhaps only the London version of myself had agency, had choice. This shadow of myself was doomed to be controlled by outside forces. I felt along my arms and shoulders, subconsciously checking for puppet strings attaching me to a master puppeteer. I couldn't feel any. But maybe they were invisible and untouchable. How was I to know? Nothing made sense in my mind any more. Perhaps Mother really was in that tent, coiled like a snake, ready to spring up and stab me in the heart as she had intended. Whatever was to happen, there was no escaping my fate.

The air of a prophecy was draped like a vampire's cloak over that tent. I knew that whatever happened in that godforsaken place would stay with me forever. There was no erasing it. Like Mother, it would stick to me as a second shadow, trailing my steps wherever I went. Even the chaotic jumble of sounds around me couldn't drown the sudden chorus of whispering that erupted in my head.

I don't remember covering the entire distance of the field. But somehow we found ourselves standing outside the tent. The air was dense around it, thick floating molecules infiltrated my mouth and nose, suffocating my lungs. I felt as if the volume had been turned down, the yelling children, animal cries, and musicians had all been muffled as if swaddled in cotton wool.

"Come on," Emma whispered, sensing the shift in atmosphere. She lifted the flap and entered the tent.

This tent was shabbier than the others. It was a dark canvas brown, without a drop of extra colour, as if the artist had merely forgotten about its existence. The entrance flap was sewn crudely on with jagged black stitches lacing its perimeter. I couldn't let Emma go in there alone. I lifted the heavy cloth and stepped inside.

I could hardly breathe. Incense clogged my nostrils and lungs whilst smoke churned in my eyes, making them water. The tent was split into two sections, separated by a beaded curtain. A woman was sitting in the middle of one of the sections on a threadbare carpet on the grass. The grass was sickly yellow and looked like it was wilting with every passing second. Her kohl-ringed eyes were closed but her back was ramrod straight. Jewels glittered in her hair and dangled from her ears and wrists. An eerie humming filled the corners of the tent.

Suddenly, her eyes snapped open and the humming stopped. She stared at both of us. Her eyes quickly flitted up and down Emma before fixating on me. Although it was hot and muggy in the tent, her eyes sent an icy chill down my spine. I could feel her inside my brain, sifting through my thoughts, perusing my feelings. Her eyes were black and endless, like two dark tunnels spiralling on forever. I averted my gaze, fearing I would get lost in those tunnels.

"You," she said in a hoarse voice to Emma. "Go to the next room. Sabina will read your fortune. And you," her cutting gaze slicing back to me, "stay here."

Emma nodded immediately and dipped behind the glittering beaded curtain. I heard murmurs on the other side. Although she was only a few metres away, she might as well have been on the moon. The room was like a vortex, pulling me to its centre where something dark was lurking, waiting for me.

"Sit," the woman said. Her face was ageless but her eyes looked as though she had lived a thousand years and witnessed a thousand more horrors. The black pits were soulless, no light was able to peek through.

My limbs automatically followed her orders as I sat down in front of her. I tried not to look at her eyes, but they reeled me in like floundering, helpless fish strung up on a rod.

"Palm," she demanded, outstretching her own scarred, jangling hand. Jewels dotted her fingers, intertwined with those stacked on her wrist. Strange symbols were painted on her hands. The palm of her right hand was webbed with scars. I wondered what had caused such a disfigurement.

She took my palm in her rough hands and stared hard as if she were reading a detailed map to find the hidden treasure. Perhaps that's what my hand was to her, a map of my soul, a path to my future or perhaps absolute nothingness and she was a mere trickster, creating illusions out of smoke and mirrors.

Her thick dark brows knit together whilst her eyes flitted from my face to my palm. "You're one of us," she said in a raspy whisper. "A gypsy. You belong on the outside, free to wander, free to travel wherever you please. But..." Her voice trailed off as she peered closer at my hand, seeing beyond the skin's surface. "There's something else. Something different about you. There is a darkness that will consume you whole one day. I see the shadow of death stalking you, mocking you and taunting you. But it is not after your life."

"Then what is it after?" I blurted out, unable to control myself.

She stared hard into my eyes until I felt like I could see those dark pools swirling around and around in circles, making me dizzy.

"Your soul," she replied slowly. "You are surrounded by a thicket of poisonous thorns. A prophecy of doom hovers over your head and you are fated to it."

I tried to yank my hand away from this cruel, old woman. I wanted to slap her so hard that the little gems would fly from her hair. She clasped my hand firmly in her mutilated claw.

"You are both in danger and a danger," she hissed, her eyes boring into mine, emptying the dark abyss of her soul into me.

I shook my head without realising it. An avalanche of tears was pouring down my face.

"You are not safe here, and others are not safe whilst you are here," she continued. "But there is hope, for when you die, it dies with you. Listen well and take heed, never bring another into this world. Ensure you take your cursed soul to the grave with you. Your mother was right. Never bring life into this world. You must remain childless. All the devils in Hell will be unleashed if you do not take heed."

With all the force I could muster, I snatched my hand from her iron clasp. I stumbled out of the tent, my head reeling with smoke, incense and her vitriol. A deep creaking laughter filtered through the gaps in the cloth folds of the tent. Was that the ominous laughter of the wicked fortune teller? Or was it Mother from the world beyond revelling in my misery? Or was it coming from within me? All I knew was that the laughter was inside my head and all around me, drowning out all other sounds.

I lurched away from the tent. I needed to get as far away from it as possible. The menacing laughter faded until it was a distant echo. I felt fingers grasp my arm. I jumped and spun around.

Emma's innocent face was peering into mine. Her clear summer green eyes shone with a purity that had clearly never witnessed the shadows that creep in the dark.

"Are you all right, Rose? You've gone as white as a sheet. What happened in there?"

"Nothing. I left before she could start," I said, mustering up the most convincing smile I could. "I just got a really bad headache. I think I should go rest."

"Well, let me walk you home at least," Emma said.

"No, no, you stay! The fun has only just got started here. The sun is still up so no need to worry about me. I want to be alone, clear my head a little."

Emma nodded, still unconvinced.

"It's a short walk. You don't have anything to worry about," I said, placing a reassuring hand on her arm. "I'll be fine."

"If you're absolutely certain," Emma replied, her voice wavering slightly.

I gave an affirmative nod and turned around. I felt her soft, mellow eyes follow me through the crowd until I was able to slip away and melt into the shadows where I belonged. I knew I couldn't stay. I knew I didn't belong. I knew it was time for me to leave.

"You're a danger," the voice rang in my head. It continued, like a poisonous snake hissing in my ear, *"You killed Mother, you know."*

"I didn't," I mumbled to myself as I was walking away from the circus. "She killed herself."

"No, she killed herself because of you. You kill people. That's what you do, Erosabel."

"That's not true!" I said louder, covering my ears with my hands.

A small girl stared up at me, her eyes wide with fright. Her mother came quickly and ushered her away from me like I was a disease.

I placed my hands by my sides, imagining nailing them there, preventing them from doing anything strange. I walked quickly, cutting through the crowd.

Suddenly I heard a familiar voice shouting, "Where are you going, Belle of the ball?"

I closed my eyes, debating whether to stop and turn around or to ignore him and keep going. It was too late. The decision, like so many, was out of my control. I felt his hand graze my shoulder. I turned around and met Alexander's cool, deep-set eyes, focused on me.

He repeated his question, this time in a more concerned, serious manner. "So Belle, where are you really going?"

My eyes filled with tears. I had known a glimmer of happiness in this town which felt as if it had sprouted out of nowhere. But it was an illusion. It wasn't real. I wasn't meant to be here. I was an awkward puzzle piece that wouldn't fit. Not only that but I was dangerous. I would wreak havoc on this tranquil small town. It didn't deserve that. It didn't deserve the likes of me.

"Away," I said plainly.

Alexander nodded, still staring at me. "You're a wanderer, a traveller, much like the gypsies here. Take this," he said, holding out a heavy velvet drawstring purse of coins. "Hide it well. John may not be around next time to sneak it up his sleeve." He winked.

The corners of my mouth lifted involuntarily. He had known where my secret coin stash was. In that moment, I wanted to hug him.

"I can't take this from you," I said, as he tried to place the purse in my hands.

"Oh, don't worry, you're not taking this from me. These coins are the hard-earned coins of all these good people you see around you. You're taking it from them." A slanted grin began to spread across his face.

"You mean... You've been stealing from these people!" I said, lowering my voice and giving his arm a punch.

"Not stealing, just borrowing. And now I have a good cause for it. It's for you. Please take it. I've seen how resourceful and clever you are but it's a tough and dangerous road for a single young woman."

I didn't have the strength to resist. I pocketed the purse. "Thank you, Alexander."

"No, thank you. I haven't forgotten what you did for my arm," he said, showing me the jagged scar the stitching had left behind. "Without you, I probably would have lost it. Listen," he continued. "I know of a gypsy camp not far from here. They're travelling north towards Birmingham but they usually camp out in towns or villages during the winter. If you head that way you may bump into them. They're a friendly bunch and I'm on good terms with the leader of the group, a man named Willowen Woodlock. Tell them that you know me, Alexander Tadbury, and they will welcome you with open arms."

He gave me rough directions and some landmarks to look out for along the way so that I would know I was on track. I looked up at him, my eyes welling with tears. I nodded, choking back the lump in my throat, as I threw my arms around him in gratitude.

"No need for any of that." He laughed as he wrapped me in a much-needed embrace.

Just a moment's contact before I travelled alone into an unknown world was all I needed.

"Please just take care of yourself, Belle," he said, his words tinged with sadness.

"I will," I croaked. "You take care too."

He nodded and raised a hand in farewell. I gave him a watery smiled, turned and left. I quickly headed up to the room where I had been staying at Emma's and packed the few things I had in a cloth sack. I wrote a letter explaining how grateful I was to them and how I would miss them dearly. They had provided me so much warmth and happiness but I knew I could never reciprocate it. I wrote an extra note to Emma who had been my first close girlfriend. I told her I would keep her in my heart and memory for as long as my time on earth would permit.

With that, I gathered my scattered thoughts and emotions and silently crept out of that peaceful, sleepy town. My mind swilled with what the evil fortune teller had said. I hated her. I hated that tent. And yet I couldn't help but think she was right. How did she know about me? How did she know about Mother?

Mother's stab wound glistened and oozed through my memories leaving a thick, slimy trail behind, muddying all my other memories. I had to leave. I didn't want to hurt anyone else. Everything I touched was stained with blood, and the voices within agreed.

PART III

HOPE

Gypsy Camp, 1829

Chapter 13

I WAS BACK on the open road. This time the weather was cooling down rapidly. Instead of trudging through sticky heat, I was trembling through biting winds. With each passing day I felt the temperature drop a little more. My extremities felt it first. I started doubling up the socks I was wearing and plunged my hands deep into my pockets to prevent them from going numb. Even with my extra layers, the wind crept through and seeped into my bones.

I had to spend more nights in taverns and inns to prevent turning into a statue of frost and ice overnight. Although it was still possible to walk during the day, the nights were brutally cold without the sun's meagre appearance. The moon in all her cold glory showed no mercy for the likes of me. Although I chose the cheapest places to stay, my purse felt drastically light. I still tried to sell my wares in the towns and villages I passed through, but less people were willing to brave the weather for my tonics. I made more remedies for common winter maladies, such as coughs and sneezes. These sold relatively well and managed to keep me from utter destitution.

During my lucid moments, I wondered what Emma and her family had thought of my sudden disappearance. My heart was heavy, burdened with regret, at the thought of leaving them without even having the grace to say a proper farewell. They had opened their door and hearts to me and I had repaid them with abandonment. I wondered if John was curious as to where I was journeying or if he was now preoccupied with his new life in the quaint small town. Alexander had understood. Like Lucifer, he seemed to have a second sense when it came to understanding people. Alexander knew I had to leave, that I didn't have a choice. What he didn't know was the extent to which I was rapidly descending into an underworld of madness. A world which had consumed Mother whole. A world I had spent my entire life trying to fight.

I frequently heard laughter reverberating in the air, neurotic and wild. It would take several long, stretched out minutes before I realised the manic laughter was my own. Even after this realisation, I was not able to quell it immediately. It had to run its course and dwindle away of its own accord. I started writing notes on any bits of scrap paper I could find. I thought I could write away what was going on inside my head, pouring my insanity into words. Once written I thought that perhaps the madness would stay there on the page and stop haunting me. When I went back to read these scraps, I was shocked to find they were nothing more than the ramblings of a lunatic.

My grip on reality was tenuous at best but even I could see I was starting to have more bad days than good. Even when I stopped at a tavern for the night, I stopped brushing through my hair or cleaning my face. I didn't see the point. Potential customers scurried away when they saw the scruffy wreck I was deteriorating into. My clothes were worn and had tears slicing through them. Cuts and bruises peppered my arms and legs although I had no recollection of how they had sprung up there. Even the bitter wind eventually stopped penetrating my thick skin. I was impervious to it, surrounded by a protective shield.

It was during a speck of clarity that I asked an innkeeper for a map to get to Birmingham. He eyed my tousled hair and grubby hands in what looked like pity. After a moment he drew me a map and told me the roads I needed to take to get there. He warned me this winter was a cold one and only someone with a death wish would journey there alone on foot. I bit my lip to prevent the laughter bursting between the seams of my teeth. Didn't he see, I was no longer alive to have a death wish? At this point, I was already a ghost.

With a resolve I didn't know I still had, I thanked him for the map and journeyed on. If I came across other stragglers on the way I would ask them if they knew of a gypsy camp headed by a particular Willowen Woodlock. I clung to that name with all my mental and physical strength combined, as if it held all the answers I had been seeking. Before going to sleep, I would recite it over and over again until I drifted off into my troublesome dream worlds. That name was my redemption, my last saving grace. That name prevented the feeble thread of sanity I still had from completely snapping, untethering me from reality once and for all. I needed to find that camp. If I continued alone, I feared I would wander into a vast realm of nothingness, unable to reach others or be reached by them. I was not ready for that moment of complete and utter aloneness.

I don't know how many days, nights, weeks or perhaps months passed before I came across a toothless woman dressed in rags. She was limping, leaning on a wooden stick as she walked. Her back was arched over and thin wisps of hair hung like limp weeds around her face.

"Hey, you," my voice croaked.

She didn't glance up but continued hobbling on. I grabbed her shoulder roughly, making her almost lose her balance. I held on to her to prevent her from toppling over.

"Willowen Woodlock and his gypsy camp. Do you know where it is?"

She lifted her head and revealed a gappy smile. A single tooth hung on by a thread, swaying with her sour breath.

"Yeaaa," she managed, pointing down a mud trail off the road. "Dow' da row. Walk da' way an' you'll fine 'em."

I could hardly make out her garbled mutterings but I saw where she was pointing. I nodded and patted her bony arm in thanks.

"Baa," she called after me, waving her stick in the air as I hopped over the fence and muddled my way down the trail.

I heard and smelt them before I saw them. The sounds of clattering pots, laughter and brazen shouts weaved amongst the dense trees. The air was soaked in the mouth-watering scent of cooked food, tinged with a biting acrid metallic smell. I spied where their camp was based on the thin tendrils of smoke curving heavenward. As I walked closer I could feel the air thicken around me. The cold was melting away. I felt I was shedding a heavy, cold layer of skin like a snake.

I stumbled onto the campsite. There was a large clearing in the woods. Several rickety, brightly painted caravans dotted the clearing.

Children were running around playing some sort of chase game. Two tall men were stoking the fire, whilst several others were patching up the scratches and broken wheels of a lopsided-looking caravan. I watched as three women chattered whilst scraping the pots, pans and bowls clean. I stared at the commotion, unable to interject myself into the humdrum scene unfolding before me. It wasn't until one of the children collided into me that I was able to find my voice.

"Careful there," I said to the child.

She simply looked up and stared at me, curiosity brimming in her eyes. An older boy joined the girl and put a protective arm around her. "Who're you?"

As I was about to answer, one of the women who had been scraping the pots came over. She placed a hand on her hip.

"Who're you?" she said, repeating the boy's question.

"Erosabel. Is Willowen Woodlock here? I've come to see Willowen Woodlock. The highwayman, Alexander Tadbury, said I could find him here. He said if I mention his name then Willowen Woodlock would give me food and shelter for a while. I've been wandering for months all alone and just need some food and shelter for a little while," I gushed.

The woman stood there, staring at my jutting bones, manic eyes and ragged clothes.

One of the tall men who had been stoking the fire walked over. "I heard you saying my name," he said in a voice as tranquil as the sea on a windless day.

I looked up at him and did a double take. He had the most peculiar eyes. They were so light it almost looked as if there was no pigment there at all. There was the merest hint of a lavender grey hue swimming in his orb-like eyes. I felt if I looked deep enough into those crystal balls, I would be able to see what my future held.

He was tall and solidly built, with a straight back, tucked-in chin and strong, muscular arms. His skin was rough and tanned. Silver streaks combed through his dark hair, which he had knotted in a ponytail that fell elegantly down his back. His mystical eyes scanned me from top to bottom, making me feel that all I ever was and all I ever could be was imprinted on my body and soul in a language that only he could read. I realised he was waiting for me to speak.

"Alexander Tadbury," I blurted out. "He said you knew him and that you would grant me lodgings for a while if I told you Alexander is my friend."

"You know Alex?" Willowen said, raising a thin, faint brow. The hairs were so fragile I imagined them being whisked away on the next breath of wind.

"Yes, I know Alex. I fixed his arm. It was about to get infected and he would have had to have it sawn off. I'm a healer. I have potions here in my sack that really work. I healed his arm and we became friends. But I left the town we were in. He told me if I had to go off wandering alone, I should pass by your camp for food, water and rest. I'm exhausted. I don't think I can go much further on my own."

The words tumbled out of my mouth before I even knew what I was saying. It was in that moment I realised how utterly drained I was. It was taking the last drops of strength to stand there in front of him and speak. I felt myself swaying slightly whilst the world around me started swirling.

201

I heard Willowen's gentle voice giving instructions to the woman standing next to him. "Take her to my caravan. Make sure there are warm blankets and some broth prepared for her when she wakes up. Check if she has any wounds. Alex is a good friend of mine. We will honour his wishes and find out more about this girl later."

I remember the edges of my vision getting dimmer and clouding over. A miasma of darkness flooded my eyes. The last thing I heard was Willowen speaking to me.

"Don't worry. You're safe now."

How I wished that were true.

* * * * *

I woke up in a haze. I felt like I was floating in a sea of tranquillity. My mind was clouded in fog but amidst that fog I felt peace radiate through me. It was a sense of peace I had not felt in years, if ever. My body was weightless and my mind was like a ship, sailing towards freedom. There were no malignant whispers in the shadowy corners, no cackling laughter bubbling out of nowhere. White light blossomed inside me. I felt its glow and warmth embracing me with feathered wings.

"Here you go, dear," a disembodied voice said.

I turned my head and reluctantly opened my blurry eyes. I was not ready for this dreamlike trance to end. I wanted to cling onto this sensation for as long as possible but I knew I wouldn't be able to. It was like catching light in the palm of one's hand.

"Where am I?" I mumbled.

"You're with us, with the gypsies," a woman's voice said.

I peered up at her. She had a friendly, heavily lined face. In her hands was a steaming bowl of broth.

"Drink this. It'll perk up your strength. You looked like you've been starved, battered and left out for the dogs to pick at your bones. Poor thing."

I took the broth with my feeble, shaking hands. I gulped a long, hungry sip before guzzling down the entire bowl. "How long have I been here?"

"You've been asleep for a full day. You woke up a few hours ago yelling and screaming as if someone was tormenting you. I had to hold you down so you wouldn't scratch your own eyes out. I gave you a few drops of laudanum, and that did the trick, had you sound asleep again in no time."

I nodded, noting the name down in my memory. If it seemed to have worked wonders on me, I could incorporate it into my other remedies.

"You just rest now, dear. I'll bring you some more broth in a few hours," the kind woman said.

I nodded, letting my head sink back into the blankets and cushions. The second I closed my eyes, the white light embraced me. My angel of light had finally appeared, and her name was Laudanum.

Chapter 14

I HAD BEEN staying at the gypsy camp for several weeks. At first the others were suspicious of me but when they saw how useful I could be, their suspicions melted away. Once I had been fed and regained some weight, I was able to continue making remedies, mend clothes, cook basic dishes, clean and even build simple pieces of furniture and equipment. I forced my energies into cultivating all the skills I had gleaned throughout my life to prove to the group, and most importantly to Willowen, that I was worthy of the kindness they had shown me.

Not only was I starting to make friends and gain a sense of belonging but with the help of my angel laudanum, the voices were quieter, sometimes non-existent even. I was able to maintain equilibrium and felt more like the person I had been before the whispers had infiltrated my mind and soul. For the first time in my life, I felt the curse that trailed my every step since birth lift just a little.

"Here, I got you some of those berries and leaves for the tonic you wanted to make," Isolde said.

"Thank you," I said, smiling up at her. I was crouched over, crushing herbs and flowers to dust in my mixing bowl.

Isolde was fascinated by the remedies I made and was determined to help out whenever she could. She was the same age as me. Her mother had died in childbirth, but her father was still here, working at the camp. She was the youngest of five brothers and sisters. She had her hair cut surprisingly short, just above her shoulders. It was thick, wavy and luxurious, constantly tumbling around her face. She had a proud face with high cheekbones, narrow cat-like eyes and a small, upturned nose. Her delicate thin lips were permanently curled in a mischievous smile.

At first we worked together in silence, Isolde gathering materials and me mixing them. As the days wore on we found ourselves slipping into easy, friendly banter. I quickly found out that she was strong-willed and fiery. She would become passionate about any topic we discussed and held resolute, unwavering views.

"Here, how about you give it a go and mix the ingredients?" I said.

"Sure!" she said enthusiastically, sitting down next to me. "So have you ever kissed a boy?" she asked bluntly.

"Uh, not really," I replied. My thoughts flew to Tommy and the fumbling kiss we had shared. I wasn't sure if that counted. Either way, I didn't want to reminisce about my past. Mother was locked within the prison walls of my memories. Unlocking that prison, even for Tommy, might unleash her as well. It was a risk not worth taking.

Her eyes widened in surprise. "Oh, I thought for sure you would have! I have!"

"How was it?" I asked, scrunching up my nose. I had never had a girlfriend to talk about these sorts of things with.

"I can show you if you like," she replied in a conspiratorial tone.

I blinked in surprise. "I, uh, what do you mean?" I stammered.

She looked around to make sure no one was looking and then leaned over and kissed me full on the mouth. Her thin lips were warm. Her tongue peeped out from her mouth as she licked the inside of my lips, teeth and tongue.

I pulled back, feeling a rush of heat flood my cheeks.

"Oh, you're so sweet. You're blushing!" she teased.

"No, it's just that was unexpected and it's kinda warm, is all," I rambled.

"Warm! It's the middle of winter!"

I shrugged then we both burst into a peal of giggles.

"So who was the first guy you kissed?" I asked.

"His name was Fennix. He's a couple of years older than me. He was from a different camp. We travelled together for a while and we did a little more than just kiss!"

"What, did you actually..." I let my voice trail off.

"No!" she exclaimed. "He just got a little handsy and so did I."

I nodded, feeling a whole new world opening up to me, things I had yet to discover. So many other things had constantly burdened me, leaving little room in my mind to think about boys and romance.

"Is there anyone you like around here?" she asked. "I grew up with most of these boys. I swear they're all idiots!" she said, rolling her eyes.

I turned my face, pretending to focus on the potion so that she wouldn't see me blush again. There was one man who made me feel light-headed and fluttery inside. My skin would involuntarily heat up whenever he looked my way. I knew he must be at least twice my age but I couldn't help feeling my nerves explode whenever his penetrating, pale eyes were on me.

"Not really," I said as nonchalantly as I could. "Like you said, all the boys our age here are idiots."

She nodded emphatically in agreement. "At least we have each other." She winked. "If there's anything you want to practise, just let me know!"

"Well, I think this is just about done," I said, steering the subject to calmer waters. "Let's bottle it and put it with the rest."

"You got it."

After I had told Willowen that I was a healer, he had crafted a small medicine wagon for me. I had set up the majority of my remedies on the rough wooden shelves, categorising them according to their function. One section was dedicated to coughs and sneezes, another for insomnia. I had a large section for general pain relief and skin ailments and a growing section for beauty treatments and potions. I found myself dipping into the beauty treatments occasionally, especially if I knew I would be speaking with Willowen about something later that day.

Although it was nothing in comparison to the full apothecary I had back in East London, Rose's Travelling Apothecary still had a certain ring to it. What I also found useful was the easy, quick access I had to my new favourite panacea, laudanum. I found myself taking a pinch of it if it was in powder form or about twenty drops if dispensed from the chemist in liquid form. I found the itinerant life useful for obtaining my laudanum supplies. I noticed when we stayed in one campsite for slightly longer, the chemist gave me a strange look when I went back for more.

"Didn't you just come in here to buy laudanum two weeks ago? If I recall I sold you an amount that should last somewhat longer than that," the chemist said coldly.

An inexplicable rage rushed over me and I felt myself flushing red. I didn't want him to see that he had annoyed me so I kept my voice as calm as I could.

"I'm a healer and I use laudanum in several of my panaceas. This obviously isn't just for personal use," I replied more curtly than intended.

"I see." He let his words hang between us for several long seconds. His beady eyes darted across my face, resting on my eyes. Such direct eye contact made me feel surprisingly nervous. I held his gaze although inside my nerves were rattled. When he finally broke his gaze, I realised I had been holding my breath.

"Just a moment. Let me go round to the back and get you the amount you require."

When he left, I inhaled deeply and released a shaky exhale. The nervousness churned within the pit of my stomach and morphed into a ball of rage. Who was he to question me? What was it to him? I could be using all of the laudanum in my remedies for others. Obviously, I wasn't and the majority of it was being used as a remedy for myself but what was wrong with that? I am a healer after all. Why shouldn't I heal myself?

I channelled my anger towards him, although deep down, I knew something wasn't right. I was delighted that the voices were being kept at bay but my reliance on the substance was increasing. I took a morning dose to help me function during the day and another dose just before I went to sleep. At first it had seemed to be the perfect balance. Just as I was coming down from my euphoric state, the nightly teaspoon would pick me up and settle me into a blissful, empty, and most importantly, quiet sleep. But now, I was starting to itch for it during the day as well. I would get a sudden craving. I would try to ignore it, but my mind kept drifting back to my stash, folded within scarves heaped in a locked cabinet in the caravan. When this happened, white hot anger would flood through my body, making my nerves feel as if they were on fire. Not only was my body desperate for the substance, causing me to be irritable and annoyed, but I was also angry with myself. I was angry that the Devil's voice had infiltrated my mind in the first place. And I was even angrier that my angel laudanum had tricked me and was slowly devolving into a demon in and of itself. Wherever I turned, whichever direction I went, the dark, pointed shadows of demons were never far behind.

* * * * *

With all the busy commotion, the icy winter was rapidly melting into a vibrant spring. I found life on the encampment relatively peaceful, even with my fraught relationship with laudanum. I realised with surprise that it had been months since I had last thought about Mother. She no longer tormented me as she used to. I was settling comfortably into my new routine with my new friends and what I considered my new family.

It was a frosty morning sometime in March. We were supposed to be travelling onwards to a different campsite. I was untying the horses and preparing them for the journey when I felt someone's presence behind me.

Willowen cleared his throat and smiled as I turned around.

"Good morning. How're you?" he asked.

My mind instantly went blank. "Yes, I mean, fine. How're you?"

"Good, thank you."

My hands fumbled over the knot I was trying to untie. The horse whinnied exasperatedly, sensing my nervousness.

"Here, let me help," Willowen said. He placed his large, rough hands over mine, encasing them in a cocoon as he helped untie the horse. His touch sent bolts of electricity ricocheting through my body.

"Thanks. It's just a little cold. My hands have gone numb."

"I just wanted to check in on you, make sure everything is ok?" he said. "You really have a lot of great skills, you know. I'm glad you stumbled across us when you did."

"Thanks. Yes, everything is fine right now. I just finished a new remedy for warts. It's bottled and ready to sell."

Willowen raised his eyebrows in surprise. "Well, that's great to hear. I'm sure it'll sell well like everything else you've made."

One of the men beckoned Willowen over.

"Anyway, if there's anything you need, just let me know, Erosabel."

"Will do," I said, feeling weak-kneed at the sound of my name on his lips.

As he walked away I couldn't help but slap my forehead. Warts! Why had I mentioned that particular remedy! I had also been working on a cream to soften the skin and flower water to add to any shampoo or simply flick on the bed linen to give it a sweet aroma. But no, I had to mention warts.

Isolde came and found me later that day. "Roz, guess what!" she said excitedly. Before giving me a chance to guess she steamrolled on. "There's going to be a big meet-up in a few weeks, with other gypsy camps. Around this time of year, we always have a big celebration to celebrate surviving the winter, catch up and welcome in spring. We're going to have to make new dresses for it. It's the best time of the year!"

I laughed at the exuberance radiating off her. "Will Fennix be there?" I teased.

Isolde shrugged, pointing her nose in the air. "Doesn't matter. Either way both of us have to look amazing!"

"Absolutely," I concurred. "Well, I'm pretty good at making dresses but we better get started soon to make sure we have enough time."

Isolde jumped and squealed in delight. "I think the next place we'll be stopping at has a town centre. We can buy any extra cloth and material we need from there. We're going to look perfect!"

* * * * *

We journeyed on with a newfound spring in our step. Excitement rippled through the camp as everyone prepared for the festivities. It was not only the chance to meet new people, which was exciting, but for many they would be seeing friends and acquaintances they hadn't seen in potentially years. It was a time for gossip, sharing news, mourning those who had passed and celebrating new life.

We bought the necessary supplies for our dresses whilst some of the other older women bought special meats and cuts to prepare dishes for the festival. Isolde was using fiery red and orange silks and taffeta for her dress. I went with more subdued silvery purples. I added beads to reflect the light, making them look like little twinkling stars embedded within the night sky.

The days continued to roll on with a slowness brought on by anticipation. I had left the campsite in search of flowers and petals to crush into a perfume for the women to use on the day of the festival. Humming to myself, I bent over a particularly sweet-smelling flower and plucked it from the earth.

"*The Devil is here. The Devil is amongst us.*"

I dropped the flower as if it had scorched my skin. I stared at it lying limp on the floor. It couldn't possibly be talking to me, could it? I was sure I saw it twitch just then.

"*You fool. You thought you got rid of us that easily.*"

The voice was hissing from somewhere nearby, just out of sight. My pulse quickened. I was sure that I had taken my laudanum earlier that day. Were the voices speaking to me again from the void? Was it some new devil? Had they overridden my laudanum dose? Or was someone really talking to me, playing a cruel joke?

"Is anyone there?" I called out to the bushes. I heard a faint jeering laugh. "Show yourself! Who's there?" I demanded, my voice shaking. Just as I felt I would jump out of my skin I noticed a rustling in the bushes. I squinted hard. Was it my imagination or were the leaves quivering? "I said show yourself, you coward!" I yelled at the inanimate branches and leaves, mocking me with their shimmying.

"Hey, don't shoot." The warm voice of Willowen came tumbling out of the bushes. He was carrying an armload of firewood and smiling.

My cheeks flushed scarlet at the sight of him. I wished I had stepped into a sinkhole and been consumed by the mud and earth. As it stood, all I was consumed with was my own embarrassment and feelings of stupidity.

"Sorry, I didn't know it was you. I thought I heard someone else. I wouldn't have shouted all those silly things if I'd known," I rambled.

"That's ok. You sounded very brave actually," he replied.

I blinked several times before letting my gaze fall to the firewood he had been collecting. I felt annoyed at myself that I couldn't maintain his gaze without blushing. Taking several silent deep breaths, I tried to steady my nerves.

"What are you doing out here all by yourself? Collecting more stuff for your cures?" he asked.

"Actually, I was gathering some flowers and roots that I thought I would crush together into a perfume. I think the women would like it for the festival." I felt an iota of relief as I heard myself speak. My voice was calm and steady. I was able to have an ordinary conversation without turning into a gushing fool after all.

"Your skills are very impressive. I'm sure the women will love it."

Just as I thought I had reined in my emotions the compliment shook my newfound sense of ease.

"Thank you," I said, squirming inside.

"I have a lot to thank Alex for what with all the help you've been around here," he continued. I felt the heat of his gaze on me. He was watching me. I couldn't tell if he was just being friendly or if there was a flirtatious undertone to his words.

Before I could reply, I felt my foot catch on a protruding tree root. My basket tumbled out of my hands as I fell forward. I heard the sound of wood clattering to the floor and felt a pair of strong arms around me. Willowen caught me before I fell to the ground. I turned to look up at him as he had me in his warm, protective embrace. I wasn't sure if I was breathing or not. A strange expression between warmth and longing flitted in his pale eyes. His face was inches from mine. I could smell fresh grass and wood emanating from him. I wanted to lean in closer, to see what it really meant to be kissed by someone. Before the magic of the moment carried me away, I disentangled myself from the embrace.

"Thank you. Sorry, I can be so clumsy," I said, as I gathered my petals and flowers from the ground.

He knelt beside me to help. "No need to apologise."

"We should be getting back," I stated.

"Absolutely."

He picked up the firewood and we walked back to the campsite together. An electric silence hung in the air between us. Several times I tried to think of something to say to fill it, but my befuddled mind couldn't string a coherent sentence together. We got back to the campsite as the sun was setting, drenching everything in liquid gold.

"I'm glad I bumped into you. Take care now. Don't go falling where I'm not there to catch you," Willowen said, smiling.

"I'll be careful," I replied, a flush threatening to creep up my neck.

Then he bent down and kissed me, brushing my cheek ever so gently. He lingered a little too long for it to be considered a friendly peck. My face burned as I blinked several times in confusion, standing stock-still.

He smiled. "Goodnight, Erosabel."

My name on his lips was the most melodic music to my ears. When he was out of earshot, I let out a deep sigh, expelling all the pent-up nervous energy.

I began to make my way to the caravan Isolde and I were sharing when I heard a rustle behind me. Quickly I spun around. There was nothing there, although I was sure I could hear a faint jeering cackle of laughter. I shook my head several times and hurried to the caravan. I wanted the relief my laudanum gave me. I wanted it now. I needed it. The magic of the moment kindled a warm glow within me. I wasn't prepared to let the voices steal that from me. Not tonight.

* * * * *

It was the day of the festival. Excitement pulsated through the camp. Everyone was making last-minute preparations for that evening. Isolde and I were trying on our dresses, sashaying around inside one of the caravans.

"I love yours. You chose such nice colours. They really suit you," I said, admiring Isolde's dress.

It was nipped in at the waist and puffed out from the hips downwards. The sleeves went down to her elbows and were slightly off the shoulder. As she twirled the skirts fanned out, lending her the appearance of a flower in bloom. A web of thin lacy gold adorned the dress, sending sprays of light across the roof of the caravan.

I fixed my dress and smoothed out the material.

"Roz," Isolde said, staring at me. "Wow, you look amazing." She stopped spinning and gawped at me, letting her arms fall to her sides.

I felt the heat rushing to my cheeks. "Really? Thanks."

"You are going to have boys stuck to you like flies." She giggled.

I stared at my reflection in the small broken mirror, adjusting it so that I could see myself from different angles. The strands of silver that laced through the dress made my eyes sparkle a brighter blue. My dress wasn't puffy like Isolde's but clung to my figure, melting in a silky puddle on the floor. The lacy sleeves covered my shoulders, swooping down to reveal a generous amount of décolletage. I then realised with our colour schemes, Isolde was the brilliant sun and I was the elusive moon.

The sun was setting and it was time to go. Quietly and quickly I sneaked off to my travelling apothecary and fixed half a spoonful of laudanum. I knew that meant I would be taking an extra dose since I would also take one before I went to sleep but it was a special occasion.

Why couldn't I enjoy this evening free of demonic voices? Was I not entitled to a fun, light-hearted evening like everyone else? I felt myself getting angry before realising that I was having this internal dialogue, this argument, with myself. No one knew of my secret addiction, if I even dared call it that. I may have been increasing the amount I was taking, and I knew I couldn't go a day without it, but laudanum helped. It healed me. At least I thought it had done until I heard the voices return that day I bumped into Willowen. A nagging doubt paired with guilt settled in the pit of my stomach, heavy as lead.

I decided to re-join Isolde in an attempt to dispel the uncomfortable feelings that were making me jumpy and nervous. I found Isolde helping the other women carry platters of food, instruments and cards for the night's entertainment. A campfire was already burning at the meeting spot, its flames leaping high into the air. A pale full moon watched us passively, her fluid light rippling across the field. A gust of wind swept past me. I couldn't help but feel that was no ordinary wind. It carried with it the scent of change. A sixth sense whispered to me that this was no ordinary night. Unseen forces were at work. Destiny was calling to me on the breeze. I could sense it as clearly as dogs can sense a sound too high-pitched for the human ear to perceive. I would be on my guard, ready to face whatever fate had in store for me.

Whoops of excitement, cheers and greetings met my ears as we got closer to the bonfire. People were hugging, crying and laughing all at once. I heard snippets of stories being exchanged, catching up on several years' worth of events. As more people joined in, the hum of conversation pulsated loudly through the night.

"Over there, it's Fennix," Isolde said excitedly, pointing to a tall man with a mane of unkempt fiery red hair.

"Go and talk to him," I said, giving her a nudge.

"No, I can't. Are you sure? Should I wait for him to see me?"

"No, just go over there and say hi," I said, laughing. I had never seen her this uncertain or nervous. "You look beautiful. He's gonna be stunned speechless."

Isolde inhaled sharply. "You're right. I'm going to do it. Wish me luck!"

"Good luck, but trust me, you don't need it."

I watched as she sauntered over to Fennix. As I had predicted, I saw his jaw drop and no words come out for a good ten seconds. I smiled to myself as I turned my gaze to several gypsies who had started playing a variety of woodwind instruments. The leader of their group was sitting on the earth, strumming on a guitar whilst singing in a language that I did not recognise.

Several women had sets of tarot cards and were flicking through them, trying to catch the elusive spectre of the future. I turned away from that crowd, knowing I would never want to dabble in that again. After my last experience, I preferred for my future to remain in the realm of the unknown and unscripted. I was the author of my future, not a set of flimsy cards nor an old, wizened trickster with kohl-rimmed eyes.

I walked closer to the warmth emanating from the bonfire, around which men and women were dancing and twirling. Against the black night, the jewels around the women's necks and in their hair scintillated, looking like a blur of stardust. Mesmerised, I watched as they moved in perfect unison like they had choreographed and practised the dance before coming. I was so enraptured I didn't notice a second shadow flickering next to mine.

"Hello, Erosabel," a calm, deep voice reverberated from behind me.

I heard the faint sound of destiny knocking on the door, if I would only let it in. I spun around and had to catch my breath. It was Willowen, his tall imposing frame barely inches from mine. He was wearing a smart waistcoat, draped over his usual shirt and trousers.

"You look beautiful," he said softly.

"Thank you," I said, grateful that the dim light was disguising the blush that instantly flushed my cheeks.

"We have a lot in common, I believe," he said.

"We do?"

"Yes, you prefer your own company to that of others. You're a lone wolf like me. You are self-reliant and do what you need to do to survive. And we were both orphaned at a young age."

I blinked, surprised at his unusual candour. "How old were you?"

"I think around seven years old," he replied matter-of-factly. "Both parents died from a disease as did all my siblings. I don't know why I survived it but I did. I did a lot of things I now regret to survive. But it led me to this," he said, gesturing to the moonlit festivities around us. "I wouldn't change it for the world."

"You're lucky," I said. "You found your calling, where you're meant to be in the world. My fate seems to be leading me down some strange paths."

"You may not be able to understand it yet, but in time, when you look back, you will see those paths made perfect sense. Those paths were inevitable. You just need to have faith."

I smiled. "You're very reassuring. I can see why everyone here admires you."

"Does that include you?" he asked, peering down at me with those translucent eyes that set my skin on fire.

I looked down, scuffing my feet in the dirt. "I, um, yes of course. Like everyone here, I respect you and everything you've done for this community, this family."

A half-smile played on his lips. He extended his hand as he said, "Would you do me the honour of dancing with me?"

"I don't know how," I said, baffled. "Everyone seems to know exactly how to move. I have no idea."

"I'll teach you," he said, taking my hand in his.

The music shifted from the upbeat, energetic tones to a more subdued, tranquil beat. The woodwind instruments sent a ripple of calm through the crowds. Willowen pulled me closer to him and put his hand around my waist. I couldn't tell if I was still breathing. My hands trembled slightly as I put one on his arm and one on his shoulder. I could feel the heat of his gaze on my face but kept my eyes averted. If I looked up into those mystical eyes whilst his hands nestled along the curves of my body, I was sure I would faint.

It happened as if it was fated. The stars had aligned, and everything was as it was meant to be. If there was one moment in time that I could freeze for all eternity, it would be this one. I wasn't surprised when he leaned in to kiss me as the final musical notes melted away into the vacuum of the night. My body automatically pressed against his. His lips were soft and warm whilst his body was muscular and hard. I felt an ache deep within me awaken. My soul had been wandering in search of his. I knew it with a certainty that scared me. We were two pieces of a puzzle that fit perfectly. When he withdrew I felt the breath of my soul being taken with him. I knew from that moment onwards he and I were connected by the strings of fate and destiny.

"Let me play you a song," he whispered in my ear. He picked up a flute that had been abandoned by a fellow musician and began to play.

It was a song of the ancient moon bathed in its silvery glow. A song of earth's eternal woes and the clouds' perpetual tears. It was a song of shattering heartbreak and melancholy echoing throughout this time and beyond. It stretched its threadbare wings, embracing the universe one last time before disappearing forever. It was the song of my soul. It went on forever, an endless melody into an endless night. Even when he lay down the flute, the notes continued to play in my ears. Whenever I closed my eyes and blotted out the world, the song would come back to me, a loyal old friend.

We were married just before my sixteenth birthday.

Chapter 15

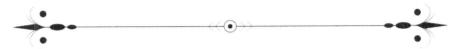

WHEN I THOUGHT the pain was over and the baby was out, a second wave of pain and nausea reeled through my body.

"There's another one coming!" the midwife shouted.

I was having twins. I screeched in pain as I pushed with all my strength and might a second time. I gritted my teeth with such a ferocity I was sure they would shatter. Sweat mingled with tears poured down me, drenching my clothes and the sheets. With a final roar I felt the second one slide out of me and into the world.

I couldn't tell if I was sobbing or laughing when I heard two high-pitched wails, crying out in unison.

"Tell Willowen that everything's looking good," the midwife said hurriedly to her helper. The young girl darted off to inform my husband of the healthy arrival of our twins. "One healthy boy and one healthy girl," the midwife said softly to me. "You did it."

I couldn't talk, my throat felt constrained, and my lip trembled. All I could do was stare at these tiny little bundles, each nestled in the crook of my arms. Silent tears slid down my cheeks as I watched their small mouths open and close as they made little animal-like sounds.

"Let's get you cleaned up so Willowen can come in and see the little babes," the midwife said.

I nodded silently. As the midwife took each baby to clean, I felt a part of me was being yanked away. I stared at her as she lifted their little limbs and wiped them down, worrying if she was being too rough with them.

"Don't you worry now," she said, as if reading my mind. "They may be small but these two are tough little fighters. There we go, all clean." She then turned her attention to me. With a bucket of water and a towel, she washed me and changed my clothes and the sheets. Even the slightest movement for me was painful.

"It'll take a good couple of months to recover," the midwife chattered on. "But recover you will and then you'll have forgotten all about the pain you went through and will be ready to have another."

That evening I was transferred back to our caravan. The midwife had said I could stay the night with her and she'd watch over me, but I wanted to be back with Willowen. His face was pale when I saw him.

"You're all right?" he asked.

The two bundles had been placed in cradles on the floor.

I nodded, feeling exhausted and breathless. "Just feeling tired," I replied.

"Of course. You lie down and rest."

He propped up the blankets and pillows for me. He then turned to look at the sleeping bundles. Very delicately, he stroked each of their tiny cheeks. I watched, feeling a flood of love and happiness sweep through my exhausted body.

"It's a good thing we picked our favourite names for both scenarios," I said quietly to Willowen. "What good fortune we can use both of them."

Willowen smiled at me. "Logan and Joni it is."

"Logan and Joni." I repeated the names under my breath several times. Inexplicably I felt a sudden weight descend upon me. Amidst all the commotion, exhaustion, joy and awe something didn't feel quite right. It was a warning, a sign that I had not obeyed the prophecy. I was wreaking havoc with fate and would pay the price down the line.

I turned slowly onto my side to get a better look at the twins. For a moment, Logan opened his large brown eyes and stared intently at me. I had brought these precious lives into this world and it was my responsibility to care for them and protect them, no matter what.

"Don't worry, sweetheart," I whispered so softly only he could hear me. "I'll keep you safe."

With that, his eyelids drooped, and he drifted off to sleep.

* * * * *

Despite gaining so much weight to the point where it had been difficult to walk towards the end of the term, I had enjoyed my pregnancy. Willowen and the others had showered attention and love on me. The little movements I had felt within sent a palpitating thrill within my heart and, best of all, the voices had slunk away again, as if banished. I had been radiating with joy. I had fallen pregnant immediately after the wedding and couldn't have been happier. I noticed that whilst I had been pregnant, I didn't even need as much laudanum, which Willowen disapproved of anyway. He didn't quite know the extent of my laudanum use before I got pregnant. When I started showing, however, he became more invasive, asking questions, checking my stash to make sure I wasn't overdoing it. He had repeatedly told me that there was nothing a good walk and fresh air couldn't cure. Usually, those things would aggravate me, causing me to snap or lie just to avoid his penetrating gaze and annoying questions. But when I was pregnant, I was too happy to care. Besides, the voices had drifted off of their own accord. There was no space for them whilst I had my twins brewing within.

Now, however, now things had changed. I felt the shift almost immediately. After delivering the twins, it was as if the voices were in overdrive, compensating for time lost. The months that followed passed in a sleep-deprived, hazy blur. I'm not entirely sure what happened during this new period of motherhood. Before the memories had the chance to form and consolidate they were consumed by a vicious acid. I was taking more and more laudanum to maintain my balance. Desperately, I clung onto the one thing I felt could restore my mental equilibrium, keep me sane. But the voices had started creeping back in and, what was worse, they were talking about my babies. The demons were hungry and my babies were the prey. I had to take laudanum to silence them before they spilled out of my head like tendrils of poisonous smoke seeking to harm those who meant the world to me.

225

Isolde and I had been chatting together whilst weaving baskets to sell in the next village when I heard them.

"*You disrespect the prophecy, fool.*"

Startled, I looked up. "Did you say something?" I asked, glancing around.

"Hmm? No," Isolde replied, not looking up from her work.

Beads of perspiration formed a garland on my forehead.

"*You think you can escape us that easily. Now you and those children will pay the price.*"

"No!" I heard myself yelling out.

Isolde's head snapped up. "No what? I didn't say anything?" She was staring at me strangely. Or could she hear them too? Was that why she looked so perplexed? She could hear the demons that tormented me! Or, perhaps, she knew what they said, and she was on their side. Maybe she was helping them destroy me and my family. I felt a sudden rage rise within me. My hands tightened over the coils I was using to weave the basket together.

"Are you ok, Roz?" Isolde asked slowly, a hint of fear flickering behind her eyes.

I shook my head. I had to get out of there. I had to leave before I did something I would regret. I tossed the basket aside. "Sorry, I don't feel too well. I have to go," I said, without making eye contact.

I stumbled out of her caravan. She was saying something, calling after me, but I couldn't hear what she said. The words were disjointed. I couldn't connect them into meaningful sentences. I needed to get to the apothecary. My hands were shaking when I got there. Where was it? I had placed the bottle right here, under a loose floorboard in my travelling apothecary. My stomach was tied in knots as nausea travelled up my throat. I shoved the other vials aside, barely even noticing the spray of glass as one smashed to the floor. I heard a light, dry cough behind me.

Willowen was standing there, and he was holding my bottled angel, my laudanum. I stared at it, raw hunger shining in my eyes.

"Is this what you're looking for?"

"Yes," I said, trying to sound calm. When he didn't give it to me, my calmness instantly evaporated and I tried to snatch it from him.

"Roz," he said, taking a step back from me. He slipped the bottle in his pocket.

My eyes traced his movements, watching as the little bottle left an indent in his trouser pocket.

"Roz," he repeated louder, trying to get my attention.

My eyes snapped up to meet his momentarily, before being dragged down again to his trouser pocket where my angel was being held hostage.

"You've been taking too much of this stuff lately. I've told you before, it's not good for you," he said.

"I'm the healer here. I know what I'm doing and I know the right dose I need to take," I snapped.

"You're not yourself any more. It's this poison. It's making you act insanely!"

He didn't understand. He never would. My laughter surprised me as it cracked through the tense atmosphere in the caravan. It was a mirthless, mocking laughter tinged with a bitterness that was new even to me.

"This poison is what keeps me sane," I hissed. "I need it. Now give it to me."

Willowen stared at me for a long time. I couldn't read his expression. I could barely see anything other than the outline of the bottle in his trouser pocket. After what felt like an eternity, he took the bottle out and placed it on the shelf. I visibly relaxed, my tense muscles uncoiling as if I had already swallowed several teaspoonfuls of the substance.

"The twins are crying," Willowen said flatly. "They need their mother."

I hadn't even heard their pitiful cries from the caravan right next to us. I had been so focused on getting my laudanum back. Now that I heard them, I felt their cries were mounting to a crescendo, so loud my eardrums would burst.

"Coming," I said, diving for the bottle. "I'll be right there."

Willowen left the caravan. I took a draught of my medicine and exhaled a sigh of relief. I let it sink into my system before picking myself up to find the twins. I could only be their mother on laudanum. If I didn't have laudanum, I feared I would become my own worst nightmare. I would become untethered. I would become Mother.

* * * * *

Soon after the incident I fell pregnant again. I couldn't help but feel that Willowen thought pregnancy was a solution to my strange problems. He didn't understand what was wrong with me and I hadn't told him about the voices. But he noticed that when I was pregnant, I was calmer, less dosed up on laudanum. He had tried to talk to me several times about the strange afflictions I suffered but I couldn't face the conversations. I told him it was headaches that got so painful I was sometimes delusional. I told him I had them for as long as I could remember and there was nothing to worry about. As long as I was on laudanum, they were manageable. Either way, pregnancy suited me fine and I was willing to be continuously pregnant if that kept the voices at bay.

It was spring and I was out with the twins, enjoying the sunshine. I knelt by them as they played. My bump was getting so large I could feel I was due any day.

I laughed as Joni picked up a flower and held it right next to her eye, inspecting it closely. Logan wobbled over to her to see what was so fascinating. They seemed to speak to each other in a language only they understood, full of glances, gestures, sounds and giggles. It was magical to watch.

I was sitting under the warm breath of the sun, absent-mindedly picking daisies and linking them together in a daisy chain. Joni squealed with delight when she saw the little daisy crown I had made for her. I placed it gently on the top of her head. Within seconds Logan snatched it. The daisies crumpled in his little fist just as Joni let out a wail of grief at her fallen flower crown.

"There, there, Joni," I cooed, scooping her up in my arms. "Your brother was only playing."

Logan's eyes started to water as he watched his sister cry.

"Not you too, sweetheart," I said, sweeping him onto my lap. I bounced the pair of them on my knees as best I could until they started giggling again, the whole unseemly business of the crushed crown completely forgotten.

I stretched out my legs, switching positions trying to get comfortable. It was difficult when my belly was this swollen. I patted it as I felt a gentle nudge from inside. I couldn't help but smile. Another pair of pattering feet was on the way. My dreamy haze was interrupted by the harsh squawk of a bird. I turned around distractedly, searching for the culprit who had rudely disturbed my peace.

It was a large, ugly black raven. Its feathers were ruffled as if it was agitated. Its beady dark eyes were focused directly on me. I instinctively moved closer to Logan and Joni to protect them from the gruesome being. As I turned to check on the twins, I heard a low ominous hiss. The children were sitting facing each other, hitting a mound of earth in front of them and laughing. I turned to face the bird. From my experience, birds didn't hiss.

I watched it closely. A strange, heavy atmosphere descended, closing in on myself and the bird. When I glanced at the twins, I saw them as if they were in a bubble of their own. They were still playing under the glow of sunlight whilst I was cast in this shadowy prison, trapped with the bird.

It remained perfectly still, continuing to stare at me with its deep harrowing eyes. The low strange hiss permeated again from its beak. This time I heard what it said.

"*Erosabel*," it whispered.

It was so faint and distant it could have been a figment of my imagination, a distant memory or an echo reverberating from the bottom of a deep long-forgotten well. But then I heard it again, stronger this time. The bird knew my name.

"Erosabel, don't trust them. You can't trust them."

I backed away from the bird in horror as it moved its beak, spitting out its venomous words. I didn't know who it was referring to but my instinct was to grab the children and run. I jolted myself violently out from the invisible egg-like membrane the bird had enveloped me in. I rolled onto all fours and crawled towards my babies.

"Come on, sweethearts," I said hurriedly.

They looked up at me in surprise as I grabbed them and heaved them up, one balanced on each hip. I was in a clearing all by myself, with only an ominous feathered beast for company. I had to head back to the campsite before anything else happened. With a squirming twin on each hip I struggled back to where everyone else was, where there was laughter and light. Before I left the clearing, I turned around. The raven was still there. It continued to watch me as I stumbled along and finally disappeared into the muddle of caravans and horses.

I put the twins down for a nap when I reached our caravan. With a shaky hand I poured myself half a teaspoon of laudanum to calm my frazzled nerves. What had just happened? Ravens weren't supposed to open their beaks and start talking in the real world. Had I imagined it? Or was this not the real world? My head was spinning as Willowen walked in.

"Quiet," I whispered, trying to keep up a semblance of normalcy. "I just got them to sleep," I said, gesturing at my sleeping angels.

As Willowen turned to look at the slumbering twins, I discreetly tucked away the laudanum. He never prevented me from taking it but whenever he saw me swallow a teaspoon or two, his mood would sour, and he would avoid me for the rest of the day. The next day I would be sure to hear a lecture on the importance of fresh air and brisk walks. It was easier that he didn't know. At least that was what I told my guilty conscience.

Willowen turned to face me. He smiled and wrapped his arms around my expanding waist.

"And how're you?" he said softly. "You look tired."

"I feel tired," I said. Perhaps that was it. Perhaps I was tired and had dreamt the whole talking raven thing.

"You are the most wonderful mother to those lucky children."

"They're my everything," I said, staring at their serene sleeping faces.

"And you're my everything," he said, planting a long kiss on my forehead.

I felt strength and vitality surge through me anew. With Willowen by my side, I could conquer anything. A sense of peace floated through me like a cloud on a breeze. Either Willowen's soothing words or my soothing laudanum was working its magic.

"I might try and take a nap now, whilst they're sleeping," I said.

"Rest well. You're going to need your sleep before this one comes along," he said, patting my round belly.

"Lord help us." I giggled.

I snuggled up in the blankets as Willowen left the caravan. I could hear the sweet, gentle sounds of the children's breathing. They even breathed in unison. They would be attached at the hip as they got older. I smiled to myself. Just as I was about to close my eyes, I could have sworn that I saw the shadow of a bird flit past the caravan window. I placed an arm around the twins, shielding them from whatever dark forces lay in wait out there.

Chapter 16

T HE SQUEALING CRY of a new-born permeated the
caravan. Tears of relief and exhaustion sprang from my eyes.

"Is he ok, Florence?" I asked the same midwife who had
delivered the twins.

"Yes, he's perfect," she said.

I desperately wished Willowen was nearby. I needed his calming
presence, but the baby had come early. Willowen had travelled alone to
another gypsy campsite to strike up a deal and share provisions. Several
of our horses had fallen sick and two had already died. He was hoping
they would have a couple of horses to spare. I had wanted to take a look
at them but Willowen had refused. He didn't want me getting near sickly
horses in case I caught something and somehow harmed the unborn
baby growing within me. The poor horses had stopped eating and had
been feverish for the past few days. By the time I had concocted a remedy
that I thought could help, it had been too late for two of them. I gave

the panacea to the boy who cleaned out their stables and told him to feed it to the horses that were showing symptoms.

Willowen was supposed to be back from his trip in time for the birth but our baby had other plans.

"Let me see him," I said, managing to lift myself up. The screaming bundle was placed in my arms. "My sweet little boy. My Danior."

He looked into my eyes with a strong, solid gaze. I was taken aback by the tenacious expression that lingered within.

"You're a tough little one, you are," I said, as I gazed down at the strong-willed baby in my arms.

Florence and her helper, Vadoma, took him from me to clean him up whilst I fell into a heavy slumber. It had been a long delivery. Both Logan and Joni had been out within an hour of pushing but Danior had taken his time. I had been in labour for nearly twenty hours before he made an appearance. But he was out now, safe and healthy which was all that mattered.

Willowen made it back by nightfall. He looked tired and exhausted but his face lit up when he saw me cradling Danior in my arms.

"A boy?" he asked.

"Yes, just as I thought," I said in hushed tones. "Our little Danior."

"How are you feeling?" he asked, stroking my hair.

"I'm fine. Just happy that Danior is healthy. He took his time coming into this world."

Willowen nodded. With a single finger he patted the baby's soft, velvety head. "We are blessed," Willowen said softly. "Me, you, Logan, Joni and Danior. Our family couldn't be any more perfect."

I smiled, but my mind was already whirring. The angel, laudanum, lurked in the back of my mind. Whatever happened to my body during pregnancy usually kept the worst of the voices at bay. Without a baby within me, I had to go back to my old friend, my crutch, my laudanum.

"Are you all right?" Willowen asked.

"Yes, fine, just in a bit of a daze," I said quickly. "How did it go with you?"

"I think they're willing to give up one of their horses," he said, with a shrug, attempting to make light of the issue.

I knew one wouldn't be enough, especially if more of ours fell prey to this illness.

"We'll figure it out. Don't worry, you've got enough on your plate right now," Willowen said, noticing my expression.

Just then Danior started to squirm in my arms. He let out a low wail, signalling an impending crescendo.

"I better feed him before he brings the place down."

"Where are the twins?" Willowen asked.

"They're with Isolde. She and Fennix are taking care of them for the night."

Isolde and Fennix had married around the same time Willowen and I had got married. They had a son, Leo, and Isolde was now several months pregnant with their second child.

Willowen nodded. A hushed content settled around us like soft confetti us as I fed baby Danior. I hoped things could stay this calm and tranquil forever. My mind was silent and the babies were safe and happy. There was nothing more I wanted in this world.

Chapter 17

IT WAS A bad day. I couldn't usually tell when I was having them. It was in retrospect that I could see how unhinged I had behaved or how scattered my thoughts had been. But today, since the morning, I could feel myself becoming undone. The little threads that were woven together keeping my mind composed were being unpicked by a being beyond my control. The threads unravelled faster and faster, drifting away in the breeze like a kite without a string. I watched it go, helpless to stop it.

The weather was starting to cool down. I felt the urge to be outside, somewhere without walls pressing in on me. Soon we would have to remain huddled up in the tight caravans to ride out the winter. I needed to be amongst nature, amongst the trees before that time came.

"Children," I called out. "Let's go for a walk."

"But we're playing with Leo and Clem," Joni called out. "Logan is supposed to be catching us!" Leo was about the same age as the twins and Clementina was just a couple of months younger than Danior.

Just then Logan collided into Joni. "Caught you!" he yelled triumphantly.

"No, silly! I'm talking to Mummy. That one doesn't count!"

"I don't mind going for a walk," Danior chimed in.

"We're all going for a walk," I said emphatically. "Let's go altogether."

Logan and Joni were grumbling whilst Danior skipped in step with my brisk stride. I felt a pang of guilt as Logan and Joni waved to Leo and Clem who were both clearly disappointed at losing their playmates.

"They'll be back to play soon," I called back to them. "I'll pass by your mother after our walk, and we can all have some bread and jam together."

"Ok," Leo replied, both his and Clem's faces perking up at the prospect of jam.

"Why do we need to be altogether all the time?" Logan moaned. "There's plenty of grown-ups to watch us."

Joni mumbled her agreement.

"I feel better when we're altogether," I replied curtly. "A brisk walk will do us all good before the winter sets in."

"Aren't you going to be cold, Mummy?" Danior asked, looking at my bare arms whilst he huddled in Logan's old coat and scarf.

"I'll be fine, sweetheart," I reassured him.

"Where are we going, Mummy?" he asked.

"You see that trail that leads into the woods? We're going to follow that. We can collect nuts and gather firewood for Daddy along the way."

Danior nodded as if given his marching orders. Although he was only four years old, he was always trying to act older than he was. He took everything very seriously. A slight crease formed between his brows as his eyes keenly searched for hefty pieces of wood to carry back. Logan and Joni cheered up as they continued playing their chase game, running rings around Danior and me.

"Slow down, you two," I called out to them as they continued to dash farther and farther ahead.

"Yes, Mummy," they trilled in unison.

I picked several flowers and roots which could be used in my remedies. I placed them in the deep pockets woven into my dress.

"What about this?" Danior asked, holding up an oval-shaped, smooth stone.

I couldn't think of a single use for such a small stone. "That's perfect, Danior. Hang on to it and keep looking," I said, patting him on the back.

A gust of wind sent a rustling murmur through the trees. Several golden-brown leaves detached from the spindly branches and fluttered in eddies around us. Danior was momentarily distracted from his task and began stomping on as many crunchy leaves as he could, laughing in delight at the sharp crackling sounds they made.

The wind discomfited me. I could hear whispers, faint and distorted, travelling on the tail end of the breeze. The voices were here, in the forest, encircling my family and me.

"Logan, Joni, come back now," I called out.

A wall of silence was my only answer. Panic swelled in my chest. Had the voices reached them? Had they drawn them into a black hole where I would never be able to find them?

"Logan, Joni!" I yelled, more frantically this time.

Danior glanced up nervously, clearly noticing the rising panic in my voice.

"Mummy, Mummy!"

I could hear the distant cries of the twins. Their call was muffled, lost in the army of trees blockading my way. I could sense the malign intent oozing through the sap of the trees, determined to separate me from my babies. I broke into a sprint, tree branches viciously whipping my arms as the wind cackled behind me.

I tumbled through the woods and saw them.

"Look, Mummy, it's so pretty," Joni was saying. She was pointing to a still lake twinkling under the late afternoon sun. A blurred string of clouds was reflected on its glass-like surface.

"Yea, so pretty," echoed Logan.

I heard strained panting breath behind me. Danior had been trying to catch up as I dashed off after the twins. I could tell he was close to tears but was stubbornly fighting them off.

"Come here, dear," I said, scooping him in my arms. "Look at the lake your brother and sister found. Isn't it pretty?" Guilt intermingling with relief rushed through me. Everyone was here, safe and sound.

Danior rubbed his eyes and nodded before nestling his face in my neck. I rubbed his back, my ears pricked, listening intently for the voices. Had we outrun them? Perhaps they wouldn't find us today. I wished I had my stash of laudanum on me. My nerves felt brittle and frail. I sat down on a log whilst Logan and Joni played near the lake. I started picking at the dry skin around my nails, nervously thinking about how long it would take to walk back so that I could get my laudanum.

"Look, I can make the stones bounce, like Daddy," Logan said, throwing a stone haphazardly into the lake. Inevitably, it plopped beneath the smooth surface and sank to the bottom.

"That one didn't bounce," Joni said. "Let me try." Hers also met the same fate, sinking deep into the bed of the lake.

I felt my eyes glaze over as I watched this repetitive game. Logan and Joni would take turns trying to skip the stones over the lake's glassy surface.

I couldn't pinpoint the precise moment when I stopped seeing them. I had been watching. My eyes were open and I was right there. How could I not have seen them? I heard their giggles and loud exaggerated sighs as the stones continued to break the lake's calm surface and sink. I felt Danior as I continued to rub his back and hold him close to me.

Time seemed to expand and contract around me. It drifted in and out of focus. It could have been day or night, I couldn't tell the difference. All I know was I roused back to the land of living by piercing screams. Even when I heard the screams, my body was immobilised, my muscles frozen in place like a statue made from stone. My eyes wouldn't focus, and my senses collided in confusion all around me. I tried to search for the source of the screams but felt as if I was miles underwater, pushing my way through a blurry mass of oblivion.

I heard crashing through the undergrowth behind me, as if it were coming from far far away. There was a splash and the sound of crying.

"Erosabel! Erosabel!"

Someone was shaking me violently and yelling my name so loudly it tore through my conscience, rousing me back to reality.

My vision finally cleared, and I was able to focus on my surroundings. The first thing I saw was Willowen's luminescent eyes, radiating with a cold fury I had never seen before.

"How could you, Erosabel! You were sitting right here!" he was yelling at me.

I felt disoriented. The sky was pitch black and I was shaking from the cold.

"The children, where are the children?" My voice came out in scratchy rasps as I scanned my surroundings frantically.

Willowen stared at me in shock. I saw all three of them dripping wet, bundled under his coat. They were shivering and crying softly.

"Why are they crying? What happened?"

"You don't know?" Willowen asked incredulously. "You were right here watching it all."

Confusion and fear seeped like a cold poison into my bones. "No, I don't know. Why are they crying?" I tried to stand up but collapsed. My muscles were stiff and ached from sitting in the same position for so long. Willowen caught me in his strong arms.

"Danior nearly drowned, Erosabel. And you were just sitting here, staring. I saw it. It was getting late and you hadn't returned. I asked where you'd gone and Isolde's children told me you went this way. I followed you as best I could and then I heard the screams. Danior fell into the lake and the twins tried to jump in and save him. They could have all drowned if I hadn't got here in time."

My hands were shaking as tears poured down my cheeks. I felt breathless, as if someone had punched me with an iron fist in the stomach. "I don't understand. I was here. I was watching them the whole time. They were playing. No one fell in the lake," I said shakily.

"Erosabel, they were all in the lake. Why were you out walking anyway? And at this time of night? You put them all in terrible danger."

I was shaking so badly I couldn't speak. Fear and nausea swept through me in sickening waves. I had put my babies in danger and couldn't even remember it.

"Come on, let's go home," Willowen said in a gentler tone. "Why did you go out like this in the first place? You must be freezing."

Willowen gathered a sobbing, shivering Danior in his arms and kept the twins close on either side. I felt his furtive glances land on me like a hail of accusatory stones. Each glance reminded me of how my children had been put in danger under my care. I couldn't make sense of it. The voices hadn't followed us. We had outrun their whispers in the woods. I had been sure of it. My mind felt like a shattered ornament, the sharp, broken pieces scattered in a million different directions. And I was scrabbling to gather them together, make them fit so that I could remember. I walked slightly behind Willowen and the children in a dumbfounded trance. No matter how much I tried to rearrange the

244

scene in my mind, I didn't understand. Why couldn't I remember? Where had the time gone? It had simply slipped past me like a slick thief in the night.

When we reached our caravan, the campsite was silent and still. Most people had gone to bed. I helped change the children into warm clothes and bundled their small, shivering bodies under the blankets.

"I'm so sorry, my loves," I whispered to them. "It'll never happen again. I'm so sorry." I hugged and kissed each one of them.

"What happened to you, Mummy?" Joni asked softly before I turned to get ready for bed myself. "It's like you were there, watching us but you weren't in your body. You were like an empty shell. Me and Logan screamed at you and pulled at you to get your attention but you just weren't there. You couldn't see us any more. It's like we didn't exist."

I tried to hold back my tears but they spilled out of the corners of my eyes. "I'm so sorry, sweetheart. Sometimes Mummy doesn't feel well. It was like I was sleeping with my eyes open, I think. I was just feeling a bit tired. But don't worry, I will get better. You and your brothers have nothing to worry about. You're safe with me. I'm so sorry I frightened you today." I stroked their hair and kissed them again. "Goodnight. I love you all so much," I whispered.

Willowen was perched on a stool in the corner of the caravan watching me as if I were a ticking time bomb.

"Roz," he said finally. "What happened?"

I crouched down and rested my head on his knees. Silently I sobbed all the pain, fear and confusion of the day away. The tears melted down my face, a continuous stream of sorrow. I cried until I fell into a tumultuous sleep. Willowen carried me and tucked me under the blankets near the children.

Willowen always tried to see the good in people, the silver lining outlining the dark storm cloud. Even when it was clear I was losing my mind, he believed in me with a force so strong I nearly believed it myself that I could get better. But he was wrong, and I was wrong, and for that lapse in judgement, we both paid the ultimate price.

Chapter 18

AS TIME WENT by, Willowen put an ever-increasing number of restrictions on what I could and couldn't do, where I could and couldn't walk, how far I was allowed to go, and the list continued. I could understand it for the most part but sometimes it filled me with such an irrational anger I felt I might rip at the seams. It was especially difficult when he restricted my laudanum.

"Where is it?" I snarled.

"I told you, you can have one third of a teaspoon a day. You had it this morning," Willowen replied in a deliberately calm voice, which only infuriated me further.

"No, I didn't," I retorted. I tried to hide my shaking hands by shoving them into my pockets.

"Yes, you did. I gave it to you."

"It wasn't a third," I spat back.

Willowen stared at me with a look of incredulity playing across his features.

"You don't know what I suffer. If you did, you would not be so cruel," I said, changing tactic. If my rage wouldn't move him, I would beg. "Please, I only need half a teaspoon more for my nerves. They rile me up to the point where I feel my head might explode. It's a sickness and this is my medicine."

"Medicine should not make you react this way. It should help you get better not worse."

"But I'm not worse when I have enough of it," I replied, desperation creeping in. I felt we were going around in circles and he was deliberately not understanding my plight.

"But you keep needing more, Erosabel. It used to be one teaspoon, then two, then when the lake incident happened, I think you had totally lost count."

"That's not true! I was always in control," I said, through gritted teeth. A murderous rage began to ebb and flow within my soul. I tried to keep it at bay. I had to at least pretend to be calm if that would get me my laudanum.

Willowen simply shook his head. "I can't keep arguing with you," he said sadly.

"Then don't and just give me what I need," I replied, hoping that he was coming around.

"The answer is no." He turned and left the caravan. I heard a click behind him as he locked the door.

I flung myself at the door, rattling the handle. "You can't do this, Willowen! Let me out!" I yelled after him.

"Unless you want to scare the children even more, I would keep it down if I were you. I'll open the door when you're calm," Willowen said. "This is for your own good."

My head was swirling. There was no laudanum. My angel had deserted me. Or it had been stolen from me. The rage seeped into my blood, setting it on fire. Just as I was about to release a bloodcurdling shriek to get him to open the door, I heard it.

"He won't come back, you know. He doesn't love you like we do."

"Who's there?" I said, spinning around.

"We're your friends. We want what's best for you. Unlike him, we want you to be happy."

"No, no, no!" I sat down in the middle of the caravan, rocking backwards and forwards. My hands were balled into fists, shaking.

"Don't be afraid of us. We're looking out for you. They're the imposters. That husband, those children. They aren't real like we are."

"Stop," I said, through clenched teeth. Without realising it, I began pummelling my head with my quivering fists. It needed to stop. I had to get them to stop.

"But why? We're here for you when they aren't. They will rob you, bully you and stab you in the back the first chance they get."

"They're my family!" Tears started rolling down my cheeks. I was crying oceans of tears. Soon the contents of the locked caravan would be swilling around in my sadness, drowning.

"That's an idea."

"What is?" I stammered.

"You could always end it all. Kill yourself before they kill you."

I couldn't breathe. It was as if I was already under a wall of water, gasping for air. I looked up, expecting to see an undulating vision of light reflected on the surface of the pool smothering me. Instead, a ghastly black bird flapped its wings above my head. It was moving as if in slow motion, its immense wings moving up then down, hypnotising me. Its head shifted in my direction. A dagger-sharp beak and black pearls for eyes bore down on me. I tried to move but couldn't break the spell. It was getting closer. I could feel the puff of air as the wings of the grotesque bird continued to fan me. Then it let out a wicked, ominous caw. The caw stretched and lengthened, cutting through space and time. It continued, rising in volume, becoming increasingly high-pitched. I wanted to cover my ears, protect myself from the evil that reeked from it. Then my blood froze. The bird was no longer cawing. The screeching caw, like nails on a blackboard, had turned into something worse. It was laughing. I recognised that laugh.

The beak morphed into a knife, dripping with blood. The black pearls turned a luminous blue. Tendrils of fiery red sprouted from its head. The neck of the bird snapped. It was contorted, twitching manically. Its wings bent backwards, and its legs twisted like the knotted roots of a tree.

The laugh became louder. It felt tangible, as if it was taking up space in the caravan, consuming it. As the bird became more distorted in shape, human arms and legs emerged from the wrecked, crumpled plumage. Before I knew it, Mother was crouched in front of me, laughing deliriously. Her voice sent bullets of ice ricocheting through my body.

"You thought you got rid of me. You thought it was over and you beat the curse. It's never going to be over. Not for you. Now give me those children!"

She lunged at me with her claw-like nails aiming at my stomach. This time the scream was mine. I let out a howl of fear and horror. I didn't stop until I felt strong arms embracing me, rocking me gently. The vision of Mother disintegrated like dust particles breaking apart and scattering in the wind.

"It's all right, everything is all right," I heard Willowen's soothing voice in my ear.

I was trembling violently. A waterfall of tears continued to pour down my cheeks as I muttered incoherently, trying to explain to Willowen what I had seen.

"I'm sorry! I should never have locked you in," Willowen was saying. "I only thought I was doing what was best."

After Willowen tucked me into bed, whispering platitudes that meant absolutely nothing to me, he finally relented. I couldn't hear his justifications or explanations. His cautions and words of warning went over my head. All I knew was he was giving me the merest pinch of my angel dust, my saviour. I finally felt my brittle nerves relax as my head sank into a feathery pillow.

"The children?" I asked, before Willowen left the caravan.

"They're fine," he replied. "You just rest."

* * * * *

Willowen continued to monitor my laudanum but decided to take a gentler approach as he tried to wean me off it. I became confused, scattered and sometimes delirious. My appetite also increased dramatically. I started gaining weight. Along with the weight gain came a subtle calm, a stillness within my mind. I recognised that stillness and what usually came with it.

"Willowen," I called out one afternoon.

"Yes, love?"

"I think I might be with child," I said, rubbing my bloated belly.

Willowen looked from my face to my belly. A huge smile split across his face. "We're adding another one to the brood!" he said, with childlike enthusiasm.

"I think so!" I said, trying to mirror his excitement.

"I know we said we didn't want any more. But this feels like a blessing," he said happily. "This is just what we need."

I nodded uncertainly. I wasn't quite sure what he meant by the baby being just what we needed. I felt there was a burden, an expectation, weighing on the baby to fix something before it was even born. Then the realisation hit me. Willowen expected it to fix me. I was the broken one. Something inside of me had snapped, an umbilical cord tying me to reality, attaching me to the wisdom of the earth was gone. I was untethered, drifting away like dandelion seeds in the wind. Before the new baby arrived I had to change. I needed to get better.

"We'll be travelling up north soon," Willowen's voice echoed through my mind, but it sounded muffled, as if it was travelling a long way through space and time to reach me.

I shook my head.

"Are you all right?" he asked. His face was inches from mine.

I blinked, startled. "Yes, I'm fine. We're to be travelling soon?"

"Yes, up north. We'll try get most of the travelling done now, before winter sets in. I know a campsite where we can settle for the winter."

"I'll prepare the children and the caravan," I replied.

The children were thrilled at the plan when I told them we would be journeying on.

"We were getting so bored of this place," Danior said. 'Will there be giants and wizards and grizzly bears where we go next?"

I laughed. Danior had always had a wild imagination.

"No, silly," Logan replied. "Giants and wizards aren't real and there are no grizzly bears around here."

Danior furrowed his brows in disappointment.

"Maybe we'll see a woodland fairy or two on the way," Joni whispered to Danior, winking. "I heard they like the cold north air."

Danior considered this and shrugged his shoulders, somewhat satisfied with the promise of seeing the icy woodland fairies.

It was bright and sunny when we finally started our journey north. The children were running and squealing with laughter, playing some sort of game with Leo and Clem. I felt calm, at ease in myself and with the world. I gently placed a hand on my belly, rubbing it absent-mindedly.

By the time evening rolled around, we had set up a campfire and heated up some broth for dinner. The children gulped theirs down and then rested their sleepy heads on my lap. I stroked their hair and hummed a tune absent-mindedly, waiting for Willowen to return with more firewood.

There was jovial laughter from the others in the camp. Isolde was sitting next to me, watching the dying embers of the flames.

"How've you been feeling lately?" Isolde asked.

She knew about my laudanum habit and constant migraines, as I called them. It was common knowledge in the camp that I wasn't well but only Willowen knew the extent of my illness. Even he didn't know what really went on inside my mind. I knew I would never be able to confide in him or anyone. Saying stuff like that aloud made it concrete, real. By keeping it locked in my head, I was able to separate myself from it, pretend it was all a dark fantasy.

I realised Isolde was waiting for an answer.

"I'm fine. Just weary but also excited for this little one," I said, patting my stomach.

"Do you think it's a boy or a girl?"

"My heart tells me it's a girl. We'd have two boys and two girls that way."

"The perfect family," Isolde said, smiling.

"What about you? Do you want more?"

"Honestly, I'm quite happy with the two. But I wouldn't be surprised if another popped up sooner or later. Fennix still can't keep his hands off me." Isolde giggled.

Just then Clem came running barefooted towards Isolde. "I had a bad dream," she cried.

"There, there," Isolde soothed, scooping Clem up in her arms.

"It was really bad," she said between sobs.

"Let's go. I'll tuck you back into bed and scare all the bad dreams away," Isolde replied. "Duty calls," she said to me before walking back to the caravan with Clem in her arms.

I caught snippets of their conversation as they walked away.

"What happened in your dream?"

"They were dead! All dead," Clem replied shakily.

"Who was dead?" Isolde asked, her voice growing fainter.

Just as Clem answered, I felt a sudden jolt of pain in my stomach. Wincing, I shifted my weight as gently as I could so as not to wake the children. Danior muttered something in his sleep. I slowly rubbed the spot where the pain had shot through me. Like a ball of knotted tension, it slowly released and I could breathe again.

I let out a long exhale when I heard Willowen's muffled voice. Craning my neck, I tried to see who he was speaking to. When he drifted out of the shadows I could see he wasn't alone. A thin, wiry girl was standing next to him. She had a strange gait, limping slightly as she walked. I had the strange impression that she looked bent out of shape, as if her joints folded in the wrong directions. I squinted through the cloud of darkness trying to get a better look at her. Gently Willowen led her towards the children and me.

"Roz," he said quietly so as not to disturb the pile of sleeping children in my lap. "I was out getting the firewood when I saw this young woman who needs our help." He lowered his voice to a whisper so the woman with the strange gait couldn't hear. In the light, her features looked even more youthful than what I had initially thought. The firelight reflected off her waxy skin and hollow eyes. Willowen could have been yelling and it wouldn't have made a difference. She was in another world.

"I don't know what happened to her. I found her crouching in the bushes like an animal. She's got scratches all up and down her arms and legs. I was thinking tomorrow you could have a look at her and help heal her wounds."

I nodded, my eyes fixed on her absent expression.

"I don't know her name or where she came from. She hasn't said a word yet. She seems to understand when I speak to her. I was hoping you could try speaking to her tomorrow. I told her she can travel with us and we can keep her safe for now. Poor thing seems scared of her own shadow."

"Of course. I'll take a look at her scratches tomorrow. I can't really move right now with these ones all over me, but there's still some broth in the pot if she wants some."

Willowen nodded, ladling a generous amount of broth into a cracked clay bowl. He gestured for her to come and sit with us and handed her the bowl.

She sat on the warm, dry earth cautiously. Although angular bones were jutting from her face, jaw and collarbone, she ate slowly, with trepidation. She reminded me of a fragile little bird, taking tiny sips of the broth to fill what must be a tiny stomach. Her furtive eyes met mine. I tried to give her a friendly smile but she quickly averted her gaze, fixing her eyes on the dancing fire instead, lost in a world I couldn't see.

The only sound to punctuate the silence was the crackling fire and occasional sigh from one of the sleeping bodies nestled in my lap.

"How about we call it a night? We'll be on the move tomorrow. Best to have a good night's rest," Willowen said in an overly cheery tone.

I nodded as he scooped up one sleeping child after the other. As he was walking off to the caravan with the final sleeping child, I felt a stabbing pain shoot through my stomach again. It felt like a burning fire searing a hole through my skin. I clenched my teeth and breathed. Icy fingers of fear pricked my skin as the pain continued. I hadn't felt such pains with my other pregnancies, not even with the twins.

Suddenly I felt a warm hand stroking my arm. The woman had soundlessly crept to my side and was stroking me, as one might a cat. She rubbed my back with surprising strength. She was whispering something under her breath. I couldn't make out the words but it had a melodic rhythm to it, soothing my mind and body. Within a few moments the pain receded. As if she could tell her job was done she removed her hand and withdrew silently.

"Thank you. That really helped," I said.

She nodded, her eyes darting nervously between my face and belly.

"Come, there's space in the caravan for us all to sleep," I said, heaving myself up.

She shook her head and gestured to the ground.

"There's no need for you to sleep out here."

She gave the merest hint of a smile in response but stayed where she was.

"Well, let me at least get you a blanket." I hurried off to the caravan and pulled out a blanket I had made several years ago.

When I returned, she was already lying down, her eyes fixed towards the stars. The embers of the fire glowed, illuminating her waxy skin. She reminded me of an unblinking china doll as she lay in complete stillness. I placed the blanket next to her.

"Here, in case you get cold. I'll take a look at your wounds tomorrow and make sure they don't get infected," I said.

She didn't turn to look at me but the shadow of a smile flitted across her face as her gaze remained heavenward.

* * * * *

The next morning we set off. The children stared at the latest addition to the group, questions pouring out of them in loud whispers.

"Who is she?"

"Where did she come from?"

"Is she a fairy of the woods?"

"Why is she covered in scratches?"

I tried to explain in undertones but each explanation just led to more questions.

"She just came out of the bushes? But where was she going?" Logan asked.

"I don't know that yet, darling."

"Why can't she tell you?" Joni piped in.

"She hasn't really spoken yet."

"Why not? Can't she speak, or she won't?" Danior pressed.

"I don't know, honey."

Eventually I scolded them for being so nosey and ignored the barrage of unending questions. The pain in my stomach ebbed and flowed, cutting my patience short. I couldn't understand what was causing it. Perhaps it was simply the fact that I was older for this pregnancy and my body less adaptable. I breathed deeply, focusing on each inhalation and exhalation as we walked on.

"She hurts you," a husky voice said from behind me.

I turned around, surprised to find the hollow-eyed woman walking like a shadow behind me, watching me closely.

"I don't know," I spluttered, surprised. "I am in pain but why do you say *she*? You can tell it's a girl?"

"It's a girl."

The woman spoke in strange, flat statements. There was no flow in her voice, no cadence.

I nodded, unsure of what to say. "This pregnancy is definitely more difficult than my others," I said eventually, rubbing my belly.

"Yes."

Her speech was like a knife, cutting each conversational attempt short. I tried again.

"What's your name?"

"Bertha."

"How did you get all those scratches and scars?" I asked. I had dressed her wounds earlier that morning. Although they looked painful she didn't flinch once as I dabbed them with my ointments and bandaged them up.

"Long story."

For someone who spoke in two-to-three-word sentences, I doubted she would be disposed to tell me a short story, let alone a long one. I simply nodded again, and we walked in silence side by side.

I was lost in my thoughts when I heard it. It was the ruffling of wings. The feeling of being watched. A tingling sense of foreboding crept over me, pouncing on every nerve in my body like a black cat on the prowl. My eyes were glued to the path ahead of me. I didn't want to look up. I knew what would be waiting for me when I did. Perhaps if I ignored it, shut it from my eyes and mind, it would simply disappear. Then I heard it. It refused to be ignored. It would not allow me to shut it out. The piercing sound of a raven's caw permeated the innards of my heart and mind. I had heard its voice and it was forcing me to look its way. It would never give up. I tore my eyes from the safety of the ground and with great effort looked up.

A large raven was perched on our caravan as it bumped along the uneven road ahead of Bertha and me. Despite the sudden jolts, the bird remained as still as a statue, its wings folded tightly across its body, like a strait jacket.

I could feel something inside me churning. I couldn't tell if it was the baby, fear or something else. All I could feel was this connection, this unwanted, hated connection between me and the black sentry of impending doom. I felt the energy being sapped out of me. My life force was draining away the longer the bird continued to stare. I didn't know if it was my distorted imagination, but the bird seemed to be growing, getting bigger and fatter the longer it stared whereas I felt I was becoming smaller and more wizened. It was feeding off my spirit like a parasite.

Then the bloated bird opened its beak a crack. A low hissing emanated from it.

"*Don't trust them. They're not yours,*" it whispered.

In a state of shock I didn't see the branch in my path. I stumbled and nearly tripped. Bertha grabbed me by the arm.

"Thanks," I said shakily, transported back to the physical world.

She was looking into my face, a picture of concern. I glanced up, towards the caravan. There was nothing there. No bird. No black omen. No sentry of doom.

"Beware."

"Beware? Of what?" I asked her, my mind in a muddled haze of confusion.

261

"Be aware of the path," she replied simply, releasing her vice-like grip on my arm.

My heart was racing, thumping so loudly I was sure she could hear it. I glanced around, my eyes searching for my children. An irrational fear took hold of me. In my mind's eye, I could see the monstrous demon swooping out of a tear in the sky, an angel of doom, snatching my children in its talons and taking them to a place far away. I shivered violently at the thought.

Joni and Logan were pushing each other in what could have been a mock or real fight. Danior was trailing after them, kicking up dirt and stones. I sighed with relief. The raven was tormenting me and me alone. That I could handle. As long as nothing happened to the children I could breathe easily and retain some scrap of sanity.

Chapter 19

THE WEATHER WAS cooling down rapidly.

"My toes are frozen," Danior moaned as we traipsed along the hardened cracked ground, continuing our journey north.

I glanced down at his feet. The soles of his shoes were flapping.

"I'll mend them tonight."

"But what about right now? My toes will freeze off before night!" he complained.

"Wrap them in extra cloth. I have some rags in the caravan" I replied, exhausted.

"But then I'll be uncomfortable and won't be able to walk properly," he persisted, his frustration rising at my incompetence to solve his problems.

"At least your toes will be warm," I replied weakly. My head was spinning. I felt ever more exhausted with each passing day. My bulging stomach seemed to be carrying an extra weight. My child was in there but so was something else. There was an additional weight lodged within my womb, growing next to my child. It was a nameless, swirling substance. Just at that moment, Willowen magically appeared by my side.

"What if I carry you the entire way, like a baby!" he exclaimed.

"No, no, I'm not a baby," Danior stated emphatically, stomping a badly clad foot on the ground for added effect.

"It sure sounds like you are one," Willowen replied, scooping Danior up in his arms and flinging him over his shoulder. "You are either a baby or a sack of flour!"

Danior was laughing hysterically. "No, I'm neither! I can walk!"

"Oh no you can't! Babies and sacks of flour can't walk. I think you're going to have to stay like this forever!"

Willowen turned and winked at me as Danior writhed, laughing in his arms. I managed a faint smile. It had always been music to my ears to listen to my children's squeals of delight. Now I could barely hear it. I saw Danior laughing but couldn't hear the music. Everything around me was warped, muffled. All I could feel were shooting pains in my back and legs, making every step torture. I continued to drag my feet until blinking lights popped in front of my eyes. A husky voice floated around me.

"Stop! She's fainting."

My vision blurred. All I could see were my scuffed, worn shoes. Voices swirled around me and then all went black.

* * * * *

I woke up delirious, beads of sweat dripping down my face and back. At first I thought I was soaked in sweat until I looked down. The sheets were stained with dark, crimson pools. I didn't know where I was or how I had got there. Fear pulsated through me as I stared, fixated on the blood.

"She's awake," a disembodied voice said.

I glanced up. The face was blurred, distorted but I recognised the hollow eyes of Bertha. A warm hand clung onto mine.

"You're going to be ok. The baby will be ok," Willowen kept repeating shakily.

And then I felt it. A fire ripped through my entire body, searing every single nerve within. I screamed.

"It's happening. She's having the baby," an unfamiliar voice called.

The pain receded. In that moment free of pain I realised what was happening.

"No," I whispered, tears streaming down my face. "Willowen, no! It's too early. Much too early!"

"You'll be ok. You're strong and so is the baby. We're going to get through this," he replied shakily.

"But it's too early," I sobbed.

The scorching pain tore through me again mercilessly, and I completely lost sense of where I was, who I was with or who I was. The room around me was spinning. Darkness flooded every corner, lit up by needles of light. Pellets of rain were shooting from the sky and ricocheting off the tear-stained windowpanes. They came crashing down with such force, it sounded like rocks were slamming into the walls and ceiling.

I was being battered from the inside out. Around me a storm raged, and within a searing pain flooded my senses. I opened my eyes and for a moment all I could see were pinpricks of light dancing in front of my eyes. The stars faded, falling from my vision like confetti from the black, wizened sky.

Then I saw them. There were two of them. Standing there, at the bottom of my bed. They were perched on the bedposts, the sentinels of death, watching me. Waiting for me. I no longer felt the burning pain within me. My body seized up in a fear which turned my blood to ice. The ravens were whispering to each other, the dark holes of their eyes fixed on me. Everything around me went quiet. There was no more pain, no more screams, no more worried sobbing. All I could hear was the brazen whispering of the ravens.

"*It's a mistake. You know it's a mistake,*" one of the ravens hissed directly at me.

"What is?" I asked in a newfound state of calm.

"*You should never have had them. They're not yours. You are cursed and now they are too,*" the other replied.

My gaze darted between the two. "I don't understand. I haven't done anything wrong," I said, tears rolling down my cheeks.

"*The curse will claim you. And all those you love. You were selfish. It was a mistake. They belong to the curse now.*"

Tears were streaming down my face, blurring my vision. The shaky image of those monstrous ravens became hazy. All of a sudden, I could hear shrieks and screams as reality crashed back in around me.

"Do something, Willowen! Make her snap out of it," a voice yelled. "She'll lose the baby!"

"I'm trying! Roz, Roz, it's me, Willowen. You have to listen. You have to push! Roz, can you hear me?"

Claps of thunder burst through the room. I blinked and stared at Willowen. A flash of lightening illuminated him in a silvery glow. His face was drawn and pale. Panic was etched in his eyes. Then the pain flooded back, inundating my mind and body. I had to push. I had to push. If there was anything I had to do in that moment, it was push the baby out and into the safe hands of Willowen. I screamed as I pushed with all my strength.

"Good, now wait a moment before pushing again," the unfamiliar voice was saying.

I let the voice guide me. Someone was dabbing my forehead with a damp cloth whilst Willowen stood by me, not letting go of my hand. After what felt like an eternity of pain, I heard a yelp of joy.

"I see it! It's coming out. Just one more big push, dear, and you're done!"

I let out a final scream before pushing the baby out. A flurry of hands reached out and grabbed it. An ominous silence hung in the room.

"Why isn't she crying?" I asked desperately. "Where's her cry?"

The woman who had scooped her up as she came out was rubbing the baby's back, patting it softly. The silence stretched on as panic welled up within me. The birds were right. Everything I had done in my life was a mistake and now I was being punished. Remorse and self-hatred wrapped their arms around me, squeezing me tightly until I couldn't breathe. And then I heard it. A small cry shattered the wall of silence that had built up within the room. There was a collective sigh of relief. I wasn't being punished after all, I thought wildly. At least, not today.

I lay back and began to take in my surroundings. I was lying in a blood-soaked bed in a small room. The only other bits of furniture included a wooden chair, a chest of drawers and buckets of scarlet water with bloody rags hanging limply over the sides. It was pitch black outside but the storm was losing its force. Its willpower was ebbing away into the night. There were three other people in the room, Willowen, Bertha and a matronly woman in her mid-forties.

The woman placed a very small baby on my chest. "You have a beautiful baby girl right there," she said, smiling.

I held her close but felt a strange pang of fear in the pit of my stomach. The feelings of relief and joy I had felt with the other three were missing. I stared down at her, this perfect new life, and felt a divide between us, an awning gulf stretching into oblivion. Willowen's hand weighed on my shoulder. I looked up at him, wondering if he was feeling it too.

His eyes shone with tears. "She's perfect. Well done, Roz. I knew you had it in you," he whispered gently. "You just get some rest now."

"Where are we?" I asked.

"After you fainted, Bertha went to look for somewhere safe and comfortable for you. She had a feeling you were going into labour. Luckily she found this cottage close by and Mr and Mrs Miller here were only too happy to help."

"Of course," a tired-looking Mrs Miller said. "Let me clear this up and get some fresh bed sheets for you."

"You're too kind," I said. Tears of gratitude stung my eyes. There was still good in the world. The shadow of the ravens hadn't darkened everything in my path.

"Oh, now, none of that blubbering," Mrs Miller replied kindly.

Mrs Miller and Bertha heaved the water pails and rags out of the room and tottered downstairs.

"What shall we call her?" Willowen asked.

I stared at the bundle in my arms, my mind drawing a complete blank. I shrugged my shoulders after several moments, waiting for a wave of inspiration which did not come.

"Not to worry," Willowen replied. "We'll think about it later. You just sleep now, you must be exhausted." He scooped up the baby as Bertha and Mrs Miller entered the room.

"Will she be all right?" I heard an anxious Willowen whisper to Mrs Miller. At first I thought he was talking about the baby until I heard her answer.

"She lost a lot of blood. She will probably need to be on bed rest for quite some time."

I felt people heaving me up and gently tugging off my blood-encrusted clothes. I was laid back down in fresh, clean sheets and within seconds fell into a deep slumber.

* * * * *

My recovery was slow and painful. I bled heavily afterwards and felt a constant dull pain in my pelvis, stomach, joints, neck and back. I couldn't make sense of time as all the days blurred into one. The rest of the camp had to move on and find somewhere proper to settle for the winter. As I couldn't travel, Willowen, Bertha and the children stayed in Mr and Mrs Miller's guesthouse. They had a small farm and garden which needed tending to. Willowen helped out on the farm and Bertha helped in the home. Logan, Joni and Danior ran errands and helped whoever needed it.

I was supposed to be recovering and looking after my new-born but most of the time I found myself staring off into space, waiting for the next visit from the dreaded ravens. Bertha was a godsend during that time, helping with the naps and crying. Absent-mindedly I was able to feed her but even then, she sometimes slipped from my grasp. Luckily Bertha was there to catch her if she fell.

"She needs a name," Bertha stated.

It had already been a month, possibly longer, since she had been born and we still referred to her as "the baby".

I nodded, staring at the sleeping baby as she lay swaddled in blankets. Her features were relaxed into an expression of peace and serenity. Although I had given birth to her, which my battered body could assuredly vouch for, I couldn't help but feel she did not belong to me.

She belonged to some other entity, someone or something else. I didn't have the right to bestow a name on something that did not belong to me.

"Were you close to your mother, Bertha?" I heard myself ask.

"Yes," she replied emphatically. "You?"

"No, not at all," I replied. "What was your mother's name?"

"Edwina."

"Edwina," I echoed, testing out the sounds on my tongue, listening to how it landed on my ears. "It's a beautiful name," I concluded.

"What was your mother's name?" Bertha asked.

"Esther," I replied, spitting out the name like poison. "Edwina sounds so much prettier, a kinder name."

"Why weren't you close?"

I snorted in derision. "No one could be close to Mother. It took me a long time to realise it, but she was entirely mad. She was going to drive me mad too but I got away."

Bertha's eyebrows furrowed for a split second before she smoothed them over and assumed her usual expressionless expression.

"Your mother was kind, you say?" I asked.

Bertha nodded in acknowledgement.

"Well then, what better name than Edwina for this little one," I said, peering at the sleeping bundle. "Yes, Edwina is perfect," I whispered to myself.

"It's better than *the baby*," Bertha replied, a small smile tweaking the sides of her thin lips.

"That's settled. Edwina it is."

"My mother would be pleased," Bertha said.

"Where is she?" I asked, realising how little I knew about Bertha.

"Dead," she replied simply.

"I'm so sorry."

"She was a good woman. But poverty makes you desperate," Bertha continued.

"What did your mother do, if you don't mind my asking?"

"She went with bad men for the money," Bertha replied. "She did it for me, to put food in my mouth."

"Is that why you had all those bruises and scratches on the day I first met you?" I asked. "Were those injuries from one of those men?"

A flashback of a memory from a lifetime ago struck me. I had seen what some of the men did to the prostitutes at Madam Stark's brothel. If they were overly intoxicated or just thuggish by nature, they could inflict serious damage on the women working there. Madam Stark was a better brothel-keeper than most as she never tolerated that sort of treatment. Once one of the men crossed the line, he would not be welcomed back.

"It was my stepfather," Bertha was saying. "A year ago, one of the men married my mother but he was just as bad as the others, if not worse. When she died, he turned to me."

I let out a heavy sigh. It broke my heart to hear such tragedies befalling such good people. Bertha deserved better.

"He kept me locked in a room for ages and treated me worse than an animal. I lost track of time and have no idea how long I was in there for. It could have been weeks or months. Luckily, one day he came back dead drunk and forgot to lock the door. I escaped then with nothing but the clothes on my back and the shoes on my feet."

"I can't believe that," I said, tears welling up in my eyes. "That's so terrible. You must have been so scared."

Bertha shrugged, withdrawing into her cocoon of silence. She had shared what she needed to share and now she was done.

A soft knock came from behind the door.

"Come in."

Danior peeped around the side of the door cautiously.

"Come in, sweetheart. Quietly now, she's sleeping."

Danior tiptoed into the room and clambered into the bed with me. He stared down at the bundle in my arms.

"We've decided on a name. She's going to be called Edwina, after Bertha's mother. What do you think?"

He scrunched up his nose and contemplated the name. Finally he replied, "Yes, I like it. It works."

"Indeed it does. I think our family is perfectly complete."

Danior nodded. "Will you be happy now, Mummy?" he asked, his big round eyes staring into mine.

I blinked, shocked at the question. Bertha picked up a pile of rags and blankets and slipped out to wash them, leaving me alone with Danior and his question, which I had no clue how to answer.

"Of course I'm happy," I said as cheerfully as I could. "Why would you ask that?"

Danior shrugged. "You're sad a lot of the time. And then I heard Daddy talking..." He trailed off, examining the dirt under his fingernails.

"What was Daddy saying?" I asked, suspicion creeping into my voice.

Danior shrugged again before continuing. He spoke slowly, weighing his words. "He was talking to some man. He kept calling him Doctor. The man called Doctor said he would come back."

"What did Daddy tell the doctor?" I asked, trying to remain calm.

"I couldn't hear. They were talking very quietly."

Anger bubbled within me. He had no right to be talking to some doctor on my behalf and not tell me about it.

Danior sensed a shift in atmosphere in the room. "I'm going to play now," he said quickly, jumping off the bed. The sudden motion jolted Edwina awake and she immediately began her mewling cry. Startled, Danior glanced at me. "Sorry, I didn't mean to wake her up."

"It's fine, dear," I said, barely hearing her cries. "You go play."

Danior shot one last look at me before slinking off. Bertha immediately came into the room, as if she had been waiting on the other side of the door. She glanced at Edwina.

"I'll take her," she stated, scooping Edwina out of my limp arms.

"Hmm," I replied, my mind travelling down a multitude of avenues all at once. What was Willowen thinking? Did he really think something was wrong with me? Why hadn't he spoken to me about it first? The more I thought of these questions, the more the rage seethed within.

I didn't hear Bertha slip out of the room. I didn't see as the sun slipped past the window to be replaced by an iridescent moon. The stars shone brightly, little pinpricks in the sky. I sat completely still in my bed. I was waiting. I was expecting them this time. The outline of two large ravens graced my windowsill. I met their dark gaze calmly, waiting for them to speak.

"*He's always been against you,*" one of them whispered, its voice seeping through the cracks around the window.

"He saved me," I replied, remembering the night Willowen found me and offered me a new life.

"*It's all been a lie. He's lied to you from the beginning,*" the other raven rasped.

"Why would he do that? I'm his wife. The mother of his children."

They emitted a gurgling croaking sound in unison. It took me a moment to realise they were laughing.

"*The mother of his children, she says,*" one of them finally wheezed.

"*That's the biggest lie of them all,*" the other replied.

"What are you talking about? I am the mother of his children. I carried each of those babies inside me. I've fed, protected, cared and loved them all."

"*Those changeling children are not your own. He's cursed them. They are false children.*"

"They're mine!" I yelled. "I would know if they weren't!"

The door banged open. Willowen was standing in the door frame, glancing around the room.

"Roz, who are you talking to?" he asked cautiously.

My gaze flitted between Willowen and the window. The shadowy outlines of the ravens were gone.

"I wasn't talking to anyone," I mumbled.

"You were. I heard you shouting," he insisted.

"I must have been dreaming," I replied.

Willowen continued to stare at me doubtfully. The intensity of his stare made me doubt myself, my mind, my sanity.

"Who were you talking to earlier?" I said accusingly, the anger returning to replace the confusion swirling around in my mind.

"Earlier? When?" he asked.

"Danior said that you had been talking to a doctor about me. You didn't think it was important to talk to me before talking to a doctor on my behalf?"

"Roz," he said gently, coming to sit next to me. "You had a difficult birth and you don't seem yourself. You've been very... absent," he said after a moment's thought.

"Absent? What does that even mean?" I snarled.

"You used to be so involved with the children. You used to have so much energy. I understand you're still recovering from the birth. I just thought the doctor could help you with the recovery."

He was speaking so calmly it irritated me, as if he were trying to placate a petulant child.

"He can also help you recover your spirits and ease your mind," Willowen continued.

"My mind?" I snapped, latching onto the word.

"You know what I mean, Roz," Willowen replied in that same gentle, irritating tone that sent ants crawling all over my skin.

"No, I don't. You need to be more specific," I said in an ice-cold tone.

"This isn't the first time where you've split. It's like your mind becomes separated from your body and I can't reach you. I can't help you, Roz, and there's nothing more in this world that I wish I was able to do. I want you to be happy and healthy. You are the most important person in this entire world to me."

Willowen was clutching my hand in his, his pale eyes boring into mine. I could see the desperation and concern that lay buried deep within them. The expression in his eyes struck a latent fear within me. I broke his gaze, not wanting to see what else lay unspoken within the depths of his soul. I nodded.

"When will this doctor be coming to see me?" I asked, defeated.

"By the end of the week," Willowen said.

"And what will he do?"

"I'm not sure. I think he'll examine you with his tools. Apart from that we'll have to see what he recommends."

I continued to stare fixedly at a point just over Willowen's shoulder.

"This is for the best, Roz. You'll see. We'll get you better in no time and then we'll be able to join the rest of the camp soon enough."

I could hear the false cheer ringing in his voice, creating a gulf, widening between the two of us. I decided to play along. I smiled at him as I met his gaze.

"You're right. Of course, you're right," I replied.

He nodded. "I'll go down and fetch you some soup. Mrs Miller made some great oxtail soup with Joni's help."

I gave him my most angelic smile as he left the room. The smile immediately faded as the door closed behind him. From that moment on, I knew a dynamic had changed in our relationship. We were play-acting. We were characters in our own show, playing happy family. But it was a lie. The ravens were right. Everything was a lie.

* * * * *

By the end of the week, the doctor arrived as promised. I was feeling drained. Dreams, nightmares and strange noises were constantly interrupting my sleep. I couldn't tell if they were real or part of the dream spilling over into reality. The result was that I was permanently exhausted. The doctor who came to visit me was old and bent. His beady blue eyes darted over me as he mumbled something to Willowen who was hovering uncertainly by the door.

"Hello, I'm Doctor Williams," the stooped man said, with a cold, unfeeling smile. "I'm here to help you get well again." He spoke to me slowly as if I were a child.

An immediate dislike gripped me. I shifted in the bed away from him, repulsed by his stature, his eyes, his ancient decrepit energy that swirled around him like a stale odour.

"I'm just going to examine you," he said, sitting heavily on the side of the bed. He took out some tools with thick, gnarled hands. I watched as he fumbled with the instruments. First, he listened to my heart. Then he put down his blunt tools and used his fingers to press into my skull. After several drawn-out "hmms" and muttered "I see's" to himself he announced with certainty, "I think I know what can help here."

"Yes?" Willowen asked immediately.

"I've studied phrenology," he said in a lecturing tone. "I can tell her cranium is enlarged, causing her erratic behaviour. A routine course of blood-letting should put her to right." He was talking as if I were not there. As if this decision was one the men should make because I was too insignificant or feeble-minded to be in charge of my own treatment.

"Are you sure?" Willowen asked, a hint of scepticism in his voice.

"Are you the doctor?" Dr Williams quipped back severely. "She has excessive amounts of blood in her veins which flow to the brain causing the delusions and bizarre behaviour you were talking about. If we can drain away the excess then she would be left with typical amounts and would be just as sane as you or I."

I glared at Willowen who was pointedly not meeting my gaze. So he had told this doctor that I was a lunatic with delusions. My blood was boiling with rage. I didn't trust this old man claiming to be a doctor and I didn't trust Willowen any more, especially as he seemed to be going along with his gruesome recommendations.

"We should start as soon as possible. Today I will use my knife and bowl to catch the blood. Next time I will bring a number of leeches to aid with the patient's comfort. Many patients prefer leeches to being sliced." He said the last sentence with a creepy lingering smile. Whilst the patients preferred leeches, he seemed to prefer the slicing technique.

Willowen nodded vacantly as if unable to process everything the odious man was saying.

"I don't want leeches on my body or to be cut by your blunt instruments," I said firmly. "I'm a healer and I've never used this as part of my practice."

The doctor turned to Willowen. "Don't worry, she won't feel a thing. I'm highly skilled in blood-letting and have been doing it for decades."

I felt my fists clench at his dismissive remarks. He still didn't even have the decency to address me directly.

"Excuse me," I said louder. "But I do not want this treatment."

"Roz, he's the doctor," Willowen said in what was intended to be soothing tones, but it only served to fuel my rage.

"I said no!" I yelled.

"I see what you were saying. Definitely too much blood in her veins. Just sit still now," the doctor said, leaning towards me with his knives.

"No!" I yelled even louder, kicking and flailing wildly.

"Now we can't have this," the doctor said in an ice-cold tone. "You will abide by my treatment."

"I will not!" I was yelling. I lashed out at Willowen as he tried to settle me and hold me down. "You're a liar! You and him, you're working together against me!" I shrieked. "You don't want to help me. You're trying to kill me!"

"She's delusional. We need to sedate her," I heard the doctor state angrily at Willowen.

A sweet smell permeated the room. I knew what was coming. I struggled even harder. Willowen was repeating something in my ear but I couldn't hear him. I lashed around wildly, trying to avoid what was coming. The doctor grabbed the back of my head in a vice-like grip, smothering my mouth and nose with a handkerchief doused in the sweet-smelling liquid, chloroform. Within seconds my eyelids drooped like black heavy curtains being drawn against the light of day. The world around me was clouded over in a thick, suffocating black fog.

It was dark outside when I awoke. I looked around blearily. It was hard to move. I felt as if weights were tied to my limbs. A sharp pain shot through my arm. I glanced down and saw several angry red lacerations running like bumpy, crusty veins trailing down my forearm. I was too tired to feel angry, too exhausted to feel indignant.

I stared at the cuts and smiled. I liked the way they looked. Furious, manic, violent. It was as if the wounds I felt that were blazoned within me, that burned the insides of my eyes and brain, had found a release. Everyone could see them now. My mental angst had physical representation. My fingers caressed the jutting scars as softly as a feather skimming on the surface of water. A strange calm settled somewhere deep within me. Perhaps this was the solution. Perhaps the demons would find their release this way, through the cuts in my arms. I fell into a dreamless sleep with the embers of a newfound hope smouldering within.

Chapter 20

TIME TUMBLED IN fragments all around me. I felt the seasons shifting. I didn't notice the weather but I saw the landscapes change from icy blue with purple hues and dark misty shadows to clear skies with liquid gold lining the undulating hills. The doctor came less frequently as he deemed I was getting better. The blood-letting sessions took place only a few times a month now. I felt weak and frail but my mind felt tranquil. More than tranquil, it felt empty. There was blissful emptiness and silence. I couldn't concentrate on much for long but when I tried to listen to the voices all I could hear were muted whisperings. My mind and body were weak and defeated, feelings I relished.

Willowen allowed me to go for walks in the fresh air, despite the doctor's warnings against it. The doctor claimed my constitution was not yet ready for walks and that I should remain, for the better part of my day, on bed rest. I was pleased when Willowen defied his orders and led me gently around the Millers' vegetable patch for the first time since

Edwina's birth. A sense of equilibrium descended on me. Willowen and I were on the same team again. Everything was how it should be.

The Millers were delighted with my progress. I hadn't noticed, but they seemed extraordinarily fond of the children and grateful for Willowen's and Bertha's help during the difficult winter season.

Early one morning, I sneaked out of my stuffy room to enjoy the sunrise. Crimson waves rippled throughout the sky with splashes of fiery oranges and deep pinks. The fresh morning air left a dampness on my cheeks as it whipped past me. I clambered over the fence outlining the vegetable garden and found a tree to nestle under. I watched as the sun rose and chased away the shadows of night.

The crunching sound of footsteps alerted me that I was not alone. I turned and saw the kindly face of Mr Miller.

"Good morning to you," he said cheerily. "Beautiful out here in the early morning."

"Good morning, it really is stunning," I agreed.

We remained like that, me sitting under the tree, Mr Miller leaning against its sturdy trunk, both looking out at the splendid show of nature gently unfolding around us.

"I'm sorry if I've made things difficult for you and your wife," I said, breaking the peaceful silence that ensconced us. "I know I've got a lot of children which means additional mouths to feed and I haven't been very helpful these past few months."

"Not to worry at all. That husband of yours is the most skilled hunter I've ever seen. We had more food this winter than any other I can remember. Not to mention his knack for raising animals and taking care of the cattle. None of our animals caught any sickness or disease this winter. He's been a great help."

I nodded, reassured. Willowen certainly was skilled.

"He also pretty much rebuilt the stables which were falling apart," Mr Miller continued. "And those children of yours are absolute angels. Never seen such well-behaved little ones."

"Are you sure we're talking about the same children," I said, smiling. "Either way, I am sorry if I have been difficult. I wasn't myself for quite some time but I am feeling better now."

"Well, that's all that matters now, isn't it?" he replied. "We all have our ups and downs. As long as you've made a full recovery, all you need to do is look towards the future and have faith."

I looked up at him and smiled. "Yes, have faith. I agree."

"Those vegetables won't tend themselves now, will they?" he said jovially. "I best get back to it. Idle hands make the Devil's work," he said with a wink. Spade in one hand, he trudged back to the vegetable patch.

Perhaps that was my problem, I thought to myself, mulling over what Mr Miller had just said. Perhaps I wasn't busy enough and had spent too much time locked in my own head. I was suddenly feeling invigorated by life and ready to plunge into a new venture. Something that would hopefully keep my hands busy and my mind still. I would go back to healing and re-vamp my travelling apothecary, I decided. I would make fresh ointments and potions and redecorate everything, from the style of the jars to the colours and paints used. It would be clean and simple to reflect my newly found inner peace.

I decided that same day I would start re-building my practice as well as be more present for the children. I felt ashamed to admit it but I hadn't bonded with Edwina at all during her first few months of life. I had been distracted, stolen away by my delusions, fears and anxieties. But I had to put things right now. I would return to healing others as well as myself.

I crept into the kitchen and began preparing breakfast for everyone, a small way to express my gratitude to all these kindly people who had stuck by me during my convalescence. I prepared some skillet bread with shredded herbs and onions, whipped up porridge, eggs and boiled a fresh pot of tea.

"What's that smell?" an excitable voice exclaimed, ringing through the hallway.

Danior was the first to burst through the door, followed by a pair of drowsy-looking twins. I observed them closely as they crowded around the table, snatching the food, crumbs exploding everywhere as they talked and laughed. They were growing up and I felt I was only just noticing it. The twins were budding into adolescence and Danior was almost ten years old now. They were no longer little babies for me to protect but hurtling into adulthood where they would have to look after themselves.

"What are you staring at, Mummy?" a moody-sounding Joni asked.

"Nothing, my dear. Just admiring how beautiful you all are and how much you've all grown. Soon you won't even need me any more."

Joni made a noncommittal sound in the back of her throat as a response. Just then I heard a wail as Willowen came in with a bundle of Edwina in his arms.

"Well, she clearly needs you," Joni said, nodding her head in the direction of the screaming baby.

"Wow, you prepared all this?" a tired-looking Willowen asked.

"Sit down, let me take her," I said, scooping up Edwina into my arms. "Help yourself to the food. There's plenty to go around."

Relieved, Willowen piled his plate up high and began wolfing down his breakfast. I sipped a cup of steaming tea as I rocked Edwina gently in my arms. Her screaming abated. She opened her big eyes, puffy from crying. I felt within her stare the sharp blade of an accusation. The accusation of being absent, of abandoning her to the care of others, of loving her brothers and sister more. Like a thick, dark substance, guilt oozed through my bloodstream. I glanced away from Edwina's intense glare as Bertha and Mrs Miller entered the kitchen.

"My oh my, would you look at this!" Mrs Miller exclaimed. "Now, which one of you prepared this feast?"

"It was Mummy!" Danior piped up, looking towards me for approval.

I tousled his hair and smiled. "Yes, just a small way for me to say thanks for everything you have done for us," I replied.

"Well, this is absolutely lovely. Thank you for putting in all this effort. You really didn't have to," Mrs Miller said warmly, reaching for the teapot.

I looked towards Bertha who nodded, as if in approval, the corner of her mouth twitching. She picked up a bread roll and began nibbling the edges, watching everyone else eat with her round, alert eyes.

I sneaked up to Willowen as everyone was chatting and munching cheerfully. "You know what I was thinking of this morning," I said tentatively.

"What's that?"

"I want to start up my apothecary again. I could help out the local people around here until we are ready to move. I was thinking it could have a new look, less vibrant and colourful. Something a bit more mellow. What do you think? I could give free samples to the Millers. It could also be my way of repaying them for everything they've done." I glanced up at Willowen and was relieved to see he was beaming.

"Roz, I think that's a wonderful idea! We're going to be rolling into winter again soon so I don't think we should be travelling now. That would be a wonderful way for you to keep busy until we're ready to leave. I'll help with whatever you need. If you need me to make any stands, bottles, just tell me."

"I will," I said, feeling warmth and excitement spread through my veins at the prospect of firing up my passion once again. During the winter, people would need *Rose's Remedies* for the routine coughs and sneezes that roll on the back of the icy winter winds and rain. My mind was already abuzz with potential new creations, ointments and healing syrups.

Bertha sidled up to me. "I'll take her," she said, gesturing to Edwina who had fallen asleep in my arms.

"Oh, thank you. I guess she's ready for her nap," I replied hastily, fully aware that I did not know my own daughter's feeding or sleeping routines at all.

Bertha nodded before whisking away Edwina to her crib upstairs.

I also sneaked out of the warm, cosy kitchen and headed outside where our caravan was parked. I clambered inside. The air was frigid in comparison to the heat of the kitchen. I reached for some of my old books, stashed in a corner. Plumes of dust glittered in the shafts of cold sunlight that infiltrated the smudged windows. I flipped through the pages and made mental notes of what to create, what to change and what to discard.

I pulled out the last heavy, thick book, nestled in the corner under the pile of healing books I had written over the years. My hand froze as I dusted off the cover. The beautiful lettering swam as tears gathered in my eyes. It was Lucifer's book of fairy tales. My first-ever book which had been my pride and joy for so long had been discarded, gathering dust in the grimy corner of our caravan. I had tucked it away, hoping to keep the events of my childhood at bay. I sat and stared at it, all the memories of the past flooding back to me, the good and the bad. Carefully, I flipped through the pages. The illustrations were faded and some of the ink had smudged but as I read certain passages, I could hear Lucifer's deep, reassuring voice in my head. His puppets danced in front of my eyes with their buttons for eyes and wire for hair.

A nostalgic sadness weighed on my shoulders and inside my soul. It was so heavy it felt tangible. A hopeless yearning for Lucifer and Tommy gripped me. They had been my first true friends in this world. So much had changed since I had seen them. I wondered if they were the same, living the same lives in the slums of East London. A tear trickled down my face as I wondered if they ever thought of me, that grubby, wiry little girl who had a madwoman for a mother. It had been a long, long time since I had thought of Mother. All that darkness, all those shadows I had bestowed to my past, to a childhood I longed to forget.

I flipped through the book and landed on a fairy tale I could not remember reading. It was not written with the beautiful lettering of the other fairy tales, nor did it have a colourful illustration to go with it. Instead it was written, almost as if it was an afterthought, in scratchy handwriting on loose sheets of paper, crammed at the back. I propped the book up in my lap and began to read.

"The Witch of Shadows"

Once upon a time there was a young girl who went by the name of Bela Rose. Bela Rose had streaming dark hair and dark eyes to match. From an early age she was orphaned and sent off to live with wicked aunts and uncles who forced her to work all hours of the day. The labour was back-breaking and endless. Plates of gruel were delivered outside her dingy closet of a room in the evenings as she was not welcome at the family dinner table. For any misdemeanour, no matter how small, she was given twenty lashings with a rider's crop.

Broken and bruised, one day Bela Rose decided to escape. She waited for the cover of night to clamber out of the window. Submerged in shadow, she crept along the hills like a whisper. The shadows were her friends, concealing her from the brash lights her wicked aunts and uncles used when they realised she had disappeared into the night.

After that escape, she fell in love with the night, with the tall stretching shadows of the dark. During the day she found honest labour in towns and shops but at night, she tinkered with ancient spells, jinxes and curses.

One day a tall, handsome man stepped into the shop where she worked. It was instant. Like a bolt of lightning had hit her, she felt her pulse quicken, her heart race. Their eyes locked and from that moment they knew they were to be married.

It was as if Bela Rose had awoken from a long, dark slumber. She had finally found happiness. Light and laughter filled the house as the pitter patter of little feet resounded between the walls. Bela Rose awoke at dawn to care for and love her children and slept at sunset, as darkness stole into the house. Bela Rose no longer needed her midnight fantasies, spells and shadow friends. She had a real family and real happiness, as solid as the oak tree they had planted in their back garden.

The wave of happiness and love carried her along until one day tragedy struck. Its vicious fangs sank deep into her life. There was an accident. A fire. Her husband and two of her children were obliterated in a blaze of smoke and hot ash.

Her life, everything she had built, immediately melted back into the shadows. Her surviving children were nothing more than empty outlines of her children, unreal to her. She retreated far from the world and its cruelties. Her head became her sanctuary where the echoes of the past dragged her back in. Spells and witchcraft became ever more enticing as she experimented with deeper and darker spells into the dead of night.

One day, her two surviving children came to her hungry and crying. She saw the pain in their eyes and in their fragile bodies. She had to protect them. At midnight she told them to lie in the centre of a meadow and draw a circle around themselves in chalk, twigs or anything they could find. Tonight she would cast a spell on them to protect them forever. The outline children were not her real children but their shadows, those precious shadows, she would protect. She recited the incantation in a low voice:

"I speak to thee, blackest of shadows,

Come to me, out of the darkness grow,

No longer tied to that mortal skin,

Let this spell set you free from deep within.

Tear yourself from those physical souls,

Apart you come, my shadows, you are now whole."

The children awoke the next day, gaunt and empty. They quickly realised that they had been torn apart from their shadows. Not only had their shadows left their sides, but so had their feelings, their personalities, the essence that made them who they were. They really were outline children.

Bela Rose captured the shadows and kept them within the dark confines of her underground hideout so that nothing would ever harm them. No good was able to reach them either. They lived out their shadowy existence within the dungeons Bela Rose had trapped them in. Bela Rose did not hear their pleas to return to the real world, to their outlines that needed them. She was deaf to all reason. She could not see beyond her own grief, beyond the insanity that had gripped her mind.

As her shadow children withered and died, disintegrating into dust one day, Bela Rose let out a howl of misery. From that day on, she prowled the streets at night, stealing children from their beds and detaching them from their shadows. Eventually all the residents moved away when they saw what was happening to their children. And she was left utterly alone with only her own addled thoughts for company. No one ever dared settle in that neighbourhood afterwards, even after Bela Rose died and melted into the history of time. That place was forever believed to be cursed by the heartbreak and insanity of the Witch of Shadows.

I slammed the book shut, my heart racing. There was something sickeningly familiar about the story. It was as if I was having a bout of déjà vu. It made me feel nauseous. As I was reading it I knew this was not a story written by Lucifer. Someone else had written it and crammed it in with the other fairy tales. But who would do that? And who would come up with such a vile story? It sent goosebumps shivering down my arms. Lucifer had written dark tales and acted them out with what most people would see as creepy puppet dolls. But somehow, this story was different. It left me with a strange feeling in my stomach. It was the familiarity that crept under my skin, unsettling me. I shoved the book back in the corner.

I tried to shake the story from my mind. I had other things to focus on, like getting my business up and running again. I busied myself for the rest of the day experimenting with new solutions, mixtures and combinations to create the perfect remedies but whenever I stopped for a single moment, my mind drifted back to that gruesome story. I didn't know what it meant. It was like a question mark hanging over me, an unfinished story that I was somehow responsible for completing.

PART IV

MADNESS

Dover, 1849

Chapter 21

WE HAD SETTLED into a calm routine. Winter rolled by. We were supposed to travel that summer but Danior had broken his leg falling out of a tree. Although it had healed fast, we had to wait another winter before we could travel. Willowen was getting restless. He was happy I was better and flourishing with my reignited passion for healing and my business. He, however, was aching for the open road. Several friends from the camp visited us and gave us updates on where they were going, who had recently given birth and who had sadly succumbed to illness. A heavy sadness hung over Willowen after these visits. I knew he was missing the group, travel and freedom that went with the whole lifestyle. I could sense that the shaky semblance of peace we had found here was coming to an end.

It was a chilly autumn evening and I was packing up the vials and pots from my stall. I had established quite a name for myself and a reputation for making fast-healing ointments and remedies.

"Need any help?" Willowen asked.

"No, I think that's the last of it," I said, packing the last few bottles into a wagon.

"Let me take that to the caravan," he said. "I just wanted a few moments to talk to you about something."

I nodded, waiting for him to speak.

"We should be travelling soon. It'll probably take several months before we are able to meet up with the group. Although I have a rough idea where they are, I'm not entirely sure."

I nodded again before answering. I knew he was right. We couldn't stay here forever. And yet, there was something about being back on the road, the uncertainty that went hand in hand with the freedom that filled me with a heavy dread.

"You're right," I said, after several moments of mental deliberation. "We've stayed here long enough. Where is the camp heading?"

Relief flooded over Willowen's features as his face broke into a smile. "I heard from Johnny that they're on route to a town in Dover. I think if we leave soon, we can join them either on the road or in the town itself."

"How soon should we leave?"

"Well, within the next few days." Willowen shrugged casually.

"It'll be a shock for the kids, to just up and leave that quickly," I said, before I could stop myself.

Willowen looked at me surprised. "They're used to this life, Roz. It's these past couple of years that have been the blip in their lives. We've been waiting for you to get back on your feet, then Danior, quite literally, and now you both are ready, it's the perfect time to move on. The kids will be delighted. They'll be able to see all their old friends. It will be like going home."

I couldn't help but silently disagree. A lump lodged itself in my throat, preventing me from answering. I smiled up at him, pretending to agree. It certainly had not been just a blip. We had stayed with the Millers, been a part of their family for nearly two years. That was a lifetime for the children. I sensed they wouldn't be quite as understanding as Willowen was making out.

I knew this day had been coming though. I couldn't put my finger on what exactly was holding me back. I could never admit to Willowen that I actually preferred the settled down life, the calm simplicity, the predictability of each day. I had never experienced such a life. Deep down I had known all along that these moments, these past couple of years, were stolen. Like a thief in the night, I had crept into someone else's life, adopted their possessions, pilfered their routine. But now it was time to give all those things back. Willowen was right. This life was never truly mine to have. It was time to move on.

I broke the news to the children the next day.

"We're leaving? But why?" Joni and Logan said in unison.

"This was never a permanent thing. We were only supposed to stay until I had recovered from Edwina's birth and then Danior had to recover from his injury. Well, both of those things have happened. We can't stay with the Millers forever."

"Do they not like us?" Danior asked, confusion, like a dark cloud, spreading over his childish features.

298

"They love you, sweetheart," I replied.

"Then why are we leaving?" he persisted.

"Won't you be excited to see your friends Leo and Clem again?" I said, trying to change tack.

Danior didn't seem convinced.

"Daddy and Auntie Bertha? Coming too?" Edwina piped up.

"Of course they are," I replied, pleased that I could say something reassuring.

Edwina nodded, seemingly satisfied with the state of events.

"When do we have to leave?" Logan asked, a shadow of sullen obstinance crossing his face.

"We can start packing up our things today and be ready to leave the day after tomorrow."

"That soon?" Joni cried. "No, I don't want to go that soon. I have friends here!"

"We can come back and visit one day," I said weakly. "Listen, this is your father's decision and it's final." I couldn't help but feel a bitter satisfaction shifting the blame onto him.

"Well, he can go and we can stay here with the Millers," Joni replied, just as stubborn as her twin.

"No, sweetheart, you're coming with us," I said softly.

Joni burst into tears and stormed out of the room. As if joined by an invisible tie, Logan followed her, his brows knitted together.

"You're ok with this, right?" I asked Danior, putting my arm around him.

He shrugged, his eyes glued to the floor. "I'll start packing my pebble collection," he said suddenly, gently pushing my arm off him.

"Ok, darling. Let me know if you want any help packing," I said, a hint of desperation creeping into my voice.

"At least you're not mad at me," I said to Edwina when all the others had left the room.

Edwina smiled a wide happy smile. "Not mad, never mad!" Then she started babbling to herself in a language only she understood.

* * * * *

We left the warmth and security of the Millers' house a couple of days later.

"We will miss you and the little dears," Mrs Miller said tearfully.

The tall, rake-thin Mr Miller nodded solemnly in acquiescence.

I took Mrs Miller's hand in mine. "Thank you for all you've done. We will never forget your kindness."

Mrs Miller smiled as several tears rolled down her cheeks. The twins were scuffing their feet on the ground, standing close together. Danior was trying to put on a brave face but was clearly fighting back tears. The only one oblivious to all the upset was little Edwina. Even Bertha looked tearful.

"How can we ever repay you for your generosity?" Willowen was saying.

"It's simple Christian charity to help those in need," Mr Miller said. "Besides, you did more than your fair share of work whilst you were staying here. It's us who should be thanking you."

"You take good care of yourselves and the little darlings," Mrs Miller said, patting the twins on the shoulder and giving Danior a big hug. Danior let out several muffled sobs. I felt my heart would break at the sound.

Finally, we managed to gather up our belongings and part ways with the Millers. I wondered if I would ever see them again or if they were to be consigned to the graveyard of my past from this moment on. I took one last look at the cottage. An aura of peace draped over it, keeping all its inhabitants safe. Now we were heading back into the cruel jaws of reality, fighting with the merciless forces of nature.

Autumn leaves outlined with glistening morning frost were scattered on the cracked ground. Winter was approaching fast. I understood Willowen's need to go back to the camp but we could have ridden out one more winter in the safety and warmth of the cottage, I thought, exasperated. Stress and anxiety gnawed on my nerves. What if we couldn't find food for the children? What if they got sick from the cold? When I had shared my worries with Willowen he had simply laughed.

"Even in winter I can catch fish and rabbits and keep us fed. And look at you with all your healing lotions and potions! You've built up quite the reputation reaching far and wide. You'll have plenty of buyers in the new town and probably on the road there as well. Neither of those things are going to happen!"

It was true. We did make a good team with our combined skills. But still, one could never predict when an accident or tragedy may strike. Despite his constant reassurances, I couldn't shake off the ominous feeling I had. I was not as young as I used to be and the constant trekking, stumbling and ducking through hedges exhausted me.

"You're tired," Bertha stated one particularly icy morning.

"A little," I said, trying to offer up my best attempt at a smile.

"We should have stayed."

"I agree, but you know Willowen. Once he has an idea in his head, that's it. There's no two ways about it."

"This isn't good for you," Bertha said, her brows furrowing in the middle.

"Do you know how much longer it'll take us to reach the campsite? I've started losing track of days and time." I sighed.

"*And reality,*" a malevolent, gritty voice whispered in my head.

I froze.

"At this pace, it'll probably take a couple more weeks or so," Bertha replied.

I couldn't hear her. I couldn't see where I was. I could no longer feel the cold as it swept over my skin. I had heard it, as clear as a bell. Panic gripped me with its iron fist.

"Are you ok?" Bertha's voice echoed from somewhere far away.

Willowen and the children were further up and hadn't noticed anything.

I nodded automatically. "Yes, fine. I'm just tired," I said hurriedly.

"You look like you've seen a ghost," Bertha replied, unconvinced.

I hadn't seen it. I had heard it. The whispering ghosts that I thought I had shut out were clamouring to find their way back in. They sensed weakness and fear. This was their cue. This was how it all started. Soon their voices would rise, vying for attention, shifting me further and further from reality. I didn't have the strength to fight them any more.

"Where's Mummy?" a high-pitched childish voice floated from further down the road.

My head snapped up. Edwina was spinning around on Willowen's shoulders, her wide dark eyes searching the barren landscape for me.

"I'm just behind you, sweetheart. Mummy's just a bit tired today," I said, hearing the false cheer ringing in my voice.

"I want to be with Mummy," Edwina continued, kicking her chubby legs in the air.

"All right, all right," Willowen said, setting her down. "Go keep Mummy company."

Edwina ran towards me, her cheeks flushed pink from the cold.

I scooped her up in my arms. "Hello, darling," I whispered into her thick, curly hair.

Her solid presence in my arms reminded me that I had to carry on. I didn't have a choice. Through sheer willpower I would silence the demons. My mind whirled with potential remedies. I had tried laudanum, been dosed up with chloroform and had blood drained from my veins with knives and leeches. There were still scars riddling my arms where the doctor had nicked my veins in an attempt to dispel the bad blood. Perhaps the vile blood had piled up again. Maybe I needed to do my own blood-letting. But I couldn't do it now. It had made me feel desperately weak at the time. I needed physical strength to keep going. If there was a doctor or healer at the next campsite, I decided I would be sure to pay them a visit.

We continued on like this as time slipped past me. Seconds, minutes, hours sprinkled around me like miniature snowflakes. I kept my head down and continued to plough forward, battling with multiple forces, both internal and external. I was an exhausted warrior, slicing through the cold, dispelling the tiredness from my aching bones and wrestling with the whispers that kept penetrating my mind.

* * * * *

It was one of the last sunny days of the year when we reached the camp. Our shadows stretched tall in the cold glow of the midday sun. Tendrils of smoke from a nearby field promised warmth and food for our empty stomachs.

"Who's hungry?" I asked my jostling group of children.

"Me, I'm starving!" Danior said immediately.

"We've both been hungry for days," Joni said, rolling her eyes.

Logan nodded in agreement. Edwina simply shrugged as if food and basic sustenance meant nothing to her.

"Well, you see that smoke over there," I said, pointing. "That's were our friends are. It looks like they're making lunch and keeping warm."

"Stop calling them that," Logan muttered mutinously.

"Calling them what, sweetheart?"

"Friends!" he exploded. "We don't even remember them really. They're not our friends."

I stared, feeling hurt, empty and powerless.

"We had friends back when we were staying at the Millers," Logan continued.

I expected outbursts from Joni but not Logan. Although he always sided with her, he was not the one to lash out at me. The thought that I had upended their lives and caused even a hint of pain left me feeling broken.

"I know you did," I replied softly. "I'm sorry about all this. But you'll make new friends. You'll get used to this lifestyle again. It's full of adventures."

"I like adventures," Danior stated, as if that solved all our problems. "Do you think they'll remember us?"

I smiled. "I'm glad, dear, and yes, I'm sure they'll remember you."

I heard an eruption of cheers and laughter from the area where the smoke was rising. Willowen had been ahead of us and must have reached them. Bertha, who had been drifting by my side like a silent shadow, squeezed the palm of my hand. She gave me one of her rare reassuring smiles.

We followed the noise and commotion until we tumbled into the campsite. Immediately we were inundated with hugs and whoops of joy. I couldn't help but feel overwhelmed with emotion as I saw familiar faces I hadn't seen in years. The joy was infectious and soon even Joni was smiling and chatting to the other children.

Isolde spotted me and ran to give me an embrace. She kissed my cheeks. "It's so good to have you back! We have so much catching up to do!"

"Yes, we definitely do," I replied.

We fell into easy conversation, as if we had not been separated for over two years.

Later that evening, we sat around the fire, keeping warm and eating piping hot stew until sunset. With a full stomach and the warmth of the fire embracing me, I felt that maybe things would be all right after all. Edwina nestled into my lap and closed her eyes. Absent-mindedly I stroked her hair. Perhaps I had worried unnecessarily. Perhaps this new chapter in our lives wouldn't be so bad. I caught Willowen staring at me from across the fire. His rugged features looked tired but happy. He raised his glass and smiled at me. I smiled back, feeling that this was a new beginning, the start of our new lives.

* * * * *

Days after we had settled in that campsite, we were on the move again. We needed to find somewhere to ride out the winter which threatened to come early this year. There was a town near the port called St Margaret's at Cliffe which Willowen had heard was friendly to gypsies. Being located by the port, the town was used to receiving gaggles of people from strange lands, near and far. Willowen had already established work for the men by the port. There was also space by the cliffs to park the caravans and set up camp. All the pieces of the puzzle seemed to be falling into place.

The children were excited to be settling down again. I could tell they hadn't inherited the travel bug from their father. At least for the next few months I felt relieved that I could promise them the illusion of stability.

We made it to the town on a bitterly cold day. The winds buffeted our caravans back and forth as if they were made of nothing more than straw. The horses whinnied, stomping their hooves nervously, rocking the caravans even more. One nearly bolted, but Willowen managed to grab the frantic horse by the mane, whispering calming words into his ear whilst stroking him gently.

Most of the inhabitants of the town were tucked away behind closed doors, hiding from the impending storm. The wind screeched as we drew closer to the cliffs where we would be camping. Swollen dark clouds loomed closer, chasing us, amidst the leaden grey sky. As soon as we reached the cliffs, the downpour began.

"Is the caravan going to break?" Danior asked, his wide eyes shining with fear.

"Scaredy," Joni taunted, although I detected a quiver in her bravado.

"The caravan will be fine. It's withstood worse than this," I said, in what I hoped was a confident voice.

A bolt of lightning slashed through the sky, striking the sea's heart. Danior jumped. The twins shifted closer together. Edwina, however, moved closer to the window, her eyes glued to the flashing light.

Thunder rolled in the background. I felt its vibrations as the caravan quivered.

"It's just a storm. It'll pass." I unpacked a flurry of blankets I had made earlier in the year. "Here, everyone get cosy and we'll ride out the storm together."

"Where's Daddy?" Danior asked.

"He's just doing the rounds, checking on everyone else. I think Elsie's caravan has a leak and he's working on that. That's what Daddy does. He looks after everybody. How about you play a game?" I suggested, hoping to take their minds off the storm.

Logan fished out a deck of cards from his pocket. "I found these a while back. Let's do something with them," he said.

"Good idea," I replied, my gaze drifting over the cards. They looked like tarot cards. "Where'd you get those?" I asked absently, glancing at Edwina, who was still staring out of the window.

"I just found them," he replied, sitting cross-legged on the floor. "Who wants this creepy skeleton one?"

"Me," Joni said immediately.

"Which one do I get?" Danior chimed in.

Soon they were all in a circle, flicking through the cards, making up their own rules to the game which would certainly end in bickering.

I couldn't concentrate. My attention was drawn to the outdoors. Something was shifting along the cliff edge. It fluttered and perched on a broken, bent tree branch. It faced the window where I was staring. Even amidst the waterfall of rain, I could make out the blurry image of a slick, black bird. Its beak opened just as an eruption of thunder reverberated through the air. I knew if it weren't for the thunder, I would hear the harsh, cruel laughter bubbling from the bird's open beak. I glanced down.

To my horror Edwina was still there, staring transfixed at the same broken tree branch. At the same gruesome bird. At the same foreboding delusion. I grabbed her, glancing quickly back at the tree. There was nothing on the sodden horizon. No bird, no wicked laughter. It was just a blurry mirage with the scenery melting off the water-sloshed canvas. Edwina's eyes traced the broken tree branch before looking up at me. She smiled a strange smile.

"What were you looking at, sweetheart?" I asked.

"Same as you, Mummy," Edwina said, before babbling in her own language.

* * * * *

The storm raged for several days. Its unrelenting onslaught prevented us from exploring the village, establishing work and mingling with the townsfolk as we usually did when we first arrived in new towns. I knew some of my fellow travellers had started up seances in basements and in the dark corners of public houses. They used the weather to their advantage with the erratic flashes of light and ominous thunder enhancing the spooky atmosphere. It brought back memories of the seances Mother used to do. Several of the women had asked me if I wanted to join them. One of them said that my blue eyes could help create a sense of atmosphere. I didn't think I'd ever be ready to re-join that dark, shadowy world and politely declined each request.

I tried to focus on my remedies but found my concentration ebbing slowly away from me. I could spend countless hours staring at the waves beating the cliffs in fits of passionate rage. Just as the children were about to tear the caravan apart from boredom, the storm finally subdued.

"Can we go out and play today?" Danior asked, as the cold morning light spilt through the caravan.

"Yes, all of you out!" I said in a mock serious tone. "Make the most of the calm weather before the next storm sets in."

All at once, they tumbled out of the caravan onto the damp earth.

"Be careful. Don't go too near the cliff edge," I said, eying the perilous drop from the cliffs.

"We'll be careful," Logan shouted over his shoulder.

I saw several of the other children being jostled out of their respective caravans. I felt a sense of peace as I watched them run around and play games with wet leaves, twigs and stones. My eyes cast over the scene and landed on where Edwina was sitting, alone on a tree stump. She looked as if she was talking to herself. I felt unsettled as I watched her. I would have to keep a closer eye on her and talk to Joni and Logan about including her in their games. Just as I was about to go outside and state my new dictates, Willowen burst into the caravan.

"Hello, love," he said breathlessly. "It's cold out there but at least there's no rain."

"At last we have some respite," I agreed.

"I've rallied up the men and we should be heading to St Margaret's port now. A bunch of sailors are apparently docking this week. It's said to be a huge crew. They set off to Asia over two years ago and are coming home."

"That should be nice for their families," I said, not quite absorbing what Willowen was saying. My attention was still focused on Edwina.

"I'm sure so. There's going to be celebrations all around the town. We should prepare something. Perhaps some music or food for the festivities."

"Good idea," I replied.

"You ok?" Willowen asked suddenly, slicing through my thoughts. "You've been a bit absent lately."

I noticed the familiar note of concern creep into his deliberately calm voice. I shook myself out of my reverie and turned to face him, giving him my full attention. "I'm fine. I'm just glad there's something to do now the weather has cleared. I'll talk to the other women and see what we can do for the sailors and their families."

"Perfect," Willowen said, beaming. "It'll be the ideal opportunity to ingratiate ourselves with the community."

He pecked me on the cheek before slipping out to prepare the port. Like a magnet, my gaze drifted back to the tree stump where Edwina had been sitting. To my relief it was vacant. Edwina was playing chase with her brothers, sister and a couple of the other children. I smiled. There was nothing to worry about. It wouldn't be the first time a child had an imaginary friend.

I decided to fulfil my promise to Willowen and talk to the other women regarding what to do for the celebrations. I would start with Bertha and Isolde. I wrapped myself up in several layers of blankets and shawls before braving the cold. As I stepped out, the distinct sound of a raven's caw rattled my composure. My head spun around so quickly I heard something click. Rubbing my neck, I scanned the horizon. No birds. No ravens. Perhaps it was one of the children mimicking the ominous black bird's tongue. I scuttled off to Isolde's caravan.

"I could do my fortune telling in a tent somewhere during the festivities. Everyone always wants their fortunes told," Isolde said excitedly.

"True," I replied. I had always had an aversion to fortune telling. I found that it was bad enough experiencing life events once, let alone being prepared to experience them and then being forced to deal with them.

"What about you? What will you do?" Isolde asked. "Why not hold a seance? Some of the women were saying you used to do those. I can imagine you being very convincing."

"That's a little dark for a homecoming," I replied hastily.

"I know, but they're always popular." Isolde shrugged. "Will Willowen play the flute? I'm sure the townsfolk will love it. The way he plays the flute is magical."

"I'll ask him."

Willowen was skilled at playing many instruments but especially the flute. He had the power to transport listeners to another time and place where reality released its vice-like grip, if only for a few minutes.

"When will the ships arrive?" Isolde asked.

"Within the next few days. It's pretty good timing what with us just arriving. We'll create a festive atmosphere they'll never forget!"

"And hopefully in turn, they'll give us food and a place to shelter for the winter. It seems like we're in for a really nasty winter this year," Isolde added.

"I'm sure it'll all work out." I smiled.

Just then a shiver snaked its way down my spine. I pulled the blankets tightly around my shoulders, feeble protection from the sense of foreboding that was growing within.

* * * * *

The ships arrived on a moody, overcast day. The clouds hung low over the sea, threatening a deluge. From my vantage point I could see the port and the crowds gathering. They moved as grey smudgy blurs. Willowen would be part of that bustle. He and several others had gone to help unload the crates from the ships. I could imagine the excitement of seeing loved ones sweeping contagiously through the crowds.

The children were weaving dolls and handkerchiefs to sell. They were with Isolde as she had more lace and materials than I had. I slipped outside. The biting wind immediately crept under my layers of clothes and blankets. I perched on a smooth rock lodged securely into the cliff edge, watching the waves crash into the cliff rocks beneath me. I stared into the watery depths of the ocean, mesmerised by its timeless beauty. As I was staring transfixed, I heard them. My children's voices floated to me from the ether beyond. My mind was immersed in a thick dense fog. I strained my ears to hear what they were saying. They were upset, pleading. My heart thumped wildly in my chest. Why couldn't I hear them? Instinctively I turned to the tree next to our caravan. To my horror, four birds were perched there. One of the ravens opened its break and spoke.

"*You've trapped us. You need to let us be free,*" it said in Joni's voice.

"*Let us be free, Mother,*" said the one balancing next to it, speaking in Logan's voice.

"*Why don't you listen to us?*" Danior's voice pleaded.

"*Because she thinks they are her children,*" the smallest raven said in Edwina's voice, pointing her beak over her shoulder. "*She's wrong. We are.*"

In a daze, I turned to see who the Edwina raven was gesturing towards. Everything was happening in slow motion. My movements required momentous effort, and the seconds stretched as I turned to look over my shoulder. I saw the twins, Danior and Edwina tumble out of Isolde's caravan, carrying bundles in their arms. As if the spell was broken, my head snapped back to the entourage of birds. The slow, sludgy feeling disintegrated. All but one, the smallest one, were gone. Her beady eyes bore into mine. Although the bird's beak remained tightly shut, I heard her voice in my head. Except it wasn't Edwina's soft, childish voice. Her voice was hard, like a pile of rocks thundering down on me.

"*You know we're right.*"

With that the bird flew away, swallowed up by the dark, menacing horizon.

"Look what we made!" Danior exclaimed excitedly.

"Do you think people will buy this?" Joni was asking dubiously.

"Yes, they're lovely," I said vaguely. I did my best at pretending to inspect the handkerchiefs, scarves and dolls the children had made. I tried to focus on the colours and stitching but my mind was still swirling with a hazy fog, dragging me into pools of darkness. Why did the birds say what they had just said? Why did they claim to be my children? Had I trapped them somehow? Questions swirled around until I couldn't make sense of what I was thinking.

I tried to busy myself that day by cooking and preparing for the evening's celebrations. All the while my eyes were continually drawn to the tree where the birds had perched menacingly. I couldn't get their voices, my children's voices, out of my head. I was waiting, hoping, that the ravens would come back. We needed to continue the conversation.

Willowen returned from the port just as I was swaddling the children in scarves and hats.

"I don't need all these layers," Logan was grumbling.

"Take them off then," Willowen stated in a low voice. "There are no celebrations tonight."

I swivelled around, not recognising the surly note in my husband's voice. His face was the colour of ash and there was a hollowness that lurked behind his pale eyes.

"Children, inside," I said instinctively. Whatever was going on, I could tell it was not meant for children's ears.

"What! But we made all this stuff. Aren't we going to sell it?" Joni demanded, not wanting her hard work to go to waste.

"Not today," Willowen replied sharply.

Immediately all the children piled into the caravan, tension intermingling with their whispers. Willowen was rarely sharp with the children. He was the soft, gentle one. The one who took care of them when Mummy couldn't.

"What is it? What happened at the port?" I asked as I heard the caravan door slam shut.

Willowen looked down, rubbing his hands together for warmth. I noticed his fingertips looked blue. I took his icy hands in mine and rubbed them to bring back the circulation.

"What is it?" I asked again. "You're scaring me."

Willowen lifted his gaze to meet mine. "It was terrible, Roz," he replied slowly. "So many families, mothers, wives, children were there to greet the sailors. There was such excitement. When the first ship docked I just felt something wasn't right. Some of the men and I went on deck to see if we could help unload crates or barrels. There were only a few crew members on board the first ship. There should have been at least fifty men on that ship. There were twelve." Willowen paused, seemingly lost for what to say next.

"Where were the rest?" I asked, feeling a chill seep through my bones.

Willowen sighed before continuing. "They had stored the bodies of several of the men who had died recently, within the past day or two. They would have thrown the bodies overboard but were afraid they would wash up on the shore here since they were so close. There were at least ten corpses on the lower deck."

"And the rest of the fifty?"

"Thrown overboard after they succumbed to some strange illness. The sailors that were still alive said the men started dropping like flies after they had left some island in Asia. Not all the families have been told yet. Only the ones whose bodies were kept so that a proper burial can be arranged."

"How terrible. What a tragedy for the town," I said, thinking of all those hopes dashed and tears of joy morphing into tears of heartbreak. "I have to do something for these people. Are the twelve sailors on the first ship well? I imagine if they were exposed to the illness, they may need something to help them heal."

"I don't think it's a good idea that you get involved," Willowen said in a warning tone. "I don't want you to get sick."

A bitterness twisted within me at that comment. I had been sick my whole life, just not with the physical type of ailments that the sailors had.

"I want to help," I said firmly. "I'll pay the twelve from the first ship a visit first thing tomorrow and see how they're doing. I'll bring along my best remedies and cures."

"Roz, I don't like the sound of this," Willowen said again cautiously.

"You said we need to ingratiate ourselves with the townsfolk. It doesn't look like there will be any celebrations but let me help in this way, in a way I know how."

A sceptical expression remained on Willowen's face as he observed me. He knew once something was lodged in my mind I would follow through with it. I had always been stubborn that way.

"You'll have to be careful. Don't get too close to them. They could be carrying the disease."

"Of course. I'll get to work now."

I was almost relieved for the distraction. The birds with the voices of my children had been playing on my mind in a continuous loop. I couldn't count the number of times I had gone outside simply to stare at the tree, willing the birds to come back and validate what I thought I had heard.

Now I had a mission, to help cure the sailors or at least dress the wounds they had surely got at sea. I worked the rest of the day and into the night, my mind so full of ingredients and mixtures there was no space for anything else.

Chapter 22

IT WAS EASY to locate the twelve sailors. Most of them were in their homes being nursed by mothers and wives. They were relieved when I showed up with my healing paraphernalia and watched as I dressed the wounds. The first three I visited displayed similar symptoms of fatigue, nausea and mild fever. I recommended herbs and tonics to help ease their symptoms.

I reached the next house on my list, immediately recoiling as the door was opened. The stench of urine and vomit wafted from the belly of the diseased home. I tied a scented handkerchief around my face to make the stench slightly more bearable.

"Help him," a frail thin women pleaded. Pale wisps of blonde hair peeped out from under her tattered bonnet. Her eyes were equally pale with dark circles spreading like bruises underneath.

"You're his wife?" I asked.

She nodded, a solitary tear gliding like a smooth pearl down her gaunt cheek. Several young children were huddled in a corner in the kitchen. Their glasslike eyes were empty and staring. Fear and death mingled within the air of the house. Suddenly I felt suffocated. I just wanted to turn and run far from this place. I had come to help, I reminded myself. And this family certainly needed it.

The wife led me to her husband's room. The smell was overpowering, assaulting my nostrils and mouth. I could taste the sour vomit that caked the floor by the bed. A bucket full of bloody urine sat underneath the cracked window.

"How long has he been like this?" I managed to ask without choking on the smell.

"He was weak when he arrived. He had a fever and a bad rash all over his body. He got worse overnight. You can see the rash has turned into these bumps and he's been vomiting non-stop. He can't keep anything down. He was a bag of bones when he arrived but now he's naught more than a skeleton." The woman knelt by his side, oblivious to the odour. Gently she wiped the corners of his mouth congealed with dried vomit.

Just from looking at him I knew this was beyond my healing abilities. I could help heal the living, but this man was one step away from the grave.

"Here, I have a tonic to help ease any pain he may be feeling," I said in a low voice so as not to disturb his slumber. His eyes were closed but I could see flickers of movement behind the taut, nearly transparent eyelids. "Also, there's this ointment for his skin. I don't think it'll make the rashes and bumps go away but it may make them less irritated."

The wife nodded and began to weep silently. "There's nothing that can be done?" she asked between sobs.

"Try these and pray. Death can be a mercy sometimes," I said, staring at the skeletal man lying within sheets covered in grime and filth. His breath came in ragged rasps. Was this how the other men had died, I wondered. How harrowing it must have been for the other sailors to have had to deal with so many gruesome deaths, trapped aboard that ship, a floating mausoleum.

"I'll help you change the sheets if you want," I said, trying to think of any way that I could be helpful.

She nodded. "I boiled the only other sheets we have the other day. They should be dry by now."

She tiptoed out of the room to fetch the sheets. The man groaned, opening his mouth as if unable to breathe the air within the room. Angry red sores lined his mouth. I turned away, unable to look at the decay and rotting flesh.

His wife returned and ever so gently we managed to roll him over and slip the grimy sheets off the bed. I noticed his back was covered in a battlefield of scars and peeling scabs. Together we placed the fresh sheets under him. He didn't open his eyes. I would have thought him already dead if it weren't for the few moans and gurgling breaths he emitted.

"Thank you," the woman said as she returned me to the door. "How much is it for the tonic and ointment?"

I waved my hand, dismissing the offer of payment. "Nothing. Let's just pray he gets better." I was not religious, but I felt prayers would be just as helpful as my tonics for this man, and perhaps more so for the wife.

"Thank you. Bless you," she said quietly before shutting the door.

I spun around and walked briskly home. I let the cold fresh air pierce my lungs as I whipped off the scented handkerchief. After that, I decided I would be done for the day.

When I reached home, I was surprised to see Bertha pacing outside the caravan. She reminded me of the horses, stamping their feet, emitting low whinnies when nervous.

"Bertha," I called out. "Is everything all right?"

Cutting to the chase, as was her usual manner, she replied, "I have bad news."

A wave of exhaustion swept over me. Bad news seemed to be stalking us lately like a shadow. "Come in," I said.

The interior of the caravan was hardly warmer than the exterior. I handed her a pile of blankets to keep warm.

"What's going on?" I asked, not wanting to hear the answer.

"I went to church," Bertha stated.

I nodded, encouraging her to continue. She took a deep sigh as if preparing to run a marathon.

"I went to church," she repeated. "The preacher, George Hillock, was talking. He does not like our presence here. Says we have brought the Devil to this village. He has heard of our palm reading, fortune telling and seances. He says this is Satan's work and the town will be punished for allowing us to remain here."

"But that's absurd. The townsfolk have been asking us for seances and palm reading. Surely they don't suddenly believe this is the work of the Devil? We're just supplying the already present demand," I replied.

"I couldn't tell everyone's reaction. But people in the congregation were nodding. We're not safe here."

"We'll stop holding seances then if they're so disturbing. The men can still help with repairs and unloading the ships docking at the port. I don't think we need to leave just yet because of the ramblings of one preacher."

Bertha twisted her bony hands, rubbing her swollen knuckles. "Hillock said we were a band of witches," she said finally.

I let out a sharp burst of laughter. "No one would believe that. Witchcraft is a thing of the past. Look, I'll tell Willowen and see what he thinks. Winter is around the corner. It's not a good time to be on the road."

"The open road seems just as good as here, if not better," Bertha continued.

I couldn't help but be surprised by her argument. She rarely strung two sentences together but now she would not let this go. As if to prove her point, an icy gust of wind blew across the surface of the sea, rattling through the entire caravan. Bits of paper were buffeted around as empty vials toppled over.

"You're right, this could be something serious," I conceded. "I'll talk to Willowen tonight about it. I promise."

Bertha nodded, not looking reassured. "I must go," she said suddenly.

"Stay for dinner," I countered, immediately regretting it. We only had a ration of potatoes and hard bread packed away.

"That's ok," Bertha replied, without providing any excuses or reasons. "Talk to Willowen."

"I will," I confirmed.

Exhaustion rippled through my senses as Bertha headed to the door. It had been a long day. I felt my energy had been sapped by that house where death lingered within its cracks and crevices. The poor man probably only had days if not hours left to live.

"Take care," Bertha said earnestly, before slipping outside. A current of bitter cold air swept through the caravan again as Bertha left.

I lay down, bundled under a pile of blankets. I was just going to close my eyes for a minute. Within seconds I fell into a deep sleep no amount of noise from the children or Willowen stomping around the caravan could wake me from.

* * * * *

The next day, I went to the houses of the twelve sailors, checking to see if they were getting better. To my horror, all their symptoms had gone from bad to worse overnight, even the ones who had barely presented with symptoms in the first place. The day after, eight of them had died in agony. There was to be a mass ceremony for them that coming Sunday. I decided I would attend. It seemed the right thing to do as I had been the one trying to heal them in their last few days of life.

It was a chilly day, one of the coldest so far this year. The sky, a heavy leaden grey, hung low overhead. I had lost track of time that morning and was going to be late for the Sunday ceremony. I couldn't remember why I was late or where I had been. I only knew that I was supposed to be at the funeral and, for some reason, I wasn't there. I was experiencing more and more blank chunks of time where I couldn't recount where I had gone or what I had been doing. The familiar sensations of fear and confusion swept through me. I tried to convince myself that this was due to the stress and anxiety of the oncoming winter. Not to mention the long hours I had spent trying to heal those who were already damned to the grave. I couldn't help but feel the weight of their loss of life as a personal burden and failure. Even as I was thinking of all the excuses I could possibly make, I could tell my mind was again slipping away from me, bit by bit.

I walked to the church, hearing whispers in the bony, naked trees. They were watching me, accusing me. I arrived too late for the sermon but found the gathering huddled in a black bundle outside. The flimsy wooden coffins were being lowered into the cracked, dry mouth of the earth.

"This is the fate of those who put their trust in anyone's hands but God's," a bellowing voice erupted from the centre of the black shroud of people.

There was a cruel harshness in the voice that made me stop in my tracks. Wrapping my scarves around me, I leaned against a nearby tree. I tried to see who was speaking. Judging by his tone, I guessed it was the same preacher, Hillock, Bertha had told me about a couple of days ago. Guilt as well as a sense of foreboding began to swell within my chest, constricting my breath. I had meant to talk to Willowen the same night Bertha had warned me about the village. Instead, I had slept and completely forgotten my promise the next day. But had it been two days ago? Or was it a week? The structure of time into hours, days and weeks didn't seem to make sense any more. Everything was happening all at once. The past, present and future were all mashed together, raining down on me in a downpour of confusion.

"These unfortunate souls lost their way. We cannot blame them. But we must learn from their fates. God is the Almighty and only God can give and take life."

A small murmur or agreement rippled through the crowd.

"This illness, this disease, is of no earthly origin," Hillock continued in a more sombre tone. "Satan is amongst us because we have strayed from the path of righteousness. Satan has many faces and it is only through prayer and our Holy Bible that we can find redemption."

"But we have all prayed every day for their safe return. We have all attended service," a woman managed between sobs. "Where is it we have gone wrong, Father?" She held her handkerchief to her face and wept. Another woman placed a comforting arm around her.

"It is not you, good women and men of this village, who have strayed from the path of God and light. But you have let evil into this village without knowing it. They came under shadow of darkness with curses and spells we know are in league with the Devil. They have brought this curse to us. The band of witches and heathens infiltrated our God-fearing town with all the stealth of a black cat out for the kill."

"But they've been helpful to us. They helped rebuild some of the ships," a small, thin man piped up.

"Yes, the ships that brought in the disease," bellowed Hillock, as if proving his point.

Mutterings erupted throughout the congregation.

"The last person to see my husband was that dark-haired woman, a Mrs Woodlock, if I do recall her name correctly," a pinched-face woman exclaimed.

"And mine, she was last to see mine," another shouted.

"She gave some strange potions to my husband. He died within a few hours after her visit!" a disembodied voice yelled.

My head was swirling. I had to get out of there. I felt powerless to move my legs. Rooted to the spot I heard accusation pile on top of fresh accusation. I heard my friends' names mentioned, the seances held in shadowy basements, how the townsfolk had been duped into believing them.

"My children, my children," Hillock said, in his booming voice. "Do not fear. We will root out the evil that has settled in our pure town. We will save your mothers, fathers, husbands, wives and children from this curse. We will bring them to justice!"

This didn't feel like a funeral. This felt like a witch hunt. The crowd was being whipped up into a frenzy of hysteria and madness. At last I regained control of my legs. I spun around, wrapped my head, face and shoulders in the scarves lest someone should recognise me. I fought my instinct to break into a run, terrified they would chase me down the road then and there, demanding their twisted form of justice. Whatever those men had died of, it wasn't any curses from the gypsy camp. My heart thumped in my chest as I walked as quickly as I could without drawing attention to myself. It felt like the longest walk of my life. I kept my head down but could hear voices trailing me. I couldn't tell if they were the villagers' voices or the demons in my head. Everything echoed around me. It was so loud I squeezed my hands over my padded ears.

"They're right."

"It's your fault."

"Murderer!"

By the time I reached the cliffs I was wild-eyed and panting. To my immense relief, Willowen was outside, a pile of timber in his arms.

"What's wrong?" he asked as soon as he saw me approaching.

I opened my mouth and immediately burst into sobs.

"Roz, you're scaring me," Willowen said, wrapping his arms around me. "Calm down and tell me what happened."

After several moments of chest-heaving sobs, I managed to calm down enough to speak. "The preacher, this town," I stammered. "We're not wanted here."

"What do you mean?" Willowen frowned.

"We're in danger," I continued, choking on my tears. "I went to the funeral of the sailors. I was late so kept my distance. Hillock was saying terrible things. He was saying we are in league with the Devil."

"You are," a sly voice whispered in my ear.

I frowned and shook my head, trying to focus on what Willowen was saying.

"From what I've gathered about this town, Hillock is a pretentious man who sees sin everywhere, in everyone and everything. People don't respect him here," Willowen tried to reassure me.

"They were listening to him this time!" I cried hysterically. "They were listening and even agreeing! My name came up as well."

"What do you mean?" Willowen asked, a note of worry creeping into his voice.

"They said I was the last to see their husbands alive. They implied that I killed them!" I was shaking uncontrollably.

Willowen was silent a moment before replying. "Don't stay here tonight. There's a husband and wife, Mr and Mrs Davies. They live near here, along the cliffs. They have a storage hut. I've been using it for some of my tools as I redo parts of their house. Their roof was falling in a few weeks ago and I fixed it. Take the children there. Tell them you're my wife. They are friendly and will take care of you." Willowen's face was as white as a sheet.

I nodded. A deathly calm had suddenly stolen over me. My eyes were transfixed at a spot just behind Willowen.

"Roz, did you hear me?" he asked, speaking louder.

"Yes, yes, I'll take the children there tonight," I said.

"Good, you go there. I will warn the rest. We'll probably have to leave within the next few days. Although I suspect this will turn out to be nothing more than general scare tactics, I don't want to take any risks. We shouldn't stay somewhere we are not welcome. We'll gather supplies for the road and be on our way."

He squeezed my arm then left to make the rounds. I remained rooted to the spot, suddenly impervious to the cold salty winds whipping my bare face and hands.

"Will you keep us safe, Mummy?" I heard Danior asking.

I turned my head slowly. Danior was nowhere to be seen. Instead, the big black ravens were perched in a row. Slowly, I walked closer to them.

"Of course," I heard myself reply.

"*We are your children. You must keep us safe, not those other ones,*" Joni's voice said disdainfully.

"What do you mean the other ones?" I asked, confusion spreading across my mind like a thick, dense fog.

"*Those imposters. They're not your children. We are,*" Joni's voice continued. "*You must protect us.*"

"I will. But how did they come to be imposters?"

"These townspeople are the devils, Mummy, not us. They have cursed us. They think you killed their husbands, so they placed your children inside the bodies of ravens. It's their ultimate revenge to punish you."

"I'll protect you," I stated emphatically. "You just follow where I go. Stay close to me."

The ravens ruffled their feathers as if in agreement. I stared at their sleek, black, beautiful coats. Their deep, soulful eyes penetrated my heart. Their delicate movements as they fluttered their wings and swayed on the branches inspired my desire to keep them safe, protect them at all costs.

"My beautiful babies," I whispered.

"Mummy, who are you talking to?"

I spun around. A boy who looked like Logan was standing there, with a strange expression playing across his face. I turned to look towards the tree. The ravens were gone. An unexplainable fury simmered within me. He had scared my babies away.

"No one," I snapped. I remembered what Willowen had said. It was time to play-act. Fear had evaporated from within me, replaced by a steely calm. I couldn't even remember what I had been afraid of in the first place. Everything was fine as long as my ravens were fine. It was time to play the role of worried wife and devoted mother to these imposters.

"We have to pack a few things and go to Mr and Mrs Davies' house down the road," I heard a voice that sounded like mine saying.

I walked past the child who looked like Logan, ignoring the strange expression that remained on his face like a mask.

I felt as if I was moving through water as I prepared a few cases of things to take with us. I kept checking over my shoulder to see if the ravens had reappeared. We left the caravan and carried our small cases. It was about a twenty-minute walk before we reached what I presumed was the Davies' house. I could see the hut squatting in a corner along the cliff edge. That must be where we would camp out along with Willowen's equipment and tools.

I knocked on the door and, as Willowen had promised, was greeted by warm, smiling faces that meant nothing to me. They ushered us in and fed us dinner. Although we talked and laughed I couldn't remember any of the conversation. It melted away almost immediately, as fresh snow does when it comes into contact with the skin. I was distracted. My gaze was continually pulled towards the windows, searching for the ravens I had sworn to protect. Where were they?

When Willowen returned that evening his face was grave. Mrs Davies gave him broth as he recounted what he had seen in the village.

"They have these wagons with cages. Human cages," Willowen said, trying to control the emotion in his voice. "I saw the police dragging women who had led some of the seances and palm readings from their caravans and shove them into the cages in front of their own children. I don't know where they've taken them. I don't want to ask even more of you, Mr Davies, you've already been so kind, but do you think you could find out where they're being held?"

"I will look into it," Mr Davies assured Willowen. "I'll pull every string I can to get answers. I don't understand this sudden mania," he said, shaking his head sadly.

"It's that wicked preacher Hillock," Mrs Davies chimed in. "He's the one full of sin, telling us villagers to persecute and drive out our new neighbours." Her face was aflame with anger.

Willowen turned to me. "You seem distracted. Are you feeling all right?"

I had been gazing out the window, barely listening to the conversation. "Yes, yes, I'm fine," I said, feigning tiredness. "It's just been a long, strange day."

All I wanted was to be left alone with my thoughts. I needed to hear the voices. I knew now they had been the voices of my babies all along. I had tried to silence and quiet them when really, I should have been listening. I had to set them free.

"That it has," Willowen concurred.

I didn't know what he was agreeing with or who he was talking to. I let my gaze drift past him. Who was he anyway? Was he even real or was he a figment of my imagination? Perhaps he was a character in one of Lucifer's stories come to life. For some reason that thought made me want to laugh. I let out a spluttering cough, unsure of how brazen laughter would be met with these strangers sitting next to me. But then again, did I actually care?

"We've set up mattresses in the hut. Unfortunately, the whole upper floor needs repairs so we can't offer you to stay here," Mrs Davies said apologetically.

"You are most kind," Willowen replied.

The children were already in the hut. I stared at it as we approached. It looked as if it might tumble into the sea at any given moment. Balancing between this world and the next gave it a certain ethereal beauty despite its small, squat stature. Something that could potentially be so temporary always had an added beauty to it. It was wild and free. It was exactly where I needed to be.

"You coming?" Willowen asked, as I paused before entering.

"I'll be there in a minute. Just need some fresh air to clear my mind."

"All right," Willowen replied, slightly concerned.

I had seen a flash of black wing and feather. I had to make sure the ravens had found our new home. Reluctantly, Willowen bowed under the entrance of the hut and shut the door behind him.

"We're here," I heard it whisper from behind a smooth stone rock wedged into the cliffs edge.

I knelt down on the cold surface of the stone. Although I knew it was cold, I had lost all sensation to the feeling. "You followed. Well done," I said proudly as I saw all four birds balancing on the rocky surface of the cliff edge.

"Of course. We will follow you anywhere," the girlish voice of Edwina said.

"Smart girl." I smiled as I reached out and stroked her feathers. They were soft and silky.

Just then Willowen peeped around the door. "Get inside, Roz! It's freezing out here," he exclaimed, frowning.

The same anger I had felt earlier bubbled within me. He was trying to separate me from my babies. I got up slowly and drifted into the hut.

"Are you sure you're feeling all right?" Willowen asked, concern melting away his anger.

"I'm going to sleep," I replied, not meeting his gaze. He wouldn't understand. The villagers were wicked and they had cursed my children. But they didn't know that I would move heaven and earth to get them back.

Chapter 23

W E STAYED IN the ramshackle hut for two more days as we stocked up on necessities. Willowen had rounded up some of the group who were camping out close to the Davies' house to escape with us when the time was right. Isolde and Fennix were the latest arrivals, along with their children, Leo and Clem.

"Thank goodness you're here," Isolde said as she embraced me. "I was so worried they got you too. My God, you're so thin though. Have you been eating anything at all lately?" Isolde added, staring at me.

I couldn't read her expression. It felt accusatory. Suspicion made the hair at the back of my neck stand on end. I was sure she had been my friend for a long time, but everything felt unclear. Was she concerned? Or was there a sinister note in her tone, a mocking laugh behind her words?

"I'm fine," I replied automatically. "I'm glad you're here." I was wracking my brain for what a normal person, a friend might say to another friend. Even as the words came out, they fell flat, lacking any real emotion.

Isolde continued to stare at me. "You've changed, Roz," she said. "Something about you is different. Are you sure you're all right?"

"We're being persecuted by a bunch of mad villagers. Of course I've changed," I quipped a little more harshly than intended. I seemed to have said the right words though. Isolde's expression immediately softened and saddened.

"I know. I can't believe it either. We've never been through something so terrible." Tears welled up in her eyes as she continued. "I'm not even afraid for myself. It's the children I'm worried about and what all this madness is doing to them. We had to hide in the cellar of the public house yesterday. The police were bashing on doors, yelling for us to come out. Luckily, Frederick, the owner of the place, took pity on us. It was awful though." She was speaking in little more than a whisper. She kept darting nervous glances at Leo and Clem who were sitting in the corner of the hut, subdued. "We were packed in there like cattle. I could hear the footsteps of the police above as they smashed things in the pub, accusing Frederick of being on our side. You know, there was a baby down there with us. It was the most terrifying moment when it opened its mouth to start crying. I can't tell you how fast my heart was beating. I thought I would pass out and throw up at the same time."

Silent tears were trickling down her face at this point. I watched, trying to stir up some feelings of sympathy or sadness. All I was met with was a gaping, hallow emptiness within me.

"Thank goodness Naomi had food and fed her immediately. That quietened her down. I keep saying this, but I can't believe this is happening to us."

"I know what you mean," I finally said. "It does feel like we're play-acting a role, that this can't possibly be our real lives."

"Exactly," Isolde said, wiping away the tears.

I nodded absently. I looked out of the window, always in search of my ravens. My real life was out there, waiting for me.

"Anyway, we'll let you rest. I believe the others are just down the road. We'll go stay with them. You look after yourself and make sure you eat something," Isolde said, as she stood to leave.

"I will," I said, unsure of what I was even agreeing to.

"I think we have to leave tonight or tomorrow," she continued. "I know Willowen wants to leave with as many of the group as possible, but we have to go before they catch us all."

"Yes, I'll speak to him," I said, trying to force my brain into action.

There was real, tangible fear in her voice and expression. I tried to awaken myself to it, to feel it. Nothing. All I felt was endless nothingness.

* * * * *

That same night they came for us. Someone had informed a villager who had informed another, who had spoken to Mrs Davies telling her that they were coming to inspect their house by the cliff.

Mrs Davies had run back to the house as fast as she could. It was getting late. "They're coming, they're coming," she said frantically to

Willowen. "You don't have time to run. They're on horseback. You must find somewhere to hide."

Willowen's face paled. Something in me was also shaken. I felt as if I was losing my balance. The persecution was real. It wasn't happening to other people. It was happening to us. If I was taken away, who would set my babies free from their raven bodies? I had to stay. I had to be with them. They needed me.

"Roz, get the children," he said immediately.

At first I wasn't sure which children he was referring to. Then I remembered he didn't know about the curse and the ravens. He was busy scanning the hut but there was nowhere within the small, squat place to hide. He went outside, looking around wildly. Thunderclouds swooped low over the horizon, enveloping the area in velvet black.

"I know where to hide. We're going to jump off the cliff."

"What are you talking about?" I asked, following him outside. "We won't survive a jump like that. There are rocks at the bottom and the waves are vicious."

"I don't mean we jump into the water. I mean we climb over the cliff and find a ridge to stand on. I doubt they will look for us there. Get the children," he said, with urgency.

I nodded. I had to get the children. I felt my body shift into action before my mind was able to keep up. As I ran to find the twins, Danior and Edwina, I realised my face was wet. I patted my cheeks. They were drenched with tears. My children. I had to protect my children.

"Logan, Joni, come here," I said, grabbing them from where they were playing. "Where's Danior and Eddie?"

"I'm here," Danior said.

"Go, follow your father. We have to hide," I cried. All the panic I had been numb to earlier was now suddenly tearing through my body, threatening to rip me to pieces. "Go now!" I yelled at their stunned faces. "I have to find Edwina."

With that they sprinted off in search of their father who was scouring the cliff edge, looking for a safe place for us to hide.

Edwina was huddled behind the hut, her arms wrapped around her legs. She was perched on such a narrow ledge I thought she may tumble over.

"Come here, sweetheart," I said shakily.

Edwina looked up at me. "We're in trouble?" she asked.

"Just come with me. We're going to be fine," I said, half believing it myself. I caught her by the hand as she stood up and slung her over my hip as I ran to Willowen.

"Quick, get down," Willowen called out to us in hushed tones.

"Are they all here?" I asked, my heart in my mouth. I didn't know if I preferred the calm indifference I had felt earlier or the sheer terror I was feeling now. They both felt equally dreadful.

"The twins and Danior are here," Willowen replied.

Joni and Logan were hugging each other tightly, whilst Danior had his eyes tightly shut. I felt my heart crumbling at the sight. My children were in pain. I was sure they were my children. Imposters couldn't possibly look and act this real, could they?

"I'll go down first, then you give me Edwina," I said, as I shifted myself over the cliff and onto the tight rope ledge. Edwina had her thumb in her mouth. A fat tear rolled down her cheek.

"There, there," Willowen said softly. "We'll be ok, Eddie, hush now."

"Pass me Edwina," I called up to Willowen.

"Are you sure? You're on steady footing?" he replied.

Just then, the ominous sound of horse hooves came clattering into earshot.

"Yes, yes, give her to me!" I cried out over the crashing waves beneath me.

I felt the solid body of Edwina in my arms. She was shaking. I could feel her wet tears in the crook of my neck. This was real. I started shaking uncontrollably. I gripped Edwina tighter as Willowen gestured for us to be quiet before silently lowering himself onto the ledge. They were here.

"Get out," a gruff voice yelled, presumably at the Davies.

"Filthy rats, we'll find you," came a second, sneering voice.

A sudden crash indicated a door being broken down. There were muted sounds of smashing and clattering. The wind and waves were being whipped into a frenzy, making it difficult to hear what was going on.

Time inched forward. Any moment now they would peer over the cliff edge. I was sure I would see their jeering faces smirking at us, throwing us in their cages and dungeons.

I could hear their voices again, but they were more muted. I couldn't make out what was being said. A sudden clanging of metal on metal nearly made me jump. Several rocks by my feet crumbled and toppled down. Willowen lay a firm hand on my arm.

After what felt like an eternity, Mr Davies called down softly.

"They're gone. It's over. You can come up now."

Willowen clambered up first, half pulling, half carrying the rest of us up. We were all shaking badly.

"Come inside and have some warm broth," Mr Davies said.

We bundled up inside and drank the broth in silence. After we had recovered slightly, I felt it was time for action. Mr Davies had said a storm was brewing. It would be the perfect time for us to travel.

"Children, go get any of your toys or trinkets you have that are lying around in the garden. Edwina, if you've left any of your dolls up in the tree, I think you should bring them down if you want to take them with you," I said. We had to leave. Whatever the circumstances were, we couldn't stay another day here. I ushered them outside.

"Mother, do you think we'll be able to do it? To get away without them noticing?" Joni asked fearfully.

"Yes, sweetheart, I think exactly that. We'll manage. You heard Mr Davies, there will be a storm later. The police will be too scared to leave the warm safety of their homes to chase a little gypsy family."

"What about all our friends? We're just going to leave them?" Logan asked.

"We don't know what's happened to them and we can't find out. It's not fair but it is what it is. Life isn't fair, Logan. We're simply pawns in more powerful people's games," I replied. "Now, hurry, get whatever you want to bring with you and leave the rest."

"What about you, Mummy?" a high-pitched girlish voice asked.

"My love, I'm fine," I said quietly. "I'm feeling much better today," I continued, more to myself than anyone else.

Edwina replied but I couldn't hear her. Was I feeling better? All I could feel was fear and pain. It was so strong it was palpable. It swelled within my chest like a heavy, dense object restricting my breath. It travelled up my throat with the piercing force of an acid, scorching my insides. I could taste its metallic tang on my tongue. Was this better? Surely the nothingness was better than this.

Willowen somehow appeared by my side. "Is that true? You're feeling better today?"

"No, Willowen. It's not true. Of course it's not true. Things get worse by the day, by the hour and by the minute!" I cried. Words were tumbling out from me. Words I had tried to keep locked away for years. "It doesn't stop. They don't stop!" I said before I could stop myself. I hadn't realised I was on the floor of the hut. Willowen was kneeling next to me.

"It's going to be ok. Once we get away from here we'll get you the help you need."

"Help? The only help out there for people like me is a bed with chains. You know they'll lock me up and I'll never be able to see the children again. That's worse than death for me!" I felt I was rambling, imagining myself locked away in a dungeon.

"We'll think of something, Roz. We'll manage this," Willowen was saying.

His voice felt as if it was far away, as if he was calling to me from across the ocean itself. I was alone. I had always been alone.

"Of course we will," I said automatically. Something had shifted within me. The stress and anxiety had suddenly evaporated and the calm nothingness was filling the void. "How about you gather up some food to take with us?"

"You'll be all right in here?" Willowen asked.

"I just need to rest before the journey," I said calmly.

"Sure. I'll a pay a quick visit to the Turners. They've been so helpful with getting us supplies and food. I'm sure they will grant us this last favour," Willowen was saying.

"Say goodbye to them for me," a voice that sounded like mine said.

As Willowen was about to leave, a sudden sharp pang stabbed my heart. Something within me told me that I would never see him again.

"Please be careful, Will. I love you," I said, my voice barely raised above a whisper.

"I will. I love you too, Roz."

With that, he was gone.

I wanted to call out to Willowen, tell him to stay. He had said he would be back soon. I clung onto that. As long as I could keep it together until then I would be fine. I couldn't understand what was happening. What was real and what was an illusion? It was no longer the mob of angry villagers that was squeezing my heart with a cold fear. It was the creeping voices, familiar echoes that rang through my mind. I was scattered, becoming completely undone.

Sweat trickled down my face and back despite the freezing weather outside. Icy pebbles of fear settled in my stomach. *She* was coming to pay me a visit. I felt it. I hadn't thought of her in ages. I truly believed I had erased her from my very existence. Today, on this bitter winter day in 1849, many years after her death, the face of Mother swam into view. It was as if I had only seen her yesterday.

"I told you. You're cursed," she spat. Although her long matted hair obscured her face, I could tell she was smiling a bitter, twisted smile. "Cursed. Just like your mother."

"No, no, no," I repeated, shaking my head violently, trying to dislodge the image of her.

She was laughing at my attempts to rid myself of her. Her image became blurry but her laughter was getting louder.

"You can't escape it," the voice continued, ringing with mirth. I could no longer see Mother but her disembodied voice haunted every corner of my mind. "Now look what you've let happen. Your children have been cursed and transformed into birds. Your husband has left you. And all your friends will die because you are the Husband Killer."

"It's not true!" I shrieked, stomping my feet.

"Mummy?" a faint, scared voice came from behind me.

I spun around, wild-eyed to see Joni standing there.

"Daddy said we're leaving today and need to get packed." Her eyes were fearful and she backed away as I drew closer to her. I didn't recognise the expression lurking behind those eyes. For a long moment, I didn't recognise her.

"Yes, we're leaving today. Tell your brothers and sister and start packing," I barked in a strangled voice.

"What's going on?" she said in a quavering voice.

"The villagers are blaming us for this sickness. They want to see us hanged," I replied bluntly.

"I meant what's going on with you?" Joni continued, unblinking.

I stared at her, this girl who was supposed to be my daughter. Why didn't she blink? Clearly she wasn't human at all but some other cursed creation.

"Get your brothers and sister together and start packing," I repeated.

As the door quietly shut behind her, I drew in a sigh of relief. I looked out the window at the horizon. Storm clouds were rolling in fast, shoving past each other to get to the finish line. I knew then that I was the finish line. The dark, ominous clouds, like the gang of angry villagers, were coming for me. I was the target. Dark laughter bubbled up within me. I sniggered silently to myself before bursting into peals of laughter.

We needed to leave, I reminded myself. I needed to get it together. At the very least, I had a role to play. I went into our hut to pack a few things in my case as the children gathered sticks and stones to use to start fires outside. As I entered the hut, I knew I wasn't alone. The four ravens were there, one perched in each corner.

I had been desperate to see them all day. Now they were here, I suddenly wanted them to leave. My mind was addled, confused, and they were only making it more so.

"Go away," I said, trying to keep my voice down.

"*We're your children. We can't just go away,*" one of them said.

I shook my head vigorously. "Just stop and leave me alone!"

"*We can't do that,*" another said, in Logan's voice. "*We want to be with you.*"

"Shut up, shut up, shut up," I repeated. I couldn't tell if I was shaking my head or hitting it against one of the earthy walls. Everything around me was spinning.

"*Please don't leave us,*" Edwina's sorrowful little voice said.

I looked up. "What do you mean? You're coming with us on the journey, aren't you?"

All of the birds suddenly drooped their heads, beaks pointing towards the floor.

"*We can't. It's part of the curse. The villagers cursed us to never be able to leave the cliffs of Dover whilst still in our birdlike forms.*"

Nausea rose in my throat as I started to panic. "I can't leave you. But I also can't stay! I can't leave my babies behind!" Their deep, mournful eyes pierced my soul. I could never give up my babies. "How can I break this curse? What must I do?" I asked in desperation.

"*There is one way,*" the bird that sounded like Joni said.

"*Yes, there's only one way the curse can be broken,*" Logan repeated.

"Anything, I'll do anything to keep everyone together!"

"*To give us life, you have to end theirs,*" Edwina said, pointing her beak to where the other children were.

"What do you mean?" I asked, a sinking horror settling deep with me.

"*You know what I mean. To give us, your real children, life, you must end theirs,*" Edwina repeated.

I blinked twice. In a flash my ravens had disappeared. Silently I wept, grabbing fistfuls of my own hair and yanking as hard as I could. I don't know when those silent tears shaking my body morphed into bitter, twisted laughter. I heard it as if it were someone else's. Perhaps I was someone else. I no longer was Erosabel. I felt the dirt of the floor gather between my fingers. It felt soft and cool, like the ravens' wings. I smeared that dirt across my face. Perhaps I would turn into my real self as well and be one with my ravens.

I looked outside. The storm was upon us. The heavy rainclouds began pelting down bullets of raining, hurling them at the earth below.

A silent calm settled over me as I stood up slowly and drifted outside.

"Time to come inside, children," I heard a voice say. I saw the ravens swoop around me, as if in an embrace. "There, there, my lovies. It will all be over soon," I said softly, lovingly.

The imposter children were dotted along the cliff edge, still gathering sticks and stones. As if in a dream, I floated towards them. I knew what I had to do. A dagger of lightning struck the heart of the sea. It was in that flash, just before the thunder cracked in the background, that the outlines of the children that had been on the cliff edge were nowhere to be seen.

I stood there staring at the wild depths of the waves crashing against the cliffs. The ravens continued to caw. The voices of my children were gone. The iron bell of reality struck.

About the Author

Nicole was born in England in 1992 and has lived a peripatetic life. She moved with her family to various countries, such as England, Saudi Arabia, Lebanon, and the United States. She currently lives with her husband and son in the United Arab Emirates.

Nicole has a Bachelor's and Master's degree in Psychology and is a Board Certified Behavior Analyst (BCBA®). She is the founder of Psychminds which is an online platform that encourages discussions around mental health. Nicole integrates her education and experience in the fields of Psychology and Applied Behaviour Analysis to disseminate knowledge, increase awareness and cultivate a container where people can learn something new about themselves and the world around them.

Nicole has been passionate about reading and writing for as long as she can remember and has written a multitude of short stories, poems and articles. Erosabel is the second novel Nicole has written. It is a part of The Woodlock Curse series.

You can find more information about Nicole and her writings on her various platforms:

Author Platforms:

Website: www.nicoleplumridge.com

Instagram: @authornicoleplumridge

Psychminds Platforms:

Website: www.psychminds.com

Instagram: @psychmindspodcast

Podcast: Psychminds Podcast

Acknowledgements

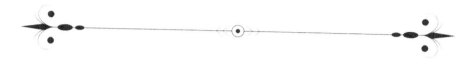

I would like to extend my sincerest gratitude to all those who helped me along the way and saw the potential in my books even when I did not.

Thank you to my mother who was my initial editor and biggest cheerleader when I first started writing. Thank you to my husband, Jad, for being the technical wizard and supporting me each step of the way. Thank you to my sisters, Layla-Anne and Alice, for being a part of my writing journey over the years.

I would also like to express my gratitude to my manuscript editor, Jane Adams. Without her feedback the novel would not be what it is today. Many thanks to my editor, Anna Paterson, for her essential work in helping me convey the heart of my stories without any awkward or jarring sentences getting in the way. Also thank you for fixing my UK and US English mix-ups.

I would like to thank my wonderful cover designer, Victoria, for the fantastic book covers she has designed. I couldn't have imagined them any better.

Finally, thank you to all the readers out there, with a special thanks to those who took the time to read, review and provide feedback on my novels. To every person who picks this book up, looks it over, flips through the pages and settles down with a cup of something to read, thank you! It is you who I write for.

Excerpt from

Healing House

Chapter 1

Samuel

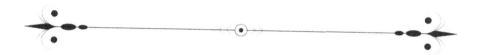

Samuel woke with a jolt and sat bolt upright, his forehead coated in a sheen of perspiration. He blinked rapidly. His heart was racing and his breath, caged in his old, decrepit lungs, came out in rasps. Samuel waited for his breath to return to normal, heart rate to slow down. He closed his eyes. The vision crept like tendrils of smoke in his mind's eye. He didn't know whether it had been a dream or a hallucination. It could have been a ghost, or it could be that at the grand old age of ninety-seven, he was losing his mind.

The man had returned. The man Samuel met on his first night at 11 Edgeware Lane, thirteen years ago. The memory of that first encounter was still fresh in his mind, as sharp and crisp as if it had happened yesterday. Samuel's memory, like his old bones and withering body, was no longer as sharp and quick as it once was. But when it came to that house, to that man, the experiences and memories would rise in unbidden waves threatening to submerge and suffocate him. Samuel could remember every detail down to the smells that hung heavy in the air, the weight of the atmosphere as it descended upon him and the fear, the ever-present fear that pulsated through his veins. Those memories were imprinted as if on a delicate tape reel which would replay over and over in his head. It didn't matter if he wanted to reminisce or not. The tape reel had a force of its own, feeding him flashes of those memories, breathing life into them until they felt tangible, real, alive.

His warm bed, the long shadows cast by the furniture, the hard, unfeeling ceiling all crumbled around him. Samuel was transported back to that first night. That fateful night at 11 Edgeware Lane, thirteen years ago. The night he met Willowen. Swollen black clouds blotted out the moon, turning everything below into liquid shadow. Samuel arrived at his new house on Edgeware Lane in the dead of winter. The roads were covered in ice, and hail had battered down on his rusted old car. Samuel remembered arriving at the front door in a flood of relief, his hands shaking from the tight grip they had had on the steering wheel for the past two hours. Samuel's eyesight, like the rest of him, had been slowly deteriorating, and driving in those conditions had been close to suicidal.

The first thing he had noticed was the putrid smell of the house as he opened the front door. The stench hung heavy in every room as if the very walls were gently exhaling the rotten odour. A strong gust of wind slammed the door shut behind him, and Samuel couldn't help feeling like a small animal clamped in the jaws of a predator that slowly caressed his body with its tongue, tasting and digesting him whole.

Samuel tried to ignore the smell and changed into warm clothes as quickly as he could. The wind and hail pummelled the roof with iron fists. Bizarrely, it felt even louder in the house than it did in the car. It was as if the hail was smashing into the house deliberately, the crashes reverberating in invisible waves through the house. Samuel could feel each and every blow in his body.

He curled up on the couch the previous owner had left behind and fell into a disturbed and fitful sleep. Samuel couldn't be sure how much time had passed, but he awoke suddenly. The house was silent and still. The storm that had been raging so violently had passed. But that was not what had woken him up. It took a moment for him to realise what had. He stretched his limbs and strained his ears. He could hear music. Slow, sorrowful music. It was the saddest song he had ever heard, filling him with a melancholy that struck him at his very core.

Slowly, Samuel got up and followed the sound of the music to locate its source. It pulled him like a magnet to the garden. The dark silhouette of a man was visible from the window. He had his back to Samuel, and he was playing what sounded like a flute. He swayed gently as he played, as if he was one with the music. The contours of his body were lit up by a puddle of moonlight. Something about the way he moved sent shivers down Samuel's spine.

Samuel gazed up at the sky. There was no sign of rain clouds, just a blank empty space with a cut-out moon plastered in the centre of the sky. The scene felt strangely surreal. When Samuel had arrived it was almost midnight. He had slept several hours after that but there was still no hint of dawn breaking on the horizon. It was pitch black, with the exception of the spotlight cast down by the moon. It was an endless night and Samuel was trapped.

Gathering his strength and courage, Samuel opened the door and called out to the man, "Hello, there. Excuse me, I'm the new owner of this house."

The man continued to play the flute, oblivious. Inexplicably, Samuel felt his pulse quicken and sweat trickle down his back even though it was mid-winter.

"Excuse me, sir," Samuel tried again. Something felt off about the encounter. It was as if the man couldn't hear him, as if he were wrapped in a completely different world separated from Samuel by more than simply space and air. Samuel reached out his hand to touch him. He was so close he could feel an electric energy radiating off this strange man's body. Before he could touch him, the man stopped playing. The note from the flute was violently cut in half, chopped by the sharp end of a butcher's knife. It left an invisible tinge of blood spreading in the gulf between them. Samuel remained as still as a statue with his hand frozen in mid-air as the man turned around slowly.

Samuel was rooted to the ground, his mouth open in shock. The man's eyes locked with his. They were a swirling lavender grey. Samuel couldn't make out individual pupils, just a mass of rotating smoke, moving like an optical illusion, defying reality. Slack-jawed, he could do nothing but stare.

The man opened his mouth and spoke slowly and carefully, as if he hadn't exercised his vocal cords in a long time. "Willowen," he said, pointing to himself.

Samuel nodded, replying shakily, "Samuel."

Willowen simply nodded, as if he already knew who Samuel was. He resumed playing his flute and turned away. He walked so gently towards the cliff edge it looked as if he was skimming over the tangled tufts of grass that carpeted the garden. Samuel blinked hard and rubbed his eyes with his gnarled knuckles. When he looked up again, Willowen was gone. The music had stopped, leaving a deathly silence looming over the garden. Samuel walked over to the cliff edge where he had just seen Willowen a moment ago. There was nothing. There was no hint he had ever been there.

In a daze, Samuel went back to the house. Had he just imagined that bizarre encounter? Was this what happened when exhausted and in need of a good night's sleep? Nothing like that had ever happened to him before.

Samuel's memory became blurred and hazy as he slipped back into the present, still sitting under his warm duvet in bed. The sensations of a cold, bleak winter night melted into the shadowy corners of his room. He thought he had left all of that behind when he sold the house. But last night, he had seen Willowen again. Although he was no longer living at the house and had nothing more to do with it, Willowen had been standing at the foot of his bed. One moment Samuel was sleeping, the next moment, whether awake or in a dream, he had seen him. The man with the swirling eyes hadn't said anything. He'd simply stared, his eyes orbs of sadness. He'd shaken his head slightly, as if in disappointment. Samuel felt tears trickling down his face.

"I'm sorry," Samuel stammered. "I'm sorry. I tried to help." The tears created rivulets interweaving through the papery wrinkles lining Samuel's face.

Samuel didn't know how long the dream lasted or how long the vision remained there. It could have been a second. It could have been an eternity. Time seemed to crumble and disintegrate into dust during these episodes. Seconds, minutes, hours, the future and the past seem to fall like heavy raindrops around him, creating a confusing blurred image of what was real and what was not. This continued until Samuel woke up and he was alone.

In that moment, Samuel knew he would never be able to leave that house in the past. Although it had been sold and the keys sent to the new owner, the house, its history, its mysteries were woven into the dark fabric of his soul. He would never escape the house. It was his prison. But would the next owner, Sophie Parker, suffer the same fate? She was not connected to the house in any way. She was not part of the dark family history. The question Samuel had been fretting over since the first day he moved into that house came flooding back to him. Should he have the house demolished or let it stand, let it continue to breathe, exhaling its memories and curses? For thirteen years, this question had flitted in his mind, swaying his opinion one way and then the other.

Samuel felt the electric current of change in the air. Willowen was back, and Sophie would be arriving soon at her new house, the house Samuel had sold to her. Samuel knew in his bones that Willowen would be there to greet Sophie, just as he had been there on Samuel's first night. Icy fear flooded his veins, while regret paralysed his heart. He cradled his head in his hands as he began to sob softly. What had he done? Had he just made a mistake that could cost an innocent girl her security, her sanity and ultimately her life?

ENTER THE WORLD OF
THE WOODLOCK CURSE...

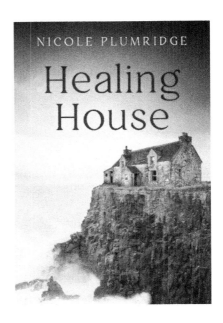

Printed in Great Britain
by Amazon

79661508R00212